Get inside

LOVE – FROM HIS POINT OF VIEW!

Three red-hot, exhilarating romances
from three beloved Mills & Boon authors

We're proud to present

MILLS & BOON SPOTLIGHT™

A chance to buy collections of bestselling novels by favourite authors every month – they're back by popular demand!

October 2009

The Parks Empire: Handsome Strangers…

Featuring

The Prince's Bride by Lois Faye Dyer
The Marriage Act by Elissa Ambrose
The Homecoming by Gina Wilkins

Love – from His Point of View!

Featuring

Meeting at Midnight by Eileen Wilks
Lost in Sensation by Maureen Child
For Services Rendered by Anne Marie Winston

DID YOU PURCHASE THIS BOOK WITHOUT A COVER?
If you did, you should be aware it is **stolen property** as it was reported *unsold and destroyed* by a retailer. Neither the author nor the publisher has received any payment for this book.

All the characters in this book have no existence outside the imagination of the author, and have no relation whatsoever to anyone bearing the same name or names. They are not even distantly inspired by any individual known or unknown to the author, and all the incidents are pure invention.

All Rights Reserved including the right of reproduction in whole or in part in any form. This edition is published by arrangement with Harlequin Enterprises II B.V./S.à.r.l. The text of this publication or any part thereof may not be reproduced or transmitted in any form or by any means, electronic or mechanical, including photocopying, recording, storage in an information retrieval system, or otherwise, without the written permission of the publisher.

This book is sold subject to the condition that it shall not, by way of trade or otherwise, be lent, resold, hired out or otherwise circulated without the prior consent of the publisher in any form of binding or cover other than that in which it is published and without a similar condition including this condition being imposed on the subsequent purchaser.

® and ™ are trademarks owned and used by the trademark owner and/or its licensee. Trademarks marked with ® are registered with the United Kingdom Patent Office and/or the Office for Harmonisation in the Internal Market and in other countries.

LOVE – FROM HIS POINT OF VIEW! © Harlequin Books S.A. 2009.

First published in Great Britain 2009
Harlequin Mills & Boon Limited,
Eton House, 18-24 Paradise Road, Richmond, Surrey TW9 1SR

The publisher acknowledges the copyright holders of the individual works, which have already been published in the UK in single, separate volumes, as follows:

Meeting at Midnight © Eileen Wilks 2004
Lost in Sensation © Maureen Child 2004
For Services Rendered © Anne Marie Rodgers 2004

ISBN: 978 0 263 87165 4

64-1009

Printed and bound in Spain
by Litografia Rosés S.A., Barcelona

LOVE – FROM HIS POINT OF VIEW!

EILEEN WILKS

MAUREEN CHILD

ANNE MARIE WINSTON

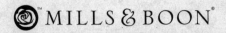

MEETING AT MIDNIGHT

BY
EILEEN WILKS

Eileen Wilks is a fifth-generation Texan. Her great-great-grandmother came to Texas in a covered wagon shortly after the end of the Civil War – excuse us, the War Between the States. But she's not a full-blooded Texan. Right after another war, her Texan father fell for a Yankee woman. This obviously mismatched pair proceeded to travel to nine cities in three countries in the first twenty years of their marriage, raising two kids and innumerable dogs and cats along the way. For the next twenty years they stayed put, back home in Texas again – and still together.

Eileen figures her professional career matches her nomadic upbringing, since she's tried everything from draughting to a brief stint as a ranch hand. Not until she started writing did she "stay put," because that's when she knew she'd come home. Readers can write to her at PO Box 4612, Midland, TX 79704-4612, USA.

This book is dedicated to my editor, Mary-Theresa Hussey, who is as extraordinary in her own way as the story's heroine. At its best, the writer-editor relationship is a partnership that deepens over time, resulting in stronger, richer stories. I've been lucky. I've worked with the best.

One

I wasn't thinking about dying. I wasn't thinking much at all, this being one of those nights when a man didn't want to listen to the noise in his head. I'd turned the radio up loud in an effort to drown out any stray thoughts, but that may have been a mistake.

Damned country music. Every other song was about loving and losing. So why did I keep listening to it?

I grimaced and drummed my fingers on the steering wheel. The wipers were slapping sleet along with rain from the windshield, and the wind was blowing hard. But I knew this road almost as well as I knew my own street. And I'd lived there all my life.

All my life…forty years now. Most of those years I hadn't lived in the big old house alone, but I was alone there now. Forty years old and alone.

And getting dumber instead of smarter, apparently. I

scowled at the strip of highway pinned by my truck's headlights. Why had I let Sorenson talk me into hanging around for a drink after we shook on the deal? I wasn't a complete idiot, though. Despite Sorenson's good-ol'-boy bonhomie, I'd limited myself to a single drink.

"Come on, have another one," the resort owner had urged. "On the house." He'd tried to make out that the weather wasn't a problem. We hadn't even had a freeze yet.

Yet being the operative word. I'd held on to tact by the skin of my teeth—the man was a jerk, but he was the jerk who'd just agreed to use my company for a major renovation job.

"Hey, a man your size ought to be able to handle his liquor. You don't want me to think you're a wimp, right? Might start wondering if you're man enough for the job."

I'd just looked at him, bored beyond courtesy. "Anyone who has to drink to prove he's a man isn't one."

I snorted, remembering that conversation. Yeah, I was some kind of man, all right. The stupid kind. The temperature was hovering just above freezing, visibility sucked, I had to be at a site at seven-thirty tomorrow morning and here I was, winding my way down a mountain road at ten minutes before midnight.

A sharp turn loomed. No shoulder along here. I took my foot off the accelerator and tapped the brakes. I intended to creep around that turn like an old man with palsy—an attitude reinforced when I saw the sign about guard-rail damage.

I hit ice halfway through.

My wheels were cut to the left, but me and half a ton of pickup kept sliding forward. The tops of a couple of pines whipped around in the wind behind the guard rails. Their roots would be thirty or forty feet below the parts I could see and beyond their roots would be a whole lot more down. I turned into the skid, then almost immediately straightened the wheel.

It worked. The rear end skated around a bit, but I'd reclaimed control. I rounded the treacherous curve, safe and sound. And through the murk of rain and sleet saw a long black whip snapping through the air. Straight at me.

A power cable. Live.

If I'd had time to think, I might have risked it. Or maybe not. The truck was grounded, but the cable might have busted my windshield and smacked me in the face with 13,600 volts. But there wasn't time then for thought, or even fear. Just action. I jerked the wheel left and hit the brakes.

Big mistake.

The truck began to spin, slick as greased Teflon. I yanked my foot off the brakes. The power cable reached the end of its arc a foot short of my bumper. I steered into the spin, more than willing to turn all the way around and head back the way I'd come.

The damned truck just kept sliding sideways.

The guard rails. I hadn't seen any damage. Maybe—

The rear of the truck thudded up against them. And stopped. The front slewed around. Jolted. And kept on going.

Even then I didn't think about dying. Didn't think at all, just flung the door open, responding to the screaming need to get out of there. But it was too late, too late to do anything but topple with the truck as it went over the edge and flipped.

Metal screeched. I turned into an object trying to bounce off the crumpling trap of the truck's cab. It was as if the darkness itself pummeled me with a giant's fist, and then a hard blow on my head—then silence. Stillness. I lay beneath a whole mountain of hurt listening to someone moan.

That irritated me. What business did this bozo have moaning when I was the one with the mountain on me? I opened my mouth to tell him to shut up. The moaning stopped.

Something in that cause-and-effect sequence woke a few brain cells. That had been *me* moaning, and I was...I was...in my truck. Only I was hanging at a funny angle.

I blinked. My right eyelid felt gummy. Slowly I put together the pressure across my pelvis and chest, the glow of the dash lights and the stillness. The nose of the truck was pointed down, but the pitch wasn't too steep.

I was alive. And I was hurt.

How bad? I couldn't tell. The pain itself addled me, made it hard to think. But my head...yeah, I remembered getting hit there. Instinctively I lifted my hand to see what touch could tell me. My shoulder exploded. Pain nearly sucked me down. I lay draped over my seat belt and shoulder harness and panted.

Okay, obviously my shoulder was hurt, too. Pretty bad.

Over the soft sound of rain I heard a creaking sound. A prickle of alarm made me lift my head. And rap it against something.

It didn't take long for me to run out of breath for cursing. Or to figure out the problem: the roof of the truck was caved in. I couldn't straighten my head.

My breath came faster. Slowly I turned my head to the right. Shards of glass glittered on the seat beside me. I couldn't see outside because light turned the starred surface of the glass opaque.

How about that. The headlights were still on. I looked to the left.

The door was bashed in.

Deep breaths, I told myself. Panic won't help. I wiggled the fingers on my left hand, then cautiously moved that arm. All right so far. With equal care I shifted my legs. Okay, good. I had three out of four limbs operational. I'd survived a tumble down a mountain and I was hurt, but I was alive, dammit. And I wasn't trapped. I could get out.

Getting out was a bitch.

The buckle to the seat belt was slippery and wet, but I got it undone, then needed to get my breath. Which was ridiculous, of course, but…my jeans were soaked. My jacket, too. And beneath the jacket my shirt stuck to me, warm and wet.

An awful lot of my blood was outside of me instead of inside.

That scared me. I reached for the door handle. My first tug didn't do a damned thing.

Fear hit, sweeping everything else out of the way. Pain didn't matter. Nothing mattered but getting out. I jerked on the handle as hard as I could, throwing my weight against it.

Metal shrieked. The door swung open and I fell out. I managed to thrust one leg out to catch myself, but the jolt as my foot hit the ground set off a charge in my shoulder that toppled my whole system.

I didn't black out. Quite. But for a while there was nothing but a red, roaring monster eating my thoughts before they could form. Eventually I noticed how cold and wet the ground was. It was a lot colder out here than in the truck. Wetter, too. Maybe getting out hadn't been such a great move, but I was here now. What came next?

The road. I had to get to the road. Not much traffic this time of night, but sooner or later that downed power line would attract attention.

Dragging myself to a sitting position left me clammy, but I made it and looked up the way the truck and I had come. Only I couldn't see the road. Too dark, and the rain didn't help. How far had I fallen?

I fought back a wave of despair. I knew where the road was—*up*. So that's where I would go.

First I used my left hand to tuck my right one into the

pocket of my jacket. There were trees, mostly pines. Not much in the way of underbrush, and the truck's passage had cleared a path through what did exist. Good. In a battle between me and a clump of weeds right then, the weeds would win.

Standing was out, so hand-and-knees it was. I started moving.

Gwen had once told me that women forget how much childbirth hurts. She made a joke of it, saying that was how nature tricked them into a repeat performance. I didn't understand then. I'd heard women swapping war stories, and it seemed to me they remembered labor pretty well.

Now I know what she meant. I remember that I hurt. Every inch up that slope equaled a yard or two of pain. But the pain itself isn't there anymore, just the imprint it left behind.

When you hurt enough, you lose hold of past and future. Like a baby or a beast, all you have is right now. I lost the knack of connecting all those nows in the usual way, like beads on a string. So some beads got lost. Others stayed stuck inside me, like a splinter the flesh has grown up around.

One of the beads that got stuck was the moment my truck finished falling.

I hadn't thought about what halted the truck's fall. Maybe that knowledge had squirmed around underneath, and that's why the creaking sound had alarmed me, why I'd been so frantic to get out. The second I heard that sharp, wooden *crack*, I knew what it meant. I craned my head to look behind me.

Branches snapped. Glass broke, and the headlights went out at last. A tangled mass of truck and tree, their shapes merged by darkness and disaster, toppled slowly, then crashed its way down the mountain. I blinked, swaying on my knees and one good hand like a suspension bridge in the wind.

That had been a damned fine truck.

I didn't mourn for long, though. I wasn't holding on to thoughts too well by then—they blew through my mind like smoke. But I had a good grip on purpose.

Up. I had to keep going up.

I remember being racked with shudders as the cold worked its way inside. At some point the shuddering stopped, but by then I was too far gone to realize what a bad sign that was. I remember thinking about Zach, but that isn't tied to any one moment. Thoughts of my son are woven through all the memory bits, like the rocks. They were everywhere, too.

I remember the angel.

That part has a beginning, a middle and an end, beads lined up neatly in order. It was the warmth that called me back. It wormed its way deep inside and tugged at me, made me notice it. And with that noticing came a thought, sluggish but complete: the warmth was real. I knew that because I started shivering again, and shivering—any movement—hurt.

I blinked open my eyes.

It wasn't her face that gave me the idea she was an angel. She was beautiful, but more exotic than angelic with her flat, wide cheekbones and tilty eyes. Her mouth was downright lush. But she had to be an angel. She was glowing.

Deeply disappointed, I croaked, "I'm dead, then."

Those full lips twitched. "No, not at all." She had a smooth sort of voice, sweet and thick like honey. And a Southern accent, which struck me as odd for an angel. "You're going to be fine."

That seemed unlikely, but even less likely things were happening right before my eyes. "You're glowing."

"I have a flashlight."

"No, it's you."

"You're imagining things. In fact, I suspect you imagined

this whole conversation." She touched my forehead. The delicate bracelet on her wrist brushed my skin, its tiny jewels winking at me. "Now, don't be wasting all I've spent on you. Go back to sleep."

I wanted to argue, but my eyes obeyed her instead of me and drifted shut. I floated away on a warm tide.

"Color's bad. Rapid respiration."

Male voices. Hands messing with me. Where was my angel?

"Nail beds are white, but it's damned cold and he's been here awhile."

"Distal pulse?"

"Can't find it."

I knew that voice. "Pete," I said, or thought I did. It came out a groan. I made a huge effort and opened my eyes. Pete Aguilar's face hovered over mine. Pete used to raise hell with my brother Charlie, but that was a long time ago. High school stuff. These days he…I blinked, trying to think of why Pete would be holding my hand.

"You with us?" He squeezed my shoulder—the left one, thank God. "Hang in there, buddy."

Oh, yeah. "Paramedic."

"That's right. Me and Joe are going to take care of you. Where do you hurt?"

Everywhere. I felt sick, dizzy, scared. "Where is she?"

"I need to know where you hurt, Ben."

"Shoulder. Head. I want…" I tried to sit up, but didn't accomplish much.

"Whoa. Stay still, or you'll open up that shoulder again."

"Dammit, I want to know—"

"I'm right here." That was her voice—close, but not as close as she had been. "Lie still and let them help you."

It's not as if I had a choice. Pete or the other man tipped me on my side. I would have belted him if I'd been able to move. As it was, I barely had the breath to curse them once they settled me on my back again.

There was something between me and the mud now. A stretcher, I guess.

"You're a lucky man," Pete told me cheerfully.

Damned idiot always had been too happy for good sense. Just like Charlie. "Not lucky...fall off mountain."

"But if you're going to fall off one, it's nice to do it just before someone with paramedic training happens along. She kept you going until we got here."

Not an angel. A paramedic. No, wait—paramedics don't glow.

A thought slipped in amidst my confusion. "Tell them... power line down. Dangerous."

"One of Highpoint's finest is keeping on eye on things until a crew arrives. Now, we've got to get you up to the ambulance where we can give you some oxygen, get a drip going. You'll feel better then."

The other man had been busy with straps. The one he fastened around my chest pulled on my shoulder. I was just getting my breath back when Pete said, "Ready? On the count of three. One...two—"

They lifted. I guess there was no way to do that without jarring me. I managed to hang on to the ragged edge of consciousness—mainly out of fear, I'll admit. I wasn't sure I'd wake up again.

I weigh about 220. They couldn't just carry me and the stretcher. They had to let the front end roll where it could, lifting it only when they had no choice. The downhill end, though, had to be lifted pretty much all the time. Pete took that end. He was a husky man, nearly as big as me, but that slope defeated him. After a few nearly vertical yards he tripped or slipped and set his end down suddenly. And hard.

I heard myself cry out. It took everything I had to fight off the black, greasy wave. Then I heard *her* voice. She was arguing with them.

She won the argument. While I was busy breathing, she took over at the head of the stretcher, leaving the downhill end to the two men. Not that I figured this out at the time. Then, I was only aware of pain. The need to stay conscious. And that she was near enough to touch me again, because she did.

"Stubborn man," she whispered. Her hand was warm on my cheek, so warm. Almost hot. That heat seemed to push me right out of myself. I lost my grip on consciousness and tumbled off into the darkness.

Two

I knew where I was before I opened my eyes. The emergency room at Fleetwood Memorial Hospital was a place of bad smells, beeping monitors and people who wouldn't listen to me.

"Deep puncture wound in the clavicular portion of the right pectoralis major," someone was saying rapidly. "Some involvement of the deltoid. Patient complained of head pain earlier."

"He was conscious? Responsive?"

"At the scene, yes. He passed out when we carried him to the ambulance. After administering Ringer's…BP holding steady. Pulse…"

The voices were fading in and out. My head ached and my shoulder was one huge, monstrous throb, but I didn't feel as sick and dizzy as I had before. Weak, though. And tired. It was hard to pay attention, tempting to let myself drift off again. But if I did, other people would be making the decisions for me. I didn't like that.

"You didn't use a neck brace." That was a prissy male voice. "The neck is to be supported in all vehicular accidents."

"He crawled more than fifty yards up a mountain," Pete retorted. "I don't think his neck is broken."

"Come on—get him on the table."

That meant they were going to move me again. I blinked gummy lids and was immediately blinded by the overhead light. "Where…" The oxygen mask muffled my voice. I turned my head and tried to dislodge it.

"Mr. McClain." A man's face hovered over mine briefly, haloed by the too-bright light. I couldn't make out his features. "I'm Dr. Meckle. You've been in an accident, and you're at the emergency room."

Well, dammit, I knew that. "Get this off me," I said, but even to me the words were unintelligible.

"You must be still. We're going to move you now."

They did. I had to pay attention to my breathing again. While I was working on that, the prissy doctor was tossing out orders like General Sherman reviewing the troops. "Get his clothes cut off. Draw some blood and get it typed and cross-matched. Aguilar, is this the only wound you found?"

"Yes, sir."

"Doesn't add up," he muttered. "This dressing is almost clean."

Someone jabbed my good arm with a needle and I realized that it wasn't strapped down anymore. Good. As soon as she pulled the needle out, I reached up and shoved the oxygen mask down. "Where is she? The woman. Paramedic."

"The paramedics who brought you in are both men," the doctor said. There was something irritating about his voice. And familiar. "Now, sir, please cooperate. You've lost a good deal of blood. You aren't thinking clearly."

Pete spoke up. "I think he's talking about the woman who found him. The officer at the scene was going to send her here. Exposure or something like that."

"What? What's wrong with her?" I needed to sit up.

"Aguilar," the doctor snapped, planting a hand firmly on my good shoulder, "if you're determined to clutter up my examination room, at least do so silently. Mr. McClain, I will promise to check on this mystery woman once I'm satisfied with your condition. Be *still*."

I subsided, unable to do much else. What had happened to her? Exposure…had she put her coat over me, and suffered for it? I couldn't remember. The officer at the scene…oh, God. Duncan. Duncan worked nights. He would hear about my accident on the police radio, and think I was dead or something. "I need—"

"What you need, Mr. McClain, is medical attention. Which I am attempting to give you. If you won't hold still, I will have you strapped down. Roberts, get that mask back on him."

The world was taking on that sick spin again, which was the fault of that prissy doctor. I wouldn't be so wiped out if he'd quit arguing and cooperate. As it was, the nurse defeated me easily, fitting the mask over my face. I decided to suck down some of the oxygen they were determined to give me, get my strength back and try again.

"Not enough blood," he muttered as he snipped at whatever was holding my shoulder together. "The man's in shock, there should be…what the hell?"

I didn't like the sound of that.

"What is it?" one of the medical crowd asked.

"Look at this. There, see?" He pointed at my shoulder, not quite touching it. I couldn't see a thing. His hands were in the way. "That's newly formed flesh. And this section is scabbed over. That's not right. It's..." He looked at me accusingly. "Mr. McClain. This is an old injury, isn't it? Several days old, at least."

Idiot. I stared at him stonily over the top of the oxygen mask.

He sighed and pulled the mask down. "Did you injure your shoulder a few days ago?"

"No. I think a tree limb punched through the window and pierced it when my truck rolled. I—"

"Impossible."

Obviously not, since it had happened. But arguing with idiots is a waste of breath, and I didn't have breath to spare. "I need to call my brother—Officer Duncan McClain."

"You did not lose any substantial amount of blood from this wound tonight."

I gave up and turned my head. "Pete, I need to call Duncan."

Pete looked at me helplessly. "I imagine someone has already called him. He'll be here soon."

"No!" I'd had enough of lying flat while everyone ignored me. I struggled up onto one elbow. Things spun for a second and my forehead turned clammy, but I made it.

"Lie *down,* Mr. McClain."

"Why? You decided maybe I am hurt, after all? Pete, I need to call Duncan myself. Don't want him worried. I—"

"This man creating a disturbance?" said a voice from the doorway.

"I tried to stop him, Doctor," said a harried female. "He wouldn't listen."

Relief hit like a slap in the face, puncturing my anger. My strength drained right out with it, so I let the nurse ease me back down. "I'm okay, Duncan."

"Yeah?" The man who cut through the medical crowd to stand by my bed was shorter and lighter than I am. Better looking, too, with smoother features and eyes as pale as mine are dark. We have the same hair, though. Dark brown and board straight.

Duncan had on his blank face, the one that makes him a good cop and annoys the hell out of me. Never have been able to read the boy when he doesn't want to be read. He put a hand on my good shoulder and squeezed lightly. "I can see that you are."

"I am," I insisted. But I was sure tired, and the pain wasn't coming in waves anymore. It was this huge, steady presence, almost solid. I felt as if I'd bounced myself off that solid mass of pain a few times too many and rattled my brains. "Truck's a mess, though."

One side of Duncan's mouth quirked up. "You've looked better yourself."

"Yeah, well...I tried to call you, but this stupid—"

"Now, now," he said.

"Belligerence is not uncommon with those in shock," the doctor said, all pompous and tolerant. "I'm afraid your brother's attitude is impeding his treatment, however. Normally I would not allow a family member to be present at this point, but if you can persuade him to cooperate, Officer, you may remain."

As if he could *stop* Duncan. I snorted.

"Belligerent, is he?" For some reason that made Duncan smile. He squeezed my good shoulder again. Anxiety nestled in the corners of his eyes, keeping the smile out, but I could read him now.

I relaxed. If Duncan didn't need his blank face, he wasn't too upset.

"You heard the man, Ben. Play nice."

"Man's an idiot," I muttered, but someone had tied weights on my eyelids. They were closing in spite of me. It was all right, though. Duncan would keep an eye on the idiot. He'd take care of things. "You'll tell Zach...make it so he doesn't worry."

"I will."

Good. That was good. The darkness beckoned, no longer threatening. "And the angel," I murmured as I let myself go. "You'll find her for me."

Doctors and nurses are not reasonable people.

No question about who was in charge, and it wasn't me. Admittedly, I wasn't in any shape to go home right away. After they'd finished poking and stitching and X-raying me, pumping me full of antibiotics and O-negative, they finally strapped me into a fancy sling and put me in a room where I could get some sleep. Then, of course, they kept waking me up.

In spite of this, I felt a lot better by late afternoon. But no one was interested in my opinion of my condition. Mostly they seemed irritated that it wasn't worse. At least that prissy E.R. doctor was out of the picture now.

I'd finally remembered where I knew him from. Twenty-some years ago, Harold Meckle, M.D., had been a couple of grades behind me in school. Harry had been a certified brain back then, so he was probably a competent doctor now. But it would take a personality transplant to turn him into a competent human being.

Harry had a real bee in his bonnet about my shoulder. At one point he'd actually wanted to do surgery in order to find out why I didn't need surgery. He was convinced I had to have some internal injury that was bleeding like a mother to account for all the blood I'd lost.

Fortunately, my own doctor had arrived by then. Dr. Miller didn't see any point in cutting me open to satisfy Harry's curiosity. Or, as he put it, he preferred a conservative approach, which meant keeping me under observation. Which meant keeping me in the hospital.

I'm a reasonable man. I could see that they needed to hold on to me awhile. I had a concussion, among other things. That's why they'd woken me up every blasted hour on the hour, until I finally stayed awake in self-defense.

I knew all that. I just didn't like it.

Shortly before supper a skinny little blonde showed up carrying a plastic sack from a department store. Her pink sweater was big enough for two of her, hiding what I knew to be a curvy bottom. She'd cut her hair again, I noticed. For some reason she liked it short. Long or short, I enjoyed looking at her hair. It was a pale, shiny blond, like sunshine on freshly cut pine.

Her name was Gwen. She was my son's mother and—as of three months ago—my brother's wife.

"I've got a book on Samuel Adams I hope you haven't read," she said, bustling up to my bed, where she deposited a peck on my cheek and the sack on my bed. "Also two magazines, a crossword puzzle book and some pajamas so you don't have to wear that hospital gown. You're looking better, I must say, though your bruises are coming out nicely. How are you feeling?"

"Hungry. Where's Duncan? With Zach?" I used my good arm to dig through the sack. The pajamas were new, of course, since I didn't own any. I wondered how much of a fuss she'd make when I paid her back for them.

"Duncan is getting something else I understand you asked for. Zach is with Mrs. Bradshaw."

"How's he taking all this? He's not too upset?"

She smiled. "We may have overdone the reassuring. He wanted to know if you'd still take him camping this weekend."

"We" meant her and Duncan. I was getting used to that. I grimaced. "We're likely to have had our first snow by the time all the dings in my carcass have healed enough for me to take him."

"Probably. He'll survive waiting until next spring. Oh, I talked to Edie. She wants you to let her know if there's anything she can do."

She might try leaving me alone. One date is not a lifetime commitment. Couldn't say that, though. The woman was a friend of Gwen's. "What about Annie? Did Duncan ever get hold of her?" I knew Duncan had called Charlie, my youngest brother, but Annie was harder to get hold of.

My little sister was currently in a tiny village in Guatemala with her husband, Jack, a construction engineer who works for a nonprofit organization. ICA builds schools and hospitals and such in developing countries. Right now, Jack was putting up a clinic while Annie taught the kids in a one-room, dirt-floor hut.

I still hadn't gotten used to her being so far away most of the time.

"Oh, yes. Sorry—I forgot to mention that. I talked to her after lunch. She's worried, naturally, but I persuaded her to hold off on buying a plane ticket."

I would have liked to see her…but that was selfish. She was needed where she was. I pulled out the book Gwen had brought. "I've been wanting to read this one. Thanks. But you forgot something."

"No, I didn't."

"My clothes."

"If I bring you clothes, you'll put them on. Duncan spoke to your doctor, Ben, so don't think you can put one over on us. You are staying here at least two more days."

I was patient with her. "I'm not planning to leave the hospital without Dr. Miller's okay. He's a sensible man, unlike the idiot in the E.R. I just want to have the *option* of leaving."

"You get the clothes when Dr. Miller releases you, and not a minute before."

"Dammit, Gwen, I'm not a two-year-old!"

"You're as stubborn as one! You've got a concussion, a banged-up knee, a big hole in your shoulder and a broken clavicle. You're not going anywhere right away, and when they do discharge you, you'll be coming home with me and Duncan."

No way in hell was that going to happen. "You live on the second floor. I'm not up to handling stairs yet."

"You're not discharged yet, either." She fussed with the flowers and stuff on the table by my bed, making room for the things she'd brought. "And once you are, you can lie around on the couch like a sultan and order everyone around. That should suit you."

Gwen had adapted well to being my sister-in-law. She sounded more like my sister all the time. Snippy. "I thought I was too banged up for Zach to see. That's why you didn't want to sneak him in here." That, and the fact that, being an attorney, Gwen has a thing about rules, and the hospital didn't allow kids under ten to visit.

"I'm sure you'll look better by the time you're released." She quit messing with the flowers and faced me. "You are not going home to an empty house in your condition, Ben. Forget that idea."

That hit too close to home. When I heard the snick of the door opening I turned to face it, relieved. Someone probably wanted more of my blood, or to see how "we" were doing, but that was okay. Better than looking at the concern in Gwen's eyes.

"You up for some visitors?" Duncan asked.

Even better. I smiled. "You're not a visitor, you're a…" My voice trailed off. I forgot what I was going to say.

He'd found her. Duncan had found my angel.

Only she wasn't, of course. Not mine, and certainly not an angel. A Valkyrie, maybe. Or an amazon. The top of her head was level with my brother's, and Duncan hits a fraction over six feet.

Her sweatshirt was blue and sloppy beneath a worn yellow parka, but couldn't disguise beautiful, half-moon breasts. Faded denim stretched tight over a couple miles of legs—firm, rounded, muscular legs. Her hair was a messy riot of brown curls tumbling well below her shoulders. She was built long and lush, strong and stacked, every inch of her pure woman.

It was a body that made quite an impact on a man. I blinked a few times before I got my gaze back to her face. That looked the same as I remembered…except, of course, she wasn't glowing.

"I don't think you two were ever introduced," Duncan said. "Ben, this is Seely Jones. Seely, this is my brother Ben—Benjamin McClain—and my wife, Gwen."

I had no idea what to say. I hadn't thought beyond finding her, seeing her again. I cleared my throat. "Unusual name."

"My mother is an unusual woman." She turned her smile on Gwen. "You have a very persistent husband. Nice, but persistent."

Gwen and Duncan exchanged one of those private smiles. "Yes, I do. I hope his persistence hasn't inconvenienced you too much. I'm very glad to meet you."

"You're okay, aren't you?" I said. "I heard you were treated and released, but no one would tell me what you'd been treated for."

"Oh, that. I'm afraid I scared the police officer who was taking my statement by fainting, so they felt obliged to bring me in."

I'd never seen a woman who looked less likely to faint in my life.

My expression must have given my thoughts away, for she laughed. "Absurd, isn't it? I've done it all my life, though. Not often, thank goodness, and no, it is not a symptom of some dreadful underlying health problem—though I did have some trouble persuading the E.R. doctor of that. You seem to be doing well."

"Thanks to you. I, uh…that's what I wanted. To thank you."

She smiled that slow, sweet smile I remembered. "Daisy says everything happens for a reason, but I never thought I'd be grateful to Vic."

"Vic?" I frowned. "You don't mean Victor Sorenson."

"Don't I?" Her eyebrows went up in elaborate surprise. "I thought I did." She ambled up to my bed, *click-click-click*.

I glanced down. She was wearing high heels. My own eyebrows went up. Got to respect the moxie of a tall woman who chooses to wear three-inch heels. "Sorenson's a worm," I mentioned, in case she hadn't noticed.

"I'll agree with you there." She spoke the way she moved—slow and easy, as if she'd never hurried in her life and didn't intend to start. "He fired me last night. That's why I left the resort so late and ended up finding you. Which is a roundabout sort of gratitude, but there you go. Roundabout is probably the only kind of appreciation Vic's likely to get."

"I didn't know Vic kept a paramedic on staff."

"I was working as a waitress, not a paramedic." Her voice didn't change but her eyes did—as if she'd closed a door, gently but firmly, on that subject. "Vic and I disagreed about the fringe benefits of the job. He thought he was one of them. I didn't."

The thought of Vic putting his hands on this woman made me furious. "I'll talk to him," I promised grimly.

Duncan gave me a level look. "Don't do anything I'd have to arrest you for."

"You should consider filing suit against him," Gwen said seriously. "Sexual harassment is wrong, and firing you for failing to agree to his demands—well, it sounds like you'd have a good case."

"Oh, he didn't fire me because I wouldn't go to bed with him. I think it was the cannelloni," Seely said thoughtfully. "It didn't go with his suit. Or maybe it was the chicken-fried steak. There was all that cream gravy, you see. He was not happy about the gravy."

A laugh took me by surprise. It hurt, so I stopped. "Dumped a tray on him, did you?"

Her mouth stayed solemn, but her eyes laughed along with me. Extraordinary eyes. Not the color—they were blue, pretty enough, but nothing unusual. Maybe it was their shape, sort of elongated, with a flirty tilt at the corners. Or the way they seemed to offer confidences, as if she and I were old friends who didn't need to put everything into words.

"I found Miss Jones at the bus station," Duncan said. "She was buying a ticket to Denver."

A frown snapped down. "You're leaving town?"

"Why not? I lost my job."

"But you have a car. What were you doing at the bus station?"

She pulled a face. "The stupid thing decided to die on me. The mechanic says it's either some gasket or the whole motor, and he can't say which without taking everything apart, which will cost a fortune. You'd think he could tell the difference, wouldn't you?"

"Head gasket, sounds like," I said, my brain clicking away on an idea. "Or the heads themselves. You must have lost compression."

"You do speak the lingo," she said admiringly.

Duncan asked her who she'd taken the car to, then assured her that Ron was a good mechanic. Gwen was looking fidgety.

"But your things!" she burst out. "I can understand leaving your car if it wasn't worth repairing, but surely you couldn't take everything with you on the bus. Even if you didn't have furniture, there's clothes, dishes, bedding…oh." An embarrassed flush sped over her cheeks. "It isn't any of my business, is it?"

Seely turned that lazy smile Gwen's way. "Probably not, but we can't help being curious about people, can we? I don't have much stuff, being more of a wanderer than a nester. No dishes or bedding. A few keepsakes and some clothes, yes, but not that many. Susan seemed happy to accept what I didn't want to take with me."

"Susan?" I said, only half my brain on what she was saying.

"Another waitress at the resort. I'd been rooming with her, but I don't think she minded my sudden departure. She's had her eye on Vic for a while. Well." She shrugged, a graceful movement that did lovely things to her breasts. "No accounting for tastes, is there?"

Things were falling into place. "You decided to leave more or less on impulse, then?"

"I do a lot of things on impulse."

"Then there's nothing waiting for you in Denver? No reason you need to be there right away?"

She used her eyebrows to ask where I was going with all this.

"My brother and sister-in-law think I'm going to need some help after I leave the hospital tomorrow."

Gwen interrupted. "*Not* tomorrow, Ben."

"They can't do anything more for me here. Besides, hospitals are unhealthy. People get staph infections in hospitals. Now, Gwen and Duncan might be right about me needing a little help—"

Duncan snorted.

"So I was thinking maybe you'd be interested. You need a job, right? And a place to stay while your car gets fixed."

"I…" For the first time, her composure was shaken. "Weren't you listening? I wasn't planning to fix my car."

I brushed that aside. "Look, if you're worried about staying with a man you don't know, I'm not in any shape to give you a hard time." Gwen muttered something about my being able to give people a hard time on my deathbed. I ignored that. "Not that I would hassle you, anyway, but you couldn't know that."

She shook her head. "That's not it."

"What's the problem, then?" I used my left elbow to prop myself up.

Everything went gray. The next thing I knew, Seely was depositing me efficiently back on my pillows. I'm not sure how she got there before Duncan, who isn't exactly slow off the mark, but she did.

"There's a line between stubborn and stupid," she said, looking down at me. "Something tells me you cross it now and then."

Duncan grinned. Gwen giggled. I scowled. "I moved too fast, that's all."

"Uh-huh," Seely said. "I can see you'll undo everyone's work, given half a chance. All right. I'll take the job."

Hot damn. "Good. That's good."

"On two conditions. First, you stay in the hospital until the doctor releases you. Second, you'll do as I tell you while you're under my care."

"Now, wait a minute—"

"He agrees," Duncan said firmly. "Don't you, Ben?"

Seely's lips twitched, but she looked at me steadily, waiting. With a sigh, I nodded. "Within reason."

Gwen spoke. "I hate to put a stick in the spokes, but you really should tell her about Doofus."

Seely did that question-thing with her eyebrows. "Zach's dog," I explained. "My son. He lives with me. Doofus, I mean." Relief had hit, followed by a wave of exhaustion. It was hard to get words lined up right. "Zach's in kindergarten. He comes over after school some days."

"My point is that Doofus is a puppy, not a dog," Gwen said. "You should be aware you're not just taking on one large, slightly snarly man. The man is at least housetrained. Doofus isn't."

"Thanks a lot, Gwen."

Seely's lips tipped up. "I think I can handle a puppy, as long as Ben can handle being bossed around."

"Within reason," I repeated. When she nodded, I breathed a sigh of relief. "All right, then. We've got a deal."

Duncan was amused, Gwen was relieved, and Seely...I couldn't tell. Her cheeks were flushed, her mouth smiling, but her eyes seemed distracted, like she was taking a serious look inward.

And me? I was satisfied...for now. "Don't you want to know how much the job will pay?"

"Money's not a big issue for me."

"Uh—you aren't rich or something, are you?"

Gwen made a choked sound that she turned into clearing

her throat. Seely laughed and tucked her hair back from her face. "I've been accused of a number of oddities, but rich isn't one of them."

The movement drew my attention to the long dangles of multicolored glass hanging from her ears. They reminded me...I glanced at her wrist.

Yes. That was the bracelet I remembered. "Pretty bracelet."

Her eyebrows lifted gently. "Thanks. The stones represent the chakras. I'm guessing by the look on your face that you know what chakras are?"

"I read." Bunch of New Age nonsense, but I wouldn't say that to the woman who'd saved my life.

Everyone wanted me to rest then. I was willing to let them have their way as soon as I'd passed on some instructions for Manny, who was going to have to run things at McClain Construction for awhile. They were right—I was tired.

And I'd gotten what I wanted.

I'd stay here one more night, then I was going home. Not to an empty house, either. Seely would be there. I didn't think Dr. Miller would give me grief over leaving the hospital once he knew I'd have trained medical help around. And I wouldn't have to come up with any more reasons not to stay with Duncan while I was recovering.

Don't get me wrong. I love my brother. Unfortunately, I also love his wife.

Three

Outside, the birds were making a fuss about morning. It was a familiar sound, even this late in the year. There were always a few who wintered over. But usually I didn't listen to their chatter from a hospital bed in the den.

I sat on the edge of that bed and glared at my knee.

I had no idea how it had gotten hurt, no memory of it bothering me during my crawl up the mountain, but it was swollen to twice its size. Soft-tissue damage, according to the doctor. The swelling should go down in a few days. I was to stay off it as much as possible.

The downstairs bathroom was two rooms and half a hallway away.

All the bedrooms in the house were on the second floor, which is why they'd parked me in the den when I came home yesterday. The den was an addition, tacked on at the very back of the house. The bathroom was opposite the laundry room.

I'd put up with using a plastic basin to brush my teeth, but I was damned if I was going to pee in the stupid urinal they'd sent me home with.

Besides, I wanted more coffee. And something to *do*. There was a TV in here, but I wasn't much for television. I like to read, but not all day. The table by my bed held sickroom paraphernalia—water, a glass, pain pills, the stuff Gwen had brought me in the hospital. My laptop, though I'd practically had to sign an oath in blood that I wouldn't use it to work yet. A little bell I was supposed to ring if I needed anything.

I grimaced at that bell. Last night I'd barely managed one game of solitaire on my laptop. Seely had come in to refill my water and see how I was doing. I'd fallen asleep so fast I wasn't sure I'd answered her.

I'd done nothing but sleep yesterday. I was sick of it.

On the floor next to the bed, Doofus was growling. He'd sunk his sharp little baby teeth into a dangling corner of my blanket and was killing it. In the kitchen, the radio was playing softly. I could hear quiet, moving-around noises, too…water running at the sink. The refrigerator door opening and closing.

That would be Seely, clearing up after breakfast. She'd brought me eggs and toast in bed.

Damned if I know why people consider breakfast in bed a treat. Even with a bed you can crank to a sitting position, it's a pain. Besides, I'd had enough of beds. I wanted to shave. I wanted a shower and real clothes, not wrinkled pajamas. I needed to talk to Manny, and my loving family had persuaded Seely not to leave the phone by my bed.

First things first. I stood slowly, having learned that I got dizzy if I tried to move too fast. It was nice, I decided, to hear a woman puttering around in the kitchen. I wondered how much of a squawk Seely would make when I joined her there. A grin tugged at my mouth.

Funny. I was in a pretty good mood, considering I'd smashed my truck and put some major dents in several body parts. But it was good to be home...good to have survived to come home.

I started across the room. Contrary to my family's fondly held opinion, I know my limits. I'd lost a lot of blood, which meant I was going to be weak, sometimes dizzy. Combine that with a knee not inclined to take much weight, a shoulder that kept me from using crutches and a body that was stiff and sore everywhere but my left big toe, and falling was a real possibility. Especially with that fool puppy running circles around my feet.

I took it slow and careful. I wanted to make a point. I also wanted coffee and conversation, maybe some answers. I limped into the dining room, frowning.

In any contest between memory and logic, logic ought to win. Women don't glow. I knew that. I'd been in bad shape when Seely found me, my perceptions skewed by a system on the verge of shutting down. I couldn't trust my memory.

Yet that one memory bead remained so clear...the curves of her face as she smiled at me, the tilt of her eyes, the way her breath had puffed out, ghostly in the cold air. And the gentle luminescence of her skin, like moonlight on snow. Not at all like a flashlight. Just as clearly I remember the warmth, a heat that had sunk itself into me instead of sitting around on the surface.

I had questions, and I couldn't let them go.

I managed to avoid tripping over Doofus as I left the bathroom, but had to pause in the doorway to the kitchen, one hand on the jamb to steady myself. The sling supported my shoulder, so it wasn't hurting too much. Unlike my knee.

Seely was wiping down the counter, humming along with the radio. She wore jeans and a blue sweater today, and her denim-clad hips were swaying to the music in a cute little be-bop that yanked my attention away from my sore knee.

Then I noticed what was playing on the radio: Kenny Chesney singing "How forever feels." The song Gwen and I had danced to five years ago, on the night we'd ended up in bed together.

The night before I left her.

All the fizz drained out of the day. I took a deep breath and limped on into the room. Doofus yelped happily, announcing our arrival.

Seely spun around, her eyes wide. "How do you do that?"

"What?" Doofus had found his water dish and was thrilled by the discovery, lapping away as if he'd been in the desert for days. I'd have to put him out soon. Or ask Seely to, dammit. I didn't like depending on others for every little thing.

"Sneak up on me when you can barely walk," she said.

"No shoes." I decided to rest a bit before making for the oak table in the center of the room. "I came out for a cup of coffee."

"I would have brought you coffee. That's what that little bell by your bed is for."

"I didn't want to drink it in bed. Besides, I thought it would help if you could see that I'm able to move around some now."

"Help what?"

"I don't want to sleep all day today."

One of her eyebrows lifted. The woman had the most talkative eyebrows I'd ever seen. "Okay. You thought I needed to be notified of this?"

Yesterday I'd dozed off every time she checked on me. That had to be coincidence...didn't it? "We have a deal. I do what you say, within reason. I wanted to show you that it wouldn't be reasonable to keep me in bed all day."

Her mouth kicked up on one side. "Well, since you're already here, you may as well sit down and have that coffee. No, wait—I'd rather you didn't go splat on the floor. Let me get on your good side first."

I didn't have much choice. She reached me before I'd taken more than a couple of halting steps and slid an arm around my waist. The warm strength of her body felt good. "How can you move so fast without seeming to hurry?"

"Long legs. It helps when my target is crippled and can't escape."

My mouth twitched. The top of her head was only a few inches below mine. If I'd turned my head, it would have tickled my nose. Her hair smelled nice—a green smell, like herbs.

We made for the table at a half lurch, and I had to admit it was easier with her help. More pleasant, too. My body started entertaining ideas I could have sworn it wasn't ready to consider yet. I sure couldn't do anything about those ideas, even if I'd been free to.

Which I wasn't. She was an employee, off-limits.

We reached the table. I spoke abruptly. "The first time I saw you, you were glowing."

"Amazing the sort of thing a mind in shock can conjure, isn't it?"

"Is that what it was?"

She let me go as I lowered myself carefully into a chair, then looked me square in the eye. Her eyebrows were expressing skepticism. "I don't know. Do you often see people glow when you aren't in shock?"

"Hardly ever." Common wisdom holds that people won't look you in the eye if they're lying. This is stupid. Since everyone knows this, someone who intends to lie to you will be sure to meet your eyes. I guess people who expect liars to look shifty haven't been around teenagers much. "That E.R. doctor was sure baffled by my shoulder."

She laughed and headed for the coffeepot. "The one you kept calling an idiot?"

"Yeah. Harry Meckle. I knew him in school." Was she dodging the subject? Or was I being given a chance to avoid looking like a fool? I drummed my fingers on the table. "I want you to tell Gwen it's okay for Zach to come over after school today."

"Uh-uh." She set a steaming mug in front of me. The multicolored stones in her bracelet glittered.

"Do you wear that all the time?"

"Hmm? Oh." She sat down, keeping another mug for herself. "The bracelet. Yes, pretty much."

"So why won't you talk to Gwen for me?"

"I never step between dueling exes."

"Gwen and I aren't dueling. We aren't even exes. We were never married." I held myself ready for the questions that were sure to come. People were invariably nosy about me, Gwen, Zach and Duncan.

Seely shrugged. "So? You're obviously ex-somethings."

I'd never thought of it that way. For some reason the notion settled me, as if some little wandering piece had finally found its spot. I took a sip of coffee. "This is good."

"Thanks."

"The thing is, Zach has had enough uncertainty in his life. I think it will be good for him to see that, yeah, I'm banged up but I'm basically okay."

"I won't argue with that, but can't you just tell Gwen yourself?"

I grimaced. "My family has some funny ideas. They think I don't know my own limitations."

She sipped her coffee, her eyes laughing at me over the rim. "Maybe you've given them some teensie-weensie reason to think that?"

"No." I was certain about that. "Couldn't have. I've never been really hurt before. A few stitches here and there, yeah, but nothing they kept me for overnight. Never been in any kind of auto accident."

"Never? Not even a fender-bender?"

I shook my head and thought sadly about my truck.

"I imagine you scared them, then. They probably don't realize it, but deep down I'll bet they think you're invulnerable."

"They're annoying sometimes, but they aren't stupid."

"Feelings don't always follow logic, do they? They probably needed you to be invulnerable when they were younger. You were all they had."

I scowled. "Who told you that?"

"Oh, it came up in different ways. While you were napping yesterday, you had visitors. Manny Holstedder—I gather he works for you?—and two of your neighbors, and of course Duncan. And phone calls. I made a list you can look at later, but I do recall that your sister Annie called, and another brother. Charlie, I think? And Edie Snelling called twice." She put just enough lift at the end of that to make it almost a question.

"A friend of Gwen's," I muttered. There are worse things than an ex-lover who's determined to fix you up. Falling off a mountain, for example. But dammit, I wished Gwen would quit trying to slide women under my door.

"Mmm. Anyway, your friends, family and neighbors all wanted me to know I was taking care of someone special. You're something of a hero, you know."

"Oh, for God's sake—"

"No, really. They all think you're pretty grand. Several of them told me about the way you took over raising your sister and brothers after your folks were killed."

Mortified, I nearly burned my tongue on the coffee. I set the mug down and cleared my throat. "To get back to the subject—I thought you could assure Gwen that I'm up to having Zach come over. That is…I never asked. Are you okay with having a five-year-old around?"

"Sure. I like kids."

"I guess you don't have any of your own. You said you weren't a nester."

She tipped her head to one side. Her curls were semitamed today, caught back in a stretchy blue thing at her nape. A few strands had wiggled free. "Are you really curious, or just paying me back for having learned so much about you when you were helpless?"

That surprised a chuckle out of me.

Oddly, she shivered. It was a delicate little thing, but I caught it. "Are you cold? We can turn up the heat."

"No," she said absently, rubbing her left palm as if it itched. "You do have a deep voice, don't you? It sounds as if it's rolling up from the bottom of a well. Oh, look—Doofus is actually at the door, asking to go out. I'd better reward that."

She liked the sound of my voice. That's what that little shiver had meant. I enjoyed that notion about as much as I did watching her as she ambled for the back door. The way those long legs carried her along put a nice little sway in her hips. Those legs…

She opened the back door and Doofus scampered out. "How did you pick Doofus?"

"The name or the dog?"

"Both, I guess. A bit of unique, isn't he?"

"That's one way to put it. No, leave the door open. He panics if you close it, then forgets what he went outside to do." A man could die happy with those legs wrapped around him—whoa. A little sexual buzz was okay, but I couldn't let myself get carried away. "I got him from the pound for Zach's fifth birthday. The vet says he's a basset mix, emphasis on the mix."

She glanced out the door. "The ears do look have the look of a basset hound. Zach comes over to play with him fairly often, I take it?"

"Two or three days a week. A neighbor's teenage daughter walks him here from the school when the weather is decent. Sometimes to Mrs. Bradshaw's, if I can't be home at that hour."

"That's your neighbor, right? She stopped by yesterday to see how you were doing."

"She keeps kids." That still didn't sit too well with me. I didn't want Zach raised by anyone other than family. But Mrs. Bradshaw was a good woman, and he liked it there. As Gwen often pointed out, at Mrs. Bradshaw's he had other kids to play with, most notably a set of twins. "You never did answer my question."

"Your…oh. About children." Doofus scampered back in, the whole back half of his body wagging with delight over his performance. She shut the door and knelt to praise and pat. "Nope, no kids of my own. No stepchildren, nieces or nephews, either. I've never been married, and I was an only child."

So was Gwen. Putting the two women together in my mind made me uncomfortable. I shifted, stretching out my bad leg. "I guess that would be lonely, being an only child."

"I had my fantasies about having a brother or sister when I was growing up. But a lot of people from big families fantasize about being an only, I think. Didn't you?"

"No more than four or five times a day. Especially when Charlie and Annie were teenagers. Not that Annie got into any real trouble, but she was a girl. There's so much *stuff* about being a girl at that age…" I shook my head. "I wanted to lock her up or send her to a convent. Raising girls is scary."

"She's quite a bit younger than you, I gather."

"Eleven years, yeah. She's the youngest." I hadn't done right by Annie. For years she'd had a kind of phobia about leaving Highpoint, and I hadn't even realized it—probably because I'd liked having her around too much to question why she'd moved back home and stayed. Jack had known, though. He'd married her and taken her off to see the world, one dirt-poor village at a time. And she loved it. I frowned at my coffee cup.

"More coffee?"

I shook my head. "No, thanks. Ah…jeans probably won't work with this stupid knee. There ought to be a pair of sweats in the bottom left drawer of my dresser, though. If you'd get them, I can have my shower in the downstairs bathroom, then get dressed."

"You are not—" she started, then stopped, shaking her head. "Who'd have thought you'd be so devious?"

I scowled. "What are you talking about?"

"I'm supposed to fuss at you, remind you of what the doctor said, et cetera. In the end, you'll give up on the shower, and I'm supposed to concede that you can get dressed. Which is what you really want."

"Are you sure you don't have brothers?"

She chuckled. "Nary a one."

Yet she obviously knew men. Well, she'd probably had plenty of opportunity to observe my half of the species. That showgirl's body would get any man's attention. Then he'd get hooked by that slow smile, or the way her eyes crinkled at the corners, laughing all by themselves. "You aren't giving me a hard time about getting dressed," I observed.

"Not much point. I knew you'd be champing at the bit today. You do realize I'll have to help you, don't you?"

"Like hell you will."

She just looked at me. For once, even her eyebrows didn't comment.

At last I sighed. "The shirt. I'll need help with that. And the sling."

"I could give you a sponge bath first."

A visceral flash hit me—her hands running a warm, soapy washcloth along my arm to my shoulder, then down my chest…she'd be bending over me, bringing those magnificent breasts close enough to… "No, you can't."

Like I said, I know my limits.

Four

I couldn't reach my left foot. I glared at my knee, washcloth in hand.

I was sitting on the toilet with the lid down. I'd managed a spit bath of sorts, pulled on my shorts and sweatpants...and one sock. I couldn't get my left sock on. And I couldn't wash my own damned foot.

Everything throbbed—head, shoulder, knee. My feet were cold. I was going to have to ask for help.

Someone knocked on the bathroom door.

"Yeah?" I growled.

"Thought you might be ready for a cup of coffee," Seely said through the door. "And an extra hand. As I recall, I had the devil of a time with shoes and socks when my wrist was broken."

I sighed. "It's unlocked. How did you break your wrist?"

The door swung open. "I wasn't a very coordinated child.

Fell from the monkey bars when I was seven. Daisy had to do everything for me at first, which sorely offended my dignity. Here." She held out a tall walking stick. "Duncan dug this up in the attic yesterday. He thought you might be able to use it."

I put down the washcloth and took the stick. It was made of walnut, a dark, burled wood that felt smooth and cool to my fingers. "How about that." I smiled, bemused. "I'd forgotten all about this thing. Funny. I must have seen my father use it a hundred times, but the one time that floated into my head just now…"

"Yes?" She set the mug on the tiny bit of counter next to the sink.

"We were in Crete. Me and my dad, that is. Annie was only a month old, so my mom wasn't able to go with my dad that year." I leaned the stick against the wall. There wasn't really room for it in this little scrap of a bathroom, but it made me feel good to have it near. "We'd climbed this little rise overlooking the dig, and he was using his stick to point out a city that didn't exist anymore. All I saw was this reddish maze of crumbling walls in the section that had been excavated. He saw so much more—the granary, the wide, dusty street leading to the temple. Maybe even the people on that street."

"He had vision. It sounds like a good memory."

"Yeah." I thought about how excited I'd been to go with him. How hard I'd tried to see what he did…and failed. "It was the first time I'd gone with him. I guess that's why that memory sticks out."

"How old were you?"

"Eleven. It was summer, of course. I remember—hey!"

She'd knelt and was reaching for my foot. "Must have been hot."

"Blazing. You don't have to do that." I tried to retrieve my foot without creating a tug-of-war.

"Quit that or I'll tickle you." She ran the washcloth over my sole. "I'll admit I'm not a real nurse, but I'm pretty sure this sort of thing is part of the job."

I scowled. This was every bit as embarrassing as I'd thought it would be. "No, you're a paramedic. So why aren't you working as one?"

"Because I couldn't hack it." She grabbed the towel. "So why is your brother married to your son's mother instead of you?"

Sucker-punched. I hadn't seen that one coming, and for a second couldn't think of a thing to say.

"I'm sorry. I shouldn't have said that." She dried my foot carefully, giving me the top of her head to look at instead of her face. Even with her hair pulled back, her hair was all crinkly, like a shallow stream wiggling over rocks.

Or like Doofus wiggling all over even when he was trying to stand still. I sighed. I felt as if I'd just kicked a puppy—and gotten bitten for it. "Don't apologize. I asked for it. I jabbed at you because I don't like needing help for every little thing. Can't complain if you jab back."

"Okay. Hand me your socks, will you?"

I did, and she pulled a sock on my left foot. It felt weird to sit there while she did that. "I'm surprised none of the busybodies you talked to yesterday filled you in about me and Gwen."

Seely looked up then, her face all smoothed out. "I really am sorry. I'm not usually such a bitch."

That annoyed me. "You're not a bitch at all."

"I can be, when my temper's up."

"I have a temper, too, but no one calls me a bitch."

She laughed. "I have a feeling no one calls you anything but 'sir' when you're mad."

"You haven't been around my family." I liked that I'd made her laugh. It was a good sound.

"You're obviously close." She tossed the washcloth in the sink. "Um...Gwen did say that you'd only known Zach for a few months. She said that was her fault."

"It was my fault as much as hers." I didn't like talking about it...but I didn't like her thinking I was the kind of bastard who'd ignore his son, either. "I didn't know about Zach's existence until last March. Gwen and I met when I was on vacation a few years ago. It didn't work out—at least, I decided it wouldn't work out. She has money, you see. Family money. A lot of it. I didn't deal with that well when I found out. She, uh, threw away my address when I left, so by the time she realized she was pregnant, she didn't know how to find me."

"How did you learn about Zach, then?"

"She hired a detective. That was after she'd been diagnosed with breast cancer." I added firmly, so she'd know the subject was closed, "She's okay now. Anyway, she brought Zach here for a visit, and while Zach and I were getting acquainted, she and Duncan fell for each other."

They'd fought it. In hindsight I could see that it must have been hell for both of them. They'd known I'd wanted to marry Gwen, and Duncan at least had accepted that I had a prior claim. But at the time I hadn't been able to see anything except how betrayed I'd felt when I found out, how thoroughly my dreams had been destroyed.

Seely rested her hand on my knee. "I'm glad you told me. If Zach is going to be here often, I wouldn't want to say or do the wrong thing."

That was a good reason for having shot off my mouth. Not the real reason, maybe, but while we were on the subject....
"You should probably know something else. If Zach starts talk-

ing about the bad man and the policeman who shot him—well, that really happened. Maybe someone filled you in on that?"

They hadn't. Useless bunch of busybodies. Why hadn't they told her the stuff that mattered, so I wouldn't have to? I didn't like thinking about that night. The strobing red of the cop car lights, the hard white light inside the store, where a crazy bastard had held Gwen and my son at gunpoint...the fear, raw and jagged like a gutful of broken glass.

I'd failed them. No matter how often I told myself there was nothing I could have done to protect them, the bitterness of my failure didn't go away.

But Seely would need to know the basics, so I told her about the holdup of a convenience store last April, and how Gwen and Zach had been among the hostages taken by a not-too-bright gunman. And how Duncan had saved them.

"My God, Ben. You said something about Zach having had a lot of uncertainty in his life, but I never imagined anything like this."

"He seems to be doing okay. Gwen took him to this guy who does play therapy. That's where kids tell their stories with toys," I explained, "and the therapist sort of plays with them, only in a way that helps them work through things."

"What about you?"

"I wasn't part of it."

"That's what I mean. There's nothing worse than being helpless when someone you love is hurting or in danger."

Uncomfortable, I said, "I don't usually blather on so much. I just thought you ought to know."

She chuckled. "You call that blathering? I don't think anything you said even qualifies as a secret. And I do know a few. It's amazing what people will say to a paramedic. I suppose doctors and nurses experience that, too."

Was that why I felt like there was something between us—because she'd saved my life? Turning the idea over in my mind, I decided it made sense.

She stood. "Seems to me you could use some play therapy yourself, but for now we'll settle for getting you dressed. C'mon, up with you. I'll take that sling off."

The moment I stood, the room shrank. Seely was standing very close, and the soft herbal scent of her hair seemed stronger. I pretended I didn't notice. "I can get this strap in front."

"Okay. Turn a bit…there." The sling came loose, and she slipped it off. "Of course, I don't know half the secrets Daisy does. If you ever met her, you'd find yourself telling her your life story in no time. People do."

My shoulder ached more without the sling's support, so I supported that arm with my other hand. "Who's Daisy? A friend?"

"That, yes. Also my mother."

"You call your mother by her first name?"

"Sure. Can you get those buttons, or do you need some help?"

I thought about letting her unbutton my pajama shirt. Her knuckles would brush against my skin…better to let my right arm dangle and fumble the buttons out left-handed. "I can do it. You did say your mother was unusual."

She chuckled again. A man could get hooked on that sound. "Unusual, yes. She used to be a flower child. The real thing, Haight-Ashbury and all that. In some ways she still is, though she's doing pretty well as an artist these days. I tease her that she's lost in the sixties. Here, we'll do the difficult arm first."

She eased the pajama shirt off my shoulder. It fit snugly over the bandages, so she had to take her time. It was ridiculous to get turned on by that, under the circumstances. But it was a good thing the sweatpants were baggy. "An artist, huh? What kind?"

"Sculpture. She's into what she calls found art these days. Some people call it junk—" her grin flashed "—but she's had two showings at a prestigious gallery in Taos. She scavenges for things people throw away, then paints this or that, puts the objects together and ends up with some pretty interesting pieces."

"Real modern stuff, I take it."

"Well, one critic called it 'an entrancing collision between the primitive and the twenty-first century,' but yes. I have a sneaking suspicion it wouldn't be your type of art." She tossed the pajama shirt on the back of the toilet, then picked up the flannel shirt she'd brought down earlier.

"What about your father? What does he do?"

"Who knows? He came down with a bad case of respectability a few years after I was born. Poor man. I don't think he ever recovered. Here, hold out your arm."

She didn't say anything else while I eased my right arm slowly into a sleeve, then my left. This gave me plenty of time to kick myself. She'd mentioned her mother several times, her father not at all. That should have clued me in.

"I know your shoulder is hurting," she said cheerily. "Turn around and let me do up the buttons. That way you can support that arm until we get the sling back on."

I did turn, but ignored the rest of her instructions. "Sometimes I don't watch where I'm putting my big feet. I stepped in the wrong place. I'm sorry."

Her eyes flicked to mine, surprised. Then a wry smile tipped her lips. "Ben, you're supposed to pretend there's nothing beneath my flip attitude but more flip."

"I'm not much good at pretending."

"No, you aren't," she said so gently she seemed to be touching on some great secret. "I think I like that about you."

She liked my voice, too. And I liked all sorts of things about her. My gaze drifted to her mouth. "I can't imagine what it would be like to grow up with so little family. I'm used to a crowd."

"But you were a lot older than the others, weren't you? You said Duncan is the closest to you in age, and he's five years younger. That's not a big difference now, but it would have been when you were growing up. You wouldn't have played together, or gone on double dates when you were teens, or—oh, all the things an only child thinks siblings are for."

"No, but that's not...they mattered. I mean, it mattered that they were around, that...hell. I don't know how to say it."

"Maybe that they were a huge part of your life? And you love them."

I nodded, relieved that she understood. "I'm not great with words."

"I think you do pretty well." She paused, then went on quietly, "I haven't seen or spoken to my father since I was eight. Um...he and Daisy weren't married."

I felt privileged, as if she'd handed me a private little piece of herself that she didn't leave lying around where just anyone might see it. "He missed a lot, then. Practically everything that matters."

"He did, didn't he?" Her smile slid back in place. "More than me, because I had Daisy."

"The two of you are close?"

She nodded, then just stood there looking up at me, curiosity and something else in those incredible eyes.

It occurred to me that I wouldn't have to bend far to taste her smile.

My heartbeat picked up. I could see the pulse beating in the hollow of her throat, too. Maybe she was having the same thoughts I was. Maybe she wanted me to kiss her. That sweet notion had my head dipping toward hers.

Had I lost my ever-loving *mind?*

Reality snapped back in place. So did my head. Panicked, trying to cover up the moment, I fumbled for the buttons of my shirt.

I forgot that I couldn't use my right arm.

"Oh, damn—*sit!*" She enforced the order with a shove.

I sat. I didn't have enough breath to curse, much less protest.

"You are *not* going to pass out on me," she informed me.

"Of course not." The first hard smack of pain had passed, but my forehead felt clammy. I cleared my throat. "I should probably get the sling back on so I don't forget and try to use that arm again."

"Probably," she said dryly, and retrieved the sling. Our conversation after that consisted of her instructions to me—turn, hold your arm out, that sort of thing. Did she know I'd been about to kiss her? I couldn't tell.

I fastened the straps myself. "I need to call Manny. He's good, but he's not used to overseeing everything."

She studied my face a moment. "Sure. As long as you call him from bed."

I scowled. "The couch in the living room—"

The doorbell rang. It must have woken Doofus; I heard his excited yips and the scrabble of his claws on the floor outside the bathroom as he skidded around the corner, heading for the entry hall.

Seely glanced over her shoulder, then back at me. "Stay put. I'll be back to help you in a minute." She left the bathroom.

I considered the ethics of my situation. I was supposed to

do what she said, but there was that "within reason" clause I'd stuck on. She hadn't stayed around to hear my reasons for not staying put.

One, I wasn't dizzy anymore. Two, the foyer was just the other side of the bathroom. Three, I wanted to see who was here.

I reached for the walking stick.

It was slow and awkward, but the cane did help. Seely was just shutting the front door when I got there, holding Doofus back with her foot so the little idiot didn't scamper out and get into the street. She turned around, tossing a set of keys up and catching them one-handed. Temper sparked in her eyes.

I had a good guess who'd been at the door.

All of a sudden she said, "Here!" And tossed the keys at me.

To catch them, I'd have to drop the walking stick. I let them sail on past. They landed with a rattle on the hardwood floor. Doofus trotted over to investigate them. "Did you miss me on purpose, or was that a happy accident?"

She looked at me like I was something the cat had hacked up on the rug. "The mechanic I took my car to just left."

I nodded, having figured out that much. "All fixed, I take it."

"Against my explicit instructions—yes!" Those sparks turned into big, blazing fires. "That man—that weasely, lowlife scum I'd *thought* was an honest mechanic—he wouldn't even tell me what the repairs had cost. Just winked at me, handed me the keys and said it was all taken care of. He practically patted my hand and told me not to worry my pretty little head!"

"Well, then. Looks like you can stop worrying."

She growled. Honest to God, that's what it sounded like. "This is not worry. This is *fury*." She stalked closer, tilting her face to snarl up at me, "You paid for it. You went behind my back and paid for the whole thing."

"I wasn't going to let you lose your car. You saved my life."

"You had no right! No right at all! You didn't even ask me!"

"If I'd asked," I pointed out, "you probably would have argued. I'm sure that wouldn't be good for me, weak as I am right now."

"It wouldn't be good for you if I were to trip you, either. Or poison your coffee. Or—or—dammit, if you don't stop grinning at me in that obnoxious way, I'm going to do something we'll both regret!"

I was grinning, wasn't I? Once she'd called attention to that, my grin widened. I was enjoying myself. A lot. Seely in a temper was something to see—eyes hot, cheeks flushed, those volatile eyebrows drawn down in a scowl. So, like the daredevil I'd never been, I plunged off the next cliff. "You are cute as hell when you're mad, you know that?"

Her mouth dropped open. It closed and opened a couple more times before she got some words out. "That knock on the head did more damage than the doctor realized."

"A lot like a kitten—hissing, scratching, growling. Cute."

"I am five feet, ten and a half inches tall in my stocking feet. I am not *cute*. And you are obviously mentally as well as physically handicapped, so I suppose I shouldn't hit you too hard."

"Well, if you're already planning on hitting me…" I said that, so on some level I must have known what I was about to do. But the thought never got up to the top of my brain where I could squash it. Something else was pulling my strings, as if some part of me I'd never known existed was suddenly in charge.

I let the walking stick clatter to the floor, cupped the back of her head and kissed her.

Her lips were soft. That wasn't a surprise. She went rigid the second my mouth touched hers. No surprise there, either. But the kick of pleasure went deeper than I'd expected. The taste of her shot straight to the primitive part of my brain the way smells do, bypassing reason. I couldn't have known that would happen. And there's no way I could have predicted the funny little sound she made just before she melted up against me.

One of us was still thinking, I guess, because she was careful of my shoulder, sliding one arm around me and letting her other hand rest on my waist. I hummed my approval against those soft lips, threaded my fingers through her hair and tilted her head so I could deepen the kiss. And she opened for me.

Automatically I widened my stance so I could snug her up closer. The stupid sling was in the way and my knee protested, but the way her fingers kneaded my waist mattered a lot more.

So did the warm, living feel of her beneath my hand. I loved the fact that I didn't have to bend over much to explore the flavors inside her mouth, and the way she stroked her tongue along mine. The long muscles of her back invited me to sample the dip at her waist, the smooth curve of her bottom.

She liked my body, too. Her hand left my waist to range up beneath my shirt and over my chest. Delight slid into need without a bump to mark the change.

I slid my right leg between hers and pressed up. She shivered. I needed more, needed her skin, her sighs, the little bud of her nipple in my mouth...where? Where could I take her? The living room was close, and the couch there was long and roomy. I started easing us both that way without taking my mouth from hers.

My foot slid out from under me.

I yelled. Doofus yipped. Seely's arm tightened around me, and somehow I managed not to fall on my stupid ass.

Not literally, anyway. Appalled by my behavior, I yanked

my hand away and stepped back. My heartbeat was doing the hundred-yard dash, my knee hurt, my shoulder hurt, and my foot was...wet. I glanced down.

"Oh," Seely said, one hand rising to her mouth to smother a giggle. She crouched to pet the droopy-eared puppy. "Oh, Doofus. You did *try* to go out, didn't you, boy?"

Saved from my own worst self by a puppy's bladder. Mortified, I said stiffly, "I apologize. I said you wouldn't have to deal with, uh, grabby hands, and then...all I can do is apologize, and promise it won't happen again."

Her gaze took a lazy trip up me while she fondled the puppy's ears. She made a tch-ing sound, shook her head and stood. "Didn't your sister ever tell you? Never apologize to a woman for kissing her—not if she kissed you back."

My ears felt hot. The rest of me was sore, aroused, exhausted and bewildered. "The last employer who made a pass at you ended up wearing someone else's dinner."

"Ben." Her smile started in her eyes and glowed its way down to her mouth. She patted my cheek. "You're not Vic, are you?"

She turned away, picked up my walking stick and handed it to me. "What you should be apologizing for is interfering in my arrangements with the mechanic. I suppose your intentions were good, but it was intolerably high-handed. How much did the repairs cost?"

"I don't know yet, and it doesn't matter."

"Probably not," she agreed easily, turning away. "Since I doubt I'd be able to repay you. I'd better get something to clean up that puddle."

"You don't have to repay me. I don't want you to."

She headed for the kitchen. "As far as I'm concerned, the car is yours now. I'll get the title switched over as soon as possible."

I frowned. Her threat about the car was annoying, but not

a real problem. If she put it in my name, I'd just put it back in hers. A much bigger worry was my own behavior.

My sister, Annie, has accused me of seeing everything in black-and-white. Maybe I do. But right and wrong have never seemed all that complicated, and if a man knows what's right, that's what he should do. Even when it's hard. Maybe especially then.

Kissing Seely was wrong. I knew that, even if she didn't. She was an employee. She was also a warm, giving sort of woman who deserved better than hand-me-downs from a man in love with another woman.

I knew that. So why had I kissed her?

No answers floated up. I stood there, aware of a number of places that hurt, and the lingering hum of arousal that defied the pain. After a moment I sighed and limped for the bathroom.

There was one bright spot. I'd stepped in the blasted puddle with my right foot, not my left. At least I could wash it myself.

Five

"Does it hurt a lot?" Zach asked.

"Not anymore."

"How much does it hurt? This much?" He used his thumb and forefinger to take a tiny pinch of air. "Or this much?" He held out both hands broadly.

"About like this." I measured a couple of inches between my finger and thumb. "More at bedtime, because I'm tired."

He nodded seriously. "When I'm sick I hurt more at bedtime. How does this thing go on?" He pointed at my sling.

We were sitting on the rear deck, enjoying what was probably one of the last warm afternoons of the year. Zach was perched on my right thigh. My left foot was propped up on a little table to keep the knee elevated. That had been Seely's idea, keeping the knee elevated, and I guess it did help. The swelling had gone down some. Doofus lay nearby, panting hopefully.

I showed Zach how my sling fastened, undoing one of the Velcro tapes and letting him restick it a few times. Velcro was one of Zach's favorite things. He wanted to know if he could have the sling to play with after I was all better.

I smiled. "Sure." God only knew what he planned to do with it. That didn't matter. The important thing was that he'd accepted I would be "all better" eventually.

He told me Doofus was lonely and clambered down to play with his pup. I handed him his magnifying glass—another of his favorite things—and pup and boy ran off to look for bugs. My throat closed up as I watched them. I'd come so close to never having an afternoon like this again.

On the other side of the sliding glass doors behind me, Seely was chopping things in the kitchen and talking to Gwen. The two of them seemed to have really hit it off. That was undoubtedly a good thing, but it made me uncomfortable. Women tell each other the damnedest things sometimes.

I couldn't stop thinking about that kiss.

Not that I thought about it every second. I had plenty of other things on my mind, like reassuring Zach, trying to set up the remodel job at the resort without leaving the house, and problems on the Pearson site.

But the memory of that kiss kept ambushing me.

I'd been eating lunch—Seely had made cheeseburgers—and all of a sudden I'd noticed her hands, the long fingers and short nails, and I'd remembered how she'd dug those fingers into my back. When Doofus tried to trip me on the way to the bathroom, I thought about how he'd nearly caused another accident.

Shoot, in the middle of a crossword puzzle the word *erupt* made me think of volcanoes, lava and heat, and I was right back with that kiss. All day long, it kept popping out at me like a jack-in-the-box with a broken lid.

I didn't like it. It's not that I expect to control my thoughts a hundred percent of the time, but I don't like being pushed around by them, either.

Maybe hiring Seely hadn't been such a great idea. I was stuck with the decision, though. It wouldn't be fair to change my mind now. I'd just have to get myself up to par as quickly as possible so I could let her go.

And then she wouldn't be off-limits anymore.

That sneaky thought annoyed me. I drummed my fingers on the arm of the chair. Once Seely's employment with me was over, she probably wouldn't be in Highpoint anymore, either. Duncan had found her at the bus station, for God's sake. And I wasn't interested in trying to persuade a reluctant woman to stay. I'd failed miserably the last time.

My chest tightened. That twitchy, brittle feeling climbed over me, the one that had ridden me too often lately, as if I were wearing my skin backward. One wrong move could split it, spilling all sorts of messy, inner bits out on the dirty ground. Yet I craved motion, action.

I was scared.

I'd wanted Gwen, wanted her for keeps. I'd gone at getting her to marry me the way I go after any important goal, giving it everything I had. And I'd flopped, big-time. She'd fallen for my brother.

Plenty of times in the last few months I'd told myself I needed to start looking for a woman to share my life. And hadn't done it. I'd begun to wonder what was wrong with me, if maybe I was too old to marry for the first time. Maybe my standards were too high, or there was something missing in me. Maybe I'd missed my chance for a family of my own.

For a long, still moment, I sat there in my wicker chair on

the deck I'd built and faced a truth I'd been dodging. Deep down, I wasn't sure I could handle failing again.

The late-afternoon sunshine hit the yard at a strong slant, dragging long shadows from the poplars along the back fence that striped the yard in plump diagonals. I hadn't mowed the grass in three weeks. It was still green but had stopped growing. The leaves on the oak showed more gold than green in the autumn sun.

By the back gate, Zach and Doofus were digging industriously. I smiled, wondering what he was digging for. Gold? Diamonds? Or the sheer joy of making a nice, big hole in the ground?

Maybe it wouldn't be so bad if I never managed to pull off the wife-and-family bit. I had Zach. I didn't have him every day, but lots of fathers were in that position these days. Didn't they say that happiness lay in being content with what you have, instead of yearning for more?

My fingers started drumming again. To hell with that. Sounded like giving up to me.

The doors behind me slid open, and a wonderful aroma drifted out.

"Thought you might like some sweet tea," Seely said. "It's a Southern tradition."

"Sure. Thanks." I accepted the glass she held out, willing to try one of her traditions. "I don't need that jacket, Gwen."

Seely took the old rocker. Gwen sat in the wicker chair that matched mine, laying my jacket across her knees. "If you say so. You know me—I'm always cold." She studied my face a moment. "You're right, Seely. He does look better. Hard to believe he's actually been behaving."

"I don't know why everyone thinks I'm incapable of taking care of myself. I've been doing it for a few years now." I took a sip of tea. "This is good. So, I guess the two of you have been, uh, getting acquainted?"

Gwen shook her head, grinning. "The look on your face, Ben! It's easy to see you think the two of us had nothing better to talk about than you. Shame on you."

"You've been talking for over an hour. In my experience, that's enough time for two women to exchange their life histories and get started on everyone else's."

Seely laughed. The rocker creaked as she leaned forward to pat my knee. "Don't worry. She didn't spill the beans about your misspent youth."

Gwen frowned. "I don't think Ben *had* a misspent youth. Or much of a youth at all, with the way he had to give up everything when…" Her voice trailed off. Maybe because of the look on my face.

The rocking chair creaked again as Seely leaned back. "Actually, we talked about your house more than you. I love old houses."

"Yeah?" I relaxed, pleased. "This one isn't all that old compared to some back east. But around here, homes over fifty years old aren't common."

"When was it built?"

"In 1935, but my grandfather used salvaged pieces from older houses where he could. That's fashionable now, but not too many people were doing it back then. The wainscoting in the entry and the mantel in the living room are about 120 years old. Came from an old bawdy house."

She laughed. "Oh, that's wonderful! And the staircase? That looks old."

"The newel post is over a hundred years old."

"It's a grand old house." She rocked gently a moment. "A pity it's neglected, but I suppose that's like the cobbler's children going barefoot. You're probably too busy building other people's homes to have time for your own."

I sat up straight. "What the hell are you talking about? Everything's in great shape!"

"I'm sure it is. Maybe *neglected* was the wrong word. It just doesn't look like anything has changed much in twenty years."

I had my mouth open, ready to blast her, when Zach came running up, chanting his mom-mom-mom mantra.

"Good grief, you're dirty," Gwen said.

"Yeah. Come see the bug me an' Doofus found. You, too, Seely," he said, politely including her in the treat. He and she had settled it earlier that he was to use her first name. "It's tre-*men*-duz."

Lots of things were tre-*men*-duz lately. I reached for my stick.

Seely stood, put her hand on my good shoulder and asked, with one lifted eyebrow, if I was sure I ought to get up. I scowled at her, but stayed put. "The steps from the deck are tricky for me," I told Zach. "I'll sit this bug out."

Everyone else headed across the yard. Over by the rear gate, Doofus was barking at the pile of dirt he and Zach had created. I assume the bug was there. Seely grinned at Zach and said something I couldn't make out. Zach giggled. Gwen smiled at him, then tilted her head to speak to Seely.

Seen side by side, the two women couldn't have looked more different. Gwen was a tidy little thing, her short hair pale and shiny in the sunlight. Seely was at least a head taller. More robust. Brighter, somehow.

I frowned. More irritating, too. What was so great about changing stuff around, anyway? Everything worked. And it wasn't as if I hadn't done anything to the place for twenty years. The couch and area rug in the living room were only five years old. Of course, it was Annie who'd nagged me into replacing them, but so what? And maybe they sat in exactly the same spot as the old ones had, but they looked good there.

The deck I was sitting on—I'd added that myself.

Fifteen years ago.

Doofus suddenly tried to catch his tail, and Seely laughed. She had a husky laugh. It made me think of a messy bed, with the sheets dripping to the floor and Seely rising above me, throwing her hair back and laughing just like that...

Whoa. That was weird, fantasizing about Seely with Gwen right next to her. But guilt was stupid. I owed Gwen family loyalty, and that was all. I was allowed to look at other women. In fact, I'd damned well better start looking.

First, though, I had to finish healing. Right now I couldn't even pick a woman up to take her to dinner. I sighed, thinking of my truck. I needed to find out what kind of hoops the insurance company wanted me to jump through before they'd issue a check.

The phone was sitting on the table beside me. I'd brought it out because I'd been talking to Manny earlier. I'd input dozens of numbers into the directory when I bought the phone a few months ago.

Not everything around here was old, dammit.

Bah. I punched up the directory. Time to put my brain to some kind of *productive* use.

Gwen slid Zach's arm into a jacket he didn't really need. "Seely, it was a pleasure meeting you. No, Ben, sit down. Don't walk to the car with us."

I shook my head sadly as I used the walking stick to lever myself upright. "What is it about me being injured that turns everyone into tyrant wannabes?"

Seely chuckled, Gwen grimaced, and Zach wanted to know why he couldn't take his bug home. To prove I could compromise, I limped to the door with them instead of going all the way to the car. "I guess I'll see you Saturday, kid." I ruffled the top of Zach's head.

He looked puzzled. "Are you goin', too?"

"Oh, Lord." Gwen rolled her eyes. "I can't believe I forgot to tell you. Duncan was going to when he stopped by yesterday, but you were sleeping."

"Tell me what?"

"Zach was terribly disappointed about missing out on his camping trip with you. Duncan managed to get some time off so he could take him."

The knife slid in so fast I couldn't guard against it. *I* was supposed to be the one who took Zach camping and hiking. I was the one who'd taught Duncan, dammit. Not to mention Charlie and Annie. Our parents hadn't much cared about that sort of thing, but I did. I always had.

My brother had everything else—why did he have to grab this, too?

"Dad?" Zach sounded uncertain.

So I smiled. "Just feeling sorry for myself because I have to miss this one. But you can tell me all about it when you get back, right?"

"Right!"

I didn't watch them drive away. I never do. That's a rule. Every time Zach leaves—especially when Gwen picks him up—I get hit with a load of might-have-beens. No point in taking a chance on Zach guessing how I felt. Kids often blame themselves when the adults in their lives are screwing up.

But I did wait to shut the door until they were both in Gwen's car.

Seely was standing behind me. "That was hard," she said. "You handled it well."

I grunted, annoyed with her for seeing too much, and hobbled toward the living room. "Not that hard. My knee's doing better."

"I wasn't talking about your knee. But I think you know that and are trying delicately to hint me away from the subject. Unfortunately," she said sadly, "I am almost immune to hints."

A quick snort of laughter snuck out before I could stop it. "That's the first time anyone's ever called me delicate. I hear blunt, rude, pigheaded and tactless from time to time, but not delicate."

"There you go. We have a lot in common. I figure you'll understand how hard it is for a basically direct person to tiptoe around a subject. Much easier to just say what you're thinking, isn't it?"

"Gets you in trouble sometimes," I said. I'd reached the couch and sat down, suppressing a sigh of relief. Stupid knee. My shoulder wasn't feeling too great, either.

"Trouble can be interesting. Here, let me help you get that leg up."

"I can do it."

"Now how did I know you were going to say that?" She ignored my scowl, putting her hands under my calf and helping me lift the leg onto the couch. "I must be psychic."

"That makes sense. It's not like I'm predictable."

She laughed and settled on the other end, curling one leg up beneath her. That surprised me. She'd mostly stayed away this afternoon unless I needed something...which I figured was my fault. Because of that kiss. With my leg stretched out between us, I couldn't jump her. That's probably what she was thinking.

And I was not thinking about that kiss again. I was just wondering if she was.

"I liked watching you and Zach together," she said. "Gave me the idea that you're crazy about him."

"Well, yeah. Of course I am. Any man..." My voice trailed off as I remembered that her father hadn't acted like he was crazy about her. I cleared my throat. "Of course, some men are jerks."

"I can agree with that."

The bitter note in her voice surprised me, though it shouldn't have. She had a right to be bitter. "Do you hate him?" I asked abruptly. "Your father, I mean."

She blinked. "I...oh, damn, I wanted to say no, that he doesn't matter enough to hate. And that's almost true. But sometimes..."

She shrugged and looked away, but not before I'd seen the unhappiness in her eyes. "It's like having a trick knee. You go along fine for days, weeks, even months. Then all of a sudden you put your weight on it, and it doesn't hold. Every now and then I still get angry. Dumb, isn't it?" Her mouth twisted. "I'm thirty-two years old. I should be over it by now."

"I don't see what 'should' has to do with it. Seems to me we can control our actions, but thoughts and feelings don't pay much attention to rules." Or I wouldn't be thinking about that blasted kiss again.

She looked startled, then smiled. "I suspect a lot of people underestimate you."

That was probably a compliment. I studied her a moment. Though her body was easy, relaxed, I thought shadows lingered in her eyes. I decided to steer us into less painful territory. "So, what would you change in here?"

"Me?"

"You said things hadn't been changed in a long time. You must have had something in mind."

"I'd paint the walls," she said promptly.

I looked around critically. "Nothing wrong with the paint."

"It's white, Ben."

"So?"

"So the room could use some color. Red would be great."

"You're kidding."

"Green would be good, too—a rich green, nothing wimpy. But this couch is a lovely, warm brown. I think red would be great with it. And maybe some molding over the fireplace to match the crown moldings. That would make the mantel really pop."

I eyed her dubiously. "You sound like an upscale decorator."

She laughed. "I'll admit to being hooked on those shows on cable."

"They have decorating shows?"

"Don't watch much TV, do you?"

"Not if I can help it."

"Well, there's a whole network devoted to it. Shows about gardening and all kinds of decorating—window treatments, kitchen remodels, painting techniques, all that sort of thing." She grinned. "A friend of mine calls it female porn. We can look and drool, but we can't touch."

"Sounds about right." I gave a thoughtful nod. "Green, maybe. I could see a pale green in here. Or purple."

"Uh…purple?"

"Sure. Put a little gilding on the crown moldings, too. It would really dress the place up."

She caught on. "Gilding the moldings! I never would have thought of that. But then, you really must use red for the walls. Chinese red. And maybe a little pagoda in the corner?"

We spent the next few minutes turning my living room into a Chinese emperor's nightmare, complete with bamboo, lacquered screens and dragons, all in the most garish cast of colors possible. Somehow that evolved into a discussion of building styles, remodeling and how to honor the architectural integrity of a building when creating an addition.

Now, all this was right up my alley. I don't often swing a hammer or hang drywall myself these days, but I've done it enough in the past. A good builder has to know a little about everything, from the right temperature to pour concrete to the current craze for paint glazes to how to shore up a damaged load-bearing wall. So it might seem like I was enjoying some shop talk and Seely was humoring me, but it wasn't like that. It wasn't about me at all. I would have talked about blueberry muffin recipes if that's what got her this excited, just so I could watch her glow.

This slow-moving woman came alive when she talked houses. Which was downright peculiar for a woman with no nesting urges.

"Your den is an addition, isn't it?" she said. She was snuggled into the corner of the couch, her shoes off and her feet tucked up. A strand of hair had worked loose to wiggle along her temple and cheekbone like a hyperactive question mark.

I grimaced. "Sticks out like a sore thumb, doesn't it? I've always meant to redo it. The roofline messes up the rear and side elevations. My father had it done, and I don't think he gave a thought to how it fit with the rest of the house's style."

"He wasn't interested in construction and architecture himself, then?"

"Sure, if it took place two or three thousand years ago."

"I've wondered about that," she said slowly. "I would have thought there would be exotic mementos scattered around from all the time he spent abroad. Pot shards, maybe, or a scarab or two."

"I've got a pretty little Egyptian lady in my bedroom, on the dresser. Most of that stuff is boxed up, though. Never really knew what to do with it. Now what," I demanded, "did I say to put that polite look on your face?"

"Who, me? Polite?"

"Like you're thinking something you're too nice to say."

"Oh." She flushed. "And here I'm trying to be tactful…it just seems like you have some issues with your parents. Maybe with the way they died and left you to raise the family they'd started."

My good mood evaporated. "I did what had to be done. That's all."

"And that was a less-than-delicate hint to close the subject. Good enough." She said that with perfect good humor, but rose to her feet. "I'd better go check on the roast."

"Don't rush off. I didn't mean to…dammit, you can't get offended every time I'm an ass, or we won't be able to talk at all."

She patted my shoulder. "No offense taken. I don't blame you for getting testy when people make a fuss about the way you took on the responsibility for your brothers and sisters. It must seem sometimes as if you're defined by what happened twenty years ago. As if nothing you've done since then matters, compared to that."

Having leveled me with a few words, she swayed gently toward the door. "Supper should be ready soon. You want to eat on a tray in here?"

I must have answered, because she left the room. God only knows what I said. I don't know how long I sat staring at the wall and seeing nothing, either.

Eventually sheer physical discomfort roused me. My shoulder this time. I mushed some pillows around to create more support for it, leaned back and waited for the fire to die down.

The blasted woman had a bad habit of saying outrageous things, then wandering off, leaving me no one to argue with but myself. That would stop, I promised myself. If she was going to drop bombshells, she could damned well hang around and deal with the debris.

But Seely wasn't in the habit of hanging around.

Never mind. People could change, right? She was big on changing walls and furniture. She could just get used to the idea of changing a couple of habits, too.

It was a helluva thing, but somewhere between Chinese-red walls and that irritating pat on my shoulder, my gut had made a decision without consulting the rest of me. For the next few days, I'd be such a good patient my family would worry about me.

Because I had to get well and fire Seely. Soon. I was going to have that woman out of my employ—and in my bed.

Six

The next day, Manny came over for lunch. He dropped off the paint we'd chosen and some painting equipment, then helped Seely move the furniture out of the living room.

I can't explain how I came to agree to this. Slippery, that's what she is. She started out by acting as if I'd already agreed. I recognized this trick, since Annie used to pull it. She'd get me to agree that music is important, mention that she wanted to spend the night with a friend, then pretend that meant I'd agreed to let her go to a concert in Denver with that friend.

When I explained Annie's teenage tricks to Seely, she looked thoughtful and said she really needed to meet my sister. The next thing I knew we were discussing paint colors.

I did protest. She wasn't being paid to paint my house, for God's sake. And I couldn't help her. She wouldn't have let me, for one thing. I couldn't pretend it would be unreasonable to forbid me to paint the living room, so I was bound by our agreement.

But that did not make it reasonable for her to do it, either. I asked if she'd ever done any painting.

"Not a lick," she'd said cheerfully. "We'll pull the couch into the middle of the room. You can lie there and supervise."

Sage green. That's the color we ended up with.

I sat on the couch with my bad leg stretched out, and scowled as Manny and Seely carried the last of the chairs into the dining room. Supervising didn't suit me nearly as well as everyone seemed to think.

"You sure you don't want me to help with the prep?" Manny was asking her as they rejoined me. "Or move the rest of the junk out?" He jerked a thumb over his shoulder in my direction.

"I'm sure I can work around the couch."

"Wasn't talking about the couch."

Seely's lips twitched.

"Manny thinks he's a wit," I mentioned. "You might not be able to tell, since his face muscles atrophied years ago. That's the only expression he's got."

Manny has an evil chuckle, like a machine gun misfiring. He employed it as he headed for the front door, advising Seely in between bursts not to let me give her a hard time. He paused in the arched entry. "Meant to tell you—that doctor called this morning."

"What doctor?"

"The one that put you back together in the E.R."

"Oh," Gwen said. "The idiot."

Manny fired another couple of bursts. "That's the one. He seemed to think you'd hurt your shoulder a few days ago instead of when you drove off a mountain. Wanted me to confirm that." He shook his head. "Weird guy."

"Yeah." I frowned as Seely walked Manny to the door. Harry Meckle was weird, but he wasn't really an idiot. Just the opposite.

The doorbell rang. I heard them talking to someone else at the door and reached for my walking stick.

"Stay put," Seely called. "It's just a delivery."

I sighed and put the stick down. A moment later I heard the door shut, then she came back into the room carrying a box. "I like Manny. I wish you'd told me, though. I'm afraid I stared at first."

"What? Oh. That's right—you hadn't met him in person." In addition to being a pain in the butt, a master electrician and the best foreman I've ever had, Manny is a dwarf. "I didn't think about it. To me he's just Manny."

She handed me the box, treating me to that slow smile. "Not 'Manny the dwarf.' Just Manny."

"Well, yeah." The logo was printed in the corner, so I knew what it held. I didn't want to open it now. "You know how it is. Once you know someone, you don't see them the same way." I decided to give her a hint. "There should be a screwdriver in the toolbox. You'll want to remove the switch plates first."

"I was hoping for a tool belt." She bent and rummaged through the toolbox. "I'm sure I'd feel more competent with a tool belt."

My lips twitched. Picturing a tool belt slung around those thoroughly female hips didn't make me think of competence.

Seely ambled over to the entry and began unfastening the switch plate there. "You like to read, don't you? I noticed that your bookshelves are heavy on history."

It turned out that Seely enjoyed history, too, though she was a slow reader. A mild case of dyslexia, she said, made a book a major investment of time for her. She considered herself lucky, since she'd been diagnosed early, and talked about a teacher who'd helped her. When I asked, she claimed paramedic training hadn't been too hard. It might take her a while to read something, but, as with many dyslexics, she had an excellent memory.

Though she usually leaned more toward historical fiction than the straight stuff, she asked if I could recommend something on American history "without too many battles," since she was more interested in people than military action.

I did, of course, and invited her to borrow my copy. By then she'd finished taping off the woodwork and was prying open the paint. She poured it into the pan. "Oh, look! Isn't that luscious?"

I looked. She'd taken the drapes down already, so light from the two tall windows flooded the room. The old pair of painter's coveralls I'd found for her completely obscured that glorious figure; her exuberant hair was braided tightly away from her face.

Which glowed. Not in an unearthly way, though. With pure delight. "Luscious," I agreed.

Maybe I did know how I'd ended up agreeing to let her paint the room, after all.

As she spread great, sweeping strokes of sage green across my walls, I found myself telling her how I'd come to enjoy reading so much. I didn't miss the architectural career I might have had; the hands-on business of construction suited me. But abandoning college before I could get my degree had nagged at me, as if I'd drawn most of a circle and never finished that last arc. So I'd started reading the kinds of things I thought would complete my education. In the process, I discovered a taste for history.

"It's full of great stories," she agreed, stepping back to survey her work. The roller work was almost done; next came the nit-picky brush work. "Daisy says we have to know where we come from to understand where we are."

"Your mother sounds like a bright woman. You missed a spot up by the ceiling in the west corner," I pointed out politely.

She glanced at me over her shoulder. "You're enjoying this."

"Who'd have thought it?" I shook my head in amazement. "I never tried sitting around watching someone else work. I like it." Especially when she bent over and the coveralls stretched tight across her round, lovely bottom.

She'd ordered me to stay on the couch. I doubt she was thinking about me making a quick tackle, then rolling her onto her back on the drop cloth. I was, though. Never mind that I'd probably have passed out if I'd tried. It was just as well that our agreement kept me from pitting common sense against the irrational optimism of lust.

Seely got the spot I'd pointed out, then stretched...an inspiring sight. "So what do you think? Will it need a second coat?"

I made myself take a good look at the walls. "Hey," I said slowly. "This looks good. Really good."

"It does, doesn't it?" She put her hands on her hips, surveying her work. The streak of green paint along her jaw curled up at one end, as smug as her smile. "Though I still say red would have worked, the green looks great. Refreshing."

She'd brought me some paint chips to choose from that morning. I'd held out for a lighter, warmer shade than she wanted, being more familiar with translating the way a color looked on a tiny chip to an entire room. "You were right about the room needing color."

"Well!" Her eyebrows rose. "A man who can admit he was wrong. Color me amazed."

"You have brothers," I muttered. "Or used to. You probably murdered them and buried the bodies."

She let out a peal of laughter. "Watch it, or you'll end up with a green nose."

"To match yours?"

She lifted a hand to her nose. The bracelet she never removed slid down her arm. "It isn't…"

"It is now."

"I must look like a little girl who's been finger painting."

"No," I said slowly. "You look like an uncommonly beautiful woman. Only *slightly* green."

The smile she turned on me was different. Hesitant.

"Why have you never married, Seely?"

Her smile faded, as if it were on a dimmer switch and I'd just turned it down. "You're changing the rules on me. Feeling safe, are you, over there on the couch?"

My heart began to pound. I didn't have to figure out what she meant. "Not safe at all. You?"

She shook her head and bent to get the narrow brush I'd told her to use around the baseboards. She took the brush and the paint tray over to the window and settled on the floor, giving me plenty of time to wonder why I'd suddenly taken us both into the deep end.

Because I wanted her to know, I decided. I didn't want her to have any doubts that I was interested, even if I couldn't do anything about it yet. I wanted her aware of me the way I was aware of her.

I wanted an answer to my question, too.

For a while, it didn't look as though I was going to get it. She seemed totally focused on the strip of wall she was painting next to the baseboard. At last, not looking up, she said, "I lived with a man for several years. His name was Steven. Steven Francis Blois."

I chewed over that for a moment, then offered, "There was a king of England named Stephen Blois. William the Conqueror's grandson."

She snorted. "Oh, yes. Every time Steven was introduced to someone he'd say, 'no relation.' When they looked confused or asked what he meant, he'd grin and add, 'to the former king of England, that is.'"

She bent and dipped her brush in the paint. "It was cute the first dozen or so times I heard it."

Sounded like she wasn't hung up on the man anymore. Encouraged, I said, "Stephen wasn't much of a king. Weak. The country was torn apart during his reign—barons chewing on other barons, eventually civil war."

"I don't think Steven knew or cared what kind of a king his namesake had been. He wasn't interested in history." She chuckled. "Actually, he was an accountant."

"An accountant." That sounded safe and dull. Of course, a builder might sound pretty dull, too. "Doesn't seem like your type."

"Do we have types?" She studied her handiwork, then shifted to touch up another section. "I thought he had an open, inquiring mind. He was very New Age, you see. Into meditation, drumming, psychic stuff."

Had he given her that chakra bracelet? I frowned. "Doesn't sound like any accountants I know."

"But he was still looking for rules, you see. Pigeonholes instead of answers. He didn't think outside the box—he just used a different set of boxes."

"So you're not still stuck on him?"

Now she looked up. "I told you about Steven because you asked why I'm not married. While we were together, I took that commitment very seriously. We were involved for six years, and lived together for five. But it ended with a fizzle, not a bang. That was over two years ago."

Steven Francis Blois must be a fool, to have had this woman for six years without marrying her. But maybe he'd wanted to get married. Maybe, for all her talk about taking the commitment seriously, she hadn't been interested in taking that last step. "So, was it you or him who thought living together was a good idea?"

Her lips twitched. "Something tells me you don't think much of living together without marriage."

"It isn't a moral thing for me. I just, ah…" Couldn't think of a tactful way to put it. Well, I'd warned her I was blunt. "It's always struck me as half-assed."

She didn't seem offended. "I take it you've never lived with anyone. What about marriage? Why have you never taken the plunge?"

"Uh…"

Her eyes lit with amusement. "Ben. You did open the subject for discussion, you know."

I guess I had, though that hadn't occurred to me when I blurted out my question. "I was serious about someone in college. Didn't work out. After that…well, for several years I was too blasted busy. Felt as if I had to set a good example—couldn't very well tell Charlie and Duncan how to act if I wasn't being responsible myself. And Annie. Lord." I shook my head. "I don't know how single parents do it. I didn't have time for much of a social life. Or the energy."

She made a listening sort of sound, and resumed painting. "Annie's the youngest, right? She's been an adult for a while now."

"I wasn't in a hurry to get tied down right away, once Annie went off to college. I guess I got out of the habit of thinking about marriage. It seemed like there was plenty of time."

"I imagine you were due a spell of blissful freedom. You'd been shortchanged on that when you were younger."

"By the time I started looking around..." I shrugged my good shoulder. "It's been suggested that I'm too picky."

She paused in her painting. Her eyes were serious when they met mine. The blue seemed darker, subdued, like a pond shadowed by trees, hiding what lay at the bottom. I wondered if she was thinking about Gwen and the child we shared. "And are you looking now? Is marriage what you want, Ben?"

"I'm forty years old."

She waited, letting her silence point out that I hadn't really answered the question.

I grimaced. I *had* opened the subject. "I want marriage, yeah. Kids to fill this old house with noise, skateboards, dolls, friends. Younger brothers or sisters to give their big brother a hard time. And a woman to share those kids with me." Someone who'd clutter the bathroom with female paraphernalia, and sleep beside me at night. Someone who would stay.

Her smile flashed, but somehow it seemed off. "Those skateboarding kids will turn into teenagers, you know. Your experience with your brothers and sisters didn't put you off?"

"It wasn't so bad. And maybe I learned a few things." I'd had about all the serious talk I could take. "What kind of teenager were you? Wild or studious? Not shy," I said definitely.

She chuckled and dipped her brush again. "Not studious, either. Though I wouldn't say I was wild, exactly—I couldn't bear to worry Daisy, so I didn't go too far. But I didn't have much sense. Is there anyone in the world as sure of themselves as eighteen-year-olds?"

We traded stories of our teenage days for a while. It looked as if she'd be able to finish up today, which wasn't bad for someone who'd never painted a room before. Of course, I'd helped a little. It didn't hurt my shoulder or my knee for me to sit on the floor and paint the strip next to the baseboards. Seely had argued some about that, but eventually she'd seen reason.

She was on the stepladder tackling the section next to the crown moldings by the time I figured out what was nagging at me.

Seely seemed open and outgoing. She swapped funny stories about growing up and spoke cheerfully about her eccentric mother. She'd told me about Steven, who I guess had been the one big love of her life.

But she'd never said which of them had preferred living together to marriage. She hadn't said anything about why she'd moved out, either, just that it happened two years ago. Yesterday she'd admitted to being angry with her father, but hadn't told me the man's name, or anything else about him. And she'd implied that anything weird I'd seen that night on the mountain must have been the product of shock.

Slippery.

Seely Jones was a much more private woman than she seemed. I could respect that, and yet…I glanced uneasily at the unopened box beside the couch.

Last year I'd gone wireless when I got a new laptop. It didn't have to be hooked up to anything to connect to the Internet. So, on my first night home from the hospital I'd ordered several books on-line, paying to have them overnighted. I probably could have gotten them, or something similar, from the bookstore on Fremont Street. Susannah would have boxed up my order and dropped them off, if I'd asked.

Or I could have gotten books from the library for nothing. I'd known the head librarian since I was five. Muriel would have looked up my card number, checked the books out to me and brought them by.

But anyone who knew me would have been startled by my current choice of reading material. I didn't want to explain. I didn't want anyone speculating about my sanity, either. I was doing enough of that.

Finding myself in the company of Harold Meckle, M.D., was a nasty shock, but like I said, he wasn't really an idiot. Just a jerk. Some of the things that happened on that mountain didn't add up, not using any of the normal ways of calculating reality.

"That bracelet you wear," I mentioned as I finished the last bit I could reach. "Did Blois give it to you?"

She didn't turn around. "Why do you ask?"

"You said the little stones were for, uh, chakras. And that Blois was into New Age stuff."

"Daisy gave it to me—her version of a 'sweet sixteen' present."

"She's into chakras?"

"Among other things."

I decided not to press for more. Not now. I'd gotten one solid answer—Blois hadn't given her the bracelet she never seemed to remove. That was something. Far from all I needed to know, though. Maybe I'm too stubborn for my own good. I've been told that more than once.

I wondered what Duncan would say about the request I planned to make the next time I saw him.

Seven

"Look, if you don't want to do it, just say so."

"I don't want to do it."

I sighed.

Duncan and I were sitting at the kitchen table with some of Seely's excellent coffee. She was upstairs getting ready.

Not that she needed to. We were just going to drop by the office—though I hadn't mentioned that part yet—then head to the building-supply center. And she already looked great. She always did.

But women have rules for that sort of thing. Not the same rules, mind—they vary from one woman to the next in some sort of changeable code. It seems to make sense to other women.

Setting has something to do with it. When Annie was doing handyman work, she'd run all over town in paint-splattered jeans or coveralls, her face bare of makeup and her hair tucked up in a cap. Dealing with clients or stopping at the gas station dressed that way was okay; going to the grocery store was not. I know this because she used to kick up a fuss if I asked her to pick up something while she was out. "I can't go to the grocery store looking like this!" she'd say, even though plenty of people had seen her looking like that already.

Apparently, building-supply centers belonged in the "get fixed up first" category for Seely. I didn't try to understand it.

I collected my walking stick and mug and lifted my left foot off the extra chair. My knee was a lot better, but I still kept that leg propped up much of the time. I limped over to the coffeepot. "Want some more?"

Duncan shook his head. He was looking tired, I thought. Night shifts didn't agree with him. Then, too, he'd pulled a double in order to free up time for the camping trip with Zach—a trip the weather had cut short. We'd had our first good freeze Saturday night, accompanied by a light dusting of snow.

Duncan's gaze held steady on me as I refilled my mug. "Maybe you should tell me why you asked. If you suspect Seely has a criminal background—"

"Nothing like that," I said quickly. "There's something she's not telling me, that's all."

His mouth crooked up. "More than one thing, probably. Women have been failing to tell men everything for a few thousand years. Police departments don't generally consider that a good reason to run a background check."

He made my curiosity sound like a man-woman thing, not employer-employee. Which was accurate but annoying. "I didn't want you to do it as a cop."

"Well, as your brother I'm advising you to drop the idea." He put the mug down. "Nosing around will just get you in trouble. Though if you really have to know something, you could hire a P.I."

No way. I'd thought maybe Duncan could find out a few things discreetly. Her father's name, for example. Some hint of why she was working at jobs way below her skill level. But I didn't want some stranger snooping around in her life. "Never mind."

"You know, this is weird."

"What?"

"You. You're acting different." He nodded toward the front of the house. "The living room. It's always been white."

"You don't like it green?"

"It looks fine. Felt weird when I walked in and saw it, though." One corner of his mouth kicked up, as if he were reluctantly amused. "Sort of like a kid who goes away to college, comes home and finds out mom and dad redecorated without telling him."

Dammit, I should have thought about how he'd feel. Charlie and Annie, too. This house was their heritage every bit as much as it was mine. "I ought to have said something. It's your house, too, and you—"

"No, it isn't."

"Of course it is. Mom and Dad left it to all of us."

"Twenty years ago, yes. But you're the one who has lived here all these years, taken care of the place. This is your home." He took a deep breath. "Gwen and I have talked about this. We want to deed my share of the house over to you."

I slammed my mug down, ignoring the coffee that slopped over the rim. "Forget it."

"There might be some tax liability for you, but she thinks we can minimize that."

"Aren't you listening?" I demanded. "Just because your wife could buy and sell this house ten times over doesn't oblige me to accept a handout."

Duncan shoved to his feet. "This has nothing to do with Gwen's money! Dammit, you hard-headed son of a bitch, will you listen a minute?"

"I'm not hearing anything worth listening to. If you don't—"

"Whoa!"

That came from Seely. Startled, I looked at the doorway.

She stood there, shaking her head. "Good grief. I can't be accused of eavesdropping with Ben bellowing like a wounded moose. I heard him from the stairs. Ben." She fixed me with a firm stare. "Do you really think Duncan offered to give you his share of this house because he enjoys flinging Gwen's money around?"

I flushed. "No. But—"

"Not your turn." She sauntered on into the kitchen, stopping in front of Duncan. "And did you really think Ben would take your inheritance from you?"

"That's not what this is about."

"It is to him." She put her hands on her hips and looked from one to the other of us. "This is none of my business, of course. But it seems pretty simple. Ben lives here. Duncan doesn't. Ben, I don't know how you're fixed financially, but could you buy Duncan's share?"

"Sure." I turned some numbers over in my head. The business had done well the past few years, and I wasn't exactly extravagant. "We'll need to get the place appraised, but I've got a pretty good idea of its current market value."

Duncan shook his head. "We don't want to use the current market value. It's worth three times what it was twenty years ago, and none of us are going to make a profit off you. Charlie suggested—"

"You talked to Charlie about this? What is this, some kind of conspiracy?"

"Exactly. Annie, too. The plan was to wait until we could all be home at the same time and tackle you together. I, uh, jumped the gun."

Seely chuckled. "Safety in numbers. A legitimate military tactic."

I glanced at her. Did she know that Duncan had been in the Army until a few months ago? Probably. If Duncan hadn't mentioned it, Gwen would have. People told her things.

"If you're all in this together," I told my brother, "you need to drop this notion of giving up your shares in the house for little or nothing. Charlie won't take a fair price for his share if you and Annie don't. The two of you may not need the money, but he does." He'd just sunk every cent he had or could borrow into a partnership in a landscaping business. I'd already tried to give him a loan. Twice.

Duncan frowned. I decided to let him chew on that a while and turned to Seely. "Looks like you're ready to go."

She looked a damned sight better than "ready to go." All that gorgeous hair spilled over her shoulders and down her back, and I could tell she'd fussed with makeup, turning her eyes sultry and her lips scarlet. She wore dark jeans and a sweater with geometric shapes in red, purple and yellow.

That sweater fit more snugly than anything I'd seen her wear before. My body took notice of this. Of course, my body had been on yellow alert almost constantly for the past three days.

"Just let me get my jacket and purse," she said, and headed for the hall.

"I'd better be going, too," Duncan said, carrying his mug

over to the sink. "What are you getting at the building supply store?"

"We're going to put up some shelves in my office here."

"I take it the 'we' means you're supervising?"

"All right, *she's* going to put them up. I'm not taking advantage of her. She's keen on all this home fixup and decorating stuff."

"Hmm." He stuck his mug in the dishwasher. "I owe Seely a thank-you."

"I'll tell her you enjoyed the coffee."

He slanted me an amused glance. "I didn't mean for the coffee."

It felt weird to sit in the passenger seat of my own car.

The Chevy was backup transportation, nearly ten years old but in good shape. Power windows, doors and steering; bench seats and a big back seat…big enough to give me some impractical ideas. Sexual frustration was bringing out the adolescent in me.

Seely drove with the same unrushed efficiency she did everything else. "I still don't know how I let you talk me into taking you by the office. You aren't supposed to be working yet."

I pointed out that I hadn't worked—I'd just checked on the work others were doing. I hadn't even insisted on going to the Pearson site.

She grinned. "I suppose you think you get Brownie points for that."

"I ought to." If sexual frustration was robbing her of sleep and nudging stupid ideas into her head, it didn't show.

"You're staring at me."

"I like looking at you."

The faintest flush mounted her cheeks. Maybe I shouldn't

have said anything. I'd been careful not to since letting her know my intentions. That was the right thing to do. Sexual innuendos were out of place while she was working for me. Besides, self-preservation called for restraint. I had to keep my eye on the line I'd drawn, or I'd find myself tumbling off another edge.

But I liked seeing that flush.

I'd spent too much time the past three days trying to figure out what was going on in her head. We had something strong and hot flowing between us. I knew that much because I'd caught her looking at me a few times, too. At twenty, I'd have assumed that meant she agreed with me, that she wanted to have an affair as soon as the employer-employee thing was out of the way.

At forty, I knew better.

At least she hadn't told me to forget it. I figured she was still making up her mind about me. I didn't say anything else until she'd shut off the engine, hoping she'd spend the time thinking about the heat between us.

I pushed open my door. "You sure you want to tackle this? Putting up shelves isn't easy. Goes a lot better with two people, and I won't be able to help much."

"You won't be helping at all," she retorted, coming around the car.

I made a noncommittal noise. No point in mentioning that there would be parts of the job where two pairs of hands would be necessary.

She matched her pace to mine—which was slow. I didn't limp anymore as long as I didn't try to outrace a snail. "This is my chance to learn from an expert," she said. "I'm not about to pass that up."

"Well, the expert suggests we get red oak. It's not easy to

work with, but it should look great." I paused, considering the state of my office. "Eventually."

"It is a bit of a mess in there."

I grunted. The doors opened for us and I crept along to the left, where the lumber was stacked. I'd pick out the wood myself, that being the reason for this trip. Well, that and a bad case of cabin fever. We wouldn't be able to take it home today, obviously, since I didn't have a truck.

And we wouldn't be able to do much with the wood until we'd cleared the place out. The room I used for a home office used to be a bedroom—my parents' bedroom, actually. I'd taken their bed out about a month after they died, unable to stand seeing it there, all made up and waiting for them. Eventually Annie had claimed their dresser. Somehow I'd never gotten around to clearing everything else out, though.

My two favorite spots in the store were the tool aisles and the lumber section. Tools are always interesting, and being surrounded by all that wood hits me viscerally. I think it's the smell—cut wood, sawdust, a whiff of sap.

Ed noticed my sling and the walking stick, so of course he had to hear the whole story, then felt obligated to spend some time assuring me I was lucky to be alive before he could put my order together. I arranged to have it picked up in a couple days. "That will give me a chance to clear the room out," I told Seely as we headed for the front of the store with the ticket. Our slow speed wasn't just due to my pace this time—she kept stopping to look at paint chips and light fixtures.

"Us," she said. "It's not as if I have much else to do. And we don't have to remove everything. You have some good pieces in there, like that occasional table with the Queen Anne legs."

"Yeah?" I smiled, pleased. "I made that when I was sixteen."

"You're kidding!"

"Shop class. It was a Christmas gift for my mom. I was trying to copy a picture I found in a magazine. Put in a lot of extra hours on it...had a lot of help, too." As I spoke I saw Mr. Nelson's face. He'd been the soul of patience, often staying late so I could work in the shop. "Lord, I hadn't thought of Mr. Nelson in years."

"Your teacher?"

"Yeah. He retired while I was away at college, moved to Albuquerque to be near his sister. He was an old bachelor, you see. I stopped in to see him once when I was there on business..." My voice trailed away as I remembered that visit. How sorry I'd felt for the old man, living alone, no one but a sister nearby. All of a sudden I could see my own future, and it didn't look much different.

I had Zach, I reminded myself. Some of the time, at least.

"What's the matter?"

"Nothing." We'd reached the front of the store. I headed for the nearest checkout. "I'm amazed that you let me get up here without buying anything else. Why is someone who calls herself a wanderer so interested in everything to do with houses?"

She shrugged. "The fascination of the exotic, perhaps. I've never rooted anywhere long enough to do much in the way of home improvement, so it seems novel and exciting. Does your interest in construction go back to that woodworking class?"

"Partly. Do you do that on purpose?"

"What?"

"Turn the conversation away from yourself and back on me. Annie tells me that all a woman has to do to appear fascinating to a man is to get him to talk about himself. Maybe that's true. But I'd like to hear about you sometimes."

A flush climbed the crest of her cheekbones. She gave me

a teasing smile. "Does that mean it's working? You think I'm fascinating?"

I'd have enjoyed her flirting a lot more if I hadn't thought she was using it to duck the question. "Look, I don't know—what is it?"

She'd gone dead pale. She was staring over my shoulder. I turned.

Someone was staring back. An old woman, every inch as tall as Seely but skinnier, like a dried-out string bean, had stopped a few feet away. She had a real lost-in-the-fifties look going, right down to the low heels and pearls. Her coat was dark-blue wool. Her gray hair had been permed, teased and sprayed into submission.

And her expression was venomous. "You! What are you doing here?"

"Buying lumber." Seely's voice was steady. Her face was blank and much too pale. "Why? What are you doing here?"

"Don't you smart off to me! You're not supposed to be here! You said you were leaving. You don't belong here. We don't want you here. Don't think you'll get a penny from me, whatever tricks you pull!"

"I don't want your money. I never did." Seely started to turn away.

"Nasty baggage! You'll listen when I talk to you." The woman started after her. "I won't have you confusing John, making him miserable again—"

"Mrs. Lake," I said loudly. "Do you realize how worried your daughter has been?"

She jolted. I don't think she'd noticed me until that second, which says a lot about how focused she'd been on Seely. I'm not easy to overlook. Faded-blue eyes blinked behind her bifocals. "What? I'm not—"

"I know," I said soothingly, and switched my walking stick to my right hand so I could take her arm. My shoulder twinged. "Not yourself these days, are you? But if you'd take your medication you'd feel better. You have to stop wandering off this way. Poor Melly is frantic."

She stared up at me as if I were mad. "If you don't take your hand off me this instant I will have you arrested."

I leaned closer and muttered, "You've drawn quite a crowd. Maybe you like scenes. If so, go right ahead and screech some more."

She looked around. People were staring, all right. The clerk had stopped ringing up her customer.

Color flooded the old woman's scrawny neck.

Seely spoke from behind me. "I can handle this, Ben."

"So? You don't have to."

The old woman drew herself up. "You'll be sorry you interfered. I'll tell the judge, and he'll see to it. As for *you*..." She leaned around me, her eyes glittered with malice. "Devil child! You stay away from me and mine."

She jerked her arm out of my grip and turned away with surprising dignity. I watched just long enough to make sure that she was really leaving, then looked at Seely.

Her lips were tight. There was a lost look about her eyes I didn't like. "I'm sorry. I didn't know...I didn't expect to see her at a place like this. I wouldn't have subjected you to that scene if I'd had any idea she might..." Her throat worked as she swallowed.

"Yeah, I'm all torn up about it." I gripped her elbow and started for the doors. "Come on."

"But—the wood! You can't...Ben?"

"Give her the ticket." I nodded at the clerk as we passed the checkout. The others in the line glared at me. "McClain

Construction," I told the clerk. "Charge it, save it, toss it, whatever. I'll call."

We went through the automatic doors at a better pace than I'd managed since falling off the mountain. No doubt my knee would complain later. I didn't care. Seely needed to get out, away from all those curious eyes.

She didn't mention my knee or my shoulder, either out loud or with her eyebrows. Which just confirmed how upset she was. She did say something about me being high-handed.

"You need to scream, cry or throw things. You don't want to do that here, so we're going home."

"I am not going to cry."

"Yeah, I figured you were more a thrower than a crier. Here we are." I released her arm and opened the passenger door.

"Wait a minute. I'm driving."

"No, you aren't." I headed around the front of the car. "Power steering, power brakes and my right leg and left arm work fine. I don't know why I let you talk me into the passenger seat in the first place."

"I've got the keys. You are not driving, Ben."

"You've got a set of keys." I used the ones in my hand to open my door, tossed my walking stick in the back seat, and lowered myself carefully behind the wheel. Damn. I'd been right about my knee. "You coming?"

She came. She slammed the door, but she came.

Eight

Seely didn't say a thing for several blocks, just sat there hugging her elbows tight to her body, as if they might get away from her otherwise.

Making her mad hadn't worked, except as a temporary fix. She'd fallen right back into whatever unhappy thoughts held her prisoner. I was hunting for another strategy when she broke the silence. "What was that bit about Melly?"

"I made that up. Got the old biddy's attention."

"It did do that," she said dryly.

"So who is she? Looked like someone freeze-dried June Cleaver's mother."

Her laugh broke out. Out of the corner of my eye I saw her arms loosen. "Don't surprise me like that! I nearly choked. Her name is Helen Burns. Mrs. Randall Burns, to be precise."

"Who's the judge she threatened me with?"

"Her husband. Who hasn't sat on the bench in twenty years, but she isn't about to let anyone forget that he used to."

"Hmm." I'd heard of the judge, of course. Didn't think I'd ever met the man.

I turned onto Oak. My street was one of the oldest in town, more level than recent construction, which has to crowd its way up the slopes that cradle Highpoint. The houses here have a settled look; some are large, some smaller, but all have good-size yards. For a short stretch, trees from both sides of the road clasped hands over the street.

We emerged from the tree tunnel onto my block. Smoke puffed from the Berringtons' chimney. Jack Robert's truck was in the driveway. Looked like he still hadn't found another position after being laid off two months ago. The Frasers were out front, old Walt cleaning out a gutter while Shirley steadied the ladder.

I knew the houses along here, the changes that had been made in and around them over the years, the names, stories and people who belonged to those houses. Some people don't like seeing the same faces and places all the time. Take my brother Charlie. He drove a truck for years because he liked staying on the move, always seeing something new. And I'm not sure Annie's husband, Jack, will ever settle permanently in one place.

That's hard for a rooted man like me to understand. Did the world's wanderers have any idea what they were missing? Or were they so busy chasing the horizon they never realized what they'd given up?

I pulled into my driveway, cut the engine and glanced at the woman beside me...one of the wanderers. I shook my head. "If you're keeping quiet in the hope that I'll be too tactful to ask why Mrs. Randall Burns hates your guts, you're out of luck."

She snorted. "I'm not such a blind optimist. Anyway,

you're due an explanation." She looked down, plucking at a snag near the hem of her sweater. "Helen Burns hates me for being born. Bad blood, you see. She's my grandmother."

I closed my mouth before any more stupid comments could escape. "Inside. We'll talk about it inside."

She didn't quite slam the door when she got out. "There's nothing to talk about."

That remark was obviously the product of wishful thinking. "I take it she's your father's mother. The father you don't know anything about."

"When I told you that I was trying to preserve a little privacy. Not a concept you have a lot of respect for...oh, do slow down, Ben. You're obviously hurting."

"I'm okay. So does he live here, too? Here in Highpoint?"

"Yes." She didn't wait for me to obey—or not—but moved up beside me and slid her arm around my waist, forcing me to move slower. "And yes, that's why I came to Highpoint—sheer, bloody-minded curiosity."

A quick jolt of heat distracted me...and a quieter warmth seeped inside, unknotting muscles I hadn't realized were clenched. The pain in my shoulder eased to a dull ache.

I frowned at the top of her head. She was looking down, as if the stairs to the porch required a lot of attention. "You wanted to meet him?"

"No. There may be a touch of masochist in me, but I don't let it take over. I wanted to see him, find out about him, that's all."

We'd reached the door. I let her use her key while I tried to sort out the difference between one kind of heat and another. "Wanting to know your father isn't masochistic."

"No? And yet you've met his mother." She swung the door open.

I limped inside. "How did she recognize you, if you haven't had any contact all these years?"

"My mother sent my father school pictures and little notes every year. I suppose he might have shown them to Granny Dearest. Or maybe she recognized me from the last time we met, twenty-four years ago." She slapped her purse down on the hall table. "Does it matter?"

Twenty-four years ago... "When you were eight? That was the last time you saw your father, you said. That was when you last saw your grandmother, too?"

"Daisy hit a hard patch financially that summer. Things were always tight, but then she had her purse snatched and there went the rent money. My father..." Her voice faltered. "He'd been gone three years by then, but hadn't yet dropped out of my life completely. She called him, asked for help."

"Did you go stay with him?"

"Not exactly. He was working toward his master's and didn't have a penny to spare. So he said, anyway. I wound up being shipped up here to stay with the judge and my grandmother. My father drove up on weekends, or sometimes we drove into Denver to see him."

"You didn't get along with your grandparents."

"That's putting it mildly." She shrugged out of her jacket and opened the hall closet. "Can we drop the subject now?"

"In a minute. Your grandmother knew you were in town. She claimed you'd told her you were leaving."

"She and the judge ate at the lodge one night. I waited on their table." She grimaced. "Not a happy encounter for any of us."

"Why didn't you—"

"Ben! Stop interrogating me. You need to sit down, get off your knee."

I didn't want to sit. I couldn't pace very well, dammit, but

I sure didn't want to sit. "If I don't ask questions, you won't tell me anything."

"Why should I?"

"Why shouldn't you? Lord, I never knew a woman so good at turning away questions! If I ask a single personal question, I end up talking about my own father. Or the best color for the hall bath, or how to repair damaged plaster."

Anger waved flags in her cheeks. "You're exaggerating." She spun and headed for the living room.

"Am I?" I hobbled after her. "You led me to think you didn't know anything about your father's side of the family. If we hadn't run into your old witch of a grandmother—"

Her laugh was short, sharp and ugly. "Oh, but she's not the witch. That's the problem. My other grandmother is. Literally."

God help me. I leaned my stick carefully against the wall. "Your mother's mother is, uh…"

"A witch." Mockery gleamed in her eyes.

"Okay." I nodded slowly. "I got that part. You mean like Wicca and all that?"

"That's what people call it nowadays. Granny doesn't, and really, I'm not sure how much a New Age witch would have in common with Granny's brand of the Craft."

She believed this. She honestly thought her grandmother was a witch. "And do you think…uh, are you one, too?"

"The word is witch, Ben. And no, I'm not. But I'm the granddaughter of one, which makes me Satan's get in the eyes of Mrs. Randall Burns. Didn't you hear the part about me being a devil child?"

"Somehow that didn't immediately bring witchcraft to mind." Muddy floors, yes. Witchcraft, no.

"I suppose not. Will you get off that damned knee?"

"I don't think I've heard you curse before," I observed.

"You could make a saint curse!"

"I'll sit down if you'll tell me about your grandmother. Your *other* grandmother, not the one I just met."

She muttered something unflattering about my antecedents, then flung up her hands. "Okay. Her name is Alma Jones. She's eighty-four and the top of her head barely reaches my shoulder. She lives...*sit,* Ben!"

"I'm sitting." I lowered myself onto the couch.

"She lives in a tiny cottage in the Appalachians and makes the world's best chicken and dumplings. Fresh chicken, mind, from her henhouse. She also makes simples, little charms and cures to sell to her neighbors, and she has the Sight."

"Ah...the Sight. That's a Celtic thing, isn't it? Irish or Scottish?"

"Her maiden name was Sullivan." The laid-back woman I'd known for a week fairly bristled with feeling. Even her hair seemed agitated. She began pacing. "She's a darling. She's helped people all her life. She didn't ask to have the Sight. Who would? But it runs in our family. Like the curse."

The curse?

Seely reached the end of the room and spun around, making her hair fly out like a curly cape. "Do you know what that self-righteous old prune called her? A bride of Satan. My granny! She taught Sunday school for thirty-two years!"

A Christian witch. Well, if you could believe in witchcraft in the first place, why not? "What curse?"

She grimaced. "I didn't mean to mention that."

"Too late now. What curse?"

"The one another witch put on my great-grandmother for stealing her man about a hundred years ago." She flung up her hands. "Why am I telling you all this? You don't believe a word of it."

"I believe several parts," I said cautiously. Her granny probably was a good, loving woman who'd taught Sunday school and made up little herbal remedies for her neighbors. And thought of herself as a witch.

Seely's expression softened as the corners of her lips turned up. "Poor Ben. You're trying so hard not to tell me that I'm nuts. If it's any consolation, I don't believe in the curse, either."

"Okay. The curse doesn't count. But you said it was passed down in your family like, uh, the Sight."

"I've heard about it all my life. I don't really believe in it, but..." She shrugged, which gave her breasts a gentle lift.

I wanted to tell her how much I liked that sweater. I didn't even let my gaze linger, an act of willpower for which I deserved a lot more credit than I was likely to get. "I know how family stories stick with you. We learn things when we're kids that cling like burrs long after we've figured out they aren't really true."

"Yes!" Her laugh was shaky. "That's it exactly. I don't really believe in the curse, yet I can't completely forget it, either. Daisy believes it." Her feet started her moving again. "She thinks my father left us because a witch cursed the women in my family to unhappiness in love."

"Hmm."

She paused by the window, shrugged. "I guess it's easier to believe in a curse than to think that he didn't really love her. Or that he's a noodle."

"Cooked, I take it."

She nodded and ran her fingers along the edge of the drapes, as if she found it easier to talk to them right now, instead of me. "I made it sound like I don't remember anything about him. That isn't quite true. He read me bedtime stories. He used to take me out in this little sidecar attached to his bicycle. I remember the way the fields smelled, the tug of the wind in my hair." She swallowed. "The sound of his laugh."

"Sounds like a noodle, all right." I came up behind her and rested my hand on her shoulder. "He loved you. For some reason he wasn't man enough to be responsible for you, but he loved you."

"You aren't on the couch."

"Nope." I folded my good arm around her and eased her up against me.

She didn't exactly resist, but she didn't relax, either. "Ben..."

I had a hunch she'd like it better if I made a pass. She'd know what to do when a man crossed that kind of boundary. Comfort was harder for her.

Tough. I stroked a hand down her hair. "So what's the noodle's name? Burns for the last half, I guess. Zebediah? Ezekiel?"

My hand was resting against the side of her face, so I felt her smile even though I couldn't see it. "Well, it is biblical."

"Mathew? Mark?" She'd relaxed against me, slightly sideways because of the sling. Her hip nestled into my groin. I wondered how long my brain could survive without oxygen, seeing that all of my blood was tied up in one part of my body. "Do I need to run through the rest of the Gospels?"

Her low chuckle delighted me. "Old Testament. Think lions."

"Lion's den. Daniel."

"Bingo." The top of her head was even with my eyes. Her hair was so soft.... I didn't nuzzle it. Surely some celestial scorekeeper was pasting all kinds of gold stars next to my name. "I'm glad Duncan turned me down. Better to hear all this from you."

She went stiff. "What do you mean, he turned you down?"

Uh-oh. Too much distraction. "Let's pretend I didn't say that."

"Oh, no." She turned, pulling out of my arms, a dangerous glint in her eyes. "I want to know what you meant."

"You weren't telling me things. Important things. So I...hell." I ran my hand over my own head this time.

"So you had me checked out? You had your brother check me out?"

"No, I told you—he turned me down."

"Oh, that's different, then! You *wanted* the cops to investigate me, but your brother wouldn't do it, so everything's fine!"

"I needed to know about you, okay? I didn't want to know. I *needed* to. And if that doesn't make sense, well, tough. Tough on both of us," I said, my voice getting louder, "because I'm *used* to making sense, only here you are, and I keep doing *stupid* things and I don't know why! I don't make sense at all anymore!"

For a second after my outburst, there was silence. I scowled at her. She was smiling, dammit. "And you like that."

Her smile just got wider. Then she lifted up onto her toes, put her hand on my good shoulder and her mouth right smack on mine.

"You..." Hard to form words with my head buzzing this way. "Why did you do that?"

"Impulse." She skimmed smiling lips across mine. "Very poor impulse control I have at times."

I, on the other hand, was great at self-control. I proved it by not grabbing her.

"Oh, dear, here comes another one. Help," she said, sliding her arms around my neck and tickling my nape with her fingers. "They're coming pretty fast now. Can't seem to stop them."

"Stop..." Her body brushed mine, scattering what passed for my thoughts. "Stop what?"

"Impulses. Wicked ones. Whoops." She slipped the top button of my shirt from its buttonhole. "See what I mean?"

"Ah…" I ran my fingers down the whole, wiggly length of her hair, then slowly wrapped my hand around a hunk of it. "This sort of thing, you mean?" And I bent my head and licked her bottom lip. "I'm not supposed to do that."

"Exactly." That word glided out on a puff of breath. "I guess they're catching."

Another button met the fate of the first. And I snapped.

My left arm clamped around her waist—and damn that sling! I couldn't snug her against me the way I wanted. But I could crush my mouth down on hers. I could catch her sigh as her lips parted and send my tongue to steal her taste, take it inside me.

I needed two hands. Hell, I could have used three or four, there were so many places I wanted to touch, but I made do with what was available. She'd fitted herself up against me as closely as possible, so I turned my left hand loose to wander.

It liked the taut shape of her thigh, the flare of her hip, the muscle and flesh of her bottom…but that sweater. I'd been looking at that sweater all day, imagining what lay beneath it. I nudged her legs apart with my knee, making a space for my leg between hers. And slid my hand up under her sweater.

"Lace," I groaned as my hand found the warmth and weight of her breast. "This damned sweater made me crazy enough. If I'd known there was lace beneath it…" I rubbed her nipple with my thumb and pressed up with my thigh.

She moaned into my mouth. Then bit my lip.

"I want this." I squeezed her nipple between my thumb and forefinger. "I want to see this."

The shiver that rippled up her spine struck me as agreement, but she shook her head as she slid one hand up my chest. "I'd have to let go of you to take it off. And I don't want to."

That was a problem, all right. I admit I wasn't much help, since I claimed her mouth again when she scraped my nipple with a fingernail. Her mouth was warm and sweet and a little wild, and though something was nagging at the back of my brain, telling me to slow down and think, I wasn't listening.

Vertical was losing all appeal. I wanted to be horizontal, where the lack of one hand wouldn't matter so much.

I also wanted her naked. "Damn," I muttered against the column of her neck as that vagrant thought finally surfaced. Reluctantly I eased away. "Hold on. We're by the window, and the drapes are open."

"Oh. I forgot. I can't believe…" She laughed unsteadily and pushed her hair back from her face with both hands. "Good grief. I'm glad you thought of it."

"Yeah." When I pulled the drapes closed, the light dimmed and softened. I smiled. "Now you can take that sweater off."

"Um…there's something I should say first."

"If you've changed your mind…" I grabbed for self-control. Never had it felt more slippery. "I won't yell. I might whimper a bit or beg. But I won't yell."

"No. Oh, no." She wrapped her arms around my waist and leaned into me. "I just wanted to make sure we're on the same page. I can't picture myself staying in Highpoint, exchanging friendly greetings with my grandmother in the produce section. And I can't picture you anywhere else."

Some emotion landed with a jolt in my stomach. "So you're saying we should have fun, but nothing serious."

"Something like that."

She'd stolen my lines, dammit. The warning I was supposed to give her. The conditions I'd forgotten about. The ones I wasn't sure I wanted anymore.

This wasn't the time to mention that. I bent and nuzzled

her hair away from her ear so I could kiss her there. "I never argue with a lady who's about to remove her sweater."

Her chuckle sounded relieved. "You've got a thing about my sweater."

"Oh, yeah. I'd do it myself if I could." I longed to strip her slowly, teasing and touching and kissing as I went. I couldn't even undress myself properly, dammit.

Which left me supervising again. I ran my tongue along the cord of her neck, then released her and waved my hand. "Up and off."

"Bossy," she observed, but her voice was husky. She grasped the hem on her sweater, peeling it up over her head.

Lace. Her breasts were cupped in it, full half-moons of creamy flesh overlaid with white lace, with darker nipples and areolas peeking through. Her hair spilled over bare shoulders, one curly strand falling in a soft hook around one dark-tipped breast.

My mouth went dry and my heart tried to hammer its way out of my chest. "Did I mention that lace makes me crazy? Never mind," I said, forgetting my plan to get horizontal. I brushed the skin above the lacy edge of her bra. "I'll show you."

"Wait a minute," she said, and stepped back a couple of paces.

Something in her voice brought my gaze to her face. Her smile was the same, that easy curve of lips. But nerves or uncertainty jumped in her eyes. I wanted to wrap her close in my arms—hell, my one good arm—and soothe her. I took a step forward.

"Uh-uh." She tossed her hair back, lifted one eyebrow. "You're not in charge here, bud."

I wasn't?

"Wait," she ordered. Her hands went to the waist of her jeans. I'm no fool. I waited.

She stripped for me. First she unfastened the jeans, giving me a peek beneath while she toed off her shoes. Then the socks, and how anyone could turn the removal of socks into a tease I don't know, but she did. Then she shoved the jeans down and stepped out of them.

A slim dip of a waist, and more lace below—white again, riding low on her hips, darker at the notch of her legs. "You have the most magnificent legs I've ever seen."

She blinked once, like a surprised cat. "Well. And here I thought it was my breasts you were fixated on." She reached behind her with both hands, which lifted her breasts in a way that nearly made me swallow my tongue. And unfastened her bra.

Magnificent was too pale a word. But when I went to her, I put my hand in the center of her chest, not over one of those bare, perfect breasts. I looked at her face. "Your heart's pounding."

She lifted one eyebrow. "I'm excited."

Her voice, her posture, that coolly lifted eyebrow—all spoke of confidence and experience. She knew her body could make a man beg. But while passion might ripen the heart's rhythm, it didn't send it tripping this fast, this hard, as if it were trying to flee. Not unless some other feelings were mixed in.

I didn't tell her I didn't believe her. I didn't follow the instinct that demanded I gather her close, stroking her back until whatever fears rode her had eased. Naked bodies didn't bother Seely. Tenderness would.

The time would come when I wanted her feelings as naked as the rest of her, but not yet. Not today. I touched her cheek and promised silently I would treasure and protect whatever she shared with me. Her body, for now.

Her eyes closed. "You are a devious man," she whispered.

I nodded. Then, at last, I cupped her breast. "You feel like rose petals." I stroked, cupped and lifted, then bent to take the hard little pebble of her nipple in my mouth.

Her breath sucked in. Her fingers fretted my hair, skimmed my jaw as I switched breasts. She made a pleased sound, then, after a moment, said, "As your medical attendant, I insist that you get off your feet. Quickly."

I licked her nipple, then blew on it. "Want to play doctor, do you?"

"Yes." She threaded her fingers through my hair, pulled my head up and kissed me. "And the doctor will see you now." Her hands went to the snap on my jeans. "All of you."

Nine

Seely believed in giving a thorough examination. And she was right—I wasn't in charge. Or in control in anyway; not for long.

The couch was warm and soft against my bare back and butt. The woman on top of me was softer and a lot warmer.

She also possessed a mean streak I hadn't suspected.

"No more," I said, then groaned as she immediately disobeyed, drawing her fingernail along the taut skin behind my balls. "Vicious," I observed when I got some breath back.

She was on her hands and knees over me. Her breasts rose and fell rapidly and her hair hung down, tickling my chest. Her lips were shiny and damp, curved in a feline smile.

It wasn't my mouth she'd been kissing. "I haven't completed my tests," she informed me. "That swelling you're experiencing is quite remarkable. Bears further study." She started to scoot back down my body.

I growled, looped a hank of her hair around my hand and tugged. "C'mere, woman."

She came, stretching out all along me. "*Tch*. You aren't supposed to grab the doctor by the hair."

"No respect for authority. That's my problem." I urged her head close enough for a kiss. While I made my point with my tongue, I nudged my hips up. The way she was straddling me left her wide open. I rubbed the head of my penis along her slick folds.

She gasped. Her eyes opened wide. "Vicious."

"Payback's a bitch," I agreed. I teased both of us until I couldn't play anymore. Not in any way. "Seely. Now. Let it be now. I need you."

She looked as if I'd said that one of us only had a week left to live. "Don't."

"Too late." I kissed that stricken look off her face, gripped her hip to hold her in place and slid inside.

She moaned. Pleasure swirled, a tactile kaleidoscope spiraling up from my groin to surround me, body, brain and soul. Her nails dug into my shoulder, a prick of pain that all but sent me over the edge. I hung on, not daring to move.

A thought floated up.

I moaned again, but not with pleasure. "I forgot. I can't believe I forgot."

"Hmm?" Her eyelids were at half-mast, her face flushed. "I don't think you've forgotten anything." She wiggled. "Yep, everything's in place, which is a wonder. I was not entirely sure you'd fit."

"I'm naked." I fought the need to move. "*Completely* naked."

"I don't...oh." Something other than passion flitted through her eyes. "Not a problem. I can't get pregnant or catch anything from you. Or give anything to you, for that matter."

Being on the pill didn't protect her from STDs. Seely wasn't stupid—she had to know that. I opened my mouth to say so, but she bent and captured it, and I lost track of words.

I did manage a weak protest after a moment, something about protecting her.

"Shh. It's all right, Ben. You can let go. This once, you don't have to be responsible. It will be okay. I promise."

It couldn't have been what she said, because that didn't make sense. Maybe it was the way she touched my face—gently, as if I were the fragile one. Or the way her hips moved, taking me in, all the way in, then rising slowly to do it again. Or the way she moaned, as if—in this one way, at least—she needed me, too.

Or maybe I lost it, all by myself. Whatever the reason, something inside me snapped. I began pumping up into her. Seely moaned, threw her head back and rode me clear to paradise.

I lay on my left side, watching Seely sleep. Her hair was all over the place. I wanted to play with it, but my only usable arm was propping me up so I could look at her. And I didn't want to stop looking.

She was cuddled up against me, her breathing soft and even. The twin fans of her eyelashes spread in tidy symmetry along the tender skin beneath her eyes. The room was murky with early twilight, as if a storm was moving in, blocking the sun.

For the first time in my life, I'd made love without protection.

Even with Gwen that hadn't happened. Zach had gotten started because Gwen had put the condom on wrong, not because I'd forgotten to use one. Or been so carried away I couldn't be bothered.

I grimaced. Seely had told me it was okay, but that didn't make what I'd done right. If she was on the pill...but she hadn't exactly said that, had she?

The possibility of her growing round with my child made a funny kind of pain in my chest, the sort of ache a kid gets just before Christmas, when he wants something so much he doesn't dare wish for it out loud.

Had I skipped protection because I secretly hoped she would get pregnant?

I don't usually waste time second-guessing myself, but I didn't know myself anymore. I kept changing my mind, doing things I'd decided not to do. First I'd just wanted to see Seely again. Then I'd wanted her to work for me, but had no intention of getting involved. Then I'd decided I wanted her even though she wasn't a forever kind of woman, but I planned to wait until she wasn't an employee anymore.

Now I was lying beside her, watching her sleep...after the most mind-blowing sex of my life.

Unprotected sex.

Must be some sort of midlife crisis. I wasn't the sort of man who fell in love every couple of months, and less than two weeks ago I'd been in love with Gwen. Besides, I didn't have any urge to sit around mooning over Seely, making up stories about how things ought to go between us. Nor was I blind to her flaws—and the infuriating woman had plenty of those.

I sighed with relief. No, this wasn't love. More like lust on steroids.

Hormones aside, though, I liked her. A lot. I got up in the morning looking forward to seeing her, finding out what she'd say, what she'd do that day. She was just plain fun to be with, and she mattered to me. Which was one definition of friendship, wasn't it?

Okay, so she was a friend for whom I had a bad case of the hots. I could live with that. But no more unprotected sex.

She went from asleep to awake in a single blink and smiled up at me.

"Hi, there." I couldn't brush the hair away from her face, so I brushed a kiss on her forehead. "I thought it was the guy who was supposed to fall asleep after sex."

"I love busting up stereotypes." She ran her fingers over my lips, as if seeing my smile wasn't enough. She had to touch it, too. "You break a few of those, too, you know."

"Yeah? Which ones?"

"You seem like a real macho man with your flannel shirts and jeans, your bossy ways and construction work. I really want to see you in a tool belt one of these days," she added. "But never mind that right now. The point is, macho men are supposed to have thick necks and tiny brains. They aren't supposed to be sensitive to others' feelings. Or be better read than me."

"You think I'm macho?" And was that good or bad?

"I think you're a man. One hundred percent man, the kind I didn't believe really existed."

Okay, that was good. I kissed her, taking my time about it.

"Well." She was satisfactorily short of breath when she flattened her palm on my chest. "Your heartbeat seems elevated."

"It was calm until you smiled at me."

The woman who'd played doctor so enthusiastically a few minutes ago delighted me by blushing. She shook her head, chiding me. "You're supposed to be flattened, drained, unable to even lift your head."

"I want you in my bed. Of course," I added regretfully, "I might need a little help getting there."

One eyebrow lifted. "Good as it is for my ego to know you're at least partly flattened, maybe a second round isn't a good idea. If you're hurting too much to make it back to the den—"

"Not the den." I stroked her back, enjoying the sweep of muscle and softness. "My bed is upstairs." The hospital bed was temporary. I wanted her in the bed where I slept every night, in the room where I woke up every morning.

"Stairs are not a good idea."

"But you can help, can't you?" I stared down at her, willing her to be honest this time. "I haven't figured out exactly what you do, but you damned sure do something."

Her whole face closed down. "I don't know what you're talking about."

"Dammit, if you aren't going to answer, then don't. But don't lie to me." I shoved up into a sitting position, which pretty much forced her to sit, too, or get shoved off the couch. She sat, eyeing me warily. Which made me furious. "What do I have to do to make you trust me?"

"You don't know what you're asking for."

"So tell me. Explain it to me." I looked around for my walking stick. It was across the room. Tough. I pushed to my feet anyway and started limping. "Everyone trusts me. The bank, my neighbors, people I do business with—the whole damned *town* trusts me, dammit. Ask anyone. Charlie's the charming McClain and Duncan's the mysterious one. Me, I'm Mr. Dependable." I ran a hand over my hair. "What good is having a reputation like that if you won't trust me!"

"I think you're charming." She uncoiled from the couch and came to me, naked and magnificently unconcerned about it. "Something of a mystery, too. Just when I think I've got you figured out, you pull a 180 on me." She slid her arms around my waist. "But I've only known you a week, Ben. It takes time for trust to grow."

"You trusted me with your body. But you can't trust me with the important stuff. Is that it, Seely? You don't think of this—" I ran my hand down her side "—as important?"

"Oh." That came out on a little puff of air, as if I'd punctured something. She laid her head on my shoulder. "Damn you. There goes another toppled preconception—bam! You aren't supposed to see that much."

"Was I being macho or sensitive?" I stroked her hair.

"Difficult." She sighed. "There was a time when I didn't much like my body. I developed early—and boy, did I develop. From the time I got breasts, I was never sure if men ever saw my face. Boys certainly didn't."

"Teenage boys are scum." Her hair looked so wild, and felt so soft. "They think with their second head."

"True. Well, at some point I decided that if I couldn't beat 'em, I'd join 'em." She lifted her head and looked at me, one eyebrow cocked. "I worked as a stripper when I was twenty."

The eyebrow, the expression, were all defiance. The eyes, though—they made me ache. So wild. And so soft. I kept petting. I didn't know what else to do. "So, were you any good?"

Her laugh broke in the middle. "I was damned good."

"Well, then." I slid my good arm around her waist and hugged her close.

She didn't say anything for a minute, but I felt the tension draining out of her. Then she sighed. "I was also young and stupid. Twenty is almost as arrogant as eighteen, isn't it?"

"Mmm." It felt good, holding her this way. "When I was twenty I ran off to get married."

She straightened, staring. "You're kidding. What happened?"

"We got halfway to Vegas and turned around. She started crying and wouldn't stop. Ruined the romance of it," I said dryly.

"I can't believe I didn't hear about that when everyone was filling me in on you."

"No one around here knows about it."

"Not even your family?" She grinned. "I sense real blackmail potential here."

"Seely…" I made a warning out of her name.

The amusement in her eyes softened. "She was the one you mentioned earlier, wasn't she? Did the aborted elopement end things between you?"

"No, we were still planning to get married after college." I shook my head, remembering. I'd been crazy about Bev, thought the sun rose and set on her. "We broke up when my parents died and I had to return to Highpoint. She, uh, didn't want to live here."

"Oh, Ben."

The ache in her voice made me uncomfortable. "It was a long time ago."

"She hurt you."

"She hurt, too. But she still had two years to go when it happened. Journalism degree. Not much opportunity to carve out a career as a reporter in Highpoint."

"And did she carve out a career?"

"I've seen her name in one of those weekly news magazines, so yeah, I guess she did. Don't look so sad. I haven't exactly been nursing a broken heart for the past twenty years. Now." I shifted my hold on her and nudged her toward the hall. "You going to help me upstairs, or do I have to crawl up there on my own?"

"Never lose track of a goal, do you?"

"Never."

That slow smile started in her eyes. "I could make you forget about going upstairs."

"Sure of yourself, are you?" We were moving slowly, with me leaning on her enough so she'd think she was helping. Good tactics, since it caused her bare body to rub up against mine.

"Damned right I am." We'd almost reached the stairs when she slipped in front of me, making me stop. Then she just stood there smiling at me...with the tips of her breasts brushing my chest with every inhalation. "What do you think?"

"You have a point. Or two." I ran my thumb over one.

Her breath sucked in. Then she got serious about making her point.

Several long, lovely moments later a thought intruded. I nuzzled her ear. "Something I almost forgot."

"Mmm." She nuzzled my throat. "What's that?"

"You're fired."

She jerked—then shook her head, grinning. "Only you would order me to trust you, then try to fire me."

What was she grinning about? "I'll help you find another position."

"No, you won't. First, I don't need help. Second, I'm not fired."

"Uh...I don't think this one is up to you."

"Sure it is." She patted me on the arm. "You can't fire people when you're naked."

I was blinking, trying to think of a logical answer to that wholly illogical statement, when the front door swung open. And there stood my little sister. Her husband, Jack. Behind them were Gwen, Duncan and Zach. And my brother Charlie, whose voice, very dry, broke the stunned silence.

"Surprise."

The woman beside me sat down on the stairs and laughed like a loon.

Ten

"If only I'd had a camera," Annie mourned.

"And here I thought I didn't have anything to be grateful for." I took another sip of coffee. Mornings after, I reflected, can be hell. Especially if you end up spending them with your sister and brothers instead of your lover. Whom I hadn't seen alone for more than thirty seconds since I slammed the door in my family's faces yesterday.

"It's not like any of us will ever forget that moment." Charlie leaned back in his chair, his hands clasped over his skinny belly. "It was a real peak life experience."

I grunted and drank my coffee. There was no point in trying to shut them up. I'd just have to let them get it out of their systems. They hadn't been able to do that yesterday because, as much of a pain as they could be, none of them had wanted to embarrass Seely.

Me, of course, they felt free to embarrass. Obliged to, even.

Seely had been great. I smiled, remembering. Not every woman could treat meeting her lover's family for the first time while stark naked as an icebreaker. She'd pulled it off, though.

And later, she'd slipped upstairs when I wasn't watching, going to bed in her usual room without giving me a chance to change her mind about that. Without a good-night kiss, either, or a single word spoken in private. My smile faded.

She was at the grocery store now with Gwen and Zach. I planned to have a talk with her when they returned.

Annie had drawn the short straw after breakfast. So far she'd managed to avoid tripping over Doofus while she cleaned up and loaded the dishwasher. You might say that the pup was excited about all the company...just like you might say that tornadoes are windy. Jack was at the coffeepot getting a refill. He was a compact man about Duncan's height, with short brown hair and an easy grin I'd seen too much of this morning.

He'd copped my new mug, the one Annie gave me last night that read: "Men. We're just better." He leaned against the counter, took a sip from my mug, and said thoughtfully, "You know how it is when you get something you've always wanted, but didn't know you wanted? It's not as if I ever dreamed of catching Ben with his pants down."

"Who would?" Duncan asked rhetorically.

Charlie nodded. "I know what you mean. I was pretty sure he put them on one leg at a time. Not positive, but pretty sure. But as for taking them off in the middle of the day—"

"Running around the house that way," Jack said.

"Bare-ass nekkid," Charlie finished with relish.

I sighed. Charlie and Jack had been best friends back in high school. They'd driven me crazy then, too.

Annie shook her head. "The things Ben's gotten up to since we left. Shocking. I had no idea."

"You've gotten up to a few things yourself." Charlie waggled his eyebrows. "Or so the presence of little Matilda indicates."

Annie got that soft look on her face I'd seen last night, the one that made her look so different from the freckle-faced tomboy I'd watched grow up. Her hand went to her stomach. If I looked closely, I could see the slight bulge beneath her T-shirt. "We may not have picked out names yet, but trust me—Matilda is *not* an option."

Annie and Jack had made their big announcement at the surprise party last night—a combination get-well-soon and belated-birthday bash. For me. That's why they'd all shown up like they had.

The surprise part had worked out a little too well, but the party itself had been great. The best part, of course, had been learning I'd have a niece or nephew in just over six months. She and Jack would be staying Stateside for quite some time, and...I swallowed the lump that kept coming back.

Annie was going to have a baby. My little sister. Imagine that.

Was there was any chance I'd be seeing Seely's tummy get round that way? She'd said not, but...

"Gertrude," Duncan suggested, straight-faced. "That's a good, solid name."

Charlie nodded. "Or Alphonse, if it's a boy. A boy named Alphonse would be sensitive, and I know that's important to you."

"Jack," Annie said, "kill those two pea-brains for me, will you?"

"Pour me some more coffee first," I said, pushing my empty mug toward him. "Before anything gets broken."

"Like me," Jack said, bringing the carafe to the table. "I can take Charlie—"

"Ha!" Charlie said.

"But Duncan?" Jack shook his head as he refilled my cup. "You know I'd do anything for you, love, but this isn't a good time for me to go into the hospital."

I started to reach for the cup he held out. The sling kept the movement to a tiny jerk. Dammit—I'd forgotten. I took the mug in my left hand and sipped.

"Something wrong with the coffee, Ben?"

"No, it's good." Not as good as Seely's, but that wasn't what had brought a scowl to my face.

I could have used my right hand. If the sling hadn't reminded me, I would have. This morning I'd woken up reaching for a woman I'd never slept beside, which was weird enough…but I'd been reaching with my right arm.

My shoulder had barely twinged. And my knee didn't hurt at all.

I'd experimented. I couldn't lift my arm over my head yet, but I could raise it up to my shoulder. It was weak, but I could use it for little things like getting dressed. Brushing my teeth. Getting my sock back from Doofus.

No way should I have been able to do all that. After pulling on my jeans I'd sat on the hospital bed, feeling cold and sick. I don't know why it shook me up so badly. I'd been pretty sure Seely had done something impossible on the mountain…but there's knowing and there's *knowing*. I guess part of me just flat hadn't believed it. Hadn't wanted to believe it.

The world wasn't the same place it used to be. Reality wasn't what I'd always believed it was. Maybe Seely's granny really was a witch. Maybe she'd turn me into a toadstool if I messed with her granddaughter.

"Hey." A hand passed in front of my face. "You in there?"

I swatted at Annie's hand but missed.

She pulled up the chair beside me and sat. Duncan had left

the room; Jack and Charlie were arguing about something. "So how are you, really?" Annie asked.

"Fine." Better than should have been possible, but I wasn't going to go into that. Seely didn't want anyone to know—hell, she wouldn't even talk to me about it. Considering how long I'd sat on that bed with my hands shaking, I could see why she wanted it kept secret. "How about you? Any morning sickness?"

"I'm healthy as a horse. Which is more than you can say right now, but that wasn't what I meant. I'm worried about you."

"Me?" I shook my head. "You're not making sense."

"Neither are you. That's what worries me. Ben." She put her hand on my arm. "All teasing aside, it isn't like you to get naked with an employee. I like Seely, but—"

"Good. Fine. I'm glad you like her. Leave it at that."

"But something she said last night made it obvious she isn't planning to stay in Highpoint. And she isn't..." She sighed. "I don't know how to put this."

"Don't put it at all." I was getting annoyed. "Look, do I tell you how to handle your relationship with Jack?"

She stared. "You have amnesia? The knock on your head loosened your brains?"

"Okay, okay. Maybe I did make a few comments back when you two first got serious."

"You threatened to break parts of his body."

"He was kissing you! Had his hands all over the place."

"We were married."

"Yeah, well, I didn't know that at the time. After that—"

"You butted in every chance you got for a good long while. And as mad as that made me, I knew you did it because you cared. So I'm claiming the same privilege. Because I care, too."

Damn. She had me pinned.

"But I'm going to try for a little more tact than you used." Her grin flashed briefly. "I guess what I really want to know is whether this is a fling, a just-for-fun affair. Because it doesn't look like one."

"What is this, feminine intuition? You haven't even been home a full day yet."

She snorted. "Feminine intuition is the amazing ability women have to see what's under our noses. From the moment I saw you two together—oh. Not the very *first* moment. Memorable as that was." Again the grin, but again it faded. Annie shook her head. "It's the way you look at her, the way...you're just different with her, Ben. That's what worries me. Because—"

Doofus leaped up, yapping loudly, and ran toward the front of the house. "They must be back," I said, relieved, and shoved my chair back. "I'll give them a hand with the groceries."

Annie's hand closed around my wrist. "You'll sit. You're supposed to be convalescing, remember? Though I must say, you're doing better than I'd expected."

Better than I'd expected, too.

"Which leads back to what I've been trying to say. I hope you're not in too deep, because I don't think Seely plans to stay around. She told me last night you wouldn't need her much longer."

Not need her? Was the woman crazy?

I shoved to my feet. We definitely needed to talk.

It was afternoon before I was able to cut Seely out of the herd.

Me, Gwen and Annie were sitting out on the deck. The weather was crisp and clear—jacket weather, if you weren't running around with five-year-old boys. Which Duncan, Charlie and Jack were doing, in a scaled-down version of softball. The twins had been invited over to wear Zach out. So far it wasn't working.

Gwen and Annie were talking about sex. They'd started out discussing pregnancy, but somehow that segued into sex. I was pretending I wasn't listening.

Not that it isn't an interesting subject, but dammit, Annie was my little sister. Besides, a man who gets into a discussion of that subject with more than one woman at a time is asking for trouble. They'll embarrass the hell out of you. When women bunch up in packs, they have no shame.

Seely had been talking with them, too, until a moment ago. She'd gone into the house to use the bathroom.

I stood. I'd given her a thirty-second head start. That was enough. "Think I'll grab another beer. Anyone else want one?"

Gwen rose to her feet. "I'll get it."

"No, you won't." I headed for the kitchen door.

"I'll take one," Charlie called from the scrap of cardboard that was serving as pitcher's mound. "Soon as I strike Jack out, these guys are dust." Jack and his two smaller teammates hooted their opinions of this prediction. I nodded and went inside.

I was leaning against the door to the laundry room when the bathroom door opened. Seely's hand flew to her chest. "Ben!"

Her hair was down, and oh, Lord, but I liked it that way. Her sweater was green with little buttons down the front. I liked those buttons, too. Though it didn't look like I was going to get a chance to mess with either her hair or her buttons anytime soon. "Surprised? You shouldn't be. You must have known you couldn't avoid me forever."

Her eyebrows expressed polite disbelief. "You may have noticed there are a few more people staying here now? I've been busy."

"We need to talk."

"Okay. You can talk to me while I peel apples." She started for the kitchen.

Dammit, she was doing it again—holding me at a distance. Avoiding me even when I was standing right in front of her. Maybe making love hadn't meant anything to her. Maybe she regretted it. Maybe she did plan to leave soon.

And maybe talk wasn't what I needed. I took two quick strides and slapped my hand on the wall beside her, stopping her.

She frowned at me. "I need to get the pies started."

I leaned in and kissed her.

She didn't push me away. Her lips were warm and soft...and they quivered beneath mine in a single, telling spasm of uncertainty. Seely, always so sure of herself, so dauntlessly confident, was frightened.

Suddenly I could admit I'd been scared, too. All day. Like thunder in the distance, fear had rumbled away deep inside, never drawing so close I was forced to notice it. Never going away, either.

I touched her bottom lip with my tongue, telling her it was okay, that I was scared, too. I feathered kisses across her cheek so she'd know I meant to be careful with her—not just her body, but all those achy inside places. Her breath caught. I brushed my lips across hers one more time, leaned my forehead on hers and sighed. "I've been wanting to do that all day."

"I don't think Annie and your brothers would have fainted if you'd kissed me in front of them."

"No, but they would have been hugely amused if you'd belted me for it. And I wasn't sure you wouldn't."

"Did you really think that? I didn't mean..." She shook her head, dismissing whatever she'd been about to say, and put a hand on my chest. "I'm sorry. I guess I've been running scared."

"Good. I'd hate to be the only one."

Her smile flickered. "I like your family."

"Me, too. Most of the time. What's wrong?"

"Foolishness. And I guess I'm a little jealous. You know I told you I was an only child? Well, my mother was, too. That's my whole family—me, Daisy and Granny."

I studied her face. She was telling the truth…but maybe not all of the truth. I touched her cheek gently. "Did you ever wonder if you had more family somewhere? Not the grandmother from hell, but your father might have married, had more kids."

Her eyelids lowered, shielding her eyes. "He did."

That sent a jolt to my stomach. "Well, hell. Did you know that when you came to Highpoint?"

Seely nodded. "He sent Daisy a birth announcement. Can you imagine that? No letter, just the printed announcement."

"Okay, he may be worse than a noodle." I hesitated. "You have a brother or sister?"

"Brother. Half brother, I mean." She sighed and laid her head on my shoulder. "I toyed with the idea of introducing myself, but when I stayed with the judge and Granny Dearest all those years ago, my father never brought his new wife and son with him when he came up on weekends. So my brother may not know I exist."

"You came all the way to Highpoint, but didn't do anything about meeting him?"

"Oh, I did something. Being a bright, mature woman, I stalked him."

I didn't mean to laugh. It snuck out.

"I agree. Pretty ridiculous. I checked out where he works, where he lives. I'd just about talked myself into going up to his door, but kept driving around his house.

Then someone else pulled up. I saw them together. All of them—my father, his wife, their son. They were...complete. A unit. I decided I had to either fish or cut bait." She shrugged. "I cut bait. That's when your brother found me at the bus station."

"Thank God he did."

She nodded against my shoulder. "It hurt. Seeing them together hurt. I didn't expect that."

"Yeah. I guess it would." I smoothed her hair back from her face.

"I came here because I was curious, not because I had any stupid ideas of a family reunion. I wouldn't have been hurt if I'd remembered that."

"There you go, being human." I shook my head and snuggled her more firmly against me. "Got to watch that. Leads to all sorts of complications."

She snorted and slid both arms around my waist. For a minute we just stood there, holding on to each other. It probably looked as if I was comforting her, but the comfort went both ways.

Fear wasn't a rumble on the horizon anymore—it was right up in my face. Seely had no intention of staying in Highpoint. Under the circumstances, I couldn't blame her. But I couldn't lose her. All at once that was blindingly obvious. Somehow I had to make her want to stay.

The thing to do, then, was to change the circumstances. But first things first. "I'm moving back into my bedroom tonight."

She pulled back to study my face, her eyebrows raised. "You've decided your sister and brother-in-law should share a twin bed?"

With all the company, the only bedroom left was the one that used to be Annie's. It was Zach's room now. Annie and Jack were in my bedroom, Charlie was in his—at least, it had been his until he quit trucking a few months ago to find himself and ended up in Arizona. And Seely was in Duncan's old room.

My heart started pounding. Oh, yeah, I was scared. Foolishly, over-the-top scared. "There's a double bed in your room. If you move in with me, they can have that one."

She didn't exactly fall on my neck with enthusiasm for the idea. "Define 'move in.'"

"Sleep in my bed. Take over the closet. Argue over who gets custody of the remote." I ran my hand along the length of her hair where it spilled over her shoulder, and my voice dropped. "Be there when I wake up and reach out for you."

Her eyes were troubled. "Ben…"

"I reached for you this morning and you weren't there."

She swallowed. "I thought you didn't believe in living together."

"I changed my mind." *Please,* I thought—maybe at God, maybe at Seely. *Please.*

That slow smile started in her eyes, spreading over the rest of her face like sunlight easing up over the rim of the world. "Changing your mind…is that anything like admitting you were wrong?"

"Pretty close."

"In that case…" She slid her arms around my neck. "I suppose a man who can admit he was wrong deserves some kind of reward."

"Is that a yes?"

"It is."

Several minutes later she was pressed against the wall, one leg curled around my thigh. Various things were unfastened. We were both breathing hard.

"Oh, boy," she said, resting her forehead against my shoulder and letting her leg slide back down. "We are not going to do this here."

"Right." I'd forgotten where we were, forgotten about my brothers, my sister and sister-in-law, my son and his friends…I was going to be really worried about my loss of control. Later. Maybe tomorrow. Right now I didn't have enough blood left in my head to scrape together a thought that didn't involve the wall, the fullness of the breast I cupped and whether it was possible to do what I wanted with only one arm.

I dragged more air in, let it out. "About that pie…apple, you said?"

Her laugh was shaky. "You are *such* a man. Here, help me put back together some of the bits you unfastened."

"I may as well peel apples. I can't go back outside yet, not in this condition. My brothers would never let me hear the end of it." They'd probably rag me anyway, but if I went out there now I'd hear way too many cracks about hauling lumber around in my jeans.

We got her bra and sweater fastened, and her jeans—which I didn't remember undoing—and my jeans, which I *know* I hadn't unsnapped—and headed for the kitchen hand in hand. I was limping a little for the first time that day.

Which reminded me. "You haven't given me any trouble about my knee and the stairs. I guess you knew it's pretty much healed."

She slid me a long, level glance. And didn't say a word.

"I'd complain about how long it took you," Charlie said, taking the bottle I held out, "but Seely has more to bitch about. You were in there too long for retrieving a couple beers, not long enough for anything else. Not if you did things right."

"You want to drink that beer or wear it?"

He grinned, lazy and obnoxious. "You're big, but I'm faster. Especially with half your body parts not working right. Speaking of which…" He waggled his eyebrows.

"Works fine," I said mildly, and took a swig of my own beer.

"Glad to hear it." Charlie tilted his bottle up.

The softball game had broken up while I was in the kitchen with Seely. Gwen and Annie were inside helping get the last few things done; the women had agreed to handle the preparation if the men took care of the ribs and the cleanup. Duncan was on his way home to shower and change into his uniform. He'd be back to eat his share before he started his shift.

I needed to talk to him, but it could wait. Right now I felt too good to worry about anything. The sky was that drenched shade of blue that makes me feel crisp and happy, as if all that color were pouring down into me, opening me up. The ribs smelled incredible. Zach and the twins were building a fort with the help of their uncle Jack, the construction engineer. And Seely would sleep in my bed tonight.

Charlie and I stood under the big oak next to the swing I'd hung for Zach, drinking beer and watching the kids. It's a good yard for kids—big, with plenty of thick grass, but a few bare spots, too. Kids need dirt. They need places that aren't all fixed up so they can build and tear down, dream and dig and make a mess.

Dreams…I'd thought I had given up on them, but they're hard to kill. This yard, like the house, was big enough to welcome a lot of kids. I was picturing a curly-haired little girl in the tire swing when Charlie said, "I like your lady."

My lady. That sounded good. "She's something, isn't she?" I remembered what Seely had said about men not noticing her face. "And I'm not talking about—"

"I didn't get a good look at them," Charlie assured me.

"You closed the door too fast. Anyway, that wasn't what I meant. Though I do have to say that if Seely stays around long, you may die young, but you'll die happy."

"Yeah." Making sure she stayed around was the trick. "I'm going to marry her."

He spewed beer all over. After he finished choking, he gave me a wary look. "You, ah, mentioned that to her?"

"Not yet." First I had to deal with the situation that had made her want to leave Highpoint.

I had a plan for that.

Eleven

At ten-thirty that night I was pacing my bedroom, which wasn't smart. I ought to stretch out in the big, comfortable bed I'd been missing and save my energy for more important things. But I couldn't settle.

The shower in the bathroom off my bedroom was running. Seely was in it.

I paused by the bed and scowled at the door to the bathroom. I was as nervous as a new English recruit watching the French form up outside a tiny village in Belgium known as Waterloo.

I grimaced. Make that as nervous as a bridegroom.

I'd always thought that when a woman moved her clothes into my closet, she'd be my wife. This living-together business was new territory for me. It didn't help that it was taking place under the amused, worried or just plain nosy eyes of my brothers and sister. Jaws had dropped when I'd announced the room changes over spareribs and coleslaw. By the time we got to the apple pie I'd almost lost my appetite.

Why did they all have to act so amazed? It's not as if anyone could have mistaken me for a virgin. I'd dated. I'd had affairs, too, some of them lasting awhile. Shoot, I'd had a fiancée back in college. Okay, so maybe my family didn't know Bev and I had been engaged. They'd known we were seeing each other. You'd think they'd have guessed there was sex involved.

What I'd never had, I realized, was a *relationship*.

No wonder I was nervous.

Relationship is a woman's word. It means that you're serious about each other, but not serious enough to get married. It means "maybe," not yes. It means that when there are problems, you're supposed to talk, work things out. In other words, make up the rules as you go along.

Jesus. I ran a hand over my hair. She sure was taking a long time in the shower.

I knew very well it was one thing to decide to marry Seely, another to pull it off. Especially when she thought she was cursed to love unhappily. She claimed she didn't believe in the curse, but I was pretty sure that deep down she did.

But maybe that wasn't such a bad deal. Women mostly liked me, some of them enough to go to bed with me. But they didn't fall head-over-heels in love, and I didn't have a clue how to make that happen. I had other things going for me, though. I was dependable. Dependable isn't sexy, but it helps when you're in for the long haul. Besides, Seely and I had the passion thing down. I wasn't going to worry about that aspect.

I could offer her a home, but I wasn't sure she wanted one. Does security matter to a woman who's been drifting around the country? But fidelity—surely that meant something. I was aces at fidelity.

And she liked me. Aside from our fireworks in bed, she liked being with me. So I had plenty to build on, I assured myself.

The sound of the water shut off. My head swivelled toward the bathroom door, but she would have more woman-stuff to do, I reminded myself. Hair, lotion, things like that. I resumed my pacing.

My gaze fell on the pile I'd brought up from downstairs—the junk that had been sitting next to my hospital bed. Including the books I'd ordered, which I'd gotten out of sight fast when my family descended on us. Books like *The Laying On of Hands*—there were two with that title—*Hands of Healing, The Women's Book of Healing* and, God help me, *Chakras, Auras and the Healing Energy of the Body.*

My fingers went to my shoulder, where a gauze pad covered the rapidly healing wound. I wasn't wearing the sling. Didn't need it anymore, though I still used it when others were around so no one asked questions I couldn't answer.

My lips tightened. I didn't mind keeping her secret, but I damned sure wanted to know what that secret was. I was pretty sure that one of the relationship rules involved being honest and open with your partner. Seely was going to have to give me some answers.

I just hoped those answers didn't involve chakras or auras.

I grimaced and caught a glimpse of my reflection in the mirror. That gave me something new to worry about. I've always been fit, and Seely seemed to like the way I was built, so I didn't think my body was a problem. But maybe I should have worn the stupid pajamas. Boxers weren't exactly romantic.

The hell with it. Normally I didn't even wear boxers to bed, much less pajamas. If a man couldn't be comfortable in his own bedroom, he—

The bathroom door opened. Seely smiled at me.

Her nightgown was made like a man's shirt, a satiny blue-green shirt that shimmered over her breasts like sunlight on water and left her legs mostly bare. Her hair frizzed around her face and spilled over her shoulders, excited by the humidity from her shower.

Her smile was shy. "Hi, sailor. Looking for a girl to show you a good time?"

I exhaled in relief. "Good. You're nervous, too."

She gave a startled laugh. "You want me to be nervous?"

"I don't want to be the only one who swallowed Mexican jumping beans." Seeing her nerves settled mine down. I moved to her and put my arms around her waist. "I like your nightgown."

"Good." Her lips tilted mischievously and she tucked her fingertips into the waistband of my shorts. "I see you're a flannel kind of a guy, all the way."

"Flannel's warm." I kissed her cheek. "And soft." I kissed the other cheek. "I like warm, soft things."

"Mmm." Her eyes were slumberous and sexy. "If I didn't know better, I'd say you were trying to distract me from my nerves."

"How am I doing?" This time I touched her lips with mine.

"Pretty good."

My body was making suggestions about the curves and softness nestled against me. I could tell she was aroused, too. But for a moment we just stood there smiling at each other.

She pulled away to wander the room, touching things as if she were getting acquainted. "It's funny. Sometimes it seems as if I've known you for ages, but I haven't. I was struck by that when I came out just now—how short a time I've known you. I've never been in your bedroom at the same time you were." She shook her head. "Even for a couple of impetuous souls like us, things have moved pretty fast, haven't they?"

"Wait a minute. I am not impetuous."

"No?" Her mouth twitched. "What do you call hiring me without checking my references? Or asking me to live with you when you've only known me ten days?"

"A good decision and a great one. I'm decisive, not impulsive."

That made her laugh. It was a good sound. "I like your room. Very masculine, but in a comfortable way. A touch old-fashioned. This lamp is a surprise, though." She touched the shade on the lamp by the bed. "It's lovely, but quite feminine."

"It was my mother's. I kind of like keeping her lamp where I can see it. She was so tickled when she bought it—it's hand-painted china."

Her ready smile tilted her lips up. "You're sentimental."

"It's not sentimental to respect the past."

"I like sentimental." She came back to me and linked her arms around my waist. "I think I'm ready to be fired now."

"Ah…" I blinked a couple times. "Because we aren't naked yet?"

"Because you don't need nursing care anymore. I can't justify drawing a salary for scrubbing your back and nagging you to take care of yourself."

Those were things a wife did. I gripped her waist. "I'll scrub your back, too."

"It's a deal."

I kissed her like I meant it this time. When I lifted my head, it wasn't because I wanted to. I've always preferred action to words, and my body was definitely not in the mood for verbal communication.

But I couldn't let this go. "One more thing we need to talk about. Why *don't* I need nursing care?"

She went still—and her face, dammit, closed down.

"I don't need the sling anymore. I ought to, but I don't. My knee is almost normal. I want to understand."

She pulled away and paced. "Why can't you just accept it? Stop asking questions, stop trying to make it fit your logical world, stop reading—oh, yes, I've seen that pile of books. Why can't you leave it alone?"

"Because you won't talk about it. You won't even tell me why you won't talk about it!"

"I want to feel normal! Is that so hard to understand?" Her voice turned wistful. "You do that for me, Ben. Here, with you and your family, I feel deliciously normal. Ordinary. As if I fit." She held out a hand. "Is it wrong to want to pretend for a while that I'm like everyone else?"

"You do fit." My throat closed up around the words, so I went to her and pulled her close. "You fit just fine."

She held on tight. "I could use some more distracting."

"I can do that." I lifted her hair with both hands, smoothing it away from her face. "I'm pretty damned distracted myself." Which might be the first lie I'd ever told her. I was hard, I was aching, but I wasn't distracted.

But pretense was what she wanted, wasn't it? She met my mouth gladly.

For the first time I was sure that she needed me…but what she needed from me was pretense, like the game of doctor we'd played the first time we made love. But no one wins when you play at denial. I knew that, and still I let her do it.

The most extraordinary woman I'd ever known longed to feel normal. It just about broke my heart.

"Ben. Ben!"

Someone shook my shoulder. I jerked and woke from nightmare.

"You were dreaming," Seely said. "Not a good dream, from the sound of it."

"No. It wasn't." I rolled onto my back and scrubbed my face. My skin was clammy.

The house was as silent as an old house ever gets, heavy with that dead-end-of-the-night feel. The old casement clock on the chest of drawers was ticking away. I heard the rustle of the covers as Seely propped herself up. I couldn't see her, except as a paler smudge against the darkness. But her hand was warm on my chest, and her hair tickled my shoulder.

"You want to tell me about it?" she asked. "Or would that violate the Tough Guy Code?"

"Not much to tell."

"Well, which sort of nightmare was it? The kind where you're being chased by hairy critters with big teeth? Or maybe a version of my personal favorite—the one where I show up for algebra class in time for the big test, but somehow neglected to get dressed first."

Okay, she'd made me smile. I reached up and tugged on one long strand of hair. "No great hairy monsters. This was more reality based."

"And…?"

I shrugged. "I was crawling along the mountain again, only I'd lost track of which way was up, so I wasn't getting anywhere."

"Reality-based nightmares are the pits." She rubbed my chest in small circles. "What happened to you was the pits, too."

"Yeah." In the nightmare I'd kept moving, just like in reality. But I hadn't been able to tell uphill from down, so moving hadn't helped. And in the nightmare, Seely hadn't found me. I'd been dying—lost, cold, alone and dying. "I guess I have to expect a few bad dreams after such a close call."

"Maybe so." Her fingers began playing with my chest hair. "Um…you need some help getting back to sleep? I'm wide awake now, too."

I felt raw, unsteady. Words seemed too frail and distant to navigate by, so I cupped her nape with my hand and brought her head down for a kiss. At the touch of her lips, need shuddered through me.

She was here. That's all I could think—Seely was real. She was in my arms, in my bed. The nightmare was false, because Seely was here.

Sex arranges itself in all sorts of ways, a grand variety of positions, styles and speeds. I wasn't thinking about style or variety then. I wasn't thinking at all. It was instinct that had me rolling her onto her back, a primitive need to cover her body with my own. It was hunger that compelled me, but a hunger unlike any I'd known.

Seely was under me. Her hands welcomed me as our legs and tongues tangled. My heart drummed an exultant riff and I took my mouth lower, drifting kisses along the cord of her neck.

She feathered her fingertips over my shoulder, where a gauze pad protected the wound. Her voice was soft and none too steady. "I should have known you'd want to be on top sooner rather than later, but your shoulder—"

"I'll be careful." I licked my way down the slope of her breast.

She shivered. "Your knee…"

"Doesn't hurt a bit." Which wasn't possible, but I wasn't going to question her now.

There was no moon that night, and my room is at the back of the house. The darkness was rich and complete, a prickling along my skin, a weightless cover woven of possibilities. In that darkness, driven by a need that both was and wasn't physical, I lost track of surfaces.

Here reality was dimensional, bodies meeting and moving in space. And as with my crawl up the mountain, reality broke up into parts—but this time each part seemed to hold the whole. I found Seely in the curve of her thigh, and the tender skin inside her elbow. She was the air that moved through my lungs, the soft cry I heard as I sucked at her breast, the hand sifting my hair. She was the dip of her navel, and the musk filling the air as I parted her inner lips and kissed her there.

At last the urgency became irresistible, pooling in one place like my blood. I braced myself over her and pushed inside. She was hot and wet, and her inner walls began contracting around me before I was fully in.

She called my name. She held on to me as my body thrust and thrust again. My own explosion hit, the universe cracking over me like a woman cracks an egg on the side of a bowl, a white-hot blow that split me open and spilled me out.

A few minutes later I fell asleep holding her and being held, neither of us having spoken another word. If I dreamed again, I didn't know it.

Twelve

One week later Annie and Jack were in Denver looking for a larger apartment; Charlie was in Arizona, planning landscapes and planting them; Zach was at Mrs. Bradshaw's; and Seely was checking out a job in the office of the elementary school near the house.

Me, I was back at work. Only for a few hours, true, but it felt great to be sitting at my desk in a chair that knew the ins and outs of my body as intimately as any spouse. My sling was draped over the back of that chair. I'd taken it off as soon as Manny left for the Patterson site, and would put it back on before I left the office. But I didn't need it. Not anymore.

In the past two hours I'd signed a few checks, talked to two suppliers and looked over bids from subcontractors. But right now I was staring out the window, wishing I was with Manny.

Deceiving Seely made my stomach hurt.

Not that I'd lied to her, but there's more to honesty than avoiding a spoken lie. I was about to do something behind her back.

I sighed, punched in the number I'd gotten from directory assistance, then listened to the phone ringing on the other end. It rang seven times.

At last a cheerful female voice sang, "Hello! This is Daisy, live and in person. Do you hate those blasted machines as much as I do?"

"Ah—I'm not too fond of them."

"Especially the ones that make you keep punching in numbers. 'Punch three if you'd like to place an order. Punch four if you hate broccoli. Punch five if you've ever been arrested.'"

I found myself smiling. "Punch five and you'll probably wind up arrested and hospitalized. Someone's sure to punch back."

She laughed. "Good point. So who is this?"

"My name is Ben McClain. I called because—"

"Seely's man! How wonderful of you to call. She has a rule, you know. I'm not allowed to interrogate anyone she dates for at least a month. But you called me, so that makes it all right, don't you think?"

"You want to interrogate me?"

"I prefer to think of it as a little get-acquainted chat."

If Seely's mother wanted to know about my intentions or my bank account, I should be okay. I had the idea Daisy Jones didn't operate on the usual channels, however. "If you want to know my astrological sign, I haven't the foggiest idea."

"Oh, I don't cast horoscopes anymore. What's your favorite member of the vegetable kingdom?"

Vegetable kingdom? I shook my head and told myself to play along. "There's this oak tree in the backyard...I guess you could call it my favorite."

"You picked a tree." She sounded delighted. "The name of your first pet?"

"Rocky. Do you really do this to anyone Seely dates?"

"Most people get used to it," she assured me. "Tell me about Rocky. Was he a dog or a turtle?"

"Why those two options?" I asked, disconcerted.

"Hedging my bets. Rocky sounds like a turtle, but I tend to think of boys and dogs."

I told her about Rocky—a box turtle I'd found when I was three. Then I told her my favorite time of day; the one food I wouldn't eat if someone tied me down and stuck pins in me; which former president I'd like to meet, and why; and what kind of vehicle I drove.

She liked trucks. Knew quite a bit about them, too, which didn't sound like any New-Age witch I'd ever imagined. But then, I wasn't clear on whether she considered herself a witch.

While we talked trucks I looked out the window at the new Dodge Ram sitting in my parking spot. The insurance company had paid up in record time, and yesterday Seely had gone with me to select the new pickup. I'd intended to get a white one, like usual, but had to admit the dark blue looked good.

A truck wasn't a good family vehicle, though. Maybe I should trade the old Chevy in on something newer....

"We may have to agree to disagree about Fords," Seely's mom said. "Now, to get back to my questions—how old were you when you had your first sexual experience?"

I didn't quite swallow my tongue. "You've got to be kidding."

Daisy's chuckle was low and wicked and made me think of her daughter. "You'd be surprised how often people answer that one. I suppose I should stop tormenting you and let you get it out of your system. Whatever you called to ask me, that is."

"Why do you think I called to ask you something?"

"Why else would you call? Unless Seely was ill or injured, and she isn't."

I didn't ask why she was sure of that. What if she told me, and I believed her? "Seely has a brother. I need to know how to get in touch with him."

There was a long pause. "Seely knows his name. Why don't you ask her?"

I ran a hand over my hair. "I'll level with you. I want to talk to the man, and I don't want Seely to know about it. Not right away, at least. It would be wrong to get his name from her if I'm going to do something sneaky with the information."

"An interesting ethical distinction. Why do you want to talk to him?"

"She's got issues." I pushed to my feet, unable to be still. "She doesn't think the deal with her father is supposed to bother her anymore, but it does. She was going to leave Highpoint without talking to him or her brother. That's not right."

"And you know what's right for her?"

"Not about her father," I admitted. "She's got some heavy-duty feelings there, and with reason. I don't understand how a man can ignore his own child. I can't sort that out for her. But her brother…she won't have the same kind of old hurt tied up around meeting him."

"Mmm. I see what you mean—the expectations would be different. But, Ben, meddling is seldom wise."

"Seely said she came to Highpoint because she was curious. I think it's more than that. Whatever pulled her here, I don't think she's fixed it yet. I think she needs to meet her brother. Find out if he smiles slowly, the way she does. If they watch the same shows or eat the same foods. If she likes him."

"He's a half-brother. She may not see that much of herself in him."

I shrugged impatiently. "Half, whole, he's still family. Does he know about her?"

"I don't know." Another pause. "I've believed for some time that she needs to resolve some of those issues you mentioned. I hadn't thought about going in the back door, so to speak, via her brother. It might work."

Relief broke over me in a grin. "You're going to help."

"I never claimed to be wise. His name is Jonathan. Jonathan Burns."

"Thanks." Still grinning, I reached for the phone book and started thumbing through it. There was more I wanted to ask, but I wasn't sure how to bring it up. "Ah…Seely told me about her grandmother."

"Mrs. Burns?"

"No, I met that one. It wasn't fun." There it was: Jonathan S. Burns, 1117 W. Thornbird. I closed the phone book. "What I mean is, Seely told me about your mother being a—" I swallowed "—a witch."

"Did she, now?"

"If she wasn't supposed to say anything—"

"No, I was just surprised. She doesn't talk about our family's heritage to many people."

"Yeah, well, speaking of the family heritage…hell. She just pulled up. I'd better go."

"Don't worry about it," she said soothingly. "I was just going to tell you to discuss it with Seely."

I was irked. "You might try letting me ask a question before you answer."

"It's more fun this way. I noticed that you had a hard time saying the word witch."

"It's a weird word. Listen, Ms. Jones—"

"Daisy."

"Daisy, then. I really have to go."

"Seely's been hurt in the past by people who couldn't accept her."

I'd suspected as much. "She wants to feel normal. I don't know what—ah, nice talking to you," I said hastily as the door opened.

Seely cocked an eyebrow at me as she strolled into my office. She had a satisfied look that made me hope the interview had gone well.

"I'll call you later," I told her mother firmly.

Daisy chuckled. "I'm tempted to ask you to put Seely on, but I'll resist. Bye, Ben. Call anytime."

I disconnected, put the phone down and gave Seely what I hoped was an encouraging smile. "Either you got the job, or you're really glad to see me."

She laughed, came up and put her arms around my neck. "Both."

"Good to know our schools aren't being run by idiots." I gave her the kiss her uptilted face invited. "We'll celebrate. Want to go to the resort for supper and sneer at Vic?"

"I like the way your mind works. But no business talk. You're not supposed to be working at all until you've been to the doctor for your checkup. Which is Tuesday, right?"

The pleasure drained out of me. "I canceled it. I'm not going to the doctor, Seely."

"You…" Her voice trailed off and her gaze flickered to the sling hanging on my chair. She swallowed and looked away. "I never meant to force you into some kind of coverup."

She was feeling guilty. Hell. And for the wrong reason—she *ought* to feel bad about not telling me everything, not because I was helping her keep her secret. "It's no big deal. I don't need to see the doctor to know I'm healing just fine."

Her head gave a single shake. "You shouldn't be forced to lie for me."

"I doubt I'll have to. Anyone who finds out I didn't go in for my checkup will put it down to me being ornery and lecture me. Hey." I put my fingers beneath her chin and tilted her face toward me. "This is not a big deal. It's not like I'm some kind of saint who never told a lie."

Her expression was odd, sort of sad and tender and wry all at once. "Not a saint, no. More like George Washington. You can't tell a lie without it troubling that great, big integrity bone that runs alongside your spine. Which is why I wondered..." Her eyes searched mine. "If I didn't know better, I'd say you were looking guilty when I came in. Maybe about whoever was on the phone?"

It took me a beat too long to reply. "Good thing you know better, isn't it? Come on." I reached out and snagged my sling. "Let's get me rigged up so we can go home and primp for our night out."

She laughed, as I'd hoped, and offered to loan me some lipstick. I shook my head and said I couldn't use her colors because I was a winter—a bit of female jargon I'd overheard. That really tickled her.

And all the while I was thinking about secrets, hers and mine, and that secrets were bad for a relationship, worse for a marriage. Mine wouldn't be a secret for long, though. Once I figured out a way to get Seely and her brother together, I wouldn't have anything to hide. But hers...

I gave her another kiss and headed for my new, dark-blue truck. She climbed into her car and we drove home sort of together, sort of alone, each in our own vehicle. Which pretty much summed up this whole relationship business, I thought gloomily.

* * *

"Look, Daddy! Look at me!"

Zach had promoted me from Dad to Daddy a couple of months ago. Whenever he called me that, my chest got warm and tight. "I'm watching," I told him from my spot on the other side of the cedar fence. "You're way up there, all right."

He and the twins were all over Mrs. Bradshaw's jungle gym, bundled up against the chill. I'd meant to bring him home until it was time for Gwen to come for him, but the three kids were having too much fun.

"So where's your pretty lady?" Mrs. B. asked.

"Inside, gilding the lily."

"Looks like you did some gilding, too. You're looking mighty dressed up."

"Now and then I leave off the flannel." My sports coat was suede the color of old buckskin, and tailored western-style. It had been a gift from Annie last Christmas. She called it "very Robert Redford." I don't know about that, since I doubt there are many men on the face of the planet who look less like Robert Redford than I do. But I was secretly proud of the way it looked. And I could wear it with jeans, which made it just about perfect. "We're going to the resort for dinner."

"Good for you. About time you took her someplace nice." Faded blue eyes twinkled behind the lavender-framed glasses. "You thinking of keeping this one, Ben? I like her."

"I'd tell you to mind your own business," I said amiably, "but I hate to waste my breath."

She chuckled. Naomi Bradshaw was a little dab of a woman with leathery skin and the most noticing eyes of anyone I knew. I guess thirty years of keeping track of kids will do that for you. She'd raised her own after her husband walked out, plus having had a hand in raising any number of other people's kids.

She was also the nosiest woman I knew. "Good to see that you're not mooning over Gwen anymore."

I scowled. "You've got a helluva imagination. And no tact."

"Don't have to be tactful with someone whose diapers I changed."

"Try another one. I was seven when you moved in next door, and you didn't start keeping children for another couple of years after that."

"The principle's the same. You haven't changed much since then—still stubborn as a mule." She shook her head. "Guess you thought the sling would mess up the lines of your pretty jacket."

Damn. I'd forgotten all about the stupid thing when I changed clothes. I didn't want her wondering why I was doing so well. "I don't need the damned sling," I growled.

"Stubborn as any mule," she repeated. "Better put it on so you don't start out your evening with an argument, because unless I miss my guess, Seely isn't…"

"Mrs. B.?" I straightened. She had an odd look on her face, as if she'd turned queasy. "You okay?"

"Fine." She waved one hand vaguely, but she didn't look any better. And she sounded winded. "Just a little…" She shook her head, looking confused. "I feel funny."

Alarmed, I said, "You go inside and lie down. I'll round up the boys and bring them over here."

"Don't be silly. Their moms will be here in twenty minutes or so. That's soon enough to coddle myself. Though maybe…" She shook her head again, frowning, and hugged her arms as if she was cold. "I had a touch of flu a few days ago. Guess I'm not as back to par as I'd thought. Boys!" she called, turning and starting for the jungle gym. "Time to go in. Carson, quit pretending you don't hear me. Zach—"

She stopped speaking. Stopped moving. And crumpled to the ground.

The fence was only four and a half feet high. I vaulted it and hit the ground running.

"Mrs. B...." She'd landed all crumpled, half on her side, with her face down. I turned her over gently, my heart pounding. The whites of her eyes showed. Her skin looked gray. I bent, putting my cheek near her mouth.

She wasn't breathing.

"Dad? Dad, what's wrong with Mrs. Bradshaw?"

Zach had vaulted off the jungle gym nearly as fast as I'd crossed over the fence. He stood nearby, the twins behind him, all of them looking scared.

"She's sick," I said, grabbing Zach. "Real sick." I rushed to the fence and dropped my son down on the other side. "Zach, go get Seely. She'll know what to do. She's upstairs. Go!"

He blinked once and took off.

I raced back to the unconscious woman, dropping to my knees beside her. Every year I refreshed my CPR training—but oh, God, I'd never had to use it. I took a deep breath and made myself sound calm. "Carson."

"Y-yes, sir?"

"Go in the house and call 911. Just push those three numbers—nine, one, one. Tell them we need an ambulance. You can do that, right?"

He nodded and pelted for the back door, his brother behind him.

A is for airway, B for breathing... I needed to make sure the airway was clear. I tilted Mrs. B.'s head back and pulled her jaw down. Her tongue wasn't blocking her airway. And I couldn't feel any breath on my hand.

I took a deep breath, pinched her nostrils shut, sealed her

mouth with mine and pushed air into her lungs. Did it again, paused—no change. She still wasn't breathing on her own.

Okay, C was for chest compressions. Fifteen of them, a little faster than one per second. I put one hand on top of the other right smack between her breasts, and pushed.

The chest should compress between an inch and a half and two inches. I tried to call up the kinesthetic memory of how it had felt to push on the dummy this way, praying I was using enough force, but not too much. I was terrified of breaking something. The instructor had told us that happens sometimes, that a strong man can crack a rib performing CPR. But she'd also said that a cracked rib is better than a stopped heart.

Mrs. B. was so small and so still. So horribly still.

…thirteen. Fourteen. Fifteen. Time for breaths again.

I'd finished two cycles and was on chest compressions again when Mrs. B.'s back door slammed open. James ran out. "They said they're coming. They're coming, Mr. McClain. Carson's still talking to them 'cause they told him to stay on the phone."

"Good." Fourteen. Fifteen.

"Is she gonna be okay? They'll make her okay, won't they?"

"I hope so." Time for breaths. I pinched her nose and bent.

"Go in the house, James," Seely called from the other side of the fence as I resumed chest compressions. "Your brother needs you to help him stay calm." I heard her climb over, but didn't look up. A moment later I saw her stocking-clad feet on the other side of Mrs. B. She dropped to her knees.

But she didn't get in position to take over the breath part. Instead she put her hands on either side of Mrs. B's neck right below the ears.

I finished the compressions and looked at Seely.

"It's bad, Ben," she said quietly. "Very bad." She bit her lip. "Will you trust me?"

"Yes."

"Then back away and don't let anyone touch her until I'm finished. Not for any reason."

Back away? Stop CPR? I hesitated. Surrendering control didn't come easily for me, and stopping CPR flew in the face of all reason.

But this was Seely. I nodded and pushed to my feet. My knee twinged sharply.

Seely put both hands on Mrs. B.'s chest, her expression calm and somehow distant. Focussed. It was the sort of expression you might see on an artist's face, or a nun at her prayers. "Oh," she said without looking up. "One more thing. If I pass out, don't let them take me to the hospital."

I took one quick, involuntary step toward her but made myself stop. Slowly, so gradually there was no way to draw a line and say when it happened, she began to glow.

Thirteen

The curtains were open at my bedroom window, but the glass gave back nothing except darkness and ghosts, vague reflections from a dimly lit room. Behind me, only one lamp was on—the pretty china one that had belonged to my mother.

It sat next to the bed where Seely slept. Doofus was asleep, too, belly-up on the rug by the bed. The pup had kept me company at first, but it was late.

Seely had been asleep or unconscious for almost seven hours.

Aside from Doofus, she and I were alone. Zach was back home with Gwen, Duncan was on patrol and Mrs. Bradshaw—

"Ben?"

I spun around, a grin breaking out. "You're back." I limped to the bed and sat next to her. "Thank God. I'm a patient man, but waiting for you to wake up…" I shook my head. "How do you feel?"

"Tired." She blinked up at me from the pile of pillows I'd arranged for her. "You were limping just now."

"I probably wasn't supposed to jump fences yet." She looked tired, all her abundant energy drained out, leaving her pale and too still. I smoothed her hair back.

"You probably weren't supposed to carry me up the stairs, either."

"Duncan did that. He came to pick up Zach this time, not Gwen." I'd had a heck of a time convincing him—and the paramedics—that Seely often fainted and didn't need to go to the hospital, too. Finally I'd asked him just to trust me, and never mind whether it made sense. After one of his long, silent moments, he'd agreed.

"Mrs. Bradshaw?"

"Doing well, last I heard. Her son and daughter-in-law are already at the hospital, and her other kids are on their way. Dr. Harry Meckle is baffled all over again. You okay?"

"Getting there." She glanced around. "How late is it?"

"About eleven-thirty."

Her eyebrows came to life, lifting slightly. "I would have expected you to panic long before this."

"I did. I called your mother."

"My…" She was speechless.

"That reminds me." I twisted around, reaching for a can of soda in the cooler I'd parked beside the bed hours ago. "She said to pour calories down you when you woke up."

"What do you mean, you called my mother?"

"Three times. She's in Directory Assistance," I pointed out, popping the top on the cola and filling a glass. "Nice lady. Different, but nice. I think she likes me. Here."

She took the glass but didn't seem to know what to do with it. "Daisy reassured you? You didn't worry?"

"Oh, I worried." The weight of all those hours returned, pressing down on me. "Daisy was straight with me about the danger. She told me to keep checking your breathing, make sure it didn't slow too much. If it had…" I swallowed. "If it had, I was to get you to the E.R. as fast as possible."

Seely touched my hand. "I really am okay, Ben. There's…kind of an edge. After a couple of bad experiences, I learned how to keep track of that edge so I don't fall over it."

I nodded, unable to speak for a moment, and gestured at her glass.

Her lips quirked. Obediently she sipped.

"I've got a sandwich and some of that cake you made yesterday, when you're ready to eat. Candy, too, if you want to take your calories straight."

"You really did talk to my mother."

"If I hadn't, you'd be in the hospital now. I didn't know enough to make the right decision on my own." I paused. "She told me a few other things, too. For example, she said you don't pass out and stay out this way unless the healing was especially hard. Unless the person was close to dying. Mrs. B. would have died if you hadn't been there, wouldn't she?"

"I don't know. There was severe damage, but they can sometimes restart a heart by shocking it. I…my best guess was that she wouldn't have made it."

I nodded thoughtfully. "You passed out after healing me. I was dying when you found me, wasn't I? I *would* have died if you hadn't done whatever you do."

She hesitated, then nodded.

I felt deep satisfaction. I hadn't imagined it. My memories of that time might be blurry and disjointed, but I hadn't imagined any of it. "So what is it you do?"

"Is this an ambush, Ben? Catch me while I'm weak and pry answers out of me?"

"Yeah, you could call it that. But I think I deserve a few explanations, don't you?"

There was a tired, defeated look in her eyes I didn't like, but I didn't see any way to get rid of it except the one I'd chosen. Finally she said, "Yes, I suppose you do. But I'd like to eat first."

I retrieved the tray I'd prepared earlier. She scooted up in bed until she was sitting, and I put some more pillows behind her, then set the tray on the bed and tried to come up with some easy things to talk about while she ate.

I talked about Mrs. Bradshaw. I figured Seely had to be interested in the woman whose life she'd saved, and I wanted her to see how many people's lives were affected because that one, nosy old woman was still around. So I told her about Mrs. B.'s grown children, and some of the other kids she'd taken care of at one time or another. Including my sister and brothers.

She had some color back in her face by the time she finished the cake, but there was still a haunted look to her eyes. Maybe whatever she did when she healed always left her that way. I didn't know, but I meant to find out.

I handed her a few of the hard candies, removed the tray and refilled her glass. "Your mom said the, ah…your family gift takes different forms, but with you it's healing. Only your gift is a lot stronger than hers or your granny's."

"My mother seems to have done a lot of talking."

"We hit it off." By the third call, I'd mostly gotten used to her habit of knowing things before I said them.

A wisp of a smile touched her lips. "Did she tell you what her form of the gift is?"

"No, but I think it has something to do with her being one hell of a good guesser."

That made her grin. It was there and gone quickly, but it was a grin. "Something like that. I guess you want me to tell you how it works. The truth is, I don't know myself. I've read some of the same books you've been reading because I'd like to understand, too. What did you think about that one?" She gestured at the book on top of the pile.

"It seemed pretty fact based," I said cautiously. "Less pseudoscience than some of them." The book was an account of a handful of well-documented cases and several anecdotal ones where the laying on of hands had apparently facilitated healing. It mentioned a study about prayer improving the chances of cardiac surgery patients, and suggested a connection.

"I thought so, too. Was anyone mentioned in that book able to do what I can?"

"It didn't sound like it."

"No. I've never found anyone else who can."

That sounded lonely. Isolating. "You've been doing this all your life?"

"It started when I was five. Little things at first—a scratch or bruise, a stomach bug. As I got older, I got stronger, until…" She shook her head, dismissing whatever she'd been about to say.

"You must have figured a few things out."

"You aren't going to let any of your questions go, are you?" She brought her knees up, wrapping her arms around them. "Okay, here's the short course. Healing 101. From what I can tell, I help the body do what it already knows how to do. I'm hell on wheels when it comes to healing wounds. Heart disease is harder, probably because I haven't had as much practice with it. But it's still a matter of helping the body heal."

She told me that she'd tried once to find out more about how her gift worked. While working as a paramedic, she'd healed a man who turned out to be a medical researcher with a Ph.D. He'd persuaded her to submit to tests.

And her gift had gone into hiding. "I couldn't heal a hangnail," she said wryly. "At first he thought I wasn't cooperating or was unconsciously blocking it. Maybe I was. We—the women in my family—have always had to hide what we were, so I've got a lot of conditioning about that. Or maybe, like Granny says, it's a God thing."

"What do you mean?"

"She thinks we aren't supposed to speak of our gift because God wants it that way." Seely shrugged. "I don't know. It was awful, though, when I didn't know if the gift would come back. Eventually Dr. Emerson convinced himself he'd imagined the whole thing, and I was a charlatan. It was spooky, watching him rewrite the past until he had a reality he could live with."

It had also been one more reason not to trust anyone with her secret. "You said you burned out as a paramedic. Too many hurt people to heal?"

She ducked her head, letting her hair hide her face. "Something like that."

I thought about what she'd said…and what she hadn't said. "There are limits on what you can do. You can't heal everything. That would be rough, thinking you should be able to save people and failing."

"Oh," she said, "you did it again…sometimes the body itself is confused. Autoimmune diseases, for example, seem to be beyond me. I can ease the symptoms of arthritis, but I can't cure it." She lifted her head and looked at me straightly. "I'm not much good with cancer, either."

My breath sighed out. So much for that faint, unvoiced hope. "It doesn't matter. Gwen's cancer is gone," I told her firmly. A thought struck. "Isn't it? Can you—"

"As far as I can tell, she's fine. I'm not a diagnostician," she warned me. "It isn't like on *Star Trek*, either. That empath who healed people by taking on their pain? It doesn't work that way."

"Thank God for that. So you don't, uh, feel what the people around you are feeling?"

"No. That would be horrible. I have to focus, to…reach out. And I have to be touching the person."

I nodded. She'd told me a lot I'd wanted to know, but she hadn't broached the important stuff. Maybe she didn't think I'd consider it important. "Something else Daisy told me about."

Seely looked down, picking at the wrapping on one of the butterscotch candies. "What?"

"She said that twit you used to live with—"

She broke into laughter. "'Twit.' God forgive me for being shallow, but I like that."

"*Bastard* seems like too important a word for him. Daisy said he talked a lot about how wonderful your gift was, seemed to accept it just fine. Until he actually saw you heal someone, and then he freaked. Things were never the same between you after that."

"That about sums it up, yes."

I said gently, "You're waiting for me to freak, aren't you?"

A spasm of emotion crossed her face. "Are you claiming you aren't already freaked? For God's sake, Ben, I know how you feel about psychic stuff!" She thumped me in the chest. "You choke on the word witch. Tell me you don't think my so-called gift is weird!"

"Hey." I caught her hand in mine. "Of course it is. But there are people called idiot savants. Some of them can't learn how to cross the street safely, but they can multiply four-digit numbers in their heads instantly. That's weird, too."

Her mouth twitched. "You calling me an idiot?"

"I'm calling you a woman with an ability that, yeah, is pretty damned strange. But it's a lot more useful than multiplying four-digit numbers in your head." I paused. "Of course, I'm hoping you'll tell me it doesn't have anything to do with chakras and auras."

"Well, I've never seen an aura—"

"Thank God."

"But chakras do seem to be a pretty accurate description of the way energy moves through the body. I don't see that energy, but I feel it."

I sighed. "I'll adjust."

Her smile flickered. She went back to messing with the candy wrapper—not removing it, just twisting and untwisting the cellophane. "You're handling all this better than I thought you would. But you haven't thought about the ramifications."

I snorted. "I've chased my brain in circles for over a week, trying to think out the ramifications. I read about chakras, for God's sake. If I haven't got it all figured out, well, you haven't given me much to work on until now."

"So think some more," she urged me softly without looking up. "If I can start a heart beating again, I could stop one, too. Doesn't that worry you? You've been sleeping next to a woman who could stop your heart in your sleep."

"If that's what the twit was worried about, I may have to upgrade him to bastard after all."

She gave the wrapper another twist. "He had reason."

"Now you're being stupid. Any woman could murder the

man sleeping next to her, if she's so inclined. Poison, a gun, a knife between the ribs—just because you could do it in a weird way doesn't mean you would."

All of a sudden she looked up, trapping me with those haunted eyes. "There's one big difference between me and all your hypothetical murderesses. I've done it. When I was eight years old, I stopped my grandfather's heart."

Shock hit, stealing my breath. Rage followed close on its heels.

"What did he do to you?" I demanded, seizing her shoulders. "What did that—that—" I couldn't think of a word bad enough. "What did he do to force you to defend yourself that way?"

"He—I—why did you ask that?" She was staring, her eyes as big as mine must have been when she healed Mrs. B. "How did you know?"

"Aw, sweetheart. How can you even ask?" Rage drained out, leaving an ache behind. I reached for her, turning her so she settled against my chest instead of the pillows, and sighed. "I don't know if this helps you any, but I feel better."

I could see enough of the curve of her cheek to know that she smiled. "You're a good man, Ben."

"Damn straight, I am." Her answering chuckle sounded damp, but real. I stroked her hair. "He must have done something terrible, something that frightened you badly."

"Yes." She hesitated. "You've already guessed, haven't you? He tried to molest me. To…feel me up, at least. I don't know how far he would have gone."

"You were *eight*," I said, sick and baffled. "You were only eight."

"It's why my grandmother hates me, of course. She refused to believe the judge could have done anything like that."

I thought about that for a moment. "He didn't die."

"No, I...once I realized what I'd done, I kept him alive until help arrived. I didn't know how to heal the damage, though. Not then." She shuddered. "It was horrible, having to touch him to keep his heart beating. But what I'd done was worse. I hadn't known...he'd exposed himself, you see. When he tried to make m-me...anyway, I screamed at him to stop. I screamed it with everything in me. I wasn't thinking about stopping his heart, but that's what I did."

I couldn't speak. I could only hold her and pet her and try to be glad for her sake that she hadn't killed the bastard.

After a while she straightened. Her eyes were moist, but she smiled. "You mustn't be picturing me as horribly traumatized. Daisy wouldn't permit that. My father sent me home to her after it happened...he wouldn't talk to me about it, but Daisy did. She helped me sort things out so that I didn't blame myself, or feel smirched."

Maybe she didn't blame herself for the way a sick old man had tried to molest her, but she was carrying a load of hurt over having defended herself the only way she could. I didn't know what to do about that. I rubbed my knuckles across her cheek, wiping away the dampness. "I knew I liked your mother."

"I like her myself."

She still looked tired, but the haunted look was gone. There was a shy sort of happiness in her eyes instead. "So." I cleared my throat. "No more big, shocking secrets to reveal?"

"That was about it," she agreed gravely.

"How'd I do? Did I pass?"

"Ben, I wasn't testing you. I wouldn't...oh, all right," she said before I could interrupt, her smile spreading slowly in the way I loved. "You passed with flying colors."

"Then maybe you'll agree to marry me." Even as her eyes

rounded I cursed myself. "Hell. I didn't mean to blurt it out that way." But I couldn't help smiling. "That's the second time I've made you speechless tonight. Must be a record."

"I think it is," she agreed faintly. "Ben, we talked about—we said we wouldn't—"

"I know you didn't want this to turn into anything serious." I captured her hands and held them between us. "But think about it. We're good together, in bed and out. Good for each other, I think. I'm not good with words," I said gruffly, "but I think you're special. Incredibly special. I'm not talking about your gift, but about…well, you. All of you."

Her eyes were getting damp again. I didn't know if that was good or bad, so I rushed forward, hoping to convince her. "I think about you when you're not around. I think about how it might be with us twenty years from now, too. And about how beautiful you'd look growing round with my child. You're great with Zach. You'd make a wonderful mother."

She jerked, nearly pulling her hands out of mine. "Ben—"

"I wouldn't be marrying you to give Zach a mother," I said quickly. "That's not what I mean. He's got a mom already. I mean—aw, hell, you're crying. Don't do that. Don't cry, Seely."

But the tears spilled over anyway. "B-Ben, I can't have children. I told you that, right at the start."

For a moment I just stared at her. Then, carefully, as if I were threading a path lined with land mines, I said, "You meant that you were on the pill."

But she was shaking her head. "I meant exactly what I said. You didn't need to use protection because I can't catch or transmit venereal diseases. And I can't get pregnant."

I dropped her hands. In the whited-out blankness of my brain, thoughts began to whirl. She'd said she didn't have any more shocking secrets, but she hadn't thought this was a secret. She'd thought I knew. That I accepted... I shook my head. "You can't be sure. Unless you've had some kind of accident or surgery—and you could fix that sort of thing, couldn't you? You could heal it."

"I tried to get pregnant, Ben. Me a-and the twit." Her smile wobbled and broke. "We both wanted a child, and we tried for years. We were both tested and the doctors didn't find anything wrong, but—"

"Then maybe there isn't anything wrong. Maybe his sperm just weren't compatible with you somehow." Hadn't I read about that sort of thing somewhere?

"It's my gift." Her voice was bitter. "The women in my family aren't very fertile. My mother had only one child. So did my grandmother and my great-grandmother. Supposedly, the gift is stronger in me than in any of them. It...maybe it 'heals' a pregnancy before it can get started. Maybe it kills the sperm as soon as they hit my womb, just as it kills viruses that enter my bloodstream. I don't know." The shrug of her shoulders was infinitely weary. "And I don't suppose it matters."

"Of course it matters." I scrubbed a hand over my hair, but that wasn't enough to quiet the screaming jitters making a mess of my insides. I pushed off the bed and began to pace. "Maybe you're wrong about your gift doing it. Maybe it's incompatible sperm."

"Steven wasn't my only lover. And I've never used birth control."

What was it about me that I had only to reach out, try to touch a dream, to have it turn to dust? "Maybe there's some way to control it. You must be able to control your gift most of the time."

"I control whether I reach out with it or not, but the gift— oh, we don't have words for this!"

"Try. Please try." Maybe she was too close to the problem. Maybe I'd be able to see something she'd missed, if only I could understand how her gift worked.

She sighed, shoved back her hair and tried. "In my own body, the gift is sort of on autopilot. It heals me automatically. When I heal someone else, I impose…call it a template, the template from my own energy field. That's why I told you not to let anyone touch Mrs. Bradshaw while I was working on her. Another person's touch interferes with the template. Once someone's body accepts my template, it knows how to heal quickly. I help that healing along, but it's like—oh, like pushing a wagon as opposed to steering it."

"Is there any way to, uh—to adjust the template?"

She shook her head. "Tampering could destroy it. Maybe me, too. I could develop cancer or some degenerative condition."

"No. God, no." I stopped, hands clenched.

"This is why I said our relationship needed to be temporary." She laughed once, mirthlessly. "Though you can be forgiven for thinking I didn't mean it, because I didn't. But if ever a man needed to have children, it's you. I knew you were in the market for marriage, but I kept hoping—"

"Wait a minute. How did you know that?"

She looked at me, a wry twist to her mouth. "One of the things I love about you is your honesty. You don't hide what you're thinking or feeling very well, even if sometimes you might like to."

One of the things she loved? My heart gave a little jump. I told myself firmly that it's possible to love some things about a person without being in love. But still…

I rubbed my chest as if I could calm a jumpy heart that way. "Okay, maybe I have been giving marriage some thought lately. That doesn't mean…" But marriage *did* mean kids to me. In my mind, in my heart, marriage and children were so intertwined I didn't know how to think of one without the other. "I have to think about this. I need a little time to think things out."

"You'll have plenty of time to do that."

Something in her voice dragged my attention away from the turmoil within. "I'm an idiot. This was no time to hit you with everything, when you're exhausted from helping Mrs. B." I went to the bed, sat down and patted her hand. "You lie down. I'll get rid of the tray and be right back. We'll work things out," I said firmly. "But in the morning, not now when we're both tired."

I was talking too much and too fast, trying to sound positive when I felt anything but. Seely was right. I wasn't good at pretending. I hadn't had much practice.

I wasn't used to running away, either, but that's what it felt like when I carried the tray down to the darkened kitchen. I took my time putting things away. And when I returned to the bedroom and found her asleep, I was relieved.

I was also genuinely wiped out, though, so maybe that was excusable. Waiting for Seely to wake up had been rough. Nothing that had happened since she did had been exactly easy, either. I closed the curtains, stripped and climbed in beside her, close enough to drape an arm over her. Tomorrow, I promised myself. Tomorrow I'd sort things out. But the ghostly sound of dreams crumbling made a dismal music to carry with me into sleep.

In the morning Seely told me she was leaving.

Fourteen

"What do you mean, you're moving out?" I growled. I was sitting up in bed. Seely was bustling around the room, removing things that hadn't been there very long.

I'd woken up to the sound of her pulling her suitcase out of the closet. Not a good way to start the day.

"Just what I said." She opened another drawer. "You need some time to think about things. Well, so do I."

"One big difference." I threw back the covers, climbed out of bed and stalked over to her. "I wasn't going to kick you out while I did my thinking."

"Oh, Ben." She stopped and looked at me, and her face was so sad it made me feel even worse. "I'm sorry. I know this is sudden. But I've done everything suddenly with you, from going to bed together to agreeing to live together."

"Those were good ideas. This is a mistake. A huge mistake."

"What's one more mistake? I've already made such a mess

of things. I thought—hoped—oh, I hoped far too many things. And without much reason," she added bitterly. "It isn't as if you led me on." She tossed a stack of T-shirts into her oversize suitcase.

"No, I just proposed to you. Dammit, quit that." I grabbed her shirts and stuck them back in the drawer. "You're overreacting. This whole relationship bit is about working things out. How can we work anything out if we aren't together?"

"I'll overreact if I want to!" She snatched up the T-shirts and crammed them into the suitcase. "Oh," she said, closing her eyes. "Just listen to me. I sound about five years old."

"You need some food in your system. Coffee. Get your blood sugar stabilized, and things won't look so—so however they look that makes you think you have to do this."

She shook her head. Her eyes were just about drowning in sadness, but her mouth was set in a stubborn line. She reached for the next drawer.

I pushed her hand away from it. "Tell me why," I said. Or maybe I was begging by then. I was beginning to feel desperate, and I didn't like it. "The least you can do is tell me why you're leaving."

She flicked me a glance. "You don't want an explanation. You want an excuse to argue me out of it."

"Don't I deserve a chance to do that?" My voice was getting louder.

"Okay. Yes. Oh, damn," she said as her eyes filled. Angrily she dashed her hand across them. "I promised myself I wouldn't cry. Here's the deal, Ben." She met my eyes. Hers were shiny with the tears she refused to shed. "I'm not as honest as you are. I went into this saying one thing, but hoping for something else. I...I hoped you'd grow to care for me."

"It worked."

"Which is why it was so wrong of me. Oh, don't you see?" She took two jerky paces and whirled to face me again. "I went after you with both barrels. I wanted you, and I persuaded myself I could have you, that you wouldn't be hurt."

"So now that you've got me, you want to throw me back?"

"I thought you knew!" she cried. "I thought you knew I couldn't have children, that you were okay with it. But that was my fault, too—that you misunderstood. I was so busy protecting myself. I didn't tell you about my gift. I didn't explain."

"If you're leaving in order to save me from myself," I growled, "don't."

"I'm not. At least, not entirely. I'm still protecting myself. I don't know what to do. I thought I could handle whatever happened, but…" She hugged her arms around herself as if she were cold. "I'm already hurting. I don't want to be hurt more."

Another kind of pain blended with the unholy mix churning in my gut. "I wouldn't hurt you, Seely. You have to know that."

"No?" For the first time, her eyebrows had a comment to make, lifting incredulously. "Tell me you still want to marry me, Ben. That it wouldn't wreck your dreams if you never had more children. That you wouldn't come to regret it—and resent me."

I wanted to say that. I *wanted* to. But… "Dammit, I need a little time to get used to the idea. From what you said, you've had years to grow accustomed to it."

"I'm going to give you time. And while you're getting your head straight, I'm going to do the same."

"But…" I rubbed a hand over my face. I wasn't going to beg, dammit. I took a deep breath and let it out slowly. "You believe you have to leave to do that."

"I do." Her chin went up another notch. "Maybe I'm wrong. Tell me one more thing. Are you still in love with Gwen?"

My mouth opened—and closed again.

She nodded slowly. "That's what I thought." She turned back to the bureau, yanked a drawer open and pulled out some jeans. They went in the suitcase. She zipped it shut.

"You aren't giving me a chance! You hit me with that question out of the blue, when I didn't have a clue you even suspected.... Dammit, how do I know? I'm feeling *everything* right now! Everything all at once!"

"Me, too," she whispered, and jerked the suitcase upright. "I'd like you to promise me that you won't call me or come around, not until I contact you."

I was shaking my head before she finished. "Forget it."

"I know you, you see." Her smile made a brief appearance, dying on a tremble of her bottom lip. "Once you've set your sights on a goal, you're as likely to turn aside as an avalanche. Look at the way you kept crawling up that mountain, when anyone else would have given up and died." Again her smile flickered—fast and uneasy, so unlike her usual molasses smiles. "It's rather awe-inspiring to be the target of all that determination. But I can't handle it right now."

I was breathing fast, as if I'd been running uphill. I forced myself to take a breath and hold it. I had to stay calm. Stay in control. We couldn't both panic at the same time—and that's what she was doing, whatever she said. "You've got money coming to you. I need to know where you'll be staying so I can send it on."

"I'll give you my address when you give me your promise. If you won't promise, I'll leave Highpoint. I'll vanish. I can do it. I'd rather not, but I will if I have to."

So I promised. It was like chewing on ground glass, but I promised. "You will call," I told her. "You said you'd call."

She nodded.

I let her carry that big, heavy suitcase downstairs herself. I didn't go with her. I stood in my bedroom and tried to make my breathing work right and listened as the suitcase thumped down those stairs behind her. Listened as the front door opened. And closed.

Then I spun around, grabbed the first thing I saw and hurled it against the wall. And stood there in among the shards of my mother's pretty china lamp, stood there and kept breathing, surrounded by thousands of unmendable pieces.

Four days later, I was returning to the office from the Patterson site. It was about six o'clock. Dr. Harold Meckle pulled into the parking lot just before I did, and the jerk took my parking place.

"Mr. McClain," he called as he got out of his shiny Lincoln. "I need to talk to you."

I was not in a good mood. I hadn't even wanted to be around my family since Seely walked out. I sure didn't have the patience for Harry. "I'm busy right now." I slammed the truck door.

"This will just take a moment. I'd like to examine you." Harry's eyes glittered with excitement. "I'm on to something. Something big."

"Yeah? I think you're just on something."

"It's that woman. I know it is." He followed me to the office door. "I don't know what she does, but I mean to find out. I understand the two of you have broken up. I had hoped you would persuade her to speak with me, but perhaps that wouldn't be feasible."

I snorted. "Since she isn't talking to me—yeah, that's a good assumption." I stuck my key in the office door.

"I treated Mrs. Bradshaw when she arrived at the E.R., you

know. She had a major heart attack, yet there is no cardiac damage."

"Go away, Harry." I opened the door.

"I can't put together a paper without solid facts. I have to examine you. You're using that shoulder normally. That shouldn't be possible."

"Consider the possibility that you've made a mistake," I said, stepping inside. "A big one."

He was still jabbering when I shut the door in his face.

I sat at my desk without turning on the light. I didn't really have any work I couldn't do at home, but I wouldn't go there until I had to. As hard as it can be to face an empty house, one filled with might-have-beens is worse.

I thought about Harry, who wanted to write a paper and get famous, and never mind the consequences to the human lab rat he proposed to write about. That made me think about Seely, of course, but there was nothing new about that. I hadn't had a moment free of her since she left me.

The worst of it was that stupid promise she'd pulled out of me. Lord! I leaned back in my chair, staring at the ceiling. How had I let myself be maneuvered into such a miserable position? If I could just go to her, talk to her…

And tell her what? I was still torn up about not having children. I hated knowing I'd never get to meet the curly-haired little girl I'd imagined swinging in the backyard. Dammit, did Seely expect me to be happy about that?

I knew where she was. She'd sent a polite little note giving me her address—a cheap, rent-by-the-week motel on the edge of town. I'd mailed her paycheck to her, but my damned promise kept me from doing anything else. I couldn't even let her know Harry was determined to make trouble for her.

Wait a minute. I couldn't contact *her*...but I hadn't promised anything about her family.

Seely's brother, Jonathan, I'd learned, was on the hospital board.

Paper crinkled as I bent and retrieved the phone book. Her stupid, polite little note was in my shirt pocket because I couldn't stand to put it away.

Jonathan Burns might be a decent sort, or he might take after his grandmother. Either way, I figured he had an interest in seeing that Dr. Harold Meckle didn't turn Seely into some sort of medical tabloid star. Maybe Jonathan would worry about what that would do to her. Maybe he'd just be worried about the consequences for the rest of his precious family.

Not that Seely would threaten to divulge what her grandfather had done, but I had no such compunctions. Besides, she still had those issues. She needed to find out if she liked her brother or never wanted to see him again.

I reached for the phone.

Seely had been gone a full week when I pulled into another parking lot. This time I was in a taxi, though. And the parking lot belonged to the Wagonwheel bar.

I'm not much for what the younger crowd calls clubbing. If I want to play pool, I go to Binton's. If I want to dance, I go to the resort. Tonight I wasn't interested in pool or dancing. I wanted to honor an old tradition and try to drink a woman out of my mind.

Not that I thought it would work, but a desperate man will try anything.

The Wagonwheel was the right spot for serious drinking. It wasn't a dive, but it wasn't fancy, either. At eight o'clock on a Thursday night the place was busy but not packed. I passed a few people I knew on my way to the bar, including a couple of men from Manny's crew. I nodded but didn't pause. I wasn't here to socialize.

I'd ordered a double bourbon when someone slapped me on the back. "Hey, there, Ben! Haven't seen you around lately."

I turned my head and grimaced. Chuck Meyers is a big, bluff, party-loving kind of guy who'd played football with me back in high school. He's one reason I don't spend much time in bars. Too easy to run into men like him. "I've been busy recuperating."

"That's your story and you're stickin' to it, huh?" He chuckled. "Don't guess it had a thing to do with that sexy nurse of yours. Saw her when I went to get my kid's school records the other day. Whew. Hot stuff." He shook his hand as if it had been singed.

"Shut up, Chuck."

"Hey, I saw her, too." That came from the man on the other side of Chuck, a scrawny little runt with a mustache. I recognized him vaguely from the hospital—he was an orderly or something. "She was at that Chinese place on Elm with this good-looking blond dude." He gave me a bleary grin. "Tough luck, McClain. Got to bite to lose one like that."

Now that was just what I needed to hear. I turned away, doing my best to ignore the two men. Seely hadn't called me. No, she'd decided to go out with some blond guy instead of working out our problems.

My drink arrived. I told the bartender to run me a tab and got my first swallow down. But Chuck and his buddy were hard to ignore. They were talking about Seely.

"Man, what I wouldn't give to have just one little taste of that," the scrawny one said.

"Some men don't know when they're lucky. Not that I'd want to stop with one taste, myself. Did you get a look at those tits?"

I sighed. "Chuck, I told you to shut up."

"I'm talkin' to Bill, here," he told me. "Since you're so unfriendly tonight."

"Well, you won't be talking about Seely anymore. To Bill or anyone else. Got it?"

"Don't see how that's any of your business. Can't blame you for being touchy, though." He slapped me on the back again, grinning. "Be strange if you weren't out of sorts after losing that piece of ass. And oh, man, those tits!" He made grabbing, squeezing motions in the air.

So I hit him.

Fifteen

There's something particularly humiliating about almost being arrested by your little brother.

"Watch your head," Duncan said.

I stopped dead beside his patrol car. "If you think I'm going to ride in the cage in back, I'll have to report you for drinking on duty."

One side of his mouth kicked up. "Guess I can let you ride up front. Though I may rethink using the handcuffs. Transporting a suspect who isn't properly restrained is against regs."

I growled and jerked open the passenger-side door. He was enjoying this entirely too much.

Duncan grinned and rounded the back of the car, got in on his side and started the engine. "I can't get over you starting a brawl in a bar. What were you thinking?"

"I didn't start a fight. I hit one man one time." Once, I

thought with satisfaction, had been all it took. Chuck had dropped like a felled tree.

"I guess those other three fellows just imagined they were in a fight."

"Some people are too suggestible."

He sighed and pulled out of the lot. It sounded a lot like the sighs I used to heave when he was a teenager. "So why did you hit Meyers?"

"The other guy was too much of a runt. Chuck is more my size."

"That isn't quite what I meant."

I knew that, of course. I gave it a couple moments, then said, "They talked about Seely in a way I couldn't stomach. About her body, really. It wasn't about her at all, just what they wanted to do with her body. I warned Chuck. He wouldn't quit."

"As a man, I understand. As your brother, I sympathize. As a cop, I ought to be reading you your rights."

"No one pressed charges." Thanks in part to my promise to pay the owner for damages, even though I hadn't broken anything. Not even Chuck's jaw, since I'd had the sense to aim for his belly. You can break your hand hitting someone in the jaw.

"Drunk and disorderly."

"I'm not drunk, dammit! I only had time for one swallow." But Duncan was grinning again, so I knew he'd just been yanking my chain.

Neither of us said anything for a few blocks. I was thinking about how pathetic it was when a man couldn't even manage to get drunk without causing all sorts of ruckus when Duncan spoke again. "I'm sorry things didn't work out for you and Seely."

"Yeah. Me, too."

"Gwen has spoken with her a couple of times since she moved out."

I was surprised, though maybe I shouldn't have been. They'd hit it off pretty well. "That's good, I guess."

"Seely wouldn't tell her what went wrong." Duncan paused. "Gwen is afraid maybe *she's* what went wrong."

"No! Tell her…" I scrubbed my face with my hand, sighed and got it said. "I had feelings for Gwen at one time. You know that. But that's in the past." Something I hadn't made clear to Seely—but she hadn't given me much of a chance, springing it on me that way.

Or maybe I hadn't made it clear because it hadn't been clear to me, either. But I was beginning to see a lot of things I'd never managed to bring into focus before. Losing Seely was a lot like dying cold and alone on a mountain. It clarified things. "Tell Gwen that the problem is me. Not her, and not Seely." I sighed. "I found out she can't have children, and I didn't handle it well."

"It isn't easy when the woman you love isn't able to bear your child."

There was an edge to his voice—not much, just a hint. And all of a sudden I knew myself for a fool.

The type of cancer Gwen had been treated for made pregnancy dangerous. It was likely that the only child she'd ever have was Zach…*my* son. I'd felt sorry for myself often enough because Zach wasn't wholly mine, living with me. But Zach was also probably the only son Duncan would ever have.

I'd never thought about what that must mean to him. And he'd never spoken about it. Duncan was the kind of quiet hero whose sacrifices were easy to overlook.

And me…I was ashamed. "You'd know about that, wouldn't you?" I said at last, as we turned off on my street.

Duncan didn't say anything until we pulled up in the drive behind my truck. Then he turned to me. "If you love Seely, you'll grieve with her for what you can't have. And it won't be just *your* unborn children you mourn. It will be hers, too."

A few more things became clear. Painfully so. After a moment I managed to say, "How did you turn into more of an adult than me, when I had such a big head start?"

He grinned, a subtle flash in the darkness. "I had a great example. Someone who raised kids he didn't father."

I nodded. "Frank McDonald, maybe? He's great with his stepkids."

"No, you jerk. You."

The Sleep-Rite Inn wasn't much, a horseshoe-shaped cluster of rooms around a courtyard of cracked and pitted asphalt, with a perpetually empty swimming pool as the centerpiece. The blinking neon "Vac-n-y" sign pretty much summed the place up.

Number fourteen was two doors down from the highway. I was scowling as I knocked on the door.

"Go away," number fourteen's inhabitant called, "or I'll call the police."

"For God's sake, Seely, what kind of place did you pick to run away to that you have to call the cops if someone knocks on your door?"

The door was so thin I heard her gasp. A moment later the lock clicked and the door opened, and there she stood in one of her old sweatshirts and the bottom half to my pajamas, rolled up at the hems. After a moment she said, "You weren't knocking, you were pounding. And it's ten-thirty at night. What are you doing here?"

"Breaking my promise. Can I come in?"

Her face had that closed, wary look that I hated, but she stood aside. I went in.

I'd never been inside the Sleep-Rite Inn's rooms before. I looked around, my scowl deepening. "This is a dump. If you needed money, why didn't you say so? We could have called it a loan," I said grudgingly.

The tiniest smile flickered deep in her eyes. "You think I

should have borrowed money from you so I could live more comfortably when I left you?"

"Since you probably wouldn't let me give it to you, yeah."

"And you came here at ten-thirty to tell me so."

I flushed. I'd swung off course for a moment. "I came because that was a stupid promise. How can you get your head straight when you don't know if I've got mine straight yet?"

She tilted her head to one side. "Have you ever broken a promise before, Ben?"

I didn't think so. In fact, I was pretty damned sure I hadn't. I began to pace. "I had this all worked out, what I was going to say and how to say it. You're throwing me off."

"Sorry."

She didn't look sorry. "The thing is," I said, halting in front of her, "that I can change course. Change my mind, that is. It may take me a while, but I get there. We'll adopt. If you want to," I added when her expression didn't change. "A very smart man helped me see that kids don't have to start out being mine to end up that way."

"You still want to marry me, then."

It wasn't a question, but I thought I heard an ache behind it. "More than I've ever wanted anything in my life. Seely…" I wanted badly to touch her, but I didn't trust myself. Sex had been too easy for us. It had broken down some walls, maybe, but at the same time sex had made it easy to think we didn't have to talk, too.

Or maybe that part was just me. I swallowed. "I'm not good with words. And I'm stubborn. Sometimes that's good, but it means I can take a while to see the obvious. You asked about Gwen. Well, it's real obvious to me now that Gwen was a dream, part of how I thought life was supposed to go. What I didn't see was that sometimes you have to let go of the dream in order to take hold of reality."

Her eyes misted. "Ben…"

"Let me finish." Now I reached for her. I couldn't help it. I put my hands on her shoulders and ran them down her arms to her hands and held on. "You're my reality, Seely. And you're better than any dream I ever mooned over. There's more *of* you—more giving, more fun, more…I don't know how say it right. Just *more*. So if you need time, I'll give you time. If you want to go back to just dating, we can do that. Just don't shut me out. Please."

She threw herself at me. She was laughing, or maybe crying.

Or maybe that part was me, too. I blinked several times, stroking her hair, savoring the feeling of having her in my arms again. "So, you want to go out with me?"

"I want to marry you, you idiot." She raised her head, and yes, her eyes were shiny wet. And her smile was huge. "I always have. From the moment I found a man too stubborn to die crawling up a mountain…that's another family tradition, you see. Knowing it right away when we meet the love of our lives. But you still haven't said what you're supposed to."

I hunted frantically through the last few minutes, trying to think of exactly what I'd said. "Did I remember to ask you to marry me instead of telling you?"

She shook her head, but it was one of those fond, he's-only-a-man head shakes women use sometimes. "You're supposed to tell me you love me."

"I…" A second's pure panic hit when the words wouldn't come. "I don't think I've said that in a long time. Give me a second."

"How long has it been?" she asked gently.

Another memory search, but this one took longer, reaching back…years.

Could it really have been that long? Surely I'd said it sometime, to someone…but you didn't say stuff like that to your brothers. And Annie—well, she knew, so I'd never had to say it. I cleared my throat. "The last time I remember saying that was to my parents. They were about to get on their plane."

"And they never came back, did they?"

"But that's stupid. I got over that a long time ago. I..." Was still not saying the words she needed to hear. There was a buzzing in my ears. I felt almost sick. "Okay, I can do this. I...I love you."

The kiss she gave me then was guaranteed to erase any lingering trauma associated with those words. After a long moment she sighed and laid her head on my shoulder. "And I love you. I fell hard and fast, so fast it nearly scared me clear out of town. If Duncan hadn't found me at the bus station..."

My arms tightened around her. "I owe him." For more than one thing.

"I wanted to call you so many times. I hated leaving. But if you didn't love me, I couldn't marry you—not when I couldn't give you the children you craved. I was afraid I'd say yes, anyway," she admitted. "That's why I left."

"You could have told me you loved me," I pointed out.

"Sure. And then you'd have felt honor bound to marry me, even if you weren't in love."

I opened my mouth to argue...and shut it again. She might be right. I couldn't say for sure, since by the time she'd walked out I'd been head-over-heels for her, even if I was too dumb to know it.

Something occurred to me. "You mean you were going to take the bus because of me, not because of the deal with your brother?"

She nodded. "Partly. Mostly. Speaking of brothers..." She gave me another soft kiss. "Thank you. I had lunch with Jonathan yesterday, and he told me you'd spoken to him. He had a talk with Dr. Meckle—who, it seems, has lost all interest in writing a paper about such an uncooperative subject."

"That's great." I hugged her. So the blond guy she'd had lunch with had been her brother. That was a relief in more ways than one. Jonathan Burns had been pretty thrown by learning he had a sister, and I hadn't been sure he would follow up on my suggestion to contact her.

I decided she didn't need to know I'd jumped to an unfortunate conclusion about who she'd had lunch with. "What did you think of Jonathan?"

"I think…" She took a deep breath, let it out. "I liked him. It will take time to build a real relationship, of course—we'll have to see how things work out. He…seemed glad to meet me. And as unsure as I was about where we go from here."

It was a start. I was getting the idea that life wasn't one long, unfolding road, but a whole series of starts and stops and then starting up again—a little smarter each time, if you were lucky.

"Are you sure you don't mind?" She searched my face. "About not having children, that is. Unless we adopt, which I would like…but you have to be sure."

"Of course I mind. I can't think of anything sweeter than watching you grow big with my child, and I'm sad that we won't get to experience it." I smiled down at her tenderly. "But that's only one part of the deal, after all, and not the most important part."

A smile slid across her face, slow as sunrise…mischievous as a puppy. "Maybe it's just as well we can't mingle our gene pools. Who knows what the offspring of two strong psychics might be like?"

I snorted. "Only one person in this room is gifted in that way."

"Ben, I don't glow."

"Of course you do. I *saw* you. Twice."

"You must have seen my aura. No one else has ever seen me glow when I heal—not me, my mother or my granny. Not the people I healed. Not the researcher who decided I'd made it all up." When I just stared at her, she chuckled. "Ask Zach or Mrs. Bradshaw if you don't believe me, but think about it. How could I have kept my healing a secret all these years if I lit up like a Christmas tree every time?"

"You don't glow."

She shook her head.

I thought it over. "Okay, you don't glow to everyone else. Just to me. That doesn't mean I see auras. Otherwise I'd have been seeing them all over the place, and I haven't. Just with you." I smiled, and it came kind of slow and easy, too. "I trust what I see when I look at you, Seely."

What I saw was real, all right. Love is about as real as you can get.

Fourteen Months Later

An invitation addressed to Jonathan and Daniel Burns:

Benjamin and Seely McClain
hope you can attend a celebration on
Wednesday, July 29 at 7 p.m.
welcoming their son, Peter Liu McClain,
into his new home.

In lieu of gifts, donations may be sent to:
Adoption Alliance.
2121 S. Oneida St., Suite 420
Denver, CO 80224-2575 USA
Phone: 303-584-9900
Email: info@adoptall.com

* * * * *

LOST IN SENSATION

BY
MAUREEN CHILD

Maureen Child is a California native who loves to travel. Every chance they get, she and her husband are taking off on another research trip. The author of more than sixty books, Maureen loves a happy ending and still swears that she has the best job in the world. She lives in Southern California with her husband, two children and a golden retriever with delusions of grandeur.

Visit her website at www.maureenchild.com.

For Susan Mallery –
a great friend and a wonderful writer.
Thanks for the good ideas and the fun plot groups.
Thanks for listening when I need to whine and
thanks for telling me what I need to hear – especially
whenI don't want to hear it. May the wind
always be howling.

One

No good deed goes unpunished.

Truer words were never spoken, Sam Holden thought. And he should have kept them in mind. Because he was even now living them.

He just couldn't figure out how he could have done anything differently.

"I owe you, man," Eric Wright said from the passenger seat. Then he reached down and rapped his knuckles against the plaster cast encasing his right leg from the knee down. "Actually, I owe you two. Saving my skin *and* driving me home for my wedding."

"No, you don't owe me." Sam glanced at his friend. A purple and yellowing bruise smudged his forehead in stark contrast to his pale face. His dark red hair stood out in a weird sort of halo around his head. Lines of pain were drawn deep around his mouth, and his eyes were tired.

"You look like hell."

"Hey," Eric said with a small grin, "if not for you, I'd be looking cold and stiff right about now."

"Yeah, yeah." He brushed the latest round of thanks aside and narrowed his gaze. "You feeling okay?"

Eric grimaced. "You asking as my friend or as my doctor?"

"Which one will get me an honest answer?"

Laughing shortly, Eric shoved one hand through his hair, then scraped that hand across his eyes as if trying to wake himself up. "I'm okay. Just tired—" he looked at Sam again "—and grateful to be alive. Like I said, I owe you."

At thirty-two, Sam was tall, leanly muscled and too impatient for his own good. A black-haired, blue-eyed doctor, he had more female patients than male but much to their dismay, Sam never noticed more about the women than the symptoms they were presenting. He had only a handful of close friends and Eric Wright was one of them.

But in the last couple of weeks, Eric had been acting more like a *fan* than a friend. Sam had never been good with gratitude. He didn't like the slippery feel of someone's admiration. *Probably shouldn't have become a doctor then, huh?* But then, he'd had no choice. He'd been interested in nothing but medicine since he was a kid. At five, he'd borrowed his grandfather's stethoscope, listened to his dog's heart and found an irregular beat. Even the vet had been impressed. And that rush of discovery had pretty much sealed his future.

But having someone look at him with shining eyes and absolute trust made him want to run for the hills. Trust was a burden he didn't want to carry…it was just too damn fragile. An odd thought for a doctor, he mused. But there it was.

"You don't owe me, Eric." He'd said the same thing he didn't know how many times since the accident. Eric never seemed to hear him, though Sam continued to try. "Hell, I was in the car. What was I supposed to do, leave you in the wreck while I ran for it?"

Eric shrugged. "Most would. There aren't many people who'll climb *into* a burning car to drag somebody out." He waved a hand at the bandage on Sam's left forearm. "With a bum arm, no less."

"Just a sprain." The bandage was an irritation and, in his mind, not really necessary. But the ER doctors had insisted on it—at least for a few days. And the night of the wreck, he'd been too glassy-eyed from shock to argue.

It had all happened in seconds—and had felt, at the time, like they were moving in slow motion. A truck swerving into their lane. Eric ripping the wheel to one side. The scrape of metal against the guard-rail. The long, eternity-filled seconds the car was airborne and the jarring slam when they hit the earth and rolled over. Sam had inched out of the broken side window, then crawled around to the driver's side. Unconscious, Eric was oblivious to the flames already licking at the undercarriage. But Sam had felt the heat against his face and the cold rush of fear in his bones. Somehow, though, he'd managed to free Eric from the seat belt and drag him to safety before the fire erupted into a blaze.

Luck was with them both that night. If it hadn't been, Eric's family would have been planning his funeral instead of celebrating his wedding.

"Still..."

Sam sighed and gave up trying to convince his friend. "Fine. I'm a hero. Super Doc, that's me."

Besides, if they were going to talk about payments due, Eric had it backward. Eric Wright had been a good friend—especially the last couple of years. By choice, Sam had always been something of a loner. More so in the last two years. But whenever Sam began pulling away from the few friends he did have, Eric had refused to allow it.

And for that, Sam owed *him*.

So here he sat, outside Eric's parents' house, with two long weeks to fill before he could head back home to L.A. Ordinarily, he would have driven up for Eric's wedding, then gone home the next day. But because of the accident and Eric's inability to drive,

Sam had somehow been suckered into a two-week vacation in northern California, specifically Sunrise Beach with Eric's family.

The prospect of which was enough to make Sam want to throw the car into gear again and peel away from the curb at warp speed. Unfortunately, he was a man of his word and there was no backing out now.

He shot a look at the Wright house. Sitting far back from the street, it boasted a deep, dark green lawn, despite the simmering heat of summer. Neatly tended flower beds, awash in splashes of brilliant color, lined the front of the old bungalow and dangled from brightly painted window boxes. The wide front porch had pots of ferns hanging from the rafters and planters with yet more flowers spilling from them perched on the railing.

The house itself was painted sunshine yellow with a dark green trim on the shutters and eaves. It looked comfortable, cared-for and sturdy, like a self-satisfied old woman. The street was quiet, tree-lined and only blocks from the beach.

To anyone else, this might have seemed like a great place for a little vacation. To Sam…he felt as if he were going into battle unarmed and naked.

"Come on," Eric said, opening the car door and taking Sam's last chance at escape out of his hands. "My folks can't wait to meet you."

"You know," Sam said, shifting his gaze past Eric to where people were already streaming out the front door like grade schoolers hearing the last bell before summer vacation, "maybe I should let you visit with your family first. I'll go to the hotel, check in, then come back tomorrow."

Or the next day, he thought wildly, watching the crowd of people pushing through the door grow and grow and grow. Just how many people were *in* the Wright family, anyway?

"Not a chance," Eric said, easing his crutches from the back seat. "If you have too long to think about it, you'll head back to L.A."

The fact that his friend knew him that well was mildly irritating, but Sam swallowed it back and forced a smile for the first member of the Wright family to reach the car.

"God, Eric, your leg!" An older woman with graying blond hair and wide blue eyes crooned the words. Eric's mother, probably, Sam thought as she reached into the car for her son.

"Look like hell, boy,"

"Thanks, Dad." Eric laughed and handed out the crutches. "Give me a hand."

The older man, burly with a square jaw, cautious eyes and a day or two's worth of gray stubble on his jaw, said, "Step back, honey." He waited until his wife was out of range, then took the crutches in one beefy fist and Eric's arm with the other, effortlessly propelling his son out of the car.

Sam stayed right where he was. Out of the swirl

of hugs and kisses and squeals. He had no doubt they'd get around to him eventually, but if he stayed quiet, he could put it off. The small mob tightened in some kind of group hug, with each of them trying to out-shout the other. Smiles, laughter, a few tears, and the family welcome celebration was in high gear. An old black Lab sat to one side and barked while a couple of kids, a boy about six and a girl even younger, danced around outside the circle of the jabbering adults, vying for attention.

It was like watching a greeting card commercial.

Outsider.

That's what he was, and at no time had it ever been clearer than right at that moment. Of course, that's how he wanted it, right? He didn't want connections. Ties. He'd done it once—made the commitment, made plans—and it had fallen apart, nearly undoing him in the process.

He'd learned the hard way that connections only left you vulnerable to pain. So whether he got lonely sometimes or not, he wasn't about to forget that lesson. He'd just sit here until the Wrights scrambled back into their storybook cottage and left him alone.

But that happy little thought lasted only moments. Until one of the women pulled away from the solid mass of humanity and leaned down to peer into the car at him.

"You must be Sam."

"Must be," he said and took one brief moment

to appreciate her—objectively, of course, as an art lover would admire a beautiful painting. Her skin was smooth and the color of rich cream. Her eyes were big and blue like her mother's. Her blond hair, pulled loosely back from her face into a ponytail, hung down on one side of her neck. The dark blue T-shirt and jeans she wore looked faded and comfortable.

"You're..."

"Tricia," she said, her lips curving as she studied him more closely. "Eric's sister. Well," she corrected a moment later, "one of them." She glanced back at the still-gleeful crowd. "There's the other one—Debbie."

He looked at the shorter, rounder blonde, currently wrapping her arms around Eric's neck tight enough to strangle.

"We're easy to tell apart. She's six months pregnant, I'm not."

"I'll remember," Sam said, though he doubted that Tricia Wright would ever be easy to confuse with anyone else.

She cocked her head, smiled and asked, "So, are you getting out of the car anytime soon?"

"Actually, I don't think so," Sam told her, suddenly looking forward more than ever to a nice, quiet night at the hotel. Give the Wrights time to enjoy their reunion. "I was just dropping Eric and his stuff off. I'll be going to the hotel until—"

"Oh, that's not gonna fly," she said, and slid into

the passenger seat. "Aah, that's better, was getting a crick in my neck."

Sam just stared at her, then shifted his gaze to where her family had calmed down enough to let the kids into the inner circle. Eric had the little girl balanced on one hip as he ruffled the boy's hair.

Family.

A part of him admired the strength in them. The bond that held them so closely. Yet, another part of him thought of those ties as binding chains that, once shattered, left a man suddenly, shockingly adrift. Better to avoid the ties altogether then, wasn't it?

"Nice car," Tricia said.

"Thanks." How to get her out of the car so he could turn on the engine and get gone?

She hit the eject button on the CD player so she could inspect the disc inside. Nodding in approval, she glanced at him. "Rock and roll, but not heavy metal. I like a man who can appreciate the classics."

Apparently, she'd settled in for the long haul. He scowled at her deliberately. That scowl had been used successfully to keep people at bay for most of his life. Apparently though, Tricia Wright hadn't gotten the memo on that one. She laughed. Not one of those dainty, musical, little wind chime laughs, either. It was full and loud and rattled around inside him until he was forced to shift uncomfortably.

"Sorry," she said, shaking her head. "Was that your 'scary' look?"

What was he supposed to say to that?

"Hey, Sam," Eric called out, "hit the trunk latch, will ya?"

Hallelujah. Anything to get this done so he could head to the hotel. He reached down by the side of the driver's seat, pulled the latch and heard the trunk spring open. Glancing into the rearview mirror, Sam saw what looked like the entire herd of Wrights assemble behind his car.

"So," Tricia said from beside him, "you're a doctor."

"Yeah." He kept his gaze fixed on the crowd behind his car. There seemed to be a hell of a lot of activity back there just to pick up Eric's two bags.

"What kind? Eric's never said, really."

He shot her an exasperated look. Those wide blue eyes were fixed on him. "Medical."

"Funny."

Sam sighed as she continued to stare at him. There was a steady patience about her that told him she wasn't going anywhere. Until he could make his escape, it looked as though he was going to be in a conversation whether he wanted one or not. "I'm a G.P."

"Good." She slid the CD back into its slot in the dash. "I hate specialists."

One eyebrow lifted. "Why?"

"I don't know," she admitted, smiling. "Maybe I watch too much TV, but specialists seem more concerned with the disease than the patient and that's not good."

"They're not all—"

She leaned back in the seat, flipped the visor down and checked her hair in the mirror. "I really do watch too much TV, you know. Comes from not having a life."

Way too much information, Sam thought and threw another look at the back of the car. Why weren't they finished yet?

"You're ignoring me, hoping I'll go away, aren't you?"

A pinprick of guilt stabbed at Sam, but he ignored it more successfully than he had Tricia. "Not really. I'm just…"

"Crabby?"

He scowled at her one more time. "No."

"There's that scary face again," she pointed out. "You should have noticed already that it doesn't work on me."

"What will?" Sam asked, desperate enough to try anything.

She chuckled and shook her head until her blond ponytail swung off her left shoulder to settle on her right. "Ah, that you'll have to figure out for yourself."

Trying to decipher Tricia Wright would take years, Sam thought. And he wouldn't be here that long. Two weeks, he reminded himself. Two weeks until Eric's wedding and then he could get back to L.A. Back to his practice. Back to the blessed stillness of his condo.

The trunk lid slammed closed and he smiled to himself. Couldn't go home yet, but he could escape to the tranquility of a hotel room all to himself. And right now, that looked like a close enough second-best.

"Sounds like they've got it all," Tricia said and swung her legs out the passenger side door. Then she looked back over her shoulder at him and grinned. "You might as well give it up and come along quietly."

"What?" He was hardly listening. Instead, he stared past her as the group of Wrights hauled luggage—Eric's *and* Sam's—toward the house.

"Hey!" He shouted it, but no one paid any attention. With no one left to ask, he glared at Tricia. "Where're they going with—"

"You didn't really think the folks would let the man who saved their son's life stay in a hotel, did you?"

He shifted his gaze to hers and saw the glint of humor sparkling at him. She knew damn well that he felt trapped. And it didn't seem to bother her in the slightest.

"So, Doc Crabapple," she asked, "you coming quietly or will I have to get rough?"

Two

Food, Sam thought, seemed to be the universal signal for welcome.

And the Wright family had it down to a science.

The big, square kitchen was roomy and tidy, with the faux wood counters practically gleaming. Cupboards painted a blindingly snowy white lined the walls while a huge, farmhouse-style table crouched in front of a wide window. Afternoon sunlight slanted through the panes and poked between the red curtains, which were ruffling in a breeze slipping beneath the partially opened window. And on the table, in that splash of sunlight, lay enough food for a battalion.

Being without the fatted calf hadn't slowed Mrs. Wright down any. Instead, she supplied a turkey, a ham and every side dish known to man. The Wright family swarm surrounded the table, balancing plates and napkins and cups filled with everything from fruit punch to beer.

Sam had been scooped up and planted in the line taking a slow walk around the buffet and, hungry or not, was clearly expected to eat his way to unconsciousness.

"Have some of this macaroni salad," Eric's sister Debbie was saying as she plopped a heaping serving-spoonful onto his plate. "Mom makes the best."

"Don't forget my fresh corn." Mr. Wright, Dan, plunked a steaming ear, slathered with butter, on the corner of his plate and smiled with pride.

"You know," Sam said, "I appreciate all of this, but I should be—"

"Want another beer?" Eric called from behind the refrigerator door.

"No, thanks."

Debbie's husband Bill helped his daughter fill her plate while Mrs. Wright, Emma, focused on her grandson's demands for more stuffing. Eric's brother Jake leaned against a wall in the corner of the room, watching the melee over the rim of his cup of beer. Tricia had already been around the table, made her selections, and now was perched on the kitchen counter, watching Sam negotiate through the minefield of family. He felt her stare and sensed her amusement.

Happy to help, he thought wryly, glad that someone was enjoying all of this.

An only child, he'd been raised in quiet civility. His parents were older than his friends' folks and they'd treated him like a short adult. They'd included him in family decisions, fostered his love of books and school and taken him on vacations to the great museums of the world.

His experience with family life was completely different from the Wrights. In his parents' home, mealtime was a quiet, genteel hour with thought-provoking discussions on current events.

This was like a day at the circus. The noise level was tremendous and the eager conversations flying around the room defied all his attempts to understand them.

But none of them seemed to have any problem keeping up at all.

"Kevin," Debbie warned her son, "no cake if you don't—"

"—he's got beans," her mother said.

"—but no meat, and boys need meat."

"Boys can live without meat." The patriarch spoke up in a tone that defied a challenge. "They need milk."

"Milk is not for everyone, you know," Eric piped up. "Ask Sam. He's a doctor, he can tell you."

"Did you call and check on the caterers for the reception?" Debbie asked the question, but Sam had no idea to whom it had been directed.

"But if you don't have milk, your bones fall apart." Eric's father defended his stance.

"Yes, they've got everything under control." Eric's fiancée Jen answered, but Sam wasn't sure if she was talking about the milk or the reception. Wasn't sure if *they* knew. Or cared.

"Just look at Eric," Debbie's husband said with a grin. "He doesn't drink milk and his leg bone snapped like a twig."

"That was a car, not a lack of calcium." Eric swung his crutch at the man, but his brother-in-law was too quick and sidestepped the half-hearted blow.

"Same thing," Dan continued, apparently not caring if anyone was listening or not. "If Eric had still been drinking milk, he might not be wearing crutches for his wedding."

Sam's head swung back and forth, trying to follow the conversational tennis match, but he couldn't keep up. Nineteen forties–style music poured from the stereo in the living room, the family dog howled from beneath the table, and Eric and his brother launched into a new argument on the merits of SUVs versus sports cars.

A movement at the corner of his eye caught Sam's attention and when he followed it he spotted Tricia. Giving her family an indulgent shake of her head, she crooked her index finger in a 'follow me' signal.

The fact that he did only served to prove the level of his desperation.

She led him through the living room and onto the front porch. Once he stepped onto the whitewashed cement floor, she closed the door, cutting off most of the noise behind them.

He took a deep breath and let it slide from him in a rush. The relative silence was a blessing...an almost spiritual event.

Tricia spoiled it by laughing.

He shot her a look. "Amused?"

"Please. *Way* more than amused." She waved a hand, then walked to the end of the porch and took a seat on the bright red swing. Patting the padded cushion beside her, she coaxed, "Take a load off."

There's a choice, he thought. Alone with Tricia or back into the fray. He glanced behind him at the closed door and thought about the herd of people within. It took only a moment to make up his mind. Still holding a plate full of food he didn't want and a cup of cold beer he did, he walked toward her. Setting his plate on a small, square wooden table, he eased back into the swing beside Tricia and nearly groaned at the relief of the quiet.

"Are they always like that?" he asked, letting his head fall to the seat back.

"Loud?" she asked with a laugh. "You bet."

"How do they understand each other?"

"Shorthand," she mused and tucked one leg beneath her. Her other foot dangled and she used the toe of her sneaker to give them a push. The swing moved into a lazy back-and-forth pattern that induced relaxation. "With four kids in the family, you learn early to say whatever you want said or you'll never get the chance."

"What makes you think anyone's listening?"

"Hah!" She leaned her head back, too, and turned slightly to look at him. "They're *always* listening. Trust me on that. I used to try to sneak a sentence in without being noticed—"

"Like?"

Her grin broadened. "Oh, like, 'Is it okay if I go to Terri's party if her parents aren't going to be there?'"

"And they heard?"

"Oh yeah. Putting one past them was never easy, but they're great."

He glanced away from her long enough to look at the living room window just a foot or so away. Behind those dark green curtains lay unfamiliar and downright confusing territory. "I'm sure they are, but—"

"—but, being in there made you look really…"

"Uncomfortable?"

"I was going to go with trapped."

He turned his head to look at her again, meeting those blue eyes with a steady stare. Damn it, he hadn't meant to offend anyone and he hoped to hell the rest of her family wasn't quite as intuitive as Tricia. "Seems a little harsh."

"I thought so, too," she said with a smile that told him she, at least, hadn't been offended. "But still, I've never seen a man who looked more in need of a rescue."

"Maybe not a rescue, but the reprieve was good. Thanks." He took a sip of his beer, warming now in the afternoon heat. "I didn't mean anything by it—"

"Hey, I'm the first one to admit we take a little getting used to," Tricia said. "Especially for someone new."

"Thanks for that, too."

"No problem."

He looked at her. "Are you always so accommodating?"

"Oh," she said with another small chuckle, "almost never. You're catching me on a good day."

"Lucky me."

"Sarcasm. Or did you mean it?"

"Right now," he said, enjoying the fact that he was outside in the sunshine with relative quiet all around him, thanks to this one pretty woman, "I mean it."

"Then, thank you."

"You're welcome."

"See, how hard was that?"

"What?"

"We just had an actual conversation."

One corner of his mouth tipped up. "It was over so fast, I must have missed it."

"See? You're already learning about chats in this family. Want to go back in?"

His features must have mirrored what he was feeling because she leaned in closer and said, "No hurry.

You're the guest of honor, so you can pretty much do whatever you want to do."

"*I'm* the guest of honor?" Honestly surprised, he just looked at her. "I figured all of that food was on Eric's behalf."

"Not completely." Reaching out, she tapped her fingernails against the wrappings on his arm. "Heroes need big welcomes."

Sam shifted on the seat, putting a couple more inches between himself and the woman still leaning toward him. And something told him it wasn't nearly enough. "I'm not a hero."

As if sensing his need for distance, she sat back, but kept her gaze locked on him. "Couldn't prove that to Mom and Dad. Or to Eric's fiancée."

"I was there at the right time," he said simply, shifting his gaze to the yard and the street beyond.

"I'm glad."

He looked at her again, saw the warmth in her eyes and felt a like response flicker to life inside him. This he could accept. "So'm I."

She smiled and something inside him relaxed a little even as his other senses heightened.

Silence dropped between them and Sam reveled in it. He'd been too long alone to be able to adjust easily to being surrounded by people. In his world, there was his condo, the freeway and his office, with no points in between. Weekends only meant being in the office clearing up paperwork and getting a head start on the following week. His nights were spent either in his home gym or in front of his big-screen TV. When insomnia struck, as it often did, he stood alone on the balcony off his living room and watched the stars fade.

He shifted in his seat, a little uncomfortable with all of this sudden self-examination. Sam had never really stopped to consider the way he spent—or wasted—his time. Now that he did, he asked himself if he'd planned to become so insular or if it had just happened …after Mary.

But then life itself had changed after Mary, hadn't it? The way he saw things, what he thought, felt, experienced. Nothing was as it had been…*before*. There'd been a pall over everything for the last two years and in response, he'd wrapped himself up in the muffling cocoon of solitude. Coming out of it now, even briefly, was as jarring as if he'd been dropped into the Amazon and told to survive with nothing more than a piece of string and a flashlight.

"You're really hating this, aren't you?"

The sound of her voice brought him back, gratefully, from his thoughts. "What?"

She chuckled, shook her head and drew her other leg up until she was sitting cross-legged on the swing. She looked completely comfortable and at ease with both herself and her surroundings, and Sam envied her.

"You heard me," she said, still smiling at him patiently as if he were a particularly dim-witted child.

"You're just trying to think of a way to answer that won't be insulting."

Irritating to be so transparent. As a doctor, he prided himself on his poker face. He never wanted patients to be able to read his diagnosis on his features before he'd had a chance to talk to them. In his personal life, he carried that trait over, keeping an unreadable—or so he'd thought—expression, unwilling to let anyone into his mind, his thoughts, his heart.

Well, except Mary.

But she'd been different.

Tricia Wright was simply…well, the word *different* about covered her, too.

"Your family seems very nice," he hedged.

"Don't forget noisy."

"That, too." Didn't seem wrong to agree if she was the one who'd said it first.

"And this isn't even as noisy as it gets."

"Don't know how it could get louder," he muttered, earning another of her low-throated chuckles. She sounded sexy, intimate, and at the thought, tension built inside him. Something he hadn't expected and didn't want.

"Oh, just wait," she teased, apparently enjoying his discomfort. "Tomorrow, Aunt Beth and Uncle Jim arrive with their three kids and then there's Grandma Joan and her new boyfriend Oliver—"

"Your grandmother has a boyfriend?"

"Well, not really a *boy*, though he is twenty years

younger than her," Tricia explained, "and let me tell you, that was a tough one for my father to take. Having a potential stepfather your own age is a big one to swallow."

Sam shook his head. He should have thanked his parents when they were alive, for being so...tame.

"And the day after, my cousin Nora gets here and she's bringing her son Tommy—lock up the matches."

"An arsonist?" he asked, appalled.

"Well, he's only seven, but he does seem to have his career picked out."

"Great."

"And there'll be *more* of us arriving during the next couple of weeks."

More Wrights? How could there be more? It made him want to run inside, grab his bag and hit the freeway, headed for home. But he couldn't, since he'd agreed six months ago to be an usher at Eric's wedding. So he'd settle for what he could get. "Good thing I already got my hotel room," he said, more to himself than to her.

But apparently, you didn't have to actually be speaking *to* Tricia to get a response.

"Oh, they'll be staying with family. No hotels allowed with *this* family. Mom and Dad will house most of them, they've got the most bedrooms. But Debbie and her husband get a few and Jake's putting up the bachelors at his place, God help them."

Sam shook his head, trying to keep the players straight, then gave it up. He'd only be here two weeks, he didn't have to know her family. But despite himself, he was caught up in the flow of her conversation. She hardly seemed to pause for breath.

"What's wrong with Jake's place?"

"Small, for one thing, and the man lives like a pig. He's never really there though, to give him his due," Tricia said thoughtfully. "He works for the government, something supposedly hush-hush. Hard to believe since he was never able to keep a secret when he was a kid." She sighed and trailed one hand along the arm of the swing. "Still, none of my business."

None of his either, Sam thought, grateful that he had an excuse to stay happily alone at his hotel room—a destination which was looking better and better all the time. In fact, no time like the present to make his escape. "With all those people coming in soon, I'll just grab my suitcase and head for the hotel after all."

"Nice try, big boy."

"What?"

She laid one hand on his arm, staying him when he would have stood up. "No hotel for the man of the hour, I already told you. You've already been assigned your quarters."

"I thought you were joking." A small sinking sensation opened up inside him.

"Nope." Tricia grinned and leaned toward him

again, and this time Sam caught a whiff of her perfume. Something soft and floral and summery, clinging to her and yet, drifting in the same light breeze that lifted the loose tendrils of her hair to curl about her face. This was not a good sign. Tricia Wright and her smiles and her scent were somehow more intriguing than they should have been.

But he wasn't going there, he decided, pushing those wayward thoughts out of his brain just as fast as they presented themselves. Holding his breath to avoid being seduced by the scent of summer flowers, he ignored the effect she had on him and concentrated instead on what she was saying.

"Yep, you'll be staying at my house."

Oh no. He just wasn't *that* good at ignoring temptation. And taking another long look at her, he decided that *any* red-blooded male wouldn't be able to ignore her for long.

"I don't think so."

"Scared?" she countered.

He laughed and didn't even manage to convince himself. "Of what?"

"Little ol' me?"

"Not so you'd notice," he said, although a part of him was very wary of both her big blue eyes and that scent that seemed to be reaching out for him, tangling him up in it as though he were being strangled by flowering vines.

"It wasn't my idea, so chill out. Mom and Dad

worked out the housing schedule." Her voice dropped. "They're really grateful for what you did for Eric. They consider you family."

He nearly shivered.

"And family does *not* stay in hotels," she said with another shake of her head. Her ponytail flipped from one shoulder to the other. "Don't worry, I didn't take one look at your masculine beauty and immediately work it so you'd be my houseguest."

He was never sure if she was serious or teasing. And right now, it didn't matter. "I didn't say that—"

"No, but you were thinking it."

"I'm not that easy to read and *no,* I wasn't."

"Ah," she said, holding up one finger like a hammy detective in an old movie, about to make his point, "but I only have your word on that, don't I?"

Sam grumbled and pushed up from the swing. Standing there looking down at her, he felt a little more in control. "Look, I appreciate the offer," he said, though God knows he didn't, "but the hotel will be more convenient all the way around."

"Can't get more convenient than my house. I live right next door," she said.

"What?" That sinking sensation widened…growing into something like a black hole.

"There." She pointed at the house just behind her. "That one's mine. Bought it a couple of years ago, thinking to get out on my own. But how on your own are you when you live next door to your parents?"

"I wouldn't know."

"Oh boy, I do," she said. Then shrugging, she added, "But it was a great deal and way better than throwing my money down a rent hole. And Mom and Dad don't just drop in, they're really good about that."

"Congratulations."

"You're very good at *that*."

"What?"

"Turning conversations around to avoid talking about what you don't want to."

Sam actually laughed. "From what I've seen, the conversations in your family are turning all the time."

"True," she said, pushing herself up and out of the swing. She stood just in front of him and when the swing rushed forward, bumping into the backs of her knees, she fell toward him.

Instinctively, Sam caught her. But he hadn't counted on the rush of warmth snaking up his arms to rattle around in the center of his chest. She was tall. The top of her head hit just below his nose. And she was close—too close. He stepped back, but not before he saw something flash in her eyes. "I just don't think—"

"You'll be a hero again."

The conversational Ferris wheel was turning again. "I'm not a—"

"Fine," she said, cutting him off neatly. "You weren't a hero with Eric. You were in the right place at the right time. But now, you have the chance to be a hero…for *me*."

Sam sighed and knew he was getting deeper and deeper into a mire he wasn't entirely sure he'd be able to get out of. She looked harmless enough, he thought—in fact, she looked the part of the quintessential, all-American girl. Which was actually trouble, not harmless. Add to that the fact that she seemed to have the unerring ability to see into corners of his soul he would prefer stayed shrouded in shadows...

She was more than he'd bargained for, that was all. Sam hadn't thought he'd be getting twisted up with Eric's family. He'd planned to be here, take part in the festivities and then leave again. But that clearly wasn't going to happen. As for now, just looking into her eyes, Sam knew he shouldn't ask what the hell she was talking about. But damned if she hadn't stirred his curiosity. "I surrender," he said. "Just how does my staying at your house qualify me for hero status?"

"If you're my guest, then I won't have to house the little fire starter."

"Your cousin—"

"Tommy."

"Right."

He thought about it for a long minute. Her eyes were wide and clear as she watched him and he knew that he'd be in trouble if he stayed around this woman for any length of time. She was a woman who saw too much, laughed too often. And made him feel...hell, made him *feel*. But he could manage for two weeks, he assured himself. Two weeks was nothing. He'd be able to have some peace and quiet. Her house was bound to be quieter than her parents' place. And he wouldn't have to spend a lot of time with Tricia. She'd be busy helping with the coming wedding. He'd have time to himself without insulting the Wright family.

It could work.

"Be a hero," she prodded. "Save the girl from a fate worse than death."

He'd probably regret it, Sam thought, as he looked down into her big blue eyes. He didn't want to be anybody's hero.

And yet, despite all that, he still heard himself say, "All right. I'll do it."

Three

The scent of cinnamon and coffee greeted Sam on his first morning in Tricia's house. Sitting up in bed, he had one blank moment when he tried to figure out where the hell he was.

Then it all rushed back to him and he remembered agreeing to move into a perky blonde's house for two weeks. At the moment, he couldn't quite recall *why* but that didn't seem to matter anymore. He glanced around the room and told himself that he could have been staying in a generic hotel room. Instead, he was sleeping in a lavender room that smelled of cinnamon, atop a bed with a scrolled iron head- and footboard. He tossed the flowered quilt to one side and swung his legs off the bed. Lacy white curtains hung at the wide windows and danced lazily in the soft breeze sliding beneath the sash. On one wall of the big room, an antique chest of drawers stood like an old soldier, while on the opposite wall, a small television crouched atop a narrow bookcase stuffed with lurid murder mysteries.

Sam smiled to himself as he rolled out of bed. He'd taken a good look at the reading selections before going to sleep last night. And even with everything he'd seen in his residency and ER rotation, some of those book covers had been enough to turn his stomach. Intriguing woman, Tricia Wright, he thought. Romantic enough to enjoy lace and antiques and apparently grisly enough to enjoy a nice, gory murder or two. What did that say about her personality?

And why did he care enough to wonder?

After a hot shower in the old-fashioned, dollhouse-sized bathroom, he headed down a short flight of stairs. His elbow throbbed from slamming it into the shower wall, and he had a crick in his neck from trying to twist low enough to have the stingy fall of water actually hit the top of his head. But he was awake and now following the delicious scent of fresh coffee and what smelled like some kind of bakery heaven.

He moved quietly through the house, enjoying the near silence and appreciating a woman who didn't seem to have the need to hear the TV newscasters shouting bad news at her first thing in the morning.

Her living room was big and square and dotted with overstuffed furniture that practically invited you to sit deep and relax. There was a brick fireplace on one wall, its mantel crowded with family pictures in a dizzying array of frames.

But he kept moving, on the trail of coffee and when he reached the kitchen, he paused in the doorway, leaning one shoulder against the doorjamb. He crossed his feet at the ankles, folded his arms across his chest and, since she hadn't noticed him yet, took a moment to watch Tricia unobserved.

Her back was to him as she worked at her kitchen counter. In the bright, overhead light, her long blond hair shone like gold in a single, thick braid that ended just at her shoulder blades. She wore a tight gray T-shirt that clung to every curve and denim shorts that exposed long, sleekly tanned legs. She was barefoot and dancing in time to the music sliding softly from the radio on the counter.

As he watched, she deftly handled a rolling pin on the marble countertop putting her whole body into the task. Behind her, on the large kitchen table, an assortment of cookies in various stages of readiness were placed assembly-line fashion—some waiting to be baked, some cooling on wire racks and some waiting to be frosted and decorated. Since she obviously had a system, this must be a familiar routine.

Sam tried to think back and recall some of the things Eric had told him about his family. But it was all a blur of information and names Sam had never paid much attention to. That should teach him to listen more.

The first light of dawn spilled into the room in a thin trickle that warred with the glare of electricity and glanced off shining window panes to lie across the field of cookies. When Tricia started singing along with the radio, he smiled at her imitation of The King.

"I'd stick to baking if I were you," he said softly, then louder, added, "Does your audience get coffee?"

"Whoops!" She practically shrieked the word and whirled around all at the same time. Slapping one hand to her chest, she left a floury handprint on her T-shirt as she gasped for breath and then laughed. "You move like a creeper."

"And you sing like a baker." He stepped into the kitchen, still watching her. She looked good first thing in the morning, he thought. Which he really shouldn't be noticing. But as a male, it was sort of a given that he would.

"Didn't mean to spook you."

"Well, now that my heart's beating again," she said, "you're forgiven."

"Forgiven enough for a cup of that coffee?"

"I would never withhold coffee as a punishment," she said, already reaching for an oversized purple mug from the cupboard to her right. "It's just inhumane."

"You're obviously a superior human being."

"I like to think so," she quipped as she filled the mug with a rich, dark brew that smelled like heaven to Sam.

Turning, she handed it to him and said, "If you want to spoil this excellent Colombian roast, there's milk in the fridge and sugar in the pantry."

He shook his head and took that first glorious sip. As the hot coffee slid down his throat, Sam felt himself waking up. "I take it black."

She grinned and lifted her own mug in a toast. "My kind of man."

Now, most men, he figured, would have taken that statement as an invitation to get to know her better. To enjoy a little flirtation. A little word play designed to entice. But Sam withstood the temptation. He wasn't here to banter, wasn't here looking for a two-week fling. And if he were, it sure wouldn't be with a woman like Tricia. She just wasn't a "fling" kind of woman. Anyone could tell that just by looking at her. She had "permanence" practically tattooed on her forehead. She was picket fences and small children and holiday dinners and huge family gatherings.

In other words, she was everything Sam was *not*.

"Don't bet on it," he said.

She laughed, took another sip of coffee, then set the big blue mug down within reach on the countertop. "I said you were my *kind* of man, not *my* man. So you can take that *Oh-my-God-how-do-I-get-out-of-here* look off your face."

Instantly, he blanked out his features, but stiffened at the fact that she'd seen right through him. Again.

"Seriously," she said, picking up her marble rolling pin and waving it at him like a professor using a pointer, "you need to relax. Your virtue is entirely safe with me."

Sam scowled a little at her dismissal. Fine, he wasn't interested, but there was a *very* small part of him that still felt the sting of a beautiful woman's indifference. His grip on the purple mug tightened slightly. "And why's that?"

She gave him a brief look and an even briefer smile. But as brief as it was, it carried power. Like the first light of dawn breaking in a dark sky, that smile indicated that more spectacular things were ahead.

"I've sworn off men." She looked at him again. "Didn't Eric tell you?"

"Why would he?"

She shrugged and set the rolling pin aside to pick up a stainless steel cookie cutter. Deftly, she pressed it into the waiting dough, then turned it and pressed again, getting as many cookies as possible on the first roll. "Because the family's worried about me. They think I'm depressed or something."

"You?" He hadn't meant to sound so astonished, but how anyone could consider a woman who even *talked* with a smile in her voice depressed was beyond him.

"Thank you." She picked up a spatula and carefully began to scoop up the cut out cookies and lay them on a waiting baking sheet. "I love my family, but try to convince them of anything."

"What're you supposed to be depressed about?" He walked closer and leaned one hip against the cold edge of the counter.

She sighed dramatically and rested the back of her hand against her forehead in a pose worthy of Broadway. "I was *dumped*."

Surprise flickered to life inside Sam as he watched her. He couldn't imagine a man stupid enough to dump a woman like her—well, unless he'd been treated to an overdose of her family. "Eric didn't mention it."

At least, he didn't *think* so. But so often, when his friends were talking to him, Sam's mind was a million miles away. Eric might have mentioned being worried about his younger sister and the words would have sailed past Sam unnoticed. He'd been too wrapped up in his own misery the last two years to pay much attention at all to the rest of the world.

And for the first time, he began to feel a little guilt over that fact.

"Well yay, him," Tricia said, finishing up the latest batch of cookies. She picked up the tray and glanced at him as she turned for the huge, commercial-size oven on the opposite wall. She bent down, yanked the door open and shoved that tray, plus another, inside. When she straightened, she set a timer on the range top and turned again. "It's no big deal," she said, "it's just that I've finally decided to accept my fate."

"And what's that?"

She plopped both flour-dusted hands onto her hips, heedless of the white powder she was dribbling on her clothes and the floor. "I just don't have any luck at all with guys. So, I've decided to give up men and have a special relationship with sugar, instead."

He smiled in spite of himself. Waving one hand at the array of goodies on the table, he said, "Apparently you and sugar are quite serious about this new relationship."

"Oh, yeah. Sugar will never let you down." She held up three fingers in a half-assed Girl Scout salute. "It may give you cavities and make you fat, but it will *always* be there for you. No matter what."

"And that's the important thing?"

"What else is there?"

What else, indeed?

Moving away from the counter, he took a closer look at the cookies on the table. In the shapes of champagne flutes and beer mugs, the cookies smelled like glory and looked like a mountain of work.

Intrigued, he glanced at her. "Your sugar comes in the shapes of champagne and beer?"

She walked over to stand at his side. "Another good point about sugar. It can come in *any* shape or size and they'll all be the right ones." Then she grinned at him. "These were commissioned by Mom. Some for the bachelor party, some for the bridal shower. You guess which are for which."

"Not too hard to do," he said. "But I don't think I've ever had cookies at a bachelor party."

She sniffed. "You will at this one."

"Apparently. Do they taste as good as they look?"

"You tell me." She picked up one of the frosted, decorated beer mug cookies and handed it to him.

Sam looked at her as he bit into it. Then he closed his eyes to better enjoy the taste rolling through him. He'd never had anything like it. Sweet, but not overly so, the cookie had an underlying flavor that swept through him and yet defied description. When he swallowed, he opened his eyes again to find her watching him with a knowing smile on her face.

"You like it."

"It's great."

She gave him a half bow. "Thank you."

He took another bite, savoring as he chewed. "What's that flavor I'm tasting?"

"Family secret."

"Seriously."

"I am being serious."

"Your mom thinks of me as family."

She looked at him for a long minute and Sam felt a new and decidedly different kind of tension build up between them. Then she spoke again and the moment was gone.

"But you're not family, are you?"

"You're not going to tell me, are you?"

"Hey," she said, "if I go around telling people my secrets, I'll be out of business instead of growing."

"This is your business?" He looked again at the table, nearly groaning under the weight of the trays and platters and racks of cookies.

She practically beamed. "I'm Cookie Lady."

He shook his head. "What?"

She sighed and a wisp of blond hair on her forehead lifted into a brief dance. "Fine. So you haven't heard of me. I'm not well-known yet. But I will be," she told him, swinging back to the counter where more dough and her rolling pin awaited her. "I'm building a reputation with parties and promotional stuff. And in a month, I'll be setting up shop in my own bakery."

"Yeah?" Intrigued by the pleasure in her voice and the excitement fairly vibrating around her, Sam pulled out a chair and sat down. Snatching up another cookie, he ate, sipped his coffee and listened as Tricia described her blossoming business.

She looked at him over her shoulder and sent him a smile that would have staggered a lesser man. But he was immune. He hadn't noticed a pretty woman in two years. So he wasn't noticing Tricia, either.

Very much.

"I got such a great deal on this retail space on the Coast Highway. It's perfect," she said as she gathered up the dough, rolled it into a ball and wielded the rolling pin again. "Big storefront window for display, nice counters and a kitchen that will really give me some room to expand."

"Looks to me like you're doing a good business already," he said, finishing off his second cookie.

"Oh, it's been great," she agreed, "and go ahead, have another one if you want—"

He did.

"—but my business is growing faster than I'd even hoped, so I just can't continue to do it out of my kitchen, you know?"

"Is that what you want?"

"Huh?"

Sam shrugged, got up and walked to the coffee pot on the counter. Refilling his purple mug, he set the pot back on the warming tray and took a long sip before saying, "Most people would appreciate being able to work out of their home."

"Yeah," she agreed, "it's been great. And handy. The store will be more expensive to run, what with rent and having to hire somebody full-time to help me out, but the trade-off is that I'll be able to do more jobs."

He didn't even remember a time when he'd been as enthused about anything as Tricia was over her burgeoning business. He saw it in her eyes, heard it in her voice and he realized that he *missed* that feeling of challenge. Of betting on yourself. Of taking a risk and putting everything on the line.

"I'll move into the shop two weeks after the wedding, so the family will be able to help do the big jobs."

"You spend a lot of time together—your family, I mean."

"Well, we all live close by," she said, "except for Eric—but you already know that. So yeah, we see each other a lot."

He didn't say anything at all and, after a moment or two, she shot him a look.

"We a little much for you, Doctor Crabby?"

"I'm not crabby," he muttered, more as a reflex than anything else.

"Okay, you haven't been this morning, but the day is young."

"Thanks," he said wryly and leaned one hip against the counter.

Even from a foot away, she smelled like flowers dusted with vanilla and cinnamon. Her skin was creamy and smooth and looked like coffee with too much milk in it. Just a soft, pale brown that told him she liked being outside, but didn't bake herself just for the sake of being tanned. Her hands were constantly in motion, working on her cookies with a capable, practiced touch. Her fingers were long, her nails short and neat. She wore no rings, but she did have huge, gypsy-like silver hoops dangling from her ears.

Her full lips seemed permanently curved into a half smile, as if she knew…

And he was getting entirely too focused on the Cookie Lady.

Moving back to his chair, hoping somehow that a little distance would ease the surprising ache that had erupted inside him, Sam sat down and focused on his coffee.

"Your arm feeling better?" She glanced at his now unwrapped forearm.

"Yeah," he said, flexing as if testing his own strength. "It's fine. Always was."

"That's good. So you're all set to help with the barbecue?"

"What?" Her ability to shift conversational gears left him constantly feeling as though he were running to catch up.

"At Debbie's. She's having a barbecue for the family and for the almost in-laws at her place. We'll have to go in about an hour. Help set up the tables and chairs and stuff."

"Sure." More family, he thought, acknowledging, at least to himself, that he couldn't remember the Wright family members he'd met already.

"Don't worry," she said, as if looking into his mind—which she had a habit of doing far too often. "They don't bite." Then she paused, cocked her head and seemed to consider that statement. "Well, Katie bites sometimes," she said thoughtfully. "That's Debbie's youngest. But don't worry, she's had her shots."

"Great."

* * *

Katie didn't bite, but she did cling.

The way a dog gravitates toward the one person in the crowd who doesn't like animals, Katie decided within the first fifteen minutes that Sam was her new favorite person. To be fair, though, it wasn't as though Sam didn't like kids. He did. He just didn't have much experience with them outside his professional life.

The little girl was almost elfin. Her long dark hair swung in pigtails hanging from either side of her head. Big blue eyes looked up at Sam with a coy flirtatiousness that told him she was going to be a heartbreaker when she grew up. At four, she was two years younger than her big brother Kevin, and obviously used to being indulged. But Sam was a sucker for the kid for a whole different reason than her loving family was.

The only children Sam saw regularly were his patients. And none of them were happy to see him, thanks to booster shots, inoculations and throat swabs. To have a child actually seem to *like* him was so novel, he really enjoyed it.

Perched on his knee, Katie leaned against his chest and opened her favorite book for the third time. Tipping her head back, she stared up at him and smiled. A powerful weapon. And the tiny girl knew it. Sam couldn't stop his own smile as he reached for the first page.

"You should do that more often," a female voice—Tricia's—said from close by.

He glanced at her as she came up alongside him. "Do what?"

"Smile," she said, apparently unmoved by the irritation in his tone. It was one thing reading to a child, another altogether reading for an audience. Plopping down on the picnic bench beside him, she reached across him to poke a finger into Katie's side and release a giggle, like air escaping a balloon.

"I smile," he said and turned back to the book and a more-impatient-by-the-minute Katie.

"Now, see," Tricia countered, stretching her long legs out in front of her. "Not so much."

"You just met me yesterday," he pointed out tightly. "And I smiled just this morning."

"Yeah, but you just don't look like you do it often enough. You don't have the 'smiler' vibe."

"And a smiler looks…how?"

"Happy," she said and grinned into his best withering glare.

The woman was as much a mystery to Sam as the books she so loved to read. Every time he turned around, she was right there. Even when they'd been hanging streamers and hauling chairs, she'd somehow managed to be within arm's reach of him. Not that he'd reached or anything. But he could have if he'd been so inclined.

Ever since their conversation that morning, when things had suddenly felt too…cozy for comfort, Sam had tried to keep his distance. But it seemed that Tricia was just as determined to close that distance.

She leaned her elbows on the tabletop behind her and tilted her head to one side as she watched him. Her blond hair shone in the late morning sun and the spatter of freckles across her nose looked like someone had sprayed her with gold dust. Her mouth was curved, naturally, and her expression was one of practiced innocence. He didn't believe it for a minute. She knew damn well that he'd been trying to stay away from her, so she'd done everything she could to keep him from succeeding.

Katie, sensing that the attention had somehow drifted away from *her*, made her displeasure known.

She grabbed a handful of Sam's dark green polo shirt and yanked. "Read a book!"

Since she'd also snatched a few chest hairs, Sam winced, patted her little hand and said, "Right. No more interruptions." That was said with a telling look at Tricia. "Back to the man in the moon."

"Good."

"Good," Tricia repeated.

"Don't you have somewhere else to be?" Sam asked, sliding her a glance.

She grinned at him and her big blue eyes actually sparkled. "I'm on a break."

"And you have to stay here?" Clearly, though, she was settling in, making herself comfortable. And making him as *un*comfortable as possible.

"Katie wants me here, don't you sweetie?"

"Aunt Trish likes a book."

"See?" Tricia grinned at the girl as though they'd rehearsed the whole scene.

He gave it one more shot. "No blood and guts in this story."

"Hey," Tricia said, still aiming that potent smile of hers at him, "variety *is* the spice of life."

And there were all kinds of variety, Sam thought, tearing his gaze from Tricia's. The trouble was, when the woman who smelled like a flower garden was too close to him, his brain was unwillingly filled with amazingly in-depth and Technicolor visions of just what kind of variety there was for two people to discover.

Four

Eric sat in a green resin lawn chair beneath the shade of a fifty-year-old elm tree. A breeze rustled through the feathery light leaves overhead, sending dappled patches of shade into a weird dance on the sun-warmed grass.

His right leg ached, and he was so tired, it was an effort to keep his eyes open. But despite everything, he felt lucky and grateful to be alive.

Whether Sam wanted to admit it or not, Eric owed him more than he could ever repay. The fact that he was sitting here, enjoying the confusion only his family could create, was a gift he'd never really thought about until today. But that debt didn't mean he wasn't worried about what was going on between Sam and Tricia.

Eric's gaze settled on his sister, his friend and his niece, all sitting on a picnic bench across the yard from him. There was too much noise from everyone else for him to catch any of what they were saying. But judging from the way Tricia was smiling up at Sam, something was definitely up.

He just didn't know what.

He hadn't said much about Tricia to Sam, knowing that his friend had been too wrapped up in his own grief and pain to be interested. But now that he saw them together, Eric had to wonder if it had been such a great idea to drag Sam upstate for a vacation. Tricia was just coming off a bad breakup and, even if she wouldn't admit it under threat of torture, Eric knew she was still vulnerable.

Tricia'd always had a hard head and a tender heart. She went her own way, wasn't afraid of speaking her mind and was usually left regretting it. She'd dated a string of guys who weren't good enough for her, and always ended up getting her heart slapped. And God help you if you tried to tell her so. She was contrary enough to date a guy you warned her away from, just to prove that she was her own woman.

So, if Eric were to take his life in his hands and tell Tricia to stay away from Sam, she'd be more than likely to find the man even more fascinating. And he'd been the one to present her with Sam. It was like dangling a candy bar in front of a chocoholic.

But even as he thought it, Eric reconsidered.

Maybe this time, Tricia wouldn't leap without looking. And even if she did, Sam at least was a good guy. He was just a man who'd been lost so long he didn't even remember how he'd gotten that way. In the last two years, Eric had watched Sam pull further and further away from everything he used to care about.

Most of the man's few friends had drifted away, but Eric had stuck. He'd tried to pull Sam back into the world of the living, but it hadn't worked. Sam had been determined to suffer. Determined to wallow in the rubble of his world.

Now, though Sam looked uncomfortable as hell, he was at least *at* the party. Surrounded by people. Sitting beside a woman who was the perfect "glass half-full" to his "glass half-empty."

Eric leaned to one side and reached down to the grass for his bottle of beer. Straightening up again, he focused his gaze on Tricia, noting her smile and the way she leaned in toward Sam. Worry snaked through him for a minute as he tried to decide who he was more concerned for—his sister, or his friend.

But the truth of the matter was, if Tricia decided to fall for Sam, there wasn't a damn thing any of them could do about it. And would he if he could? He didn't know. Tricia's heart was still bruised, but it had been bruised before and she'd survived. Plus, she had a way of enjoying life that might be just the medicine Sam needed.

So what was a brother supposed to do? he asked

himself. Just sit back and watch—wait to see if there would be fireworks?

"What do we know about him?"

"Geez!" Eric jolted in his chair. He hadn't heard his older brother Jake's approach. The man moved like a ghost. "Tryin' to kill me?"

Jake gave him a fast grin and shook his head. "Too easy a target. No challenge."

"Well, thanks, that makes me feel manly." Eric scowled at him. "What'd you say before?"

"Sam," Jake said as he went down on one knee beside Eric's chair. "What do we know about him?"

"He's a friend."

"Anything else?"

Apparently Jake's radar was on red alert, too. Hell of a thing to be a member of a close family—too many people to look out for. "Doctor. Widower. Good guy."

"Uh-huh." Jake nodded toward their sister. "Good enough for Trish?"

"Is anybody?"

Jake laughed shortly. "No. Hell, Bill's not good enough for Debbie and they're working on number three."

Eric took another sip of his beer and enjoyed the rush of cold frothy liquid before speaking again. "True. But I don't think you have to worry about Sam that way. He's…"

"Gay?"

"No way," Eric said on a short laugh.

"Blind, then?"

"No."

"He'd have to be to not see Tricia."

Blind or too far removed from life, Eric thought. He didn't say so, though. Jake was his brother, but he owed a loyalty to his friend, too. And that included not talking about Sam's problems.

"He's only gonna be here two weeks," Eric said instead, and wasn't sure who he was trying to convince—himself, or his brother. "What can happen in two weeks?"

Jake stared at him for a long minute, then laughed and stood up again. "You're kidding, right?"

Eric frowned thoughtfully. Jake had him thinking now, and even he had to admit that two weeks was plenty of time for hearts to connect…or break.

"What're you two planning?"

He shifted his gaze from his brother to his fiancée, and grinned as Jen sank to the grass and leaned back against his chair.

"Me?" Jake said, already walking back toward his father and the clutch of cousins hanging around the barbecue. "Not a thing, Jen. Not a thing."

"What was that about?" she asked, glancing after Jake.

"Just brother stuff." Eric threaded his fingers through her long, red hair. A quiet ping of guilt sounded out inside him. He should probably talk about all this with the woman he was planning to marry. But on the other hand, she'd probably think he was crazy for worrying in the first place. So instead, he hedged. "What makes you think I'm planning something?"

Jen tipped her head back and pinned him with a steady gaze. "I know you too well. Right now," she said, "you're wondering if you should rescue Tricia from Sam or Sam from Tricia."

He shouldn't have been surprised, he thought. He'd known Jen since they were kids. They'd been close since high school and had kept their relationship going even when he'd moved down to L.A. She'd been his heart for as long as he could remember. Was it any wonder she could read him as easily as she did?

"You're good," he admitted with a nod.

"Just remember that," she said and crossed her arms atop his left knee, resting her chin on her joined hands. "Wives know all and see all."

"You're not a wife yet," he teased.

"Will be in two weeks," she said, reaching for his hand.

His fingers curled around hers and held on. She was everything to him. Staring into her wide green eyes, he saw the promise of a lifetime shining back at him. He saw his future—*their* future—stretch out in front of him, and it looked great. He took a deep breath and released it on a sigh. If Sam hadn't been with him at the accident, if he hadn't been able to get

Eric out of the wreck... God, he would have missed so much.

Emotions filled him, nearly choking him with their intensity. "I love you," he blurted.

"Right back at ya," Jen said playfully, but her fingers tightened on his and he knew that she, too, was realizing just how close they'd come to losing what they had together.

Then she turned her head and looked at the three people sitting on a bench in a splash of sunshine. "So," she said, a moment later, "what did you and Jake decide about your sister and your pal?"

Eric gave them a brief glance before turning his gaze back to the woman sitting in front of him. "Jake's not talking. But I think, I'm going to remain neutral. At least for now."

"Good call."

"You think?"

Jen sighed and shook her head. "You Wrights are terrific, the way it's one for all and all for one," she said, "but you've got Tricia all wrong."

He straightened up in his chair and winced a little at the pressure on his leg. "Oh yeah?"

Jen gave him a patient, understanding smile. "She's not a fragile little woman who needs your protection, Eric. She knows what she's doing."

"In most things, sure. But about guys?"

She laughed and shook her head. "Tricia's not a wounded bird, you know."

Eric looked at his sister again and couldn't help the flicker of concern that flashed through him. "I hope you're right."

"Once we're married," Jen promised, "you'll see I'm *always* right."

An hour later, Sam realized he was actually having a good time. He hadn't expected to. Had, in fact, expected to be on the point of pulling his hair out by now. Instead, he felt himself being sucked into the crazed vortex that was the Wright family.

They were loud, funny, and almost impossible to stand against. A solitary man didn't have a chance with this group. They refused to allow anyone to be alone. Their hospitality simply wrapped around an outsider like a warm blanket on a cold night.

The scene in Debbie's backyard was one of complete confusion with a weird sense of order. Children ran and played with the old dog who looked like he wanted nothing more than to find a shady spot to collapse in. Adults dotted the yard in small conversational groups and the sun beat down on everyone, reminding them that summer was in high gear.

Sam let his gaze drift across the faces of the people who were becoming so familiar to him. The newest arrival was cousin Nora, a woman with short, dark hair, shadows under her eyes and a ready smile. A harried single mother, Nora doted on her son, Tommy. Sam kept a wary eye on the child Tricia'd told him was an arsonist in training, especially when the boy was off playing with Katie and Kevin. Surprised by the protective instincts rising inside him, Sam was *more* surprised that none of the other adults seemed concerned enough to ride herd on the kid. Even Tricia, who'd warned him in the first place, was sitting on a blanket between her pregnant sister and her mother, apparently blissfully unconcerned about potential disaster.

He had to admit that Tommy didn't look like a potential firebug. The kid had a shock of unruly brown hair, a face full of freckles and a missing front tooth. He looked like a Rockwell portrait as he ran around the backyard just like any other normal boy.

Sam frowned and glanced at the cluster of Wright men surrounding him. All of them hovered near the still-cold barbecue as the patriarch stacked charcoal in a precise pattern. While their father worked, conversations rippled like rings in a pond after a stone had been tossed in. Sam only half listened to snatches of everything.

"Football? How can you care about football in the middle of baseball season?"

"Hockey's a man's game."

"And tennis."

That statement from yet another cousin, this time a teenager, shut everyone up for a moment. Until the kid grinned and said, "Just kidding."

Jake shoved the skinny adolescent, then turned

back to trying to convince his brother that baseball was the *true* American sport. As Eric debated the issue, he swung his crutch occasionally to make a point.

"Pay no attention to them," Dan Wright said with a glance at his sons. "They've always done that. Argue over nothing just for the sake of hearing themselves talk."

Sam shook his head. "I don't think Eric even likes football."

"Probably not, but it's the argument that counts," the older man said with an understanding chuckle.

"If you say so." Sam gripped the long neck of his beer bottle, and lifted it to take a sip. The sun was warm, the breeze cool and the sounds of people enjoying themselves was almost hypnotic. It had been a long time since he'd spent a day doing nothing. Hell, he couldn't even remember when he'd last taken a day off. He frowned and sipped at the beer again.

"We appreciate you driving Eric back home," Dan said.

"No problem."

"Of course, we wanted to drive down right after the accident, but Eric wouldn't hear of it. Didn't want his mother and Jen to see him in the hospital."

Sam nodded and took a step closer to the handcrafted brick barbecue. "He looked pretty bad right after."

"Not looking real sharp yet," Dan said, sliding his younger son a concerned glance.

"Bruises fade, bones heal." Sam saw the worry in the man's eyes and understood it. Just as he understood Eric's need to keep from having people watch over him every minute. God knew, he'd experienced the same thing himself two years ago and it hadn't been pleasant.

Basically, when you felt like garbage, you just wanted to be left alone to deal with it. The last thing you needed was a group of people continually asking if you were all right. And, as a doctor, he'd been able to assure the Wrights that Eric was going to be fine. Which had kept them at a distance and given Eric a chance to heal.

"I know," Dan said, his big, work-roughened hands stacking charcoal briquettes with as light a touch as a pickpocket. "But it's never easy worrying about someone you love."

"He's fine."

Dan shot him a quick look, studied his face for a second or two, then nodded, the anxiousness in his gaze softening. "I'll take your word for it, then. And thanks."

"You're welcome." Sam pulled in a deep breath and let it slide slowly from his lungs.

"Family gatherings not your kind of party, huh?"

"I'm sorry?" Sam watched the man finish off the black pyramid of coals.

"You just seemed a little skittish earlier is all. Guess we're a bit overwhelming at first."

"I don't—"

"Not saying I blame you any," Dan said, interrupting before Sam could apologize for letting his own discomfort show. "Just said I noticed."

"I didn't mean for you to." He stared down at the beer in his hand, studying the brown bottle as if looking for just the right thing to say. Frowning again, he realized that his "poker face" was sadly lacking. Not only could Tricia read him like a book, but it seemed the rest of her family could, as well. And that told him it really had been too long since he'd spent time with people. He'd forgotten how to relax. Forgotten what it was like to stand in the sunlight and simply enjoy being alive.

The realization hit him hard. He hadn't meant to become a hermit. Hadn't intended to become the odd man out. But somehow, without him even noticing, it had happened.

Dan slapped Sam's shoulder with one beefy hand, leaving five black streaks against his green shirt. "Don't you worry," the man said. "You're getting used to us. You've eased up a lot, seem to be less on edge. Tricia'll help you through the rough spots."

Before Sam could ask what he meant by that, Dan had already turned, letting his gaze drift across the crowd dotting the lawn. Finally, he spotted who he was looking for and smiled. "Tommy!"

Sam watched the kid skid to a stop on the grass and turn to look.

"It's time, boy. Get on over here if you want to be in charge again!"

Instantly, the boy's eyes lit up and his gap-toothed grin widened in expectation.

"What's going on?" Sam asked as he watched the kid hurtle across the grass toward the barbecue.

"Oh, just our little tradition," Dan said, taking out a long-handled match from its box. "Tommy likes to be the one to start the barbecue fire." When the child stopped alongside him, Dan ruffled his hair until it stood on end. "Our little chef, aren't you kiddo?"

"You bet, Uncle Dan," Tommy said and carefully, under the watchful gaze of Tricia's father, struck the matchhead and threw it atop the charcoal pyre.

As the flames leaped, everyone applauded and Tommy beamed proudly over a job well done. Then, in seconds, he was running back to join his cousins and the dog in their continuing race around the yard.

A budding arsonist.

Right.

Sam felt like an idiot.

He'd been keeping an eye on the boy, expecting him to set the house on fire.

Shifting his gaze to where the three women sat beneath the shade tree, Sam ignored two of them and concentrated—as he had most of the day—on Tricia. She must have sensed his gaze because she turned her head to look at him.

Their gazes collided and Sam felt the power of

that collision slam into him. Embarrassment and irritation faded. It was as if they were all alone, just the two of them, linked by an invisible thread that stretched the length of the lawn and hummed with something almost electric in its power and strength.

Sam shook his head as if to clear it of the wild thoughts crowding his brain. He didn't need this, he thought, even while silently acknowledging that there didn't seem to be anything he could do about it.

Five

Sam watched Tricia walk into her house ahead of him and told himself to avert his gaze from the curve of her behind. Not an easy task. She wore a bright yellow tank top and dark green shorts that made her legs look even longer than they were. Her blond hair, freed from the braid she'd worn earlier, lay in a fall of rippled waves that looked like spilled honey and made his hands itch to touch.

Man, he'd been in the sun too long.

Getting a grip on both his hormones and his thoughts, he scraped one hand across his face and said, "An arsonist, huh?"

He hadn't had a minute alone with her to talk about little Tommy and how she'd set him up. Now that they were back at her house, with no audience listening in, he wanted a few answers.

Tricia half turned to look at him and gave him a broad grin and a wink. Then she lifted both hands into a *what do you want me to say?* shrug of innocence as she continued on into the house.

Sam followed. She'd lied to him about the kid. Worked him. All to get him to stay in her house.

He had to wonder why.

"If you could have seen your face," Tricia said with a laugh as she dropped onto one of the overstuffed chairs in her living room. "When Dad handed Tommy the match, I thought your eyes were going to bug out."

"Yeah, bet it was funny," he said and took a seat in the chair opposite her. He crossed his right foot on his left knee, drummed his fingers against the soft, faded upholstery and watched her.

Her eyes were dancing and her grin couldn't have been any bigger. She'd been chuckling since they left her parents' place for the short walk back to her house. And instead of resenting it, Sam had found himself enjoying the sound. But she didn't need to know that. His scowl deepened and she made a melodramatic attempt to sober up. She screwed her mouth into a razor-straight line and clapped one hand across her lips for good measure.

That lasted about ten seconds.

When her laughter erupted again, Sam shook his

head at her, gave up and reluctantly smiled himself. "So what was the point of all that? Making me think the kid's a firebug?"

"Fun?"

"Oh, yeah." He uncrossed his legs and stretched them out in front of him, alongside the wide, oak coffee table. "Me watching the boy all day, half expecting him to whip out a lighter and torch the yard." He nodded. "A laugh riot."

Tricia sighed and her grin faded into a soft smile. "I'm sorry. Seriously. But you do have to admit it was funny. I mean, did you really think we were harboring a psycho child?"

"Why'd you do it?" he asked, really curious. He'd forgotten about being angry that she'd lied to him and now just wanted a few answers. "Why'd you trick me into staying here?"

She studied him for a quiet minute. Her fingers smoothed the arm of the chair with long, sensuous strokes that caught his attention and held it. He shifted a little in the chair, trying not to think about those fingers caressing his skin, sliding along his body.

He scowled to himself at the wayward notion. He hadn't felt anything like this in years. It was as if his body were waking up from a deep sleep, and the first stirrings felt damn near painful. His jaw clenched and his fingers curled tight over the arms of the chair.

Outside, the afternoon sun slanted across the yard, stretching shadows as twilight crept closer. From down the block came the sounds of kids playing ball and, just across the street, someone was mowing a lawn. Just another day in suburbia.

"Okay," she said, squirming around in her chair until her legs were curled up under her and she looked like a contented cat. "Maybe I did color the truth a little."

"A little?"

She shrugged. "A lot."

"Why?" The light in the room was dimming, shrinking around them like a dying spotlight on a silent stage. In the shadows, her features looked as if they'd been sculpted from fine porcelain. A half-smile lingered on her mouth, and the slight curve of her lips was tempting. Especially to a man who'd been as good as dead and buried for two years.

"I don't know," she said finally, trying to answer his question. Her gaze met his. She stared at him for what felt like hours but couldn't have been more than seconds. He tried to figure out what she was thinking, but the workings of Tricia's mind were as much a mystery to him as ever.

Her eyes were a deep, vivid blue. Bluer than a lake, darker than the ocean. There was something compelling in her gaze. Something that caught him, held him, and Sam knew he was sliding into dangerous territory—but for the life of him, he couldn't look away.

"It's just," she said, continuing in a silky, thready voice that was almost lost in the drone of the power mower outside, "maybe I have a soft spot for crabby people."

"I'm not crabby—"

Her eyebrows arched.

"—usually," he amended, even though he knew it to be a lie. He'd had less patience with everything the last two years and hadn't even made an effort to change. Until he arrived in Sunrise Beach. And whatever change was happening inside him now had nothing to do with him and everything to do with the people around him. They simply wouldn't allow him to retreat into the shadows. Especially Tricia. She had a way of looking at him, of smiling at him that *demanded* a response.

"Look, it's no big deal," Tricia said, unfolding her legs and scooting to the edge of her chair. She leaned toward him across the magazine-littered tabletop. "You seemed nice…"

One corner of his mouth lifted at that pitiful attempt to hedge. "Thought I seemed crabby."

She fought a smile. "In a nice way."

"Gee, thanks." Sam straightened up in his chair and leaned toward her, mirroring her position.

Tricia looked into his eyes. "I love Nora, but two women sharing *one* bathroom? Not pretty."

"That bad, huh?" She still wasn't telling him the truth, but he was beginning to care less about that. All he really wanted at the moment was to keep looking at her.

"Oh, terrible," she assured him, her fabulous mouth curving again. "So terrible, I figured a nice, crabby, doctor hero-type person would be way easier to handle for two little weeks."

He tore his gaze from her mouth to look into her eyes again. "And how's that working out for you?"

"So far," she said quietly as the shadows in the room deepened, "not bad. Not bad at all. You?"

He thought about it for a minute. He could have been in a quiet, sterile hotel room. He could have been alone, watching TV, eating a boring meal delivered by an indifferent room service attendant. Right about now, he'd be pacing that small, square room and listening to the sound of his own heartbeat.

It was what he was used to.

No more than he expected.

And for the first time in a long time, he was glad things were different.

Tricia was still watching him, waiting for an answer. His half-smile felt a little rusty…but good.

"Not bad," he said. "Not bad at all."

A few days later, Sam was more tired than he'd been since his residency. There was something happening every day. Some new wedding task to be completed, some chore to be done. The influx of Wright family members had slowed to a trickle and Sam was actually reaching the point where he could identify most of them by name.

Rarely alone, Sam had become a member of the family team that met in the "war room" of the elder Wrights' kitchen every day. He wasn't sure exactly when it had happened, but somehow he'd been adopted into the family when he wasn't looking.

What was more surprising, he didn't mind a bit.

They were all still loud and overwhelming to the inexperienced, but he'd found something with these people that he'd never really known before. A sense of solidarity. Strength in numbers. And a feeling of loyalty that was so thick, so rich, it connected every family member to the next, like they were links in a solid chain—where every person was an individual, and yet an integral part of the whole.

He steered his car into Tricia's driveway and then put it in park, set the brake and turned off the engine. After a day spent helping to paint the gazebo where Eric and Jen would be married, Sam was looking forward to a little down time.

Funny, but life had slipped into a routine of sorts, and Sam appreciated it even while recognizing just how different this new routine was from his everyday world.

At home, his mornings were hurried. A quick cup of coffee, then jump into the car and head to work. Every night, he'd reverse directions on the freeway, head back to the condo and a solitary dinner, go to sleep and repeat the whole thing the next day.

Here, things were different. Morning was a leisurely time, when he and Tricia would sit at her kitchen table just before dawn and talk about what was on that day's schedule. The evenings were just as different. After that first night in her house, Sam'd given up trying to hide in his room, looking for the solitude that had been so important to him for so long. Tricia had insisted that since he was a guest, the least he could do was talk to her. She was a force of nature. She couldn't be ignored and wouldn't be denied.

Now his nights were spent here, at Tricia's house, watching old movies, listening to music or just talking.

Or rather, Sam thought, smiling, as he climbed out of his car and headed for her house, *Tricia* would talk, he would listen. The woman could talk for hours on any subject and never get tired. He shook his head as he realized just how well he'd gotten to know her in the last few days. She had opinions on everything and didn't hesitate to share them. He'd heard about her siblings, her parents, her old high school and her plans for her business.

She made him think, made him laugh...made him *feel*.

He stopped short of the front porch, stuffed his hands in his jeans pockets and stared at the pale light shining behind the living room curtains. She'd be inside, either baking more cookies or wrapping ones she'd already decorated. The kitchen table would be piled high with her labors and the air would smell of cinnamon and that other spice he still hadn't been able to recognize.

He'd walk through the house, step into the kitchen and she'd look up, meet his gaze and smile. In his mind's eye, he saw her amazing mouth curve into a welcome that had just recently become way too important to him. A warm knot of anticipation settled in his chest.

And he felt guilty as hell.

Pulling his hands free of his pockets, Sam reached up and pushed his fingers roughly through his hair. Then, just as harshly, he let his hands fall to his sides again. This small house with the tiny bathroom and the scent of perpetual baking had become…familiar. Cozy. Comforting. And he wasn't sure what to do about it.

He shouldn't even be here.

Shouldn't be enjoying himself.

Shouldn't be *eager* to see Tricia.

"Too late to stop now," he muttered thickly, nearly choking on the guilt that rushed through his body like high tide reclaiming the shore.

Even now, he felt his blood pump a little faster, his heart beat a little harder, knowing that Tricia was just inside. He hadn't felt this sort of…expectation in too many years to count.

Had *never* expected to feel it again.

He'd had his shot at happiness. With Mary.

And then he'd lost her. Regret crawled through him. In a heartbeat—everything changed forever.

Sam shook his head. "Too many ifs." Too many

lost chances and too many nights spent poring over what he had and hadn't done. And nothing ever changed.

Mary was still gone.

And he couldn't claim a life for himself, when he hadn't been able to save hers.

This time with the Wrights, with Tricia, was just temporary. A blip in his ordinary world. He should remember that. Remember that when the two weeks were up, he'd be headed back to L.A. Back to where memories of Mary still lived.

Back where he belonged.

"Is that you, Sam?"

"Yeah," he called as he walked through the quiet house, "it's me."

"I'm out ba-ack," she shouted in response, making that one-syllable word into at least two, and almost three.

He followed her voice, moving through the kitchen, slowing for a glance at the mountain of cookies displayed on the table. She'd been even busier than usual. Today's offerings were already wrapped in cellophane and tied with pale lavender ribbons. Sam picked one up and studied it. The cookie was in the shape of a bridal bouquet and the flowers were all outlined with bright piped icing. Looks too good to eat, he thought, as he set the cookie back with the others and headed for the back door.

Through the screen he saw her, sitting on the top step of the back porch. There was a plate of broken, frosted cookies beside her and a half-empty blender of something slushy. Opening the door, he stepped outside and looked down at her.

She leaned her head back, letting her golden hair spill down over her shoulders and hang in a swaying curtain of honey. She grinned up at him. "Hi. Want a margarita?"

Sam's lips twitched. Sounded to him like she'd already had several, but apparently she wasn't counting.

"Brought out a glass for you, too," she said and straightened her head so quickly, she gasped. "Whoa. Head rush."

"You okay?" he asked as he took a seat beside her. Only the tray of cookies lay between them as she handed him a now-full margarita glass.

"Oh, I'm great," she said and took a sip of her own drink before reaching for a cookie and taking a bite. "Have a cookie."

"Cookies and margaritas?"

"Cookies go with everything," Tricia said. "Trust me. I'm the Cookie Lady."

"That's right," he said, picking up one of the broken cookies and taking a bite. "Forgot I was dealing with a professional."

Tricia took another sip of her drink.

"How long have you been out here?" Sam asked, studying her profile in the wash of lamplight pouring out of the kitchen behind them. "And how many of those have you had?"

"'Bout an hour," she said softly, stretching her legs out down the steps. "Only a couple of drinks. Don't worry, you won't be dealing with a sloppy drunk."

"Good to know."

"Thought you might appreciate it."

"Any particular reason why you're sitting on the back porch drinking?"

"Do we really *need* a reason for margaritas?"

"I guess not," he said, though he did believe the frothy concoction was helping to wash the bitter taste of guilt from his throat.

"Have you ever been in love?" she demanded suddenly, turning to face him squarely. "I mean seriously, deeply in love?"

That guilt was back in a flash, slamming into his head and his heart with the force of a jackhammer. Mary's features flashed across his mind and it stunned him to realize that her image was hazy, indistinct, as though he were staring at her through a thick fog. His chest tightened as he said simply, "Yes."

"You have?" Tricia looked at him with questions gathering in her eyes and he hoped to hell she wouldn't ask them.

A moment or two ticked past before she said, "At least you've had that. I haven't. I mean, I'm twenty-eight years old and I've never seen fireworks."

Confusion grappled with relief that she hadn't asked for more information. "What?"

"You know," she prodded, "those metaphorical fireworks."

He nodded, lost.

She shook her head. "After sex? When it's all roses and puppies and bells are ringing…"

"Ah…" Sam smiled to himself, then listened up, since he'd already learned that it took all of a man's concentration to keep up with Tricia's racing train of thought.

"I've never seen 'em. Or felt 'em. Or even heard 'em, for that matter." She waved her margarita glass for emphasis and some of the frozen green liquid sloshed over the rim. "Oops." She pulled the glass close and licked up the spillage.

Sam's guts twisted as he watched her tongue slide along the edge of the glass and then across the back of her hand. A hunger ripped through him with an intensity that startled the hell out of him.

"I mean, my folks think I'm broken-hearted," she continued, oblivious to the havoc she was creating. "My sister tells me I'm too picky and my brothers want to interrogate the *next* guy I date—" She stopped and waved her glass at him again. More carefully this time. "—and that's not going to happen, because like I told you, the only relationship I'm interested in is me and sugar."

"So what's the problem?" he asked.

She sighed, tipped her head back and stared at the brilliant spread of stars across the sky. While she watched the heavens, Sam watched *her*. Her blond hair lay against her back and swung gently with every movement of her head. It was nearly hypnotic. And when her voice came again, she spoke so softly, she didn't break the spell that held him.

"The problem is," she said wistfully, "as great as sugar is," she blew out a breath, "I don't think I'll be finding the fireworks there, either."

Hell, there were a few sparklers dazzling in the air between them now, Sam thought, though he didn't dare mention it.

"And you're worried about this tonight because…"

"Not worried." She turned her head to look at him. "Just thinking," she admitted. "I was over at my folks' and they started walking really gently around me about Daly, my last boyfriend."

"Yeah?" He didn't want to think about her last boyfriend. And how strange was that?

"For some reason, they think I'm heartbroken. But I'm not and I think that's just so sad."

"That you're *not* heartbroken?" He was confused again, but that was no surprise.

"Exactly. I mean I obviously didn't love him…I don't even miss him," she said. "So, what if for some weird reason, Daly had proposed or something? God, what if I'd said *yes*?" She set her glass down beside her, then practically leaped off the porch, taking the steps down to the grass in a couple quick strides. A few more steps and she was in darkness, and he could only hear her. "I mean, I might have. You never know."

Sam set his own drink aside, stood up and followed her into the yard. She was walking the perimeter of her lot, wandering through the moonlight with a steady step that told him she hadn't had nearly as many margaritas as he'd first thought.

"But you wouldn't have said yes," he said.

"How do you know?" She whirled around and looked at him and suddenly there were only a couple of feet separating them. Her eyes looked huge and luminous in the moonlight. Her skin was pale and her lips, usually curved in a smile, or the promise of one, were straight now, and trembling.

"Because you didn't love him. You just said so."

"But I might have convinced myself I did. Is a person supposed to wait around forever...waiting for the fireworks? Or do you just settle for the flaring match when it comes along?"

She took a step closer and her perfume reached out for him.

Sam knew he should back up. Knew he should head into the house *now*. Hell, the *house*? What he ought to do was hop into his car, hit the freeway and punch it until he made it back to L.A. Back to where he knew how to act and what to do. Back to where Tricia Wright wasn't within arm's reach.

But he wasn't leaving.

Wouldn't even if he could have.

The moonlight, her perfume, and the warm summer air combined to fill him with wants and needs that were nearly strangling him.

"You should wait," he said, and heard the rough scrape of his own voice, "for the fireworks."

"Yeah?" She swallowed hard and took another step closer. "Want to help me look for them?"

Six

Sam reached for her.

She moved closer.

In the next instant, she was in his arms, pressed tightly to him, and Sam's whole body lit up like a neon sign in Vegas. Every cell came alive. Blood rushed in his veins, his head pounded and his heartbeat thundered in his ears like the roar of dozens of hungry lions.

She looked up at him and, not for the first time, Sam wondered what she was thinking, feeling. But an instant later, she went up on her toes and brushed her mouth against his. Sam pulled her tightly to him, wrapping his arms around her and holding on with every ounce of his strength. Her lips parted for him and he claimed her mouth with a fierceness he hadn't known he possessed. She sighed and he swallowed her breath, taking all of her into him. His tongue tangled with hers in a wild dance of need.

She clung to him, her fingers digging into his shoulders until he could have sworn he felt the heat of her touch branding his skin right through the fabric of his shirt. And it wasn't enough. Wasn't nearly enough.

He wanted all of her. Wanted to feel her smooth, soft skin beneath his palms, hear her sighs, watch her eyes glaze over as he slid his body into hers.

God, he wanted to feel this rush of sensation grow until it overtook him.

He wanted her more than his next breath.

Tearing his mouth from hers, Sam dipped his head and kissed her neck, running the tip of his tongue along her flesh while she shivered and whispered his name.

That broken hush of sound sent new ribbons of heat snaking through him until he felt as though the flames would simply engulf him. And still it wasn't enough.

"Tricia," he murmured, his breath dusting her skin. She tipped her head to one side, to give him easier access, and then leaned into him completely, silently offering him everything that had suddenly become so desperately necessary.

"Sam," she said quietly, "I see 'em."

"Hmm…?" Taste her, his brain screamed. Touch her. *Take* her.

"The fireworks," she whispered, and the dazed wonder in her voice caught him, held him in a grip that squeezed the air from his lungs. "They're there," she continued, her voice filled with a raw wonder, "just waiting for me. Show me, Sam. Show them to me."

He lifted his head and stared down at her through eyes hazy with passion. His breath shuddered in his lungs and an inner battle raged between what he *should* do and what he so *wanted* to do.

Sam shook his head, reached up and disentangled her arms from around his neck. His hands slid down their length until he was holding her hands in his. His thumbs stroked her palms, torturing them both…yet, he couldn't quite bring himself to let her go all at once.

"I can't."

"What?" Dazed herself, Tricia shook her head. She squeezed his hands and asked, "Why not, for heaven's sake?"

"Because I'm not the one you've been waiting for, Tricia."

She laughed shortly and looked away from him briefly. Then she dropped his hands and took a shaky step back. "I didn't *propose,* Sam."

"I know that," he said, feeling completely unprepared for the task of explaining what he was feeling—why he was turning down what any red-blooded man in his right mind would make a greedy grab at. He shoved one hand through his hair, then viciously rubbed the back of his neck. "It's just not that simple."

Her lips trembled, then firmed up again. Her features tightened as she wrapped her arms around herself and hung on. "Fine. But you can't stand there and tell me you don't want me, because I won't buy it. I *felt* just how much you *do* want me."

His back teeth ground together. Of course she'd felt his arousal. Hell, he'd held her close enough that she should, by all rights, be carrying an imprint of his body on her skin. "Has nothing to do with it," he muttered and turned, heading for the house.

He didn't think of it as running, he thought of it more as a strategic retreat. At top speed.

But Sam should have known that Tricia wasn't a woman who gave up easily. She was right behind him. He moved through the kitchen like a man on a mission. His steps were fast, but sure. He was doing the right thing.

Tricia deserved better than getting involved with him. She deserved a man who was *whole*. A man who was looking for the same things she wanted. A man who could *love* her. That wasn't him.

He hit the stairs at a fast walk and heard her bare feet on the creaky treads just behind him. At the top of the stairs, he gave it up, spun around and stopped dead. She slammed right into him and he grabbed her upper arms to keep her from tumbling back down the stairs.

She took advantage of the move by wrapping her arms around his neck again and clinging like a limpet. Her eyes were clear and deep, and the tiniest of smiles curved her amazing mouth.

"Tricia…"

"Sam…" The smile deepened just enough to make him want to see more. To see the small dimple that hid at the right corner of her mouth unless she was laughing full out.

He reached up for her arms again, determined to be strong despite the fact that every inch of his body was screaming at him to hold onto her.

"I want to know why you're so determined to stay away from me," she said with a slight shake of her head. Her hair swung gently in a soft wave of scent and color.

Sam pulled in a tight breath that barely filled his lungs. He couldn't risk inhaling that scent of hers. Right now, it would be enough to push him over the slippery edge of control.

"This shouldn't happen."

She sobered and looked him dead in the eye, as if she could read his thoughts by looking deep enough. And who knew? Maybe she could.

"Are you married?" she asked.

"No." *Not anymore.*

"Engaged?"

"No," he blurted, "but that's not the point."

"It's the *only* point," Tricia said and moved in even closer to him, pressing her body along his. "Sam, we're two adults. Neither one of us is committed to anyone else. We want each other…don't we?"

Since she could no doubt *feel* once again just how much he wanted her, it would have been pointless to try to deny it.

"You deserve better than a one-night-stand," he said tightly. "And that's all I can offer you."

"Maybe one night's all I need," she said, and he wished he could read *her* mind. What was going on in that head of hers? Did she think that maybe this, whatever it was between them, would turn into something bigger? Something permanent?

Because if she did, then he was lining up to be the next guy to hurt her. He didn't want to, damn it. He *liked* Tricia. But he wasn't the man she wanted—or needed.

"Stop thinking," Tricia urged and skimmed her fingertips down the side of his face, temple to jawline. Her touch electrified him. Damned if he couldn't actually *feel* his blood boil, hear his own breath quicken.

"Tricia—"

"Just feel, Sam," she said and went up on her toes again. Tipping her head to one side, she brushed her mouth over his. Once, and he held perfectly still. Twice, his heart crashed against his ribs. Three times, and he knew he was lost.

Surrendering to the inevitable, Sam grabbed her hard, using his arms to pin her to him. His hands slid up and down her back, possessively exploring every line, every curve. He had to feel her. Now.

His mouth took hers in a kiss designed to sweep them both over the edge of reason. His tongue stroked hers in a wild imitation of what he needed to do to her, *with* her.

She groaned and he tensed.

She leaned into him and he took more of her weight, lifting her off her feet. Tricia moaned and went with him, lifting her legs to lock them around his waist, and suddenly, she was all around him, surrounding him with sensation and a pulse-pounding desire he'd never known before. *Ever.*

This was different.

This was *more* than anything he'd ever experienced.

And as that thought flashed through his mind, he set it resolutely aside.

Sam shoved both hands beneath the hem of her tank top and luxuriated in the silkiness of her skin. Smooth, so soft and warm.

She writhed against him, burrowing closer, tighter, keeping her mouth fused with his, giving as much as she took. Sliding her hands to his face, she cupped his cheeks in her palms and pulled her head back long enough to look at him through dazzled eyes.

"Bedroom. Now."

"Right there with you," he muttered, and headed for her room. There were only four doors off the small hallway. His room, the bathroom, a tiny linen closet and Tricia's bedroom. He grabbed the doorknob, gave it a twist, then shoved the door wide.

The walls were blue. Almost as blue as her eyes. And that's all he noticed as he walked into the room he somehow knew they'd been headed for since the first time he saw her. From the moment she'd plopped down into the front seat of his car and started irritating him.

The first time she'd smiled at him.

He headed for the big bed shoved against the wall in the center of the room. Another flowered quilt lay across the wide mattress and he didn't even bother to try to pull it down. Instead, he sat down, leaned back and pulled her down on top of him.

Tricia stared down at him and he read his own hunger mirrored in her eyes. Moonlight slanted through the open curtains hanging in front of the window that faced the backyard. Its pale light suffused the room with a soft glow that seemed to shimmer all around her as she levered herself up into a sitting position.

Sam's breath caught in his throat as she straddled him. But she damn near killed him when she grabbed the hem of her tank top and slowly pulled it up and over her head. Her bare breasts were full, nipples peaked and rigid, and he could practically taste them already. All the air left him in a rush and he quickly sucked in another greedy breath. "Tricia…"

She smiled, slow and lazy, eyes glinting with a

feminine pride and confidence that slammed into him. She knew exactly what effect she was having on him and she was enjoying it.

He reached up and tweaked her nipples between his thumbs and forefingers. She groaned and rocked into his touch. Lifting both hands, she covered his, holding his palms to her breasts for one long moment.

Then she whispered on a sigh, "Now you." Reaching down, she grabbed fistfuls of his shirt and tugged the hem free of the waistband of his jeans. Suddenly hungry to feel flesh against flesh, Sam shifted slightly to help her yank his shirt up and off.

She ran the flat of her palms over his chest, sculpting him, defining every muscle, and his body lit up like a flashing neon sign. Everything in him tightened expectantly. Damn it, if he didn't have her, he just might die.

She was so unexpected.

So fascinating.

So damn…*necessary*.

"You amaze me," he said, staring up into the eyes that had captivated him from the start. His hands continued to work her breasts, his fingers teasing and toying with her nipples.

"Why?" She sucked in a gulp of air, then gave him that slow, seductive smile again.

"Lots of reasons," he murmured, his gaze sweeping over her, from the tousled blond halo of her hair to the tanned, firm thighs gripping his hips. Beneath her, he felt himself tighten further until he was hard as a rock and aching to bury himself inside her.

He skimmed his hands down her ribcage to her waist, loving the feel of her skin against his palms. She sighed and he let his hands slide across the front of her body, her abdomen and then dusting along the waistband of her shorts. He watched gooseflesh bristle along her skin and smiled to himself, knowing that he was affecting her every bit as much as she was him.

"Amazing," he repeated, deftly undoing the top button of her shorts.

She sucked in a breath of air, held it for a long moment, then let it slide from her lungs on a sigh. "You're pretty amazing yourself," she said, her voice just a tightly stretched thread.

Sam smiled to himself even as his body screamed beneath her. She squirmed, rubbing her bottom against him until he felt beads of sweat break out on his forehead and jagged spears of need slice through his body. He groaned, and she smiled, tossed her hair back in a wild cloud of blond and began to rock her hips atop him as though she were a bareback rider at a rodeo.

And damned if Sam didn't feel like a bucking bronco. He wanted to plunge into her, drive himself home and feel her body surround his. He wanted to be so deep inside her heat that some of her warmth would just naturally seep into him. He wanted to watch her eyes glaze, feel her muscles bunch and hear her sighs as he drove her over the edge of madness.

He had to have that. But first he was going to make sure that Tricia needed it as badly as he did. Patience would have its own rewards...if he didn't explode first.

As she moved atop him, he felt her heat through the fabric of his jeans and knew that he wouldn't be able to wait much longer. She must have sensed his impatience, because she did all she could to feed it.

Moving slowly, she reached for her own breasts and as he watched, she cupped them, then stroked them with long, deliberate caresses. Her fingers toyed with her own nipples and Sam's mouth went dry as his gaze locked on her sensuous movements.

And still, his brain rose up and shouted at him to be fair. To give her the chance to change her mind. To let her know that he wasn't the kind of man she needed. He had to give her the opportunity to leave him aching before he inevitably left *her* broken.

Despite the fact that if he didn't have her in the next few minutes, he was pretty sure his heart would simply explode.

"Tricia..." he said, trying to keep his voice from choking on the desire clamped around his throat.

Her hands dropped to his chest. Then she leaned toward him and laid her fingertips across his mouth. "Don't." Her mouth replaced her fingers and she kissed him, nipping gently at his bottom lip and driving his control to the ragged edge. "If you're about to say we don't have to do this," she whispered—her breath puffing against his mouth, his cheeks, his neck, as she shifted, kissing, licking, nibbling—"then you're oh so wrong."

She pushed herself into a sitting position again and made sure she was perched right over his throbbing erection. She stared directly into his eyes so that he could read the shattering passion in hers. So he would *know* without a doubt, that she was as eager as he.

Thank whatever gods were paying attention.

"I'm glad you think so," he managed to say through gritted teeth.

"Oh, I do," she whispered and ground her body against his. "I definitely do. We *so* need to do this, Sam. Right now."

"I'm convinced."

"Thank heaven."

And with the last of his doubts eased, Sam cleared his mind, banishing all thoughts that weren't directly related to this moment. Until he'd had his fill of the woman currently torturing him.

Which could effectively shut his brain down for years.

In one fluid move, he rolled her over, flipping her onto her back and covering her with the upper half of his body. His hands shifted over her, exploring, discovering, mapping her thoroughly enough that every line and curve of her body would be etched into his mind forever.

"We need to get rid of these," he said, slowly sliding the zipper of her shorts down. She lifted her hips eagerly as he peeled the fabric back, displaying a pair of pale peach lace panties. His heart almost stopped.

Sam bent his head to kiss her flat sun-tanned abdomen, just above the thin elastic strap. She shivered beneath him and sighed his name on a whisper of sound that shook him to the bone and seemed to echo inside him. He smiled against her skin as he moved further and further down her body. He pulled her shorts down her legs, then tossed them to the floor before moving again to the tiny scrap of lace guarding her center. Tan lines, creamy against her warm honey skin, told him that her bathing suit was even tinier than the panties she now wore, and he suddenly hungered to see her in a bikini, kissed by sunlight.

He touched the tip of his tongue to her belly and she jumped, moaning softly as she moved into him. "Sam..."

His name, said on a sigh of desire and passion, sent shock waves pulsing within and he gave himself up to the wonder of this moment. It had been so long, so very long, since he'd felt *anything*. Now, he was swamped with so many overwhelming emotions, he couldn't sort them out. Couldn't even identify them all.

So he quit trying.

He hooked his fingers beneath the edge of the lacy panties and in a heartbeat, he had them down and off of her. She opened her eyes and looked at him. Her tongue swept across her bottom lip and he groaned tightly. In seconds, he yanked off the rest of his own clothes, tossed them to the floor beside hers and then knelt on the mattress in front of her.

"Sam," she called his name again, insistently this time. Holding her arms out for him, she arched up, lifting her shoulders from the bed in an attempt to reach him, to pull him to her.

But Sam had other ideas.

Running his palms up and down the length of her legs, he watched her eyes roll back and her hands drop helplessly to the pale blue sheets. He stroked her slowly, then faster, each time sliding his hands higher up her thighs until his fingertips were only inches from her center. She twisted under his ministrations and tried to maneuver her body so that he would touch her core, her heat, to give her ease from the pulsing demands throbbing within.

Instead he tortured her more thoroughly.

He moved in closer, lifted her legs and rested them across his shoulders. Her eyes widened as she stared up at him. His big hands cupped her bottom, holding her firmly, despite how she twisted in his grasp.

"Sam—"

"Tricia—" he interrupted her quickly. "Shut up."

She licked her lips again, grabbed hold of the sheet with both hands as though preparing to have her world rocked, then said, "Right."

Her flesh warm and soft in his grip, he lifted her body and bent his head to claim her. His mouth covered her heat and his tongue darted out to streak across intimate flesh already sensitized.

She gasped and arched higher into him, rocking her hips helplessly as she lay in his grip.

His fingers kneaded her body as he used his mouth to conquer her. He felt the first tremors building and felt a jolt of pleasure so pure, so sharp, it nearly stole his breath. He knew what he was doing to her. Felt her response quivering inside him. Felt the heat of her, tasted her secrets and gave her more so that he, too, would feel more.

She whimpered and twisted her head from side to side on the bed. Her hands fisted the sheets, scrabbling for purchase. His tongue stroked her center over and over again and when he found the tiny nub of flesh at the very heart of her, he sucked her gently, sending her into a wild, frenzied abandon that rocketed around his insides.

When her climax erupted, he felt the tension in her body as she stiffened in his grasp. She reached up and threaded her fingers in his hair, holding his mouth to her as if half-afraid he would stop and leave her unsatisfied.

But he didn't want to stop. Sam wanted more. He wanted to taste all of her. Explore every inch of her. Claim her body as his and brand her with his touch.

When her body finally stopped trembling and she lay weak and limp in his hands, he eased her back down to the mattress and leaned over her.

"Oh, boy," she whispered, a small smile tugging at one corner of her mouth. "That was…"

"Yeah?" he whispered, slowly kissing his way up her length.

She shook her head. "I'm speechless."

He laughed shortly. "It's a miracle."

Tricia blew out a breath and stroked his hair. "Boy howdy."

"That's just the beginning," he whispered, and paused long enough to take one of her nipples into his mouth.

"Promises, promises," she teased.

He lifted his head and waited for her to meet his gaze. "Do I look like I'm kidding?"

"No," she said brokenly, struggling for air. "You sure don't." Her hands reached for him and he felt the soft scrape of her fingernails against his back, across his shoulders. Heat shot through him like a flash of lightning, and the resulting thunder pounded inside him.

Staring down into her impossibly blue eyes, he saw magic and need and knew his own eyes mirrored hers. "Good," he said. "Just so we're clear."

"Oh, rarin' to go, here."

"Glad to hear it." Sam dipped his head to her breasts again and indulged himself by taking first one nipple and then the other into his mouth.

She groaned.

His lips and tongue and teeth tormented her in a

gentle assault that had her writhing beneath him. She muttered his name on a moan that ripped through him. He sucked her and she arched her body into his, silently demanding more. Her nails scraped down his shoulders, along his arms and back up again to tangle in his hair. She held his head to her breast, then tugged him up, pulling his mouth up to hers. Hungrily, he kissed her, his tongue tangling with hers in a wild dance that fed the need erupting inside.

Now.

One thought rattling through his mind, over and over.

Now.

Sam broke the kiss, lifted his head. "Protection," he muttered thickly, cursing himself for not thinking of it sooner. For not preparing for the eventuality. But he didn't exactly travel with condoms hoping to get lucky. Hell, he hadn't planned on sex.

Hadn't planned on Tricia.

But then, how could he ever have planned on *her*?

"In the drawer," she whispered, her voice a broken shard of sound. "Over there. Bedside table. Move fast, okay?"

There was a pleading in her voice that hit his ego and pumped it higher than a helium balloon floating skyward. Knowing he'd pushed her into a torrent of emotion, of cravings, was almost as heady as hearing her sigh his name.

He shifted to one side, pulled the drawer of the

tiny nightstand table open and fumbled in its depths for a small foil package. He grabbed one, ripped it open and in seconds had sheathed himself and protected both of them.

Going up on her elbows, Tricia smiled at him again and reached down between them. Molding his length with her hand, she squeezed him gently and rubbed his hardness until Sam wanted to cry out in a guttural demand for release.

"I want you in me now," she whispered.

Sam's gaze focused on hers.

"Don't make me wait any longer, Sam," she said, closing her hand around him tightly in an imitation of the close heat he wanted so badly.

"No more waiting." The words came in a low-pitched growl as he moved to tip her flat on her back again. She opened her legs for him, welcoming him within.

As he entered her, he coaxed himself to go slow, to luxuriate, to take the extra moments and enjoy the sweet sensation of sliding into liquid heat. But the need was too much and her welcome too warm.

She lifted her hips, taking him deeper, more fully, until he felt captured by her. She held him inside a tight, hot glove of sensation and it took every ounce of his will to keep from ending it all too soon. He wanted this moment, this night, to last forever. He wanted this…*connection* to remain unbroken.

He rocked into her depths and she met him stroke

for stroke, touch for touch. They shifted into an instinctive rhythm, moving together as if they'd danced this way before.

Hunger raged, passion blossomed. And in the moonlit night, they raced in tandem toward oblivion and together, fell into the magic awaiting them.

Seven

When the madness lifted, Sam groaned and rolled to one side. His body humming, his mind racing, he fought for breath and stared up at the moonlit patterns on the ceiling. Heartbeat thundering in his ears, Sam listened to Tricia's uneven breathing and almost flinched when her leg rubbed against his.

Throwing one arm across his eyes, he blocked out the room, her, what had just happened, and retreated into the darkness. Guilt nibbled at him, gnawed at the edges of his soul and taunted him with the knowledge that he'd forgotten all about Mary in those moments with Tricia.

He winced, squeezing his eyes shut against the

pain and misery arcing through him. How could he have forgotten? Even for a moment?

And how could he *not*?

Hell, he'd never experienced anything like this before. Sex with Mary—more guilt churned inside and took a shark-sized bite out of him—was, he had to admit to himself, less exciting. Their lovemaking had been quiet. Tender. Loving.

With Tricia, he'd found hunger and passion and a need so all-consuming, his whole body ached with it anew, despite the climax still rippling through his bloodstream. Mary had been quiet fires. Tricia was explosions.

And he was surely damned for lying in one woman's bed thinking about another.

"Wow."

Naturally, Tricia wouldn't be able to be silent for long. If there was one thing he'd learned about this woman over the last several days, it was that she, like nature, abhorred a vacuum. Silence was merely the pause between conversations. The beat before the noise began. The buildup to takeoff.

Turning his head on the pillow, he lowered his arm and looked at her, not surprised at all to find her staring at him.

"That was…" She blew out a breath that ruffled her blond hair. "Wow."

He fought against the rising tide of want already reaching up to choke him again. Her lips were puffy and red from his kisses. Her hair lay like a blond halo around her head as she lay flat on her back, arms and legs splayed, as though she'd dropped from exhaustion and had no intention of moving.

Sam smiled to himself. With Tricia there was no coy grabbing of the sheet to clutch to her breasts. Another jab of guilt poked at him for yet another unfair comparison to Mary. His late wife had been shy, even when they were alone together. And, Sam recalled, he'd loved that about her even while at times wishing she'd been more open, more free to explore a deeper, richer sex life.

"You're thinking."

He stopped thinking immediately. "What?"

"I said, you're thinking," Tricia repeated. "Thinking is not allowed during sex."

"Sex is finished."

"That's what you think." She rolled to her side and reached one hand out to him. Her fingertips skimmed along his chest, trailing across his flesh, starting tiny fires just beneath his skin. Sam sucked in a quick gulp of air and grabbed her hand, holding it tightly in his.

Tricia went up on one elbow and looked down at him. Her eyes looked even bluer than usual and glittered with confusion and something else he didn't even attempt to identify.

"Okay," she said, her voice coming as soft as the moonlight shining in the room, "not exactly the response I was expecting."

"Tricia..."

Her fingers curled around his, turning his attempt to put distance between them into an intimate act, linking them together.

"Sam," she said, meeting his gaze and holding it, "what's going on? One minute you're here with me and everything's terrific and the next—"

Sam gritted his back teeth and stared up at her. He felt like an idiot. Like a cheating husband in a cheap motel. And even he knew that was ridiculous.

Untangling his hand from hers, he pulled away, swung his legs off the bed and stood up. Walking naked to the window overlooking the backyard, he stared down at the place where this had all begun and wondered why he hadn't tried harder to stop it. But then, if he had, he would never have had this time with Tricia. And even as terrible as he was feeling now, he wouldn't want to have missed it.

Bracing one hand on the wall, he kept his gaze on the shifting shadows outside as he said, "It's nothing to do with you, Tricia."

"Funny. It feels like it does."

He risked a quick glance at her over his shoulder. She was sitting up on the bed, the rumpled quilt and sheets a puddle around her. Moonlight played over her skin and danced in her eyes. She shoved one hand through her hair, pushing the thick blond mass back from her face before letting it fall again.

Turning from the window, he walked toward the

bed—toward her—and stopped just short of being close enough to reach for her. "It's me."

"Ah," she said, with a slow nod. "The old 'it's not you, it's me' routine." She went up on her knees. "Can't you do better than that?"

"What?"

Apparently unable to sit still, she scooted off the edge of the bed, stood up and faced him. The top of her head just hit his chin, but the fire in her eyes made her look ten feet tall.

"I told you, I wasn't proposing, Sam. This was sex. Great sex, but sex." She waved one hand at the bed behind her. "We're not betrothed or anything so you can relax and quit mentally racing away in your getaway car."

He stared at her for a long minute. Couldn't really blame her for taking all of this the wrong way. Reaching up, he scrubbed his palms over his face, then folded his arms across his chest. Defensive. He knew that. Couldn't seem to help it, though.

Sam pulled in a deep breath and mentally searched for the right words. When they didn't come, he settled for anything that happened to fall out of his mouth. Meeting her eyes, he blurted, "Look. Believe it or not, it really *is* me. It's the first time—"

She laughed. Shortly, sharply. Stalking past him, Tricia snatched a T-shirt off a chair near the window and yanked it over her head. The neck of the shirt wasn't even all the way down when she started talking again, her voice muffled against the fabric. "A *virgin*? You're trying to tell me I seduced a *virgin*?" She shoved her arms through the sleeves and laughed again. "If that's the case, then I hope you don't mind me saying you're an exceptionally gifted newbie."

Shaking his head, he muttered, "I'm not saying that, I'm—"

"What exactly are you trying to say, then, Sam?" She plopped both hands on her hips and tapped the bare toes of one foot against the braided rug on the floor.

Still naked, he felt decidedly at a disadvantage. If they were going to go to war, then he at least wanted some pants on. Walking around the end of the bed, he found his pants lying just where he'd tossed them. Grabbing them up, he pulled them on and didn't speak again until he had the buttons on his jeans done up.

"It's the first time I've been with anyone since my wife died." He'd half expected to choke on the words "wife" and "died." But he hadn't. They'd come out easily. And what the hell did that mean?

"Your *wife*?"

The stunned surprise in her eyes was clear, even from across the room. He nodded. "Mary."

"Mary." She repeated the name slowly, almost as if it were in a foreign language.

"Yeah."

"And she died."

"Two years ago." Yesterday. A lifetime.

Tricia pushed her hair back, smoothed her T-shirt, then folded her hands at her waist before unlocking her fingers and letting her hands hang at her sides again. "You should have told me."

"Yeah, I know."

"Well," she snapped. "As long as you know."

"Tricia—"

"No." She shook her head and pointed a finger at him. "Sam, I told you all about the losers I've dated. About how my family thinks I'm a bum-magnet. About how I've given up on men and taken up with sugar—"

"Until tonight," he pointed out.

"Okay, until tonight. Granted," she said, nodding fiercely, "as good as sugar is, it can't do for me what you just did."

"Thanks, and same to you."

A tight smile touched her lips briefly then disappeared. "Okay. We agree the sex was great. Now we just have to get past the whole why-didn't-you-tell-me-you-were-married-and-that-she-died?"

"I don't know."

"Gee, good answer."

"The only one I've got." Which was stupid, he admitted. Of course he should have told her about Mary. Should have told her when she'd asked him if he'd ever been in love. But he hadn't wanted to talk about it. Hadn't wanted to be on the receiving end of more sympathy or understanding.

Mission accomplished.

"I'm not saying it would have changed my mind about..." She nodded toward the bed. "But you should have told me—"

"Probably."

"Can't believe Eric didn't tell me," she muttered, starting her meandering again. "My brother usually has much looser lips."

Sam sat down on the foot of the bed and watched her as she walked. Her long legs looked silky, smooth, and he had reason to know just how smooth they were. Just a few minutes ago, those leanly muscled legs had been locked around his hips, holding him to her.

His body tightened and his heartbeat skipped unsteadily. Damn it, he wanted to be back inside her. Wanted to feel her warmth surrounding him again.

"I should have told you," he admitted and she stopped dead to look at him. He really wished he could tell what she was thinking. "But I hadn't planned on us ending up in bed together."

"I did."

He blinked. "What?"

"I planned it." She lifted both hands and let them drop to her sides. Shrugging, she walked to the end of the bed and dropped down beside him. She rocked her shoulder against him briefly and admitted on a sigh, "I've been thinking about doing this for the last few days. Figured hey, maybe he's crabby because he's single." Before he could open his mouth, Tricia lifted one hand and said, "No, I wasn't planning on a quote 'relationship.' I just figured, you were single, I'm single, why shouldn't we be single as a couple?"

"Be single as a couple?" Sam shook his head as if the action could make sense of that last sentence. It didn't help. "You deliberately try to confuse me, don't you?"

Tricia sighed, reached around him and draped one arm around his shoulders companionably. "Nope, it's just a gift."

"You're good at it."

"Thanks." Sliding her hand along his back and then down his spine, she let her fingertips blaze a trail that dipped just below the waistband of his jeans. "But my point here is…I don't know that I'd have done this any differently had I known about your wife."

He tensed.

"But it would have been nice of you to tell me."

"Granted."

"Anything else you'd like to confess?"

He snorted. "Now you're a priest?"

She slapped her free hand to her chest and blinked up at him in innocence. "Hey, what's said to the Cookie Lady is kept in strictest confidence."

One corner of his mouth lifted at the same time as the burden of guilt began to trickle off his shoulders. Was it the look in Tricia's eyes that did it? Was it the feel of her hand sliding beneath the fabric of his jeans? Was it the knowledge that for the first time in way too long, Sam wasn't feeling desperately *alone*?

He didn't know.

Cared less.

All he was sure of was that he needed her again. And if that made his eventual departure harder...then he'd just have to deal with that when the time came.

"I do have one confession," he said, squeezing each word past the tight knot in his throat.

Her gaze dropped to his mouth, then up again to his eyes. "Yes..."

"I found more than one condom in your drawer."

"Really?" She smiled and crawled across him to straddle his lap, wrapping her arms around his neck and bringing his mouth just a breath away from hers. "Imagine that."

He skimmed his hands up beneath the hem of her T-shirt and along her warm, soft body until he cupped her breasts in his palms.

She sighed heavily and arched into him.

His body went rock hard and ready.

She squirmed atop him and blew the top of his head off.

"How many did you find?" she asked, scraping her fingernails down his chest to slide across his flat nipples.

He sucked in air through gritted teeth. "Enough to keep us busy for the night."

"Then stop talking, Doc." She brought her mouth to his and whispered, "You're wasting moonlight."

Wrapping his arms around her, Sam fell back onto the mattress and let himself get lost in the glory of Tricia.

The next morning, Sam woke up in Tricia's bed. A spear of sunlight poked through a part in the curtains and jabbed him in the eye. He groaned and slammed an arm across his eyes, taking a minute or two to remember exactly where he was, and why.

Naturally, it all came back in a roaring flood of sound and color. He sat up, avoiding that particular spear of light, and rolled off the bed. A soft breeze drifted through the partially opened window and from outside, he heard a dog barking, kids laughing and in the distance, a growling lawn mower.

Just another day in suburbia.

Except, he told himself as he stalked around the room grabbing up his clothes, *today* was the day after he'd slept with his best friend's sister.

"Correction," he muttered as he left her room and cautiously moved across the narrow hall to the guest room, "you didn't do much sleeping."

He paused at the door to his bedroom and listened to Tricia's off-key singing coming from downstairs. He smiled to himself despite the churning emotions jangling around inside him like wind chimes in a hurricane. The woman couldn't carry a tune with both hands, but it didn't stop her from singing.

Was there a lesson there somewhere? Hell, it was too early to be looking for hidden messages. With his lover's voice still scraping his ears, he grabbed a change of clothes and headed for the shower.

A half-hour later, he was clean, shaved and nursing a knot on top of his head. Her shower had been built for pygmies.

But a headache was the least of his problems, Sam thought as he headed downstairs to face the music. Appropriately enough, an old girl-group was singing a song about begging someone to *rescue me*. He knew just how they felt. He could have used a good rescue about now.

But the plain fact was, no cavalry was on the way. He'd have to face the woman he'd made love to all night and tell her it was going no further. And despite her claims to the contrary, he knew damn well that Tricia Wright was the kind of woman who would expect what they'd shared to lead somewhere.

In a way, she was right about that.

It had led *somewhere*.

Right to a skating rink in hell, and he was about to strap on his skates.

Eight

Tricia'd been busy.

A teetering mountain of cookies lay frosted and wrapped on one end of the kitchen table, and the countertop was lined with even more cookies, cooling on trays.

"Want some coffee?"

He snapped her a look. She hadn't turned around. Her blond hair hung in a cheerful ponytail. Her long, honey-colored legs were bare beneath a pair of denim shorts with a frayed hem and her bright red tank top displayed every inch of her smooth shoulders.

Sam's insides jumped and his hands itched to stroke that satiny skin again.

She glanced back at him and offered a smile. "Coffee's hot. I've been up for hours."

"So I see." He walked into the room and reached into the cupboard for a mug. Her place was familiar now. He felt...at home here. Or he had, until this morning. Today was different. *Everything* had changed. Today, they'd crossed a line and nothing would be the same. They'd shifted into a different...he didn't want to use the word "relationship." But what the hell other word would do the job?

He poured a cup of coffee and inhaled the rich, fragrant steam gratefully. Taking a sip, he nearly groaned when the hot liquid hit his stomach like a gift from God. And he'd need all the help he could get.

"Sleep well?"

He shot her a look from the corner of his eye and caught the faint smile tugging at one corner of her mouth. A like response hovered at the edges of his mind, but he couldn't quite pull it off. Not until they'd talked. Not until she understood that despite what had happened the night before there couldn't be anything between them.

"I usually require more than twenty minutes' sleep a night," he admitted.

"Yeah, me too." She scooped up the cool cookies from the wire rack and slid them onto a wide, stainless steel tray. Stepping around him, she carried them to the far end of the table and set the tray down near several bowls of frosting. She took a seat in a splash of sunlight and got right to work. "But despite the lack of sleep, I'm feeling surprisingly perky today." She looked over at him. "Unlike *some* people I might mention."

"You want perky, I'll need more caffeine."

"As a doctor, aren't you supposed to be careful about that stuff?"

"As a doctor, sure. As a person—not a chance."

"So doctors are people, too?" In just a few minutes, she whipped a coating of bright yellow frosting over a third of the balloon-shaped cookies. "Wow. Who knew?"

He walked around the table and took a seat opposite her. "It's a closely guarded secret." Another sip, and another marginal inch of wakefulness skipped gleefully through his system.

"You know, I think we're doing a good job," Tricia said, starting on another cookie, this time with fire-engine red frosting.

"You're doing fine. I'm just sitting here."

"Not what I'm talking about."

"What then?" He knew. He just didn't want to be the one to start the ball rolling. Cowardice? He didn't want to call it that. Better to think of it as cautious trepidation.

She paused in her work, one hand holding a cookie, the other holding a pastry brush dripping red frosting. Her eyes danced with wry humor. "You know what I'm talking about. We're doing the 'morning after' dance very neatly."

"Are we?"

She shrugged and lowered her gaze to the cookie again. "We're skirting all around the subject. Not talking about it, as if not talking about it will make it go away. It's the elephant in the kitchen."

He shook his head. "Elephant?"

"A metaphorical elephant. You know, a figure of speech," she said, setting down the first cookie and reaching for another. "The one subject we don't want to talk about."

"You're right there."

"So naturally…"

"…You're going to talk about it."

"Got it in one." She flashed him a smile that sent alarm bells ringing in his brain and shouts of hallelujah echoing through his body.

Sam sucked down another greedy gulp of coffee, hoping the caffeine would kick in real soon. She'd been up for hours already, no doubt thinking about just what she was going to say. What she expected *him* to say in return. He'd been up fifteen minutes and all he was sure of was, he wasn't ready to have this conversation. But knowing Tricia, "There's no way to stop you either, I'm guessing."

"Unlikely."

"Fine." Sam set the mug on the table in front of

him and cupped both hands around the warm ceramic. Inhaling deeply, he said, "Shoot."

She laughed. "Well, that's an optimistic start."

"I didn't mean that literally."

"Just as well, I'm a lousy shot. Jake took me shooting once. He was humiliated."

"You're sliding off target now, too."

"I know." She gave him another quick look. "Just giving you time to settle into it, I guess."

"Thanks." *A year ought to be about right.*

"Oh, no problem." She picked up the next cookie and washed it with red color. "But now that you're all relaxed, why don't we jump right into it?"

Sam bit down hard, clenching his teeth. Relaxed? He wouldn't go that far.

"You want to tell me about your wife?" she asked quietly.

And so it began.

"Not particularly." Talking about Mary would only make the guilt gnawing at him more tangible. It would give it life, bring it into the sunshine-filled room and plop it down onto the table between him and his lover. Damn it. His lover. This shouldn't have happened. He should have kept his distance.

He'd had no trouble avoiding women for the last two years. What was it about Tricia Wright that had enabled her to slide beneath his radar so damn fast? Why had he been so drawn to her that he'd turned his back on memories of his late wife? And why did he want her so badly again now?

His hands tightened on the coffee cup until he wouldn't have been surprised to find the damn thing shattering in his grasp. Good thing it didn't though. He needed that coffee. He took another sip.

"Too bad." Tricia set the last red cookie down and pushed the red frosting to one side. Drawing up a bowl filled with grass-green frosting, she dipped a clean brush into the mixture and started her task again. "See, I told you about the guys littering my so-sad past. Now I want to hear about the woman you were thinking about while you were having sex with me."

That got his attention. His gaze snapped up to hers. In those blue depths, he saw pain and he winced to know that he'd caused it. Damn it. His own stupid fault. He should have fought the force of nature that was the Wright family. Should have stayed in a hotel. Should have stayed *far* away from Tricia. But it was way too late for should haves, wasn't it?

"I wasn't," he said tightly, wanting, *needing* her to believe him. "I wasn't thinking about Mary when I was with you."

After, certainly, but not during.

"That's something, I guess." Another green cookie joined its comrades.

"No, that's the problem," he said and pushed up from the table. Carrying his cup to the counter, he refilled it and stalled by taking a long sip of coffee.

She'd stopped working, turned on her chair to face him, and was now watching him with open curiosity. There wasn't enough stall time in the world to buy him a reprieve.

"Explain."

One word, but a world of questions in her eyes.

Setting the cup down, Sam leaned back against the counter and braced his hands on either side of him, fingers curled tightly around the sharp edge. "You're the first woman I've been with since—"

"Yeah," she interrupted. "I got that last night."

"And I didn't think about Mary," he blurted. "Not once."

"That's a good thing."

"Depends on your point of view."

"Whatever the point of view, it's not a crime." Her voice was soft, but firm.

He stared at her, backlit by the sunlight pouring in through the wide window. Her hair was golden, her eyes in shadow. He knew every inch of her body. Learned it during the long night they'd snatched for themselves. He knew what made her moan, what made her gasp, what made her shiver. He'd touched her and found, for a while, *life*. And she, in turn, had touched him more deeply than anyone ever had before.

Acknowledging that, Sam knew, was like a slap in the face to the woman he'd once loved and married.

"Yeah, it is. For me, it is. She was my wife. We were married for three years, together for five."

"And..."

"*And*," he repeated, still stalling. "She was sweet and quiet and kind and—she died." He paused, took a breath and said the rest. "She died and it was my fault."

Tricia blinked.

He saw it and knew what she must be thinking. The same thing he was. Bastard. He was alive, Mary was dead—because of him. And instead of remembering her, he'd spent the night bouncing on a gorgeous blonde, losing himself in her.

"I don't believe that." Tricia stood up and walked toward him.

He thought about moving away, but didn't. Instead he stood perfectly still, tightening his grip on the counter so fiercely, he felt the cold tiles biting into his flesh. "Believe it."

"Tell me what happened."

Memories rushed through his mind like water escaping a dam after the floodgates were opened. Mary's face, her shy smile, her soft, dark eyes. Her broken body. Her last quiet sigh of breath.

Sam lifted one hand and rubbed his eyes viciously as though if he scrubbed hard enough, he could erase at least that *one* memory. Though he knew it was useless. That moment was burned on his brain.

"Sam?"

He heard her, but didn't open his eyes to look at her. If that made him a coward, then he'd just have to live with the knowledge. Retreating into memory, he started talking, describing the scene that replayed through his mind at least once a day. "We'd just picked up her new car. Driving back home." To the empty condo where misery now lived as his only company. "I was ahead of her, driving slowly, since Mary never liked to go more than forty-five. Scared her."

Everything had scared her, he thought now and tasted the bitterness of disloyalty. But she'd been so delicate, so fragile. He'd had to take care of her. She'd needed it. Needed him. And he hadn't been able to do it. Hadn't been able to save her when she'd needed him most.

"Tell me."

Tricia's voice, grounding him to the moment, keeping him in the present despite his brain's attempt to drag him back into the past.

He swallowed hard. "A drunk. Crossed the yellow line, coming right at me. I swerved. Instinct, I guess. Yanked the wheel to the right. He missed me. I checked the rearview mirror…"

"And?" Her voice was tight now, as if she were afraid to ask the question and afraid not to. He still couldn't look at her.

He blew out a breath. "I watched the guy plow head-on into Mary. She didn't even turn the wheel. Didn't even try to avoid him. But it happened so fast. She couldn't get out of the way. Even if she *had* tried—" Why hadn't she tried? Why hadn't she made an effort? He didn't know. Would never know. That haunted him, too.

"Oh God, Sam."

He opened his eyes then and read the sympathy he'd seen so often in others, glittering now in her gaze. Sam stiffened against it. He didn't deserve it. "Don't feel bad for me. It's Mary who deserves your pity. Not me. Not me, because I couldn't save her. I wasn't good enough."

"Sam, that's crazy."

He pushed away from the counter, suddenly too tense, too wound up to stand still. Stalking the circumference of the kitchen, he talked, avoiding her gaze as he relived those last agonizing moments. "No, it's not. I'm a doctor. That's what I do. I save people. Hell, I saved Eric. Saved my best friend, couldn't save my wife."

She'd moved too. She stood at the head of the table and looked at him. "We were lucky that you were there for Eric. But it wasn't the same. Wasn't the same at all."

"Close enough," he snapped. "I stopped the car and I ran back to her. The front of her car was like a closed accordion. The drunk was moaning, crawling out of his car, but I didn't even look at him. All I could think of was getting to Mary."

"Of course—"

He wasn't listening. Instead, he was back on the side of the highway, rushing toward his wife in the wreckage of her car. "The airbags had opened and were already deflating. She was alive though." He remembered it all. The blood. The agony shining in her eyes. The strangled groan ripping from her throat as he tried to help her. "I got her out of the car. Shouldn't have moved her, but didn't have a choice. Had to try. Had my bag with me. Doctors always have their bags."

"Sam…"

"But I couldn't fix her. She was…broken. Inside. Internal bleeding. Someone called 9-1-1, I tried, kept trying until the paramedics got there, then *they* tried. But Mary died anyway. Because I wasn't good enough."

"It wasn't your fault."

He snapped her a look filled with the rage pulsing inside him. "Of course it was my fault. If I hadn't swerved, the drunk would have hit *me*. Mary would have been all right."

"Maybe. And maybe he would have killed both of you."

"No." He shook his head. He'd relived those few moments too many times to believe her rendition. He *knew*. He knew it in his bones. If he had just taken the hit, he could have saved Mary.

"Sam, you can't believe that."

"Yes, I do."

"That's crazy." She took a step. "It was an accident."

"That should have happened to me."

"It shouldn't have happened to *anyone*."

"True. But it did. To Mary. And I couldn't save her."

"Neither could the paramedics."

"They're not doctors. I am. I should have been able to keep her alive." He shoved both hands through his hair, yanking at it as if that small pain could ease the larger one raging within. It didn't help, though. Nothing did. Nothing could. The guilt lived and breathed inside him. Like a dragon, crouched in the shadows, it erupted now and again to flame his insides with the burning knowledge that he'd failed. And nothing would change that. Ever.

Sam stood at the window, staring out at her driveway and the trees beyond the fence separating her house from the one next door. Wind played in the leaves, dancing along the fencetop.

"I had no idea."

He flinched at the stiffness in her tone. "Now you do."

"Oh, yeah."

She walked toward him. He heard her bare feet on the linoleum and braced himself for whatever it was she was going to say.

She turned her back on the window and perched her hip on the window ledge. Staring up at him, she shook her head and said, "If I'd known, I would have treated you totally differently."

He winced inwardly, but didn't let the pain show on his features. He'd expected her to feel this way. To be as disgusted with him as he was with himself.

But hearing it was harder than he would have thought.

"I'm not surprised."

"Well I am," she said, her voice rising slightly. "I mean I knew you were a doctor. But I had no idea you were God, too."

"What?" He snapped his gaze to hers and was startled at the flare of emotion glittering in her blue eyes.

"You heard me."

"Don't you get it? Don't you understand what I'm telling you?"

"Better than you do, I think."

"Apparently not."

"Is this how Mary would have wanted you to feel?" she asked hotly. "Would she want you drowning in guilt for something you couldn't have changed?"

"No, but—"

"But nothing. For heaven's sake, Sam. You don't control the universe."

"I never said I did."

"Might as well have," she said and stood up. "You're taking the blame for what was clearly a tragic accident. Why is it your fault and not the drunk driver's?"

He scrubbed one hand over his mouth. "He was the cause, but I—"

"—couldn't work miracles?" she countered.

Sam blew out an angry breath and forgot about

trying to argue with her. What would be the point? She wasn't going to understand this. Wasn't going to see that day as he did.

He shook his head, refusing to believe, refusing to grab hold of the life preserver she was trying to throw him. How could he let go of the guilt? Let go of the pain?

They were only inches apart now. The scent of her perfume mingled with the fragrant aroma of her morning's baking and filled him, whether he wanted it to or not.

"You don't understand."

"Oh, sure I do," she countered, cutting him off before he could even finish his sentence. "You're so busy punishing yourself, you don't have to worry about actually living anymore."

Irritation flashed inside him.

"You're a doctor," Tricia said, her voice a low-pitched thread of steel that couldn't be ignored. "You did your best to save her and Mary died anyway."

"Exactly."

"Have you lost other patients?"

"Of course, but—"

"This is different?"

"Yes."

"How?"

He opened his mouth, then snapped it shut again.

"Lost for words?" she coaxed.

"She was my wife," he said.

"And she died."

"Because of me."

"Because she *died*." Tricia laid one hand on his forearm and Sam felt the warmth of her touch right down to the bone. "Not because of anything you did or didn't do, Sam."

He looked at her, staring hard, trying to read everything he saw in her eyes. There was no pity there. No censure. But he couldn't accept her words. Couldn't make himself believe it. He'd clung to his own guilt and sense of failure for too long now to be able to go on without them. And if he *did* somehow let them go…wouldn't he be letting Mary go, too?

She reached up, laying both hands on his shoulders. The warmth of her skin seeped into him, easing back the chill still coating his insides. And everything in him yearned for that warmth.

"Don't be a dope, Doc," Tricia said, with a slow shake of her head. "The accident wasn't your fault. Mary dying wasn't your fault."

"You don't know that—"

"I know that you clearly loved her. If you could have saved her, you would have." She squeezed his shoulders tightly as if trying to give him a good shake.

"Fine. Then if I'm not to blame, who is? God?"

"It was an *accident*." Tricia let her hands drop from his shoulders as she frowned up at him. "God wasn't driving that car."

"Clever. But it doesn't help."

"What does?" she demanded, slapping both hands to her hips and giving him a look so hot it could have fried an egg on his forehead. "Locking yourself away? Shutting out the world? Refusing to live because someone you loved died?"

"You don't—"

"Fine. I grant you, it didn't happen to me, so maybe I don't get a vote in how you handle it." She reached up again and grabbed two handfuls of his dark blue T-shirt. "One thing I do know though. If all you learned from loving Mary was to close yourself off, then you missed the whole point."

She went up on her toes and planted a long, deep kiss on him that left his brain spinning. When she let him go, he had to fight for balance. Shaking her head until her ponytail danced behind her, she said, "That's not what love's supposed to teach us, Doc."

Nine

The Wright family swallowed the day in one noisy gulp. Sam found himself making liquor runs, dropping by a local craft store for more decorating supplies and loading rented chairs into the back of Jake's truck. He'd ridden herd on Debbie's kids for an hour while she grabbed a quick nap and everyone else was busy with more wedding stuff. He'd helped mow the lawn and trim the flowering bushes in the backyard and was so tired at the moment, he just wanted a place to sit down and quietly die.

But at least he'd been busy.

Too busy to think about the conversation he'd had with Tricia that morning. Just as well, he thought. There was no point in going over it again and again.

He groaned tightly and scraped one hand across his face. No point in telling himself that maybe, just maybe, Tricia was right. Because he couldn't make himself believe it. And when this two-week span was up, he'd be back in L.A. Back to the world where his only companions would be memories of Mary and his own failure.

A cold stone of dread dropped to the pit of his stomach and shook him to the core. When he'd arrived here, all he'd been able to think about was escape. Now, it was just the opposite.

Sam walked out to the middle of the backyard and let the cool, ocean breeze ruffle past him. From inside the house behind him came the voices of too many Wrights, with children's laughter ringing out above the rest. It was all so…ordinary—and yet, special, too. And maybe, he told himself, that's what the extraordinary really was—taking the time to realize that the ordinary was a small miracle in itself. And families loving each other, most of all.

"Man, I've been here too long." He shook his head, then lifted his gaze to the wide sweep of summer sky. A few stray white clouds scuttled across the broad sweep of blue, blown by the same wind rushing past him. For one brief moment, he wished that wind was strong enough to blow him the hell out of there. To get him back to where he knew how to behave. Knew what was expected of him. Knew what the rules were. But even as he stood there, he realized that he wasn't sure where that was anymore.

The back door flew open, slamming into the side of the house. He spun around. Tricia was framed in the doorway and something in Sam's chest turned over.

It couldn't have been his heart.

"Hey," Tricia called out, a wide, impossibly attractive smile on her face. She hadn't brought up their earlier conversation once during the long day. Hadn't prodded or probed or tried to resuscitate their argument—as, he admitted silently, Mary would have.

Thoughts raced randomly through his mind as time seemed to stand still. Staring at Tricia's open grin, he saw instead, Mary, her eyes wounded, biting her bottom lip as silent tears coursed her cheeks. He vividly remembered the guilt along with the sense of resentment that had crowded him every time an argument had become a cold war. Mary hadn't liked dissension, as she called it, and had simply retreated whenever they'd had a disagreement. It had been infuriating and frustrating to watch the woman he loved pull away from him rather than talk to him.

Instantly, though, he gave himself a mental shake. *Resentment? Frustration?* Mary had been fragile and tender. She hadn't been the kind of woman—as Tricia was—to go head to head with a man. She'd needed care. She'd needed…oh God, so much.

Where had that come from?

What the hell was wrong with him?

"Yo, Sam!"

He snapped out of his self-induced coma, [fo]cused again on the woman now standing [on his] parents' back porch. Hands at her hips, she s[tood in] a slice of late afternoon sunlight, blond hair shi[n]ing, tanned limbs gleaming—and she made his mouth water. Even at a distance she reached him as no one else ever had. He shook his head again. "Yeah?"

"Good." She jumped off the porch, hit the sun-warmed grass with both sneaker-clad feet and walked toward him with a sway in her hips that spiked his temperature and fired his imagination. "Thought maybe you were sleep walking."

"Wide awake," he snapped, *and dreaming anyway.*

She stopped just an inch or two from him and tilted her head to one side as she looked up at him. "Wide awake and just a little on the crabby side?"

He inhaled sharply and glared at her.

She ignored it. "Well, that doesn't matter. You've been elected, and I volunteered to go along for the ride." She hooked her arm through his and started for the driveway.

His skin tingled at her touch. But that was nothing new. She seemed to electrify him on a continual basis. Tricia was a toucher. She was forever reaching out, patting his hand, stroking his forearm, leaning into his chest to laugh. He wasn't used to it, but he was getting there. Mary had never been very affectionate. At least not publicly. Her own innate shyness had kept her from it.

And damn it, why was he comparing the two women again?

"Go where?" he demanded, slipping his arm from her grasp. "For what?"

"Questions," she said, laughing. Apparently, it hadn't bothered her a bit that he'd deliberately uncoupled them. "Don't you trust me?"

The problem was, he didn't trust himself around her. But how the hell could he admit that? "Should I?"

"Oh, absolutely, Doc." She kept walking and, naturally for Tricia, *talking*. "See, I'm the one who's not afraid to look you dead in the eye and call a crab, a crab. So you should always trust the person who's not afraid to—"

"—insult you?" he finished for her.

She grinned at him. "Exactly." Rising on her toes, she dusted a quick kiss at the corner of his mouth, then headed around to the passenger side of his car. When he didn't move, she urged, "Hello? Dinner not going to walk here on its own."

He just looked at her, his mouth still on fire from the quick press of her lips. "You're not mad, are you?"

She opened the car door and paused, one hand on the door, one hand on the roof of the car. She stared at him for a long minute, then blew out a breath and shook her head. "You mean about this morning?"

"Yeah."

"What's to be mad about? We both had our say. It's over."

Amazing, he thought. "Just like that."

"Well," she said, her smile spreading, "I didn't say there wouldn't be Argument II: The Return. But, yeah, it's over."

"You're an unusual woman," he said, opening his side of the car.

Tricia grinned at him and her eyes actually seemed to sparkle. "You know," she said, "I think that was a compliment."

"It was."

"Well keep 'em coming, Doc," she said and slid onto the passenger seat. "A girl could get used to it."

Getting used to it was the problem though, wasn't it? He was getting used to Tricia, to her family, to the world he'd discovered outside his own small circle. But in less than a week, it wouldn't matter because he'd be gone and in no time at all, Tricia would be arguing with someone else.

He fastened his seat belt, fired up the engine and tried to tell himself that he didn't care.

But even *he* wasn't believing him anymore.

"It hurts!" Katie wailed, and her voice hit notes that surely only dogs should be able to hear.

Sam winced and tried to take hold of the little girl's knee. But she was so busy kicking and wailing, it was like trying to catch a live electrical wire.

Not as easy as it looked and downright dangerous to boot.

The child's wildly kicking foot narrowly missed his groin and Sam did a quick two-step to stay out of range. As a doctor, he was more than used to having to deal with frightened children. But doing so in a crowded bathroom with not only the crying child but her pregnant mother, older brother, grandparents, aunt and uncles crouched and perched around him was something else again.

And that wasn't even counting all of the advice flying around him.

"Does she need stitches?" Debbie asked.

"Should have just taken her to the emergency room," Jake muttered.

"Sam can do the job right here," Tricia said and leaned over Sam's right shoulder until her face was alongside his and all he could smell was her perfume. She turned her face at him and smiled encouragingly.

"Is she gonna bleed some more?" Kevin demanded, inspecting the bloody washcloth with incredible relish.

"No and put that down," his mother said, and clapped one hand to her mouth and the other to her distended belly. "Think I'm gonna be sick."

"Can't," Eric piped up from the hallway. "No room."

"Put your head between your knees, honey," Tricia's mother shouted to her pregnant daughter.

"I haven't seen my knees in two months," Debbie moaned.

"Well if Doctor Parker was still working we could go there." This from Tricia's father.

"He's not though, and isn't it a shame, that nice office and his practice going to waste." Tricia's mother said again. The woman leaned in and patted Sam's shoulder companionably. "It's just the right sort of practice for a young married doctor. Family close by and all…"

"Geeezzz, Mom, show a little subtlety," Eric complained, and a moment later a sharp slap sounded out, followed by an outraged, "Ow!"

"When's she gonna bleed some more?" Kevin's indignant voice rose up to rival even Katie's wailing.

"Will everyone please shut up?"

Stunned silence dropped onto the group and Sam paused to enjoy the quiet. He hadn't meant to yell, but it seemed there was no other way to get the Wright family's attention. You had two choices with them—either be overlooked or shout them down. Well, it appeared he'd warmed up to them all enough that it didn't bother him a bit to tell them to put a collective sock in it.

"Way to go, Doc," Tricia whispered in his ear. "My hero." Her breath dusted his skin and he had to fight to shrug off the sensation. After all, four-year-old Katie was the star of this show.

And the only one currently paying no attention at all to his demand for silence.

He stared into the little girl's watery eyes and felt

his heart twist. What was it about a child's pain that could slice right through a man?

"Do I hafta get a shot?" she wailed the last word, making it almost four syllables long.

He thought about it, then glanced at the girl's mother, still looking a little green around the gills. "Has she had a tetanus shot lately?"

"Yeah," Debbie said, keeping her hand firmly against her mouth and avoiding looking anywhere near the bloody washcloth or her child's scraped knee. "Last year."

"No shot then," he announced and won Katie's love forever.

"But there's gonna be more blood, right?" Kevin again.

"Oh, God," Debbie moaned again.

"That's it," her mother said and snatched her out of the bathroom as though she were a child again. "Come on, you're not being the least bit of help, here."

"How come Mom doesn't like blood?" Kevin demanded. "It's really cool and stuff and—"

"That's enough from you," his grandfather said, scooping the boy up and pushing his way out of the bathroom. "What're you, a vampire?" He tickled the boy and a trail of giggles floated like soap bubbles behind them as they went downstairs.

"Keep your chin up, kid," Jake said. "Never let 'em see you cry."

"Girls can cry," Katie argued.

"The ones I know do it all the time," Eric quipped and got another slap, this time from his fiancée. "Man. Guy can't say anything around here."

"You know," Sam said loudly, pitching his voice to cover the remaining Wrights and all of their conflicting opinions, "why don't all of you go on downstairs and Katie and I will be along in a minute."

With a lot of muttering and more than a few grumbles, the remaining Wrights finally trickled out of the bathroom. All except Tricia. But then, Sam thought with a sigh, he hadn't really expected her to leave and was rather grateful she'd stayed. She could distract Katie while he washed and bandaged the scrape on her knee.

"She's all yours, Doc," Tricia said and perched on the edge of the bathtub to watch.

"I'm a brave girl," Katie said stiffly, her bottom lip trembling with the strength of an 8.5 earthquake.

"Sure you are," Sam said, falling into his routine for dealing with scared kids. He fumbled in the leather bag Jake had retrieved from Tricia's house and came up with a grape sucker. Well, he wasn't a dentist. Why should he worry about kids' cavities? "But even brave girls like candy, don't they?"

"Uh-huh." Katie snatched it and tore at the cellophane while Sam worked quickly, quietly. She took one lick, then winced and pulled her leg back. "That hurts."

"Not a lot, though."

"Uh-huh."

"Katie," Tricia said, drawing the girl's attention from Sam's ministrations. "When Sam gets you all fixed up, you know what?"

"What?"

"It's time for me to go and pick up Sheba."

"For real?" Katie's face lit up.

"Sheba?" Sam asked, one eyebrow lifting. "As in, Queen of the Jungle?"

"That would be Shee*na*," Tricia corrected, still smiling at him.

"My mistake."

"Sheba's not a queen," Katie said, reaching out to tug at Sam's shirt to regain his attention. "She's a puppy. Aunt Tricia's puppy."

Tricia shrugged and lifted both hands as she looked fondly at her niece. "Loose lips."

"A puppy?" Sam echoed, trying to keep Katie still despite the fact that she was practically vibrating with excitement.

"We've been waiting and waiting for the puppy to be big enough to leave her mommy," Katie burbled.

"And now it's time."

"And we can go get her?" The little girl nearly hopped off her perch on the toilet seat.

"You bet." Tricia went down on one knee beside Sam and caught one of Katie's hands in hers. "So, you want to go with me to get her?"

"Oh," a brilliant, teary smile lit the little girl's face. "Just me and not Kevin?"

Sam laughed. Nothing like a little sibling rivalry to get a girl's mind off her pain.

Tricia laughed, too, and the music of it seemed to settle over Sam like a warm blanket. His fingers fumbled at his task as he shot a quick look at her. Her nose was sunburned, her hair a mess, and a splotch of something that looked suspiciously like ketchup stained one shoulder of her T-shirt. He'd never seen anyone more beautiful.

"Sure," she was saying to Katie. "It'll be just you, me and Doc."

"Me?"

She looked at him and grinned. "Don't you want to come along?"

If she kept smiling at him like that, Sam thought, he'd probably be willing to go anywhere with her. And that realization shook him right down to the bone. It took everything in him to keep from grabbing her and pulling her close. A damn good thing that Katie was there. And wasn't that a hell of a thing, a grown man grateful to be hiding behind a four-year-old girl.

"What do you say?" Tricia asked, cocking her head to one side, keeping her gaze fixed on him.

He swallowed hard, and shifted his gaze to Katie's scraped knee as he applied ointment and a bandage. Much safer that way. "I don't—"

"Don't you like puppies?" Katie asked.

"Sure, but—"

"Don't you like *us*?" Tricia asked.

He shot her a frustrated glance. "Yes, but—"

"I like *you*," Katie said, crooning the words. Then she pouted, her bottom lip thrusting out in a way that told Sam females were obviously *born* knowing how to do that.

"Me, too."

Sam looked over at Tricia and caught the sparkle of humor in her eye along with the deliberately pouty lip. Like any smart man, Sam knew when he was beaten.

"Okay," he said. "I'll come."

"Good." Tricia grinned and winked at Katie conspiratorially.

"But first, my doll fell down, too," the little girl said, thrusting a beat-up, nearly bald baby doll at him. "Fix her."

Tricia just smiled.

Katie waited impatiently.

Indulgently, Sam wrapped the same kind of bright, neon-colored bandage on the doll's knee and when he was finished, Katie scooted off the edge of the toilet seat and threw her arms around him. Holding on tight, she gave him a smacking kiss on his neck and squeezed with every ounce of her little-girl strength.

Over the child's head, his gaze met Tricia's. Warmth shone in her eyes and for a long moment, he simply basked in it as a man starved for the sun would seek out a beach. Everything in him yearned for her. Her scent reached for him. Her steady gaze warmed him.

And as the moments slipped quietly past, Sam felt himself fall a little deeper into the vortex that was Tricia Wright.

Ten

Sam lay in his bed, staring up at the moonlit ceiling. A soft breeze ruffled the curtains at the window and threw dancing patterns of light and shadow across the pale blue walls. He'd been watching those shadows for what felt like hours. He couldn't sleep. Every time he closed his eyes, Tricia's features rose up in his mind, making it impossible for him to relax enough to fall asleep.

He threw the sheet back with a grumble and swung his feet to the floor. Naked, he paced the room for a few minutes before stopping at the window. He stared briefly into the shadows below, his brain racing, his thoughts churning. A muffled whimpering reached him and he glanced over his shoulder at his closed bedroom door. Tricia's new puppy was making herself heard from the bathroom. Apparently Sheba was unhappy with her new bedroom.

A moment later, Sam heard Tricia's whispered voice, crooning sympathetic, nonsensical words. He smiled to himself, imagining her cuddled up on the bathroom floor, soothing the puppy. He wished he could join her. Wished he had the right to go to her, to help her with the puppy that he wouldn't be around long enough to watch grow.

The new puppy was just one more addition to the Wright family circus and she'd already made herself at home. Tricia and Katie had smothered the little dog with affection from the moment they'd picked her up. Sam had kept his distance, not wanting to involve himself any further than he already had.

Naturally, the midnight-black pup had unerringly attached herself to Sam, the one person *not* trying to bond with her. Tricia had even resorted to bribery, pulling out dog treats and toys—but Sheba had chosen her favorite human. And damn it, he'd had no better luck steering clear of the puppy than he had keeping his distance from Tricia. Sheba was as stealthy as her new owner. She'd slipped past Sam's defenses as easily as Tricia had.

It hadn't taken more than curling up in his lap. He'd never had pets. His parents hadn't approved of animals in the home, calling them, as he remembered it, "germ factories with legs." And Mary'd been allergic, or so she claimed, though Sam used to think that it was just her way of avoiding a discussion she wanted no part of.

He winced slightly as he realized that more and more lately, he was looking at Mary's memory without the sweet, soft-focus lens of distance. And why was that? he wondered. Why now? Why here?

But the answer was clear. Kids, dogs, Tricia...it was all crowding him.

Life seemed to pulse all around him and it was impossible to be oblivious to it when every glance at Tricia only reminded him how alive and...*alone* he really was.

He wasn't spending all his time revisiting old memories here. He was building new ones, whether he wanted to or not.

And Sam knew damn well that once he'd left town, once he'd gone back to his old life, the memories of Tricia and the puppy and the kids, and the whole damn Wright family, would haunt him every bit as much as Mary had. No, damn it—still did now.

He'd been alone for two years, shutting himself off from everyone and everything that used to matter to him. He'd sought to punish himself and he'd done a hell of a job. But in the last ten days or so, he'd been dragged kicking and screaming back into the world.

With the wedding only a few days away, all too soon he'd be going back into the cold silence of his own world, and the very thought of it nearly strangled him. How could he go back to that life? After being here, being with Tricia, how could he blindly return to the solitude that suddenly looked so empty? So depressing?

And how could he not?

"Sam?"

He whirled around and stared at the closed door for a heartbeat or two. Then a gentle knock sounded and Tricia's voice came again.

"Sam? You awake?"

His heart jumped into high gear, slamming against his ribcage like a sledgehammer on an anvil. Snatching his jeans off a nearby chair, he dragged them on but didn't bother buttoning them closed as he walked across the room in three long strides. Grabbing the doorknob, he turned it and pulled.

Tricia was right there, hand lifted to knock again.

The hallway light spilled down over her, highlighting her hair, soft and loose. She wore a pale peach-colored nightgown with thin straps over her shoulders and a lace-trimmed bodice that dipped low over her breasts. It looked silky and cool and eminently touchable.

Just like Tricia herself. Damn, why did she come to him now? When his resistance was at its lowest?

"You *are* awake." She smiled up at him.

"Or sleepwalking."

"With your eyes open?"

One corner of his mouth lifted. "Easier to see that way."

She walked past him, into his room and when she'd taken a few steps, she stopped, turned around and looked at him. "Are you really seeing me?"

"Oh yeah," he muttered, voice thick, heart now rising high enough to lodge in his throat and threaten to choke him.

"What do you see when you look at me?"

He saw images of what might have been. A life he could have had if things had been different. He saw everything that he hadn't known he'd always wanted. And so much more. "Tricia…"

"Tell me."

He couldn't. Couldn't tell her all of that because he didn't have the right. He'd long ago given up on life and now, even if he'd wanted to rejoin the land of the living, he wasn't entirely sure he could pull it off. So instead, he gave her the much shorter answer. "A beautiful woman."

"Is that all?"

He smiled tightly. "Not enough?"

"Nope."

"What do you want to hear?"

She tipped her head to one side and looked up at him. "I *want* to hear that when you look at me, you want to make love to me. That I'm the reason you're not asleep."

"I do," he ground out tightly, against his better judgment. "You are."

Tricia smiled briefly. "You weren't going to say so, though."

"No."

"Interesting."

"Glad you think so." He could hardly think himself. Moonlight speared through the lace curtains at the window and backlit Tricia as though she were the lead actress on an empty stage. She looked like a dream. A vision come to taunt a lonely man.

And God, he hoped she wouldn't leave.

"You were good with Katie today," she said.

"What?" Katie? They were going to talk about kids, now?

"Katie. She really likes you."

"Uh-huh." Confusion rattled through him. The woman's conversations were like mental Ping-Pong games. It took all a man's concentration to keep his eye on the ball and remember where he was.

"I really like you, too."

Sam groaned inwardly, but kept the sound wrapped tightly inside him. Folding his arms across his chest, he braced his feet in a wide apart stance and fought for balance. What was it about this woman that could so tilt the world? "Good." A safe answer, right?

She turned away and walked toward the window. Her bare feet didn't make a sound. The breeze ruffling the curtains danced around the hem of her nightgown and lifted it against her tanned legs. Sam swallowed hard and hoped to God he could keep from grabbing her, throwing her onto the bed and forgetting all about being rational.

"The puppy was crying a minute ago."

"I heard." There went the Ping-Pong ball again. New direction.

She turned around to look at him, silhouetting herself against the moon-washed window. "She's quiet now, though. She was just lonely. I gave her a stuffed animal and she snuggled right in and went to sleep."

"Yeah?"

"And I was thinking…" She bent forward slightly and lifted the hem of her nightgown. Drawing it up by slow, incremental inches, she tantalized him with an ever-growing peek at her legs.

"What?" One word. The best he could do. His gaze was locked on the lacy edge of satin and the ever-increasing expanse of lean, tanned thighs.

"That maybe that's all any of us need," she said, pausing long enough in her undressing to cause Sam's heart to stutter to a stop. "Not to be alone. To have someone to snuggle up to when the night gets lonely."

He shook his head and fought for clarity…and lost. "You want a stuffed animal?"

She laughed that low, luscious, music-filled laugh that reverberated inside him.

"Not exactly," she said, a moment later. "What I want is *you*."

She pulled the nightgown up and over her head, then tossed it to the side in a wide arc that had it fluttering like a half-open parachute before landing on the floor.

Beautifully, gloriously naked, her soft, smooth skin seemed to absorb the moonlight. She damn near glowed.

Sam sucked in air and knew it wouldn't be enough. His lungs felt as though they were being squeezed by a giant, uncaring hand. His heart erupted into a wild beat and his temperature shot up about twenty degrees. His mouth went dry, his hands went damp and his groin tightened eagerly.

"Tricia…"

She walked toward him with no hesitation, no coy smiles, no pretense of embarrassment. When she reached him, she stopped, lifted both hands to his shoulders and held on. The warmth of her fingers on his skin slid down inside him and filled the last few crevices of cold.

"If you don't want me," she said, going up on her toes, "just say so. Otherwise, kiss me."

Trembling with need, Sam forgot about everything but the moment. She was back in his arms when he'd thought he'd never hold her again. She was warmth and light and laughter and *life* and he wanted her more than his next breath.

Grabbing her close, he bent his head and kissed her, laying siege to her mouth in a frenzy of need that swamped them both. Tricia clung to him, turning into his kiss, pressing her body along his, rubbing herself against his chest. Heat, delicious, mind-numbing, soul-searing heat rushed through him.

He half carried, half dragged her to the bed and tossed her down onto the mattress. Yanking his jeans off, he knelt on the bed beside her and filled his hands with her. He touched her again and again, stroking, caressing, exploring every inch of her sweetly curved form.

Her breasts became a feast. One after the other, he kissed them, tasted them, taking first one nipple and then the other into his mouth. His lips and tongue tortured her gently. As he sucked her, she lifted into his grasp, arching toward him, demanding and taking more.

Her hands moved over his back, his shoulders and down along his spine. She nibbled at his shoulders, swept her tongue along the side of his neck and shifted until she could teasingly bite his earlobe. Jolts of white-hot heat splintered inside him and Sam clung to it all. He memorized the very feel of her. The way she bent into his grasp. The way her leg slid up his and hooked around his waist. The damp warmth at her center when he dipped first one finger and then another within her.

She sighed and it was music as sweet as her laughter. She gasped and whispered his name and it was a gift that swept inside him, settling in one corner of his heart.

"Sam," she called his name again as his fingers continued to tease her, push her higher along the frantic edge of urgency. "Sam, I need you inside me, now."

"Oh yeah," he murmured, inhaling her scent as he kissed and licked his way along her throat and down, down to the tips of her breasts again. He couldn't taste her enough. He couldn't feel her enough. He wanted more. Wanted *all*.

She rocked her hips into his hand as his thumb slid across a small nubbin of flesh.

"Oh!" Her eyes wide, she looked up at him with the same need pulsing inside him. "Now, Sam. Seriously, I mean *now*."

He needed her, too, but he didn't want to rush it. Wanted, in fact, to prolong it. He made no move to claim her body, to push his own into her depths. Instead, he only pressed another finger into her center, stroking, rubbing, pushing her higher, faster, until her breath exploded from her lungs and her hips rocked feverishly.

"Take this first," he whispered brokenly, caught by the passion glazing her eyes, by the parting of her lips, by the desperate grasp of her fingertips on his shoulders. "First you, then *us*."

"Not fair," she whispered, licking her lips, tossing her head from side to side. "This was my idea. Not fair to change the rules."

"No rules," he said and deliberately stroked that most sensitive spot at her core again, just to watch the tremors take her. "Not tonight."

She smiled briefly, brightly, then gave herself into his hands. "Oh, Sam…so…good. So…amazing."

"Let go, Tricia." His words came softly, gently, beneath the frantic rush of her breath and the staccato pound of her heart. "Let me see you go over."

"Can't…wait…can't…stop…"

He took her mouth when the first ripple of sensation caught her and shook her in his grasp. His tongue swept past her lips to taste her sighs, swallow her cries as she erupted beneath him, straining and reaching for the release shuddering through her.

And before the last tremor died away, Sam shifted, knelt between her raised thighs and pushed himself home. She was more than ready for him and she took him into her depths, surrounding him with a heat that branded him.

She reached for him, wrapping her arms around his neck. He moved and she echoed it. The dance was as old as time and as new as a morning. Together, they found the rhythm that sent their bodies into urgent tandem.

Sam had never known such completion. Such intimacy. He didn't want it to end. He could have stayed locked together with her forever. But as the need pulsed within, he knew his control was slipping.

That's when he remembered. "Condom."

Her eyes flew open. "Damn. My room."

He groaned tightly and moved to pull free of her.

"No, don't. Don't leave me."

The fine thread of control was frayed, and inches from snapping entirely. "Need to."

"Take me with you."

He choked out a half laugh, then grinned. "Never cease to surprise me."

She smiled back at him even as she wrapped her arms and legs tightly around him. Sam eased off the bed, bringing her with him. And holding her to him, still locked within her, he hurried from his room, across the short hall, to hers. There, he made a wild grab at the bedside table and blindly scrabbled inside the top drawer. Finding one of the dozen or more condoms there, he frantically tore it open, then lay down on the bed.

"Hurry," she whispered, and she twisted and writhed beneath him as he was forced to withdraw from her long enough to sheathe himself.

"Trust me, I am." Only seconds, but it felt like lifetimes. And then he was inside her again, pushing home, delving deep, surrounding himself with her.

"Welcome back," she said, smiling up at him. Taking his face between her palms, she drew his head down for a kiss.

"Glad to be here," he murmured.

Then their bodies took over and the flames rising

within consumed them both. And, locked together, they found the fireworks.

Later, when they could separate without shattering, Sam lay across the mattress with Tricia beside him. She flung one leg across his, one arm across his chest and breathed out a long, deep sigh. He turned his head to look at her, to simply admire her, as she lay sated in a splash of moonlight.

Emotions churned in her blue eyes, shifting, flashing across their surfaces so quickly, he couldn't identify them all. And not for the first time, Sam wished to hell he knew what she was thinking, what she was feeling. A moment later, though, he realized that he would never have to wonder what Tricia was thinking. If he simply waited her out, she'd say it.

"Doc…" She stretched languidly. "For a crabby man, you sure have a way about you."

He laughed, in spite of the situation, and damned if he could remember a time before Tricia when he'd ever laughed during or after sex. "My pleasure."

"Good to know." She pushed herself up onto one elbow and looked at him. Her hair stood up in a tangled halo around her head and her eyes were still foggy with satisfaction. She was breathtaking.

"But, the thing is…"

He cocked an eyebrow and narrowed his gaze on her. Something was bothering her. Hell, how was a man supposed to think after experiencing what they'd just shared? His body was still on fire, but his brain now raced to catch up and pay attention. The concern suddenly etched on her features worried him. "Problem?"

"Sort of."

Sam groaned.

She ignored him. "It's just that…well, I don't want you to get the wrong idea here or anything—"

"About what?"

"About *me*."

"Like?" He pushed himself up until he was braced on both elbows. Totally confused now, he watched her, and noticed the way her fabulous mouth twisted with whatever was worrying her. Then he noted her gaze shift to one side of him so she didn't actually have to meet his eyes. The last of the fire in his blood fizzled out. "What's going on, Tricia?"

She huffed out a breath and let herself flop back onto the mattress. "Stupid. But I don't want you thinking that I act like this with just anybody."

"Huh?" This was making no sense at all and he had a feeling it was about to get worse.

"This, you know…" She blew out another breath and glanced at him. "Coming in here, seducing you and everything and—"

"Seducing me?" He grinned. Couldn't help it.

"Well, yeah."

He grabbed hold of the foot she had draped across his thigh and began to rub it. "Do you really think that if I hadn't wanted this to happen, it would have, just because you'd decided it would?"

Her features screwed up as she tried to work that one out.

Sam chuckled. "Man, I have been here too long. I'm starting to sound as confusing as you do half the time."

"Gee, thanks." She pulled her foot free of his grasp and sat up on the bed, wonderfully uninhibited about her own nudity. "But you know, some guys don't like a 'pushy' woman and—"

Laughter faded as he watched her. "What man wouldn't like what just happened?"

"Well, for instance," Tricia said, "my ex-boyfriend. He didn't really like it when I made the first move and—"

Sam squeezed her bare foot gently. "He was an idiot. Don't change, Tricia. You're...*refreshing*."

She snorted. "Sounds like a soda commercial."

He smiled and shook his head. "Being with you is—"

He paused and the silence stretched on so long, she rushed to finish his sentence for him.

"Amazing? Wonderful? Inspiring?"

"Yeah," he said, nodding, wondering how it had happened that this incredible woman had come to him. What had she seen in him that had made her want to reach out? And how would he get by without her in his life? "All of those." Then, without thinking, he blurted, "Your ex-boyfriend sounds like he would have been perfect for Mary."

"What?"

"I can't believe I said that," he muttered, shoving one hand through his hair. Staring blankly up at the ceiling, he muttered, "I didn't mean to, I just—"

"Hey, I talked about my past—no reason why you can't talk about yours."

He looked at her. He'd just dropped his late wife into the bed between them and Tricia wasn't even angry. Would he ever understand how her mind worked? And did that matter? Shaking his head slightly, he started talking again, "It's just that Mary was…shy. And fragile, somehow."

"Really." Not a question. Just a statement.

He looked around the moonlit room, then back to where she lay naked and completely at ease, and smiled to himself. "Mary never wanted a light on when we made love. She even put blackout shades on the windows to block moonlight."

"Wow."

Sam winced. "I shouldn't—"

"Hey," she said with a shrug, "lots of people like the dark."

"Mary did. Until the night I couldn't see her and moved the wrong way and she ended up with a black eye."

"What?" A muffled snort of laughter shot from her throat.

Sam glared at her, instantly defensive, and irritated with himself for even starting this. "It wasn't funny," he snapped. "She—"

"I'm sorry, of course not." Tricia clapped one hand over her mouth and didn't look at him. She held up one hand, breathed through her nose, then gave up. Her laughter helplessly spilled out.

"You shouldn't laugh and—"

Still shaking her head and trying to get a grip on the giggles rolling from her throat in long waves, she struggled to breathe. "I know," she said in between fresh bursts of laughter. "I know, it's just…a black eye? Oh God, Sam, you must have felt awful."

"Hell yes," he snapped, remembering just how badly he'd felt and how much Mary had added to his guilt. She'd made him pay for that mistake in dozens of different ways, for weeks. Why hadn't he remembered that before now? he wondered. Why had he allowed himself to forget that Mary hadn't been perfect? That their marriage hadn't been an amusement park?

Tricia's laughter had faded into an occasional eruption of chuckles when he finally smiled, too. It really was funny if you looked at it objectively. And Mary hadn't been hurt, really. More embarrassed than anything. And he had the distinct feeling that if the same accident had happened between him and Tricia, Tricia would have worn the black eye like a badge of honor.

Oh yes.

Two very different women.

"Poor Mary," Tricia finally said. "I shouldn't have laughed, but Sam, dumb stuff happens to me all the time. One night, I almost knocked my boyfriend out when I turned over suddenly just as he was sitting up, and my elbow caught him right between the eyes."

"No way," he said, watching her with a smile on his face.

"Oh yeah." Tricia grinned. "He went down like a redwood."

Now it was his turn to laugh and it felt good. It felt damn good to be with a woman who could turn his insides into a molten mess one moment and make him laugh like a loon the next.

"Anyway," Tricia said, "it's sort of nice to know that I am not alone in the world of quirky happenings."

"No, you're not."

"And now that we're in the 'share' mode," she said softly, her expression shifting from amusement to serious.

Uh-oh.

"I wanted to tell you that I'm a very picky woman, Sam." She watched him through steady eyes filled with raw emotion. "I've only been with two other men and each of them meant something to me. I don't take this kind of thing lightly."

He'd known that about her from the first. Which was why he'd tried so hard to keep his distance. For all the good it had done him.

"I know." He stared at her in the moonlight and knew that this image of her would always remain with him. Twenty years from now, he'd be able to reach into a corner of his mind and pull out this one moment and relive it. The scent of her, the look of her, the very real temptation of her. But he forced himself to meet her gaze squarely and say again, "I know exactly what kind of woman you are, Tricia."

She studied his gaze for a long minute before, apparently reassured, she nodded. "I'm glad," she said finally as she shifted position, then leaned in, bracing one forearm on his chest as she rested against him. "And there's something else you should know."

It wasn't easy to concentrate when he had a warm, wonderful woman draped across him. But he did his best, trying to ignore the brush of her breasts against his chest.

"What's that?" He forced himself to ask, even though he was half afraid of what she might say.

"I found them tonight."

His guts twisted. ESP? Foreboding? He didn't know how he knew, but damn it, he *did* know what she was going to say. And he didn't have a clue as to how to respond to her. Naturally enough, Tricia didn't give him much of a chance to consider it before she started talking again.

"The fireworks I told you I was looking for? Well, I found 'em tonight."

Eleven

Everything in Sam ached.

His whole body prickled and tingled, like a long-asleep limb just waking up. Painful, irritating, impossible to ignore. Then his heart twisted in his chest and he felt a new kind of pain. He knew what she wanted him to say. And he couldn't give it to her. "Tricia, I—"

"It's funny," she said, her voice wistful as she cut him off neatly, "you spend your whole life waiting for something and then, when it finally comes along, you can't have it."

Sam sucked in a gulp of air and trapped it in his lungs, afraid that if he let it go, he might not be able to draw in another.

She was telling him that she loved him.

He knew it.

Felt it.

And there wasn't a damn thing he could say to her to make this easier.

He couldn't be the man she wanted. The man to be her husband and the father of the children he already saw shining in her eyes. She deserved better. She deserved a man who hadn't already given up on the very things she was still dreaming about.

No. He'd failed once. He couldn't live through another failure.

"It's okay, Sam." Tricia smiled and stroked her fingertips along his jaw and then across his lips. "I don't expect anything from you."

"You should, though," he said, suddenly tired right down to the bone. "Damn it, Tricia, you have a right to expect a lot from a man." He only wished he were the man to give it to her. "You have a right to expect *everything*."

"Sam—"

He slid one hand along her arm, lulling himself with the silky smooth feel of her beneath his fingertips. "It's just that—"

"Relax, Sam." She smiled slowly, intimately, and shook her head. "If you're lying there worried that I'm about to propose, don't."

He started. "I didn't think—"

"Sure you did." Her smile widened briefly. "I saw the momentary flash of panic in your eyes."

He grabbed her hand and swallowed the bitter tasting, fresh serving of guilt. He'd lost Mary. Hadn't had the ability to save her. And now, he was hurting Tricia, losing her. Yeah, he was a real prize. All he could do now was try to lessen her pain. Help her to see that she was better off without him. "I wish…"

"I'm not asking you to love me, Sam," she interrupted him, her voice a soft hush of sound. "But I *am* asking you to love *someone*."

He went completely still. He would have sworn that even his heart stopped for one hideously long moment. Then Tricia spoke again and her quiet voice shattered the stillness.

"It's not going to be me," she said. "I get that. I knew going into this that you'd be leaving. In fact, even as close as we are right now, I can feel you mentally backing away."

"No, I'm not." Yes, he was. And she knew it, damn it. What was it about this woman, that she understood him better than he did himself? How could she look at him and see beyond the face he presented to everyone else? How did she look deeply enough to see the real him and want him anyway?

She only gave him a patient smile.

"Tricia." He forced himself to look up into her eyes, to read the patience and yes, the love, written there. "I can't be the man you want."

She tipped her head to one side to study him. "How do you know what I want?"

Sam wished he could pretend he didn't know. But how could he? It would be lying to them both. "I knew what kind of woman you were the first moment I saw you." He smiled sadly. "You're picket fences and kids and a dog. You're the PTA and cookies and barbecues on Sundays. That's who you are, Tricia." Everything he ached to have and couldn't claim.

"I *do* know."

She lifted one shoulder in a half-shrug. "Maybe. But I know something about you, too, Sam." Her gaze locked on his and he felt the power of it slide right down to what used to be his soul. "You gave up too soon. You walked away from life when you should have stayed and tried harder. And now, you don't have anything left." She bent her head and kissed him briefly, gently. "Until you love again, you'll stay just a little bit dead inside."

He flinched, but she wasn't finished.

"And if that's all you want out of life, Sam," she said quietly, "then you should have crawled into that grave with Mary."

Fury still clouded the edges of Sam's mind three days later. He clung to it like a child to the string of a balloon. But the tighter he held on, the more that string seemed to slip from his grasp. Hard to keep righteous indignation going when you suspected that the person who'd made you so damn mad was partially right.

Naturally, Tricia had been acting as though nothing had happened. As though she hadn't forced him to take a hard look at himself. As though they were nothing more than casual acquaintances.

They'd continued sharing her small house. They'd worked together on the reception plans, the last-minute wedding details and he'd even helped make several cookie deliveries. He'd seen the new shop she'd be moving her business into and had even helped with some of the clean-up. He'd watched her play with the puppy, laugh with her family, and he knew he'd be imagining her doing all of those things once he was back in his own house in L.A.

And late at night, he'd ached for her when he lay in his bed alone.

She treated him as politely and warmly as she would any guest, and Sam hated it. It would have been easier on him if she'd fought about it. If she'd been as furious as he'd been that night. If she'd thrown him out and sent him to a hotel. But in typical Tricia fashion, she never did what he expected—or hoped—she would do.

She was giving him too much time to think and damn it, he didn't like the thoughts he was coming up with.

He couldn't really bring himself to admit that Tricia was totally right. That was asking too much. But at the same time, a small, rational voice in the back of his mind taunted him with reality.

He had been as good as dead for two years. He'd hidden behind the failure of losing Mary and let himself be buried in thoughts of what "might have been." Easier, safer than having to try. To face the world and pretend to care about anything other than his work. Guilt and misery had become second nature to him. At this late date, he didn't even know if he *could* change. Or even if he should try.

Say he did, Sam thought, arguing silently with himself. Say he gave it a shot, and failed. What then? Then his guilt would be doubled and he'd have screwed up Tricia's life on top of it. Did he really have the right to risk that?

The last two weeks had only been a blip on his otherwise straight and narrow highway of solitude. The Wright family had brought him out of the shadows. They'd welcomed him and made him one of them.

Tricia had made him want to really *live* again.

But he just didn't believe he deserved to.

He scraped one hand across his face, trying, unsuccessfully, to wipe away his thoughts. But nothing would be that easy ever again. He picked up the cup of coffee sitting on the table in front of him and, almost desperate for distraction, turned his attention to the rush of activity surrounding him.

The wedding had been everything a wedding should be.

Nothing fancy. Nothing over the top.

Just family and friends and a reception that looked as though it was going to rock on long into the night.

Sam sat at a table in the far corner of the Wrights' backyard, hidden by the shadows thrown from the strings of white lights stretched across the property. From beneath the overhang of one of the trees, he watched the party happening around him and, not for the first time, realized that he was already becoming the outsider again.

And he was doing it voluntarily.

Dance music poured from the stereo speakers and smiling couples whirled across the neatly trimmed grass as smoothly as if they were on a polished dance floor. The kids raced through the crowd, laughing and eating handfuls of cake. Tables rented for the occasion groaned under the mountains of food brought in by the local Mexican restaurant, and the margarita bar was standing room only.

Sam was clearly the only one *not* having a good time.

"Having fun?"

Startled to hear his own thoughts spoken out loud, Sam shifted in his seat and looked up at the groom. He forced a smile and lied through his teeth. "Sure. Great party."

"Oh yeah, I believe you," Eric said, setting his crutches aside and lowering himself into a chair beside his friend. "I came to tell you the other guests were complaining. You're having too much fun—getting a little too loud. Want to dial it down a notch?"

"Funny." Sam's gaze slid away from his friend. Hell, he was here, wasn't he? He'd stayed through the wedding when all he'd really been thinking about the last few days was escape. He was living in Tricia's house and keeping his hands off her. Torturing himself so he wouldn't let Eric down by leaving early. Talk about the mark of friendship.

"I'm a funny guy."

"Not really," Sam said, shifting Eric a quick look.

"Uh-huh. So, do you love my sister or what?"

"Huh?" Sam tensed, straightening slowly. Hell, he hadn't expected this. Should have known by now that the Wrights, every damn one of them, excelled at the unexpected. But he couldn't tell Eric the truth. Not when he hadn't had the guts to tell Tricia. His gaze met Eric's and he heard himself say, "No."

Knee-jerk. Even as the single word shot from his throat, his mind and heart argued the lie. Love. Dear God, did he really love her? And if he did…did it change anything?

No.

"Then you're an idiot."

Sam's gaze narrowed as he lifted his coffee, took a sip and stared at his friend over the rim. Once he swallowed, he said, "Stay out of this, Eric."

"Not gonna happen."

"I'm leaving tomorrow," Sam pointed out. "Problem solved."

"Think so, huh?" Eric glanced over his shoulder at the crowd behind them.

Sam followed the man's gaze until he spotted Tricia. Dancing with a man old enough to be her grandfather, she was laughing and clumsily trying out a half-hearted jitterbug, just to please the guy. Sam smiled to himself and indulged in one good stare. Her soft blond hair was loose and wild, shining in the glow of the lights. Her dark green bridesmaid dress clung to her figure, making Sam grateful for talented dressmakers.

Her laughter bubbled up again and Sam had no trouble hearing it over the crush of noise in the backyard. Something told him that for the rest of his life, he'd be half listening for that laugh—just as he'd be looking into crowds, hoping to find her.

Regret pooled in the pit of his stomach and spilled through his veins. Darkness crouched inside him and his heart ached with the numbing throb of a toothache.

"Oh yeah," Eric said, looking at him again. "An idiot."

"Go away." God, he wanted a drink. But he settled for another gulp of coffee. He'd already decided to drive home to L.A. right after the reception, so he couldn't afford to drown his sorrows in a bucket of margaritas—despite how good that sounded to him.

"I'm going." Eric pushed himself to his feet, then

settled his crutches into position beneath his arms. Staring down at Sam, he said, "I should have warned you before not to hurt my sister. Now it's too late."

Guilt, his old friend, reared up inside him. Sam stared up at Eric, backlit with the tiny fairylights strung out behind him. A summer wind shifted through the party and those lights danced as if they had wings.

Jaw clenched, Sam forced himself to meet his friend's gaze. "I didn't want to hurt her—and once I'm gone, she'll be fine."

Eric snorted and shook his head. "God, Sam. You really *are* an idiot."

Another hour or two passed before the crowd started thinning out. Eric and Jen had left for a honeymoon that would be only slightly hampered by the groom's cast. The caterers were slowly cleaning up, the music had changed from blistering rock and roll to quiet love songs and the remaining guests had splintered into small groups clustered around the rented tables.

Sam's gaze fixed on Tricia and after a few moments, she seemed to sense his attention. Turning away from the friends she'd been chatting with, she started a slow walk across the yard toward him. Like the pull of a magnet on metal, Sam couldn't resist her. He stepped out of the shadows and met her in the middle of the grassy dance floor.

Her scent reached out to him and Sam inhaled it deeply, knowing that soon, this would be all he would have of her. This night. This memory. This fragile scent that wrapped itself around his heart and held on with a tenacious grip.

"Wasn't it a wonderful wedding?" Tricia smiled, her eyes shining with happiness.

"Yeah, it was."

She sighed tiredly and glanced around at the remnants of the reception. "And a great party."

"Yeah, it was."

Tricia's lips twitched as she looked up at him again. "Jen looked beautiful, didn't she?"

"Did she? Hardly noticed her. Too busy looking at you." Stupid, he told himself. Don't dig yourself in deeper. Don't make this harder on both yourself *and* her. But he couldn't seem to help it. Just being near her was far more intoxicating than anything he could have gotten out of the margarita bar.

Her smile slowly faded, dying away as completely as the stars in her eyes. "You're leaving, aren't you?"

He nodded tightly. "Tonight."

She took a deep breath then blew it out in a rush. "Well, that's eager."

Eager? No. Safer? Oh, yeah. "I have to get back to my practice, Tricia."

She studied him. "Doctor Parker's practice is for sale, right here in town. You could work here. Be needed here."

"I know," he said. "Your mother already gave me his phone number."

Tricia smiled sadly. "Then you know you'll be missed."

No one since Mary had missed him. And knowing that these people would—that Tricia would—made leaving even harder.

She sighed. "But you're still leaving."

"It's better for both of us if I just go. Soon."

She shook her head, then lifted one hand to push her hair back from her face. "You know what's really sad? I actually think you believe that."

Another slow song started up from the CD player in the corner of the yard. The melody swam on the summer breeze and swirled around them both, drawing them inexorably closer.

"I do," he said, his voice ringing with the regret churning inside him.

"Sam—"

"Dance with me," he murmured before he could stop himself. Hell, if he had to leave, the least he wanted was to hold her in his arms one more time. Was that too much to ask? Too much to want?

She stepped in close, sliding her left hand up high on his shoulder and allowing him to fold his fingers around her right hand. They barely moved. It was more swaying than dancing, but neither of them cared.

Sam looked his fill of her, letting himself get lost in her eyes. She felt right, nestled close to him. He could almost feel her heart beating in time with his. And he knew he would miss her for the rest of his life.

"You're thinking again," she whispered.

"Yeah, guess I am."

Tricia pulled her head back and looked up at him. Her gaze met his. "You're going to miss me."

"Guess I am."

"You're going to regret leaving."

Something in his chest tightened, squeezing until he was sure his lungs were exploding. And still, he forced a smile and played their last game. "Guess I am."

"You love me."

He stopped the dance, but didn't let her go. He didn't speak. Didn't think he'd be able to if he tried.

One corner of her delectable mouth tilted slightly. "Ah, no quick answer that time."

"Tricia, I wish it could be different."

"It could be. If you wanted it badly enough."

Everything in him ached to believe her. But it had been too long. Two weeks of happiness wasn't enough to ease two years of misery. And how could he possibly believe in a future when he was still tied to the past?

She stepped back, out of his arms, but stayed close enough that she could speak softly and still have him alone hear her. "I lied before, Sam."

"What?"

"When I told you I didn't expect you to love me, but you had to love *someone*." She reached up and cupped his cheek in her palm. "I want that someone to be me."

"Tricia…"

Shaking her head again, she spoke up quickly, before he could finish. "I'm not asking you to *stop* loving Mary. You'll always love her. And you should. I just want you to love me, too."

God, she made it sound so simple. Yet, he knew it wasn't. It couldn't be that easy to put aside one life and pick up another. Could it?

Her eyes swam with emotion and he hoped to God she didn't cry. Because he was pretty sure that would kill him. "I'm sorry, Tricia."

"I know," she said. "I love you anyway."

"I know," he said and forced himself to walk away.

Twelve

The condo felt as empty as a tomb.

Sam had thought the sense of isolation would pass once he got used to being back where he belonged. But it had been a little more than a week since he'd left Tricia and nothing had changed. Every time he walked into the place, silence dropped onto him like a sack of bricks. He felt suffocated by the very stillness he'd once craved.

Before, there had been a sort of comfort in the silence. Now, there was only a profound loneliness that gnawed at him relentlessly. Reminding him that he'd had a chance to change his life and had turned his back on it. He'd walked away from the only woman who'd been able to touch his heart...his soul.

When he slept, his dreams were haunted by images of Tricia. When insomnia struck, his mind filled with thoughts of her.

There was no escape.

Waking or sleeping.

Worse, he didn't *want* an escape.

So what kind of fool did that make him?

Sam stood on the narrow balcony off his living room and stared up at the night sky. Below him, the lights of the city shone in the blackness, but he didn't notice. Didn't care. The city held nothing for him because his heart was still in a small town in northern California.

He grabbed hold of the iron railing, his fingers tightening around the cold metal until his knuckles whitened. A slight breeze whipped past him, but it was hot and airless. There was no scent of the sea, no hint of Tricia's perfume. No life in it at all.

"You're in bad shape," he muttered, just to hear the sound of a voice in the numbing quiet.

And when a man started talking to himself, things were going downhill, fast.

He pushed away from the railing before he started answering himself and stalked the narrow perimeter of the balcony. Here, he was safe. Here, no one expected him to live. To love. To be involved in anything beyond his own pain.

So why wasn't that comforting anymore?

"Why can't I stop thinking about her?" He

dropped into one of the two chairs pulled up to a small, round table. Bracing his elbows on the glass tabletop, he cupped his chin in his hands and stared off into the darkness as if half expecting to find the answers he sought.

But all he found were more questions.

His mind filled with thoughts of the Wright family and all he'd left behind. And he wondered…

Was Tricia's business settled into the new shop?

Were Eric and Jen home from their honeymoon?

Did Kevin get the stethoscope he'd sent him, as promised?

Did they miss him as much as he missed them?

Was Tricia as lonely as he was?

His heart tightened as though it were in the grasp of a huge, cold fist. Sam jumped to his feet, shoved both hands through his hair, then scrubbed his palms across his face. There was only one way to find out.

Tricia opened her front door and immediately spotted the large, pink pastry box on the porch. Sam quietly stood to one side and watched as she opened the box and gasped at the contents.

He knew all too well what she'd found.

Nine cookies. Each of them frosted and boasting a single word that, together, spelled out a simple, yet heartfelt question.

Tricia I love you. Will you marry me? Sam

Stunned, she looked up and met his gaze as he stepped out of the shadows to stand in front of her.

"Sam?"

"You look wonderful," he said, not trusting himself yet to reach out and grab her. First he had to know. Had to know if he'd ruined what they'd had. If, in his own stupidity, he'd thrown away his last best chance at happiness.

His gaze swept up and down her quickly, thoroughly. Her blond hair was pulled into a high ponytail at the back of her head. Flour dusted her nose and forehead and her blue eyes looked impossibly beautiful. She wore an old T-shirt and the denim shorts with the frayed hem that showed off her legs to perfection.

Sam's heart jolted and his blood pumped in a fury of want and need. One look at her again and he knew without a doubt.

She was his future, his present, and everything in between.

Through some incredible stroke of good fortune, he'd not only found love again...he'd found *life*.

Now he could only hope that he wasn't too late to claim it.

"Don't say anything yet," he blurted before Tricia was able to launch into one of her rambling conversational threads.

She inhaled sharply. "Okay."

He nodded, shoved both hands into his pants pockets, then pulled them out again. Pushing one palm along the side of his head, he then let it drop to his side and gave up trying to find the perfect words. Instead, he settled for speaking from the heart and hoping it was good enough.

"I love you."

"Oh, Sam..."

"Still talking," he said quickly.

She grinned. "Right."

Okay, smiling. That was a good sign, right? He kept talking, half afraid to stop now that he'd started. "I did love Mary and she'll always be a part of my heart—but," he said, swallowing hard as he said the words it had been so hard for him to accept, "she's my past. You're my future."

Her eyes filled with a sheen of tears and she blinked frantically, trying to clear them.

Taking one step forward, Sam reached out and grabbed her upper arms as if to reassure himself that she was really there. Really standing there smiling at him.

"I want to be your future, Tricia. I want to build a life with you. Have lots of babies with you. I want us to live in the middle of the Wright whirlwind, because outside it, life is just too damn lonely. Too empty. And without you, it's unbearable." He shifted his grip on her, sliding one hand up to stroke her cheek. "*I'm* too empty without you. I *love* you, Tricia. I think I have from that first moment."

"Well, *duh*."

Sam blinked and stared down at Tricia's wide grin. But he only had a moment. She dropped the pastry box and leaped at him. Wrapping her arms around his neck, she laughed and buried her face in the curve of his throat.

His arms came around her tightly and he bent his head to hers, dragging her scent into his lungs with a silent prayer of gratitude. She leaned into him and Sam held her tighter, closer, and knew there was a part of him that would never want to let her go.

"Took you long enough," she whispered brokenly, and finally pulled her head back just far enough to look up at him.

He smiled, feeling the old guilt and misery slide off his soul, leaving him feeling lighter than he had in years. "I'm a slow learner."

"Apparently." She didn't let him go, just held on as though she had no intention of ever releasing him. Rising up on her toes, she planted a quick kiss at the corner of his mouth and confessed, "If you'd taken much longer, I was going to L.A. to drag you back here myself."

"Is that right?"

"You bet, Doc." Her fingers tangled in his hair. "This is home. This is *your* home. *Our* home."

"I know that now."

"Good."

"Oh, better than good," he assured her. "I sold my

half of the practice to my partner and as soon as I contact Doctor Parker, I'll get set up here in town and—"

Tricia laughed. "Won't take long. Mom already talked to Doctor Parker and told him you'd be back to take over his practice."

"Of course she did." Sam laughed, too, and then lifted Tricia off her feet, swinging her up into his arms, close to his heart. Where she'd always been. Where she would always belong.

Her smile warmed him down to the bone and chased away any last traces of the shadows that had held him in their grasp for too many years. Sam stared down into her eyes and saw the future stretch out in front of them. He saw his heart. His life. His love.

"Welcome home, Doctor Crabby."

"Not feeling so crabby right now," he said and seriously doubted he ever would again.

"I really do love you so much, Sam," Tricia said, cupping his cheek in her palm.

"Don't ever stop," he whispered.

"Not a chance."

From inside the house, the kitchen timer rang out, its shrill tone sparking a loud, yapping response from the puppy in the backyard. Next door, at her parents' house, the old black Lab added his deeper bark to the fray and the noise hit amazing proportions.

"Cookies burning?" He shouted the question over the din.

"Whoops! It's a double batch, too!" She clambered out of his arms, then stopped long enough to grab her proposal-in-a-box off the porch. Clasping it to her chest with one arm, she grabbed Sam's hand and tugged him inside. "C'mon, Doc. Once the cookies are safe, we've got some celebrating to do!"

"Home, sweet home." Sam grinned and jumped into the whirlwind, enjoying the rush and pull of a rich, full life so unlike the silence he'd left behind forever.

* * * * *

FOR SERVICES RENDERED

BY
ANNE MARIE WINSTON

RITA® Award finalist and bestselling author **Anne Marie Winston** loves babies she can give back when they cry, animals in all shapes and sizes and just about anything that blooms. When she's not writing, she's managing a house full of animals and teenagers, reading anything she can find and trying not to eat chocolate. She will dance at the slightest provocation and weeds her gardens when she can't see the sun for the weeds any more.

You can learn more about Anne Marie's novels by visiting her website at www.annemariewinston.com.

For the Out-of-Control Croppin' Crew:
Kathy, Connie, Janis, Judi, Vick and Susan.
It was a sultry night.

One

"Please tell me this is the last one."

Sam Deering linked both hands above his head and stretched his powerful arms. He had kinks in his back from sitting so long, exactly the kind of thing his physical therapist would give him hell for, but he really needed to get somebody into the new position so he had to finish the interviews today. He dropped his glasses on top of the stack of paper before him and stood, stretching his left leg. It had never been the same since he'd been shot, but it was a lot better than anyone expected, so he supposed he couldn't complain.

"You okay?" Del Smith, the vice president of Protective Services, Incorporated, looked up from the résumé she was reviewing, her heavily lashed brown eyes focusing on him.

"Yeah." He picked up his glasses and resettled them on his nose, then nodded at the door. "Let's get this over with." It had been an exciting ride over the past few years, he thought. PSI might have started out small, but it was making up for it now. About a month ago, he'd realized they needed an assistant for their in-house undercover consultant to handle the amount of work they were getting. He liked the fact that his Virginia-based company could respond to so many different needs in people's lives, from kidnappings to home-security analyses to bodyguard services, but it kept him on his toes.

Del and him, he corrected himself. Without her, he might never have been able to put this all together.

"This is the last one." Del's husky voice sounded as relieved as he was. She laid a neat file before him on his desk, picking up the previous one at the same time. "Here's the next interview."

Sam flipped open the file, casually riffling through it as he watched her from beneath his lashes. "What do you think so far?"

Del shrugged slender shoulders beneath the oversize man's work shirt that was part of her standard code of dress. Beneath the open shirt she wore a PSI T-shirt that probably would fit Sam. He suspected there were some decent breasts under those sloppy casual clothes, but in seven years, he'd never once seen her in anything other than her jeans and shirts or a shapeless black jacket and pants she wore when they entertained clients. It wasn't exactly the kind of thing he could ask about, either. *So, Del, what size jugs you got under that shirt?* No, probably not a good idea.

Unaware of his thoughts, Del shook her head as she arranged papers in front of her own seat. "The Sanders man probably would be competent, but he didn't show me anything special, if you want the truth."

He nodded, forcing himself to focus on the potential employees they'd spent the afternoon interviewing. "I agree. Maybe we'll get lucky on the last one."

Del gave him a small smile as she turned to walk to the doorway. "Maybe."

As she strode across the floor in the no-nonsense style he associated with Del, Sam watched her go. He knew she was slender beneath the baggy jeans and shapeless shirt, but the clothes left him guessing at details. Over the years, he'd become obsessed with trying to catch her in positions that might give him a hint of what lay beneath those layers.

Today, as always, her long, shiny brown hair was braided into a single thick rope that hung from the hole in the back of the baseball cap she always wore and as she walked, it twitched from side to side, brushing across her butt rhythmically, capturing his gaze as surely as if she were stripping in front of him. What would that mane of waist-length hair look like loose and flowing around her shoulders? Hard to believe that in nearly seven years of working in each other's pockets every day, he'd never seen her with it down.

He shifted in his chair, glad he was sitting down. He doubted any of his employees had any idea how his vice president turned him on and he wanted to keep it that way. It wasn't as if he had any intention of acting on it, after all.

No, the last thing he needed was any sort of entanglement with a woman. PSI was the only mistress he had time for. A flesh-and-blood woman would never be content with the long hours he put in, the occasional urgent summons and instant response that certain kinds of cases required.

The door of his office opened again and Del ushered in a tall woman in a severe dark jacket and pants with a white button-down shirt. The jacket was a boxy, unconstructed cut and as he assessed her, he'd bet that it had been made to conceal a sidearm, although she wasn't carrying today.

Del took her seat at Sam's side with a second file. "This is Karen Munson," she said. "Karen, Sam Deering, the president of PSI."

She turned her attention to Sam for a moment. "Ms. Munson has a Criminal Justice degree from Penn State. She started as a beat cop in Miami, worked her way up to Homicide investigations and then applied to the FBI. Her background includes criminal profiling, kidnapping investigations and long-term deep-cover assignments."

"Call me Karen," the woman said, smiling at him. There was no hint of flirtation in the smile, and no hint that she recognized him as anything other than the head of the firm.

Good. The last thing he needed was an employee blabbing his whereabouts to the press. He'd had enough media attention nine years ago to last a lifetime. Even Del didn't know about his past.

He'd considered telling her a time or two, back in the early days when even the easiest of physical tasks had been such an obvious struggle for him. But she'd never asked how he'd been hurt, simply did what she could to lighten his load. And in recent years, he'd improved so much that he sometimes even forgot he'd been shot.

"Why did you get out of undercover work, Ms. Munson?" he asked, glancing at the file.

"I had a child," she said. "I wanted more regular hours."

"You might not always get them here," he warned.

She nodded. "I understand. I've read the information you gave me. But my circumstances have changed now and I have no time constraints anymore."

"None? No child care?"

Karen Munson's mouth compressed into a thin line. She looked away for a moment and he saw her take a deep, fortifying breath. "My son has passed away," she said quietly. "Frankly, Mr. Deering, the busier you can keep me, the happier I'll be." She leaned forward, all business again. "As you can see, I have management experience as well as expertise in a number of the areas you indicate you need."

The interview went on for another thirty minutes, longer than he'd spent with the other three applicants who had cleared the background checks and job-description requirements. When it ended, he'd hired Karen Munson as an assistant to his undercover ops team leader.

She shook his hand, then Del's, and Del led her to her office to give her some paperwork to fill out over the weekend. As she shut the door behind them, his intercom beeped. Punching an open channel, he said, "What's up, Peg?"

Peggy Doonen was Del's assistant and had been manning the front office during the interview.

"It's quittin' time, that's what's up!" Peggy's boisterous good humor boomed around the room. "I thought you said we had a light weekend coming up."

"We do. What's your rush?" Sam didn't generally engage in banter with his employees but Peggy was a force of nature, the office's self-appointed morale officer, class clown and party planner. He'd actually made part of her job description "employee satisfaction" a couple of years ago, and she was worth every penny of the increase. The office was a pleasant, friendly working environment, his employees a close-knit team that generally ran amazingly smoothly despite all the different personalities.

"It's Del's birthday is what's the rush," she informed him. "And we're taking her out to dinner tonight. So unless you've got something important going on in there, set her free. Matter of fact, why don't you relax a little for once and come along with us?"

"No, thanks." The refusal was automatic. "That might inhibit some people."

"That's ridiculous," Peggy opined. "If you change your mind, we'll be at O'Flaherty's Irish Pub. We're meeting at six."

"Have a good time," he said automatically. Del's birthday. For a moment, he felt vaguely guilty. She'd worked for him since he'd opened the firm seven years ago, was his most trusted employee…and he didn't even know it was her birthday. It wasn't as if he didn't have access to the information, either. He'd just never bothered to learn.

Then he shrugged it off. That was part of Peggy's job, making sure employee birthdays were recognized. She sent cards from the firm on which he dutifully scribbled his signature when she thrust them under his nose. She organized lunch or dinner get-togethers to celebrate, although he'd never attended—

His intercom buzzed again. "Yo," he said, punching a button.

"Ms. Munson's gone. She'll be here Monday at nine," Del's voice said. "I'm heading out, too, unless there's anything else you need."

"No. See you Monday."

"Have a good weekend. See you Monday."

"Hey, Del?"

"What?"

"Happy birthday."

"Oh." She sounded surprised and pleased, and he mentally thanked Peggy for clueing him in. "Thank you."

"I would sing, but we'd both be sorry," he told her.

"We'll pretend you already did," she suggested. "Thanks for the lovely serenade." She chuckled, a warm, husky sound that vibrated pleasantly through him. He'd always liked making her laugh, though she did it rarely. Del was one of the most focused people he'd ever known when her mind was engaged on a problem. And in their line of work, problems were commonplace.

"Have a good weekend," he said.

"You, too." Her intercom clicked off.

He stood there for a moment, wishing she didn't have to leave. Then he shook himself. *Don't be ridiculous, Deering. You don't need to get involved with anyone who works for you.*

That was assuming Del would even be interested in him, anyway. As far as he knew, she had never dated anyone from work. Hell, he couldn't remember her ever speaking about her personal life, so he really didn't know whether she dated at all. She'd been single when he hired her and he was pretty sure she still was. No husband would put up with the hours Del spent at work. She was with him way more than half her waking hours in any given week.

He was on his way home when the idea popped into his head and wouldn't go away. *Why not? Peggy invited you,* he reminded himself.

Yeah, but she didn't really mean it.

Sure she did. Peggy doesn't say things she doesn't mean.

The other employees wouldn't like it.

How would you know? You're always invited but you never go.

All right. Fine. So he'd go one time just to see what all the birthday hoopla was about. And because it was Del. After all, she was his second in command, and he really should recognize all the work she did for him. He swung the car off the Capital Beltway toward Fairfax, where he knew O'Flaherty's was located not far from Tyson's Corner Mall.

He glanced at his watch. Seven-fifteen. He'd be late, but that was good, wasn't it? This way, his employees would see that he just stopped to offer his best wishes, not to cramp their party style. And they'd have finished dinner by now.

He parked and walked into the Irish pub. He was barely through the front door before he saw them. There were three round tables crammed full of PSI people.

No, that wasn't right. There was a slender redhead who wasn't one of his employees. She was so unslender in one particular spot that she must have had implants, he decided. She was snuggling against Gerald Walker, a former federal agent who headed up the security-analysis team. Walker had been through a bitter divorce about a decade ago. Sam knew this because one night shortly after PSI had opened he'd called Walker to come in on an after-hours consult and the man staggered in with one of the worst hangovers Sam had ever seen on someone still standing.

"Saw my ex today for the first time in a couple of years," Walker had explained. "It was either drink or put my fist through a wall."

Sam shook his head at the memory as he wove through the crowd. There was one other woman he didn't know with the group, a petite female with a wealth of chestnut hair softly waving around her shoulders and falling down her back. She wore a strappy little black dress that exposed slim, muscled arms and shoulders and a generous amount of cleavage. Wow. None of his employees looked like *that* in a little black dress.

She had her face turned away from him, talking to the firm's accountant with whom she must have come. He couldn't see if the face matched that truly delectable body. Still, he wondered idly what a woman like that was doing with the chubby, bookish accountant.

But...where was Del? His steps slowed as he realized the birthday girl wasn't in the crowd.

"Sam! Hey, Sam, glad you could make it!" Peggy spotted him and stood up, one hand waving madly. "Look, everyone, it's Sam."

He ducked his head and made for the table, miserably aware that half the people in the place had turned to look at him. Damn! What a dumb idea.

Why hadn't he talked himself out of this? It was true he hadn't been recognized in some years now, but this would be the perfect place for it. He came to such restaurants and bars so rarely that he actually couldn't remember the last time he'd been out for a purely social function.

He forged through the room to his group's tables. Peggy already had requisitioned an extra chair and everyone at her table scooched over so he could join them. Peggy had placed the chair beside hers. Directly across the table from him sat Grover and one of the strangers.

Only when she lifted her head and looked across the table at him, she was no stranger. The girl with the long, wild cloud of hair and the incredible figure had Del's small heart-shaped face, Del's velvety brown eyes and the cleft in Del's stubborn little chin.

Holy hell. He felt as if he'd been sucker punched right in the gut. Thank God he hadn't asked Peggy where Del was.

"Hey, Del," he said, making a superhuman effort to pull himself together and act normally. "Happy Birthday. Again."

"You missed the cake," someone said.

"That's all right." He was still looking at Del,

unable to process how his efficient vice president had become this…this hot.

And hot she most definitely was. Instead of her standard old baggy shirts, she was wearing that little black dress with spaghetti straps. She filled it out beautifully, and he was pretty sure it wasn't due to surgical enhancement, either.

"Nothing to say about Del's transformation?" Peggy asked. "The rest of us almost walked right past without recognizing her."

"I'd have done the same." He forced himself to tear his eyes away from Del. "It's a good thing she doesn't come to the office looking like that or we'd have clients crawling all over each other requesting a consultation with her."

The waitress approached then and he ordered a beer. Del got another drink, too, another of the green things in a big hurricane glass with a shamrock swizzle stick. But no one else did.

"Better not," said Sally from payroll. "I've got to drive and I need to get home to feed the dogs, anyway."

"My wife held dinner for me," the personal-security consultant said.

One by one, various people made their excuses and left until all that remained were Walker and his top-heavy date, Peggy, Del and him. After a few more moments, Peg also stood. "My youngest had a soccer game tonight. I figure I'll make it just in time to pick him up if I scamper now." She leaned down and bussed Del on the cheek. "See you Monday, birthday girl. Bye, boss, bye, Walker. Jennifer, it was nice to meet you."

"Oh, you, too." The redhead spoke with a breathy baby doll voice that sounded too silly to be real. It was the first thing she'd said since Sam had arrived, and he couldn't help turning incredulous eyes to Del.

When she met his gaze, there was amusement in the chocolate depths. He could almost hear her saying *Is she for real?* Suddenly he felt a lot more comfortable. She might have transformed her exterior but underneath she was still the person with whom he shared an almost uncanny nonverbal communication.

"Bye." Del spoke in unison with him. As Peggy maneuvered through the crowd toward the door, there was an awkward silence.

"So, Walker, we hired an assistant undercover consultant today." Del was quicker at making an effort to salvage the conversation than he was. "She's got a lot of experience with undercover work, which should complement Doug's capabilities." The undercover team typically assisted with bodyguard and surveillance work and often worked closely with Walker on abduction cases.

"A woman?"

Del nodded. "A very competent woman."

"Great," Walker said. "Since we got that little girl back from the relatives in France who stole her from the mother, we've gotten more work than Doug and I can comfortably handle. Someone with additional undercover expertise is just what we need. And it's probably a good idea to add a woman to the team."

"Oooh, you work undercover?" Jennifer turned on a high-voltage smile as she batted big blue eyes at Walker. She punched him playfully on the shoulder. "You didn't tell me that. How exciting!"

"Not really." Walker looked as if he was strangling in a tight necktie, except that he wasn't wearing one.

Sam took a closer look at Walker's date. Was she even legal? Beneath the boatload of makeup, the woman looked unbelievably young.

"What kind of work do you do, Jennifer?" Del stepped into the silence once again.

"Oh, I'm a model," she said. "Or at least, I wanna-be. Right now I take classes at the Barbizon School of Modeling and I work in the makeup department at Bloomie's."

A model wannabe? Jeez, there had to be a twenty-year age gap between Walker and his date. What the hell was the man trying to prove? Then Sam jumped as a small but lethal foot wearing a very pointy shoe kicked him in the shin. He turned and glared at Del but she was smiling at Jennifer.

"Modeling can be hard work." Del did her best to sound admiring.

"Uh-huh." Jennifer leaned forward. "I bet it's really fun being a secretary for these guys."

"Del's not a secretary," Walker said. "She's my boss."

"Wow!" The redhead clearly didn't know where to go with that statement. Eyeing Del critically, she said, "You know, if you're in management, you really should learn how to maximize your assets. I could fix you up with a makeover in no time flat. You'd be even more of a knockout with a push-up bra and—"

"Well," Walker said heartily. "Jennifer and I need to get going. Del, hope it was a good one. See you Monday, you guys." And with what was clearly the haste of a man in full retreat, he dragged his date out the door.

Sam watched them go. "Maximize your assets?"

Across the table, Del couldn't contain herself any longer. She snickered, then began to laugh. Her amusement was contagious and after a moment, he joined her.

"A makeover," she managed. "If she could only see my usual attire. She'd run screaming."

"It's probably past her bedtime," he said as their laughter subsided.

"Be nice." But Del's shoulders still were shaking with laughter. "What in the world is Walker thinking?"

Sam raised his eyebrows. "Do I really have to explain?"

"Besides the obvious," she said severely. "What could they possibly have in common?"

He only looked at her. "What else do they need?"

Even as the words hit the air, he realized the comment was a mistake. There was a moment of silence that, to him anyway, felt charged with erotic particles of sensual speculation. Though he'd often wondered about Del the woman, he'd never shared with her this kind of vivid awareness, a pull that made him want to reach over and set his mouth on hers.

Sam cleared his throat. "We seem to have been deserted," he said.

"The group doesn't usually stay late," she told him. "A drink, sometimes dinner and that's about it. Most everyone has a family to get home to." She twisted around and found the strap of her purse, which had been hanging on the back of her chair. "I appreciate you coming by, but don't feel you have to stay."

"I don't," he said, trying not to stare at the way her little dress shifted every time she moved. Suddenly, going home to his empty apartment seemed unbearable. "But I'm starving. I haven't eaten. Would you like to have another drink with me while I get a bite of supper?"

"Are you sure? This isn't just birthday pity?"

He felt the corners of his lips curving upward. "Nope. This is hunger speaking. I eat alone too much. Why don't you stay?" He shouldn't be encouraging her to linger. He was used to eating alone and the last thing he needed was for his vice president to think he was coming on to her. But he found he was waiting eagerly for her answer.

She hesitated a moment longer, then finally shrugged. "Sure. I don't have anything to rush home to."

"No pets?"

"Not even fish." She slanted him a wry look. "My boss is very demanding and I never know when I'm going to be needed for odd hours and overtime."

"Hey," he said, "you never said you minded. In fact, you often work harder and stay later than I do."

She shrugged again, making the little dress cling to her curves enticingly. One strap drooped off her shoulder and she impatiently hitched it back up. "Like I said, nothing to rush home to."

He had to concentrate to form a coherent answer. "Me, neither. I appreciate the company."

And he did. He was enjoying himself. While Del was efficient and not afraid to make her opinion known at the office, they rarely had time for personal exchanges. He'd learned more about her already tonight than he had in the past seven years.

"So why the transformation?" he asked. "You look great, but it's definitely a change from your usual garb."

"My mother sent this dress for my birthday," she told him. "Usually, the things she sends are so outrageous I wouldn't even wear them when I was alone. This wasn't too bad so I took a self-timed digital picture to send to her."

"Very thoughtful," he pronounced. "Why does she send you outrageous things?"

Del's eyes darkened as she took a sip of her drink. "Because that's exactly what she's like. Outrageous."

Two

"**I**'d like to meet her."

Del shook her head definitely, sending her hair slithering over her shoulders, and he was instantly distracted. What would it feel like to have that hair sliding all over *him?*

"Not in this lifetime," she said. She picked up her drink and took another long pull on the straw. "I only see her about once a year and trust me, that's more than enough."

There was the faintest note of bitterness in her tone. He wondered what her childhood had been like, to produce a reaction like that. If he asked her outright, she'd probably refuse to talk about it. So he went around the subject. "Do you have brothers or sisters?"

She shook her head again. "No, I'm an only. I was an accident."

"Your mother didn't want kids?"

"She was afraid they'd ruin her image."

Ah, so the woman was vain. Hard to imagine how she could have a daughter like Del, who purposely played down her looks. "And did you?"

She giggled. "No, but I certainly tried."

Had she just *giggled?* He couldn't believe it. There wasn't a woman on the planet less likely to utter a girly laugh than Del. "How much have you had to drink?"

"This is only my third," she said with great precision. "They're shamrock daiquiris and they're very good."

"Only your third? In a little while, those are going to hit you right between the eyes."

The waitress came by a moment later and he ordered a second beer and his meal. Del insisted on ordering another of her green concoctions, but he silently motioned the waitress to go light on the alcohol. Then he pointed to a small booth in the corner which had just emptied. "We're going to move back there."

He rose and grabbed his beer bottle.

Del stood as he rounded the table, picking up her drink and her bag. "Why are we moving?"

He pulled her chair back and took her elbow to guide her through the maze of tables. "That table's too big for just the two of us."

This close, he could see that the black dress was short. Very short. It exposed what looked like miles of long, slim leg. And she was taller than he was used to because she wore a pair of little strappy shoes with high heels.

Oh, man, he *loved* high heels on a woman with terrific legs. And Del did indeed have terrific legs. Long, muscled thighs, firm calves and slender ankles—he'd better get his mind off Del's legs before he embarrassed himself.

"Remind me," he said, "to thank your mother for this outfit sometime."

There was a moment of startled silence. Then Del said, "Do you like it?" She tilted her head back to peer at his face and almost lost her balance. "Whoops."

Sam put his arm around her waist—why hadn't he ever realized how delicate and slight she was?—and hauled her over to the table in the corner. He set her down on the seat. "Yeah," he said, hoping he hadn't overstepped the boundary between them. "I like it." *Like* was a vast understatement. The top clung to the curves of her breasts and dipped down to reveal the shadowed cleavage between them. All he wanted to do was lean down and place his mouth right there above the gentle swellings, to taste her fine-grained skin and feast on the scent that would be simmering there.

Telling himself that would be the stupidest move he'd ever make in his entire life didn't seem to help. But he forced himself to set down his beer and slide into the seat opposite hers. It was a snug fit for a man as big as he was. His legs tangled with Del's beneath the table.

"Sorry," she said, and she sounded breathless. "They must have decided to fill up this space with a downsized version of the real furniture."

He worked his legs around so that he could stretch them out on either side of hers. Not great, but bearable. Particularly when she moved and the outsides of her slim thighs brushed against the inside of his. Oh, yeah. Definitely bearable.

The waitress came by with his meal.

"Eat some fries," he said to Del.

"I already ate."

"Let me guess, a salad?"

She glared at him. "A *chef* salad, with ham. How did you know, anyway?"

"Because that's what you always get when we take clients out or order in." There. He might not have known her birthday but he did know something about her after all. "Eat some fries."

"You're just trying to keep me from getting too drunk," she accused.

"Yeah." He didn't see a reason to deny it.

"But I want to get drunk, Sam. I need to get drunk tonight if I'm going to meet a man."

He'd just taken a swig of beer and he damn near spit it out. "What? Who are you meeting?" He wasn't letting her meet anyone she didn't know really, really well in the condition she was in.

"No one in particular." Her voice was sulky. That was another first. Del in a mood. At work, she was quiet, reasonable, occasionally insistent and rarely annoyed. But the sexy little pout pushing out her full lower lip was one expression he'd never seen before.

"Are you telling me you're planning to pick up a guy in a bar tonight? No." He shoved his food away. "No, no, no."

"Whoa. Wait!" She grabbed the table and clung as he attempted to haul her to her feet. All that did was ensure that the table came with her as he started to drag her toward the door. "Sam, stop it! You're making a scene."

If there were any words he dreaded more, he couldn't imagine what they'd be. He let her go and straightened the table. Once she'd taken her seat, he also sat again, but he leaned across the small space, shaking a finger in her face. "You are not leaving this bar or any other with anyone besides me tonight. Got it?"

She blinked at the large finger waving beneath her nose. "That's a good way to get bitten," she said mildly.

"Wha—? Oh." He gave her his most menacing look although he was prudent enough to remove his finger from close proximity to her mouth first. "You're trying to change the subject."

"Yup." She nodded, leaning across to take one of his French fries. She nibbled it delicately and the motion of her soft pink lips made him swallow involuntarily.

"Why?" He didn't get it. "With all the scary stuff that can happen to a woman today, why would you take a chance like that, picking up a stranger?"

"It's very simple, Sam." She picked up her green drink and took a sip. "Do you know how old I am today?"

He shook his head. He'd honestly never thought about her age. She was just Del. "We started the company seven years ago," he said, thinking aloud.

"Right. And I was just out of college. Today I am twenty-nine years old."

"Congratulations?" He was mystified at her apparent annoyance.

"No!" She was glaring at him again. "I am twenty-nine years old and I've never had a boyfriend, much less a lover, in my whole life. I'm an old maid. And I refuse to let another year go by without finding out why sex is such a big deal."

She might as well have hit him over the head with a plank. "You're…you've never…"

"No." Her voice got softer and the animation drained from her features. "I've never."

"Why?" Why the hell would a woman who cleaned up as nicely as Del did still be a virgin at the age of twenty-nine? He was totally out of his depth. He heard the words and knew he needed to respond like a friend, but his body was responding as if he were a stud dog and a bitch in heat had just sashayed into his run. Ruthlessly, he shoved away the surge of desire that rose. "You're a beautiful woman, Del. I can't believe you've never had a guy interested in you."

She shot him a skeptical look, her finely arched eyebrows rising. "Don't be ridiculous. You know as well as I do my normal mode of clothing isn't exactly a man's fantasy."

"So? You could have found someone if you'd wanted." *I can't believe she's still a virgin!* "You hide your looks like some people hide their money."

"That's just it," she said. "I never wanted." She hesitated, then took a deep breath. "My mother was a party girl when she was younger. There were always men and booze and sometimes drugs around. She's been married several times since my father was killed when I was a toddler but not one of the marriages has lasted."

There was a wealth of pain in the simple explanation, and suddenly it was easier to think about something other than his own gratification. "Where were you when these parties were going on?"

"In my room. But I could hear. I used to sneak out when I was younger and watch sometimes. Then one evening a man found me and made some—" she made a disgusted face "—improper advances. My stepfather of the moment threw him out. When I got older, my mother was determined to marry me off. She started introducing me to potential husbands when I turned sixteen."

Sam realized his hands were clenched in tight fists on the tabletop and he made a conscious effort to relax them, taking a deep breath. "I begin to see why you dress the way you do."

She smiled grimly, gesturing at him with a French fry like a teacher with a pointer. "Exactly."

"So how did you escape?"

"Went to college on the other side of the country from my mother. And you know the rest. I came to work for you three weeks after graduation."

When he'd just been starting out. He remembered it well. He'd spoken of his new business to an acquaintance whom he'd met while he was convalescing. The man had told him he knew a young woman with a new degree in Business Administration who would be an asset. Gave her glowing references.

He couldn't even imagine the childhood she'd described. Visions of a poorly clothed child in a filthy room fending off her mother's drug-dealing friends troubled him. Why had he never known any of this about her before?

He knew exactly why, he thought as he scarfed down the sandwich he'd ordered. He wasn't the type of person to inspire confidences on the best of days. And Del, without the inhibition-lowering dose of alcohol she'd consumed tonight, wasn't the type to share them. He gave silent thanks to whatever god had led them to this juncture tonight. Clearly, he'd been put in Del's path to keep her from making a huge mistake.

"Del," he said carefully, "I can appreciate what you've told me. And I can understand it. But why now? If you've decided you're interested in a relationship, why not go about it in a more conventional way?"

"A relationship?" She made a sour face. "No. The last thing I want is some man trying to make me believe he loves me." She laughed, but there was little humor in it. "My mother was a shining example of matrimonial bliss. Thanks, but I'll pass."

"All right. So you don't want a relationship. But why pick up a strange man in a bar?"

She looked at him as if he were insane. "Where else do you suggest I go? Church?"

"Well, maybe, but there are other ways to meet guys."

"Such as?"

Damn. He couldn't think of a single thing except—"What about online dating services?"

She cast him a speaking glance. "Would you consider doing that?"

"Not a chance." Then he realized what he'd just said, and he narrowed his eyes. "That was a trick question."

He'd had plenty of occasions to become familiar with Del's stubborn streak over the years. When she didn't respond, he could tell from the mulish look on her face—the one he knew meant *You can say whatever you want but I'm still doing it my way*—that she wasn't going to listen.

"There's nothing wrong with being a virgin," he said desperately.

"Are you?"

"Of course not! But...that's not the point." His recovery time was a beat too slow.

"Why? Because you're a guy?" Suddenly there were tears in her eyes.

Oh, hell. Tears. He *hated* tears. In the seven years they'd worked together he'd never seen Del cry once. "No. Of course not. Just because...because..." He was drowning, going down for the third time without a life vest, and Del wasn't about to throw it to him.

All of a sudden she stood up. She slung her purse over her shoulder. "See? You can't come up with a single valid reason." And she turned and walked away.

Sam sat, distantly aware that his mouth was hanging open as he watched her totter toward the bar on those ridiculously high heels. Those high heels that did such wonderful things for her amazing legs. How crazy was it that this was the first time he'd ever seen those legs? No crazier than the conversation they'd just had, he decided.

Then he realized she was sliding onto a bar stool and he stood up. No way was he going to let her do something so final. He tossed a bill on the table which would cover their drinks and his dinner along with a generous tip, and strode through the throng toward Del.

"…work for a security firm. You know, like home alarm systems and things," she was saying to a very interested guy next to her as Sam got within range. Even half-toasted and undoubtedly pissed at him, he noted that she was suitably low-key when discussing the business. They'd agreed long ago that the best advertising for their unique services was word-of-mouth, that not everyone would appreciate the kinds of things they offered.

"Hey," said Sam.

She turned to face him, frowning. "Go away."

"I'd be happy to. And you're coming with me." In one smooth move he spun her stool around to face him and hefted her over his shoulder in a fireman's carry.

"Sam!" It was a half scream.

"Hey, buddy," said the guy beside whom she'd been sitting.

Sam shot him a single, bring-'em-on look, the kind he'd once used in combat. "She's with me."

The man put both palms up in surrender. "Okay, whatever, man. I was just making a little conversation. I didn't know…" His voice faded as Sam turned and headed out of the bar.

Del was wriggling and squirming and generally being a pain. For a moment he couldn't keep his hand from lingering over the firm curve of her bottom. The skirt was so short he could slide his hand beneath it in a heartbeat—*stop it, Sam!* "Settle down," he said to her. Her bare legs were smooth and muscled beneath his arm and he ran an appreciative hand down her calf as he let the outer door swing shut behind them. "Do you run or something?"

"I am going to *kill* you," she said in a muffled voice. Probably had a faceful of his shirt and her hair.

"Nah." He set her on her feet beside his car, trying to ignore the basic hunger that surged when she shook her hair back from her face with one of those unbelievably erotic little head tosses women did without thinking. "Tomorrow morning you'll be thanking me."

"I will *not*." He'd never seen her defiant before, either. She hugged her arms around herself as if she were cold, which she probably was in that skimpy outfit, and her voice quavered when she spoke again. "Tomorrow morning I'll be even more of a dried-up old prune than I am now. No man's ever going to want me." Her breath was hitching and by the time she finished, he could see in the glow from the streetlights overhead the shine of tears making tracks down her cheeks.

God, he hated it when women cried. There was nothing in life he hadn't been trained to overcome during his years in the Navy SEAL teams—except feminine tears. "Stop bawling, dammit!" Suddenly, he was completely out of patience with her, with himself, with this whole crazy evening. Why the hell was he staying away from her? He wanted her, had wanted her for…years, maybe. He'd just never let himself acknowledge it before. "You're not going to be a prune. If you're so damn determined to lose your virginity tonight, then it might as well be with me."

"You?" It was, to his ears, a horrified whisper.

"Me," he repeated grimly. "I'm clean, I'm nonviolent—unless called for—and I'm familiar. I'm good at sex. You'll like it." *And oh, baby, so will I.* "Now get in the car."

Quickly, before she could begin to argue, he put an arm around her and ushered her to the passenger side of his vehicle. "I'll bring you down to pick up your car tomorrow. You're not driving tonight."

He closed her door, rounded the hood and slid into the driver's seat of his Jeep Cherokee. Del hadn't moved, hadn't even put on her seat belt, so he leaned across her and snagged it, buckling her in. As he did, his forearm pressed against the soft, yielding swell of her breast. She made a small, panicked almost-sound and went perfectly still. His pulse raced and his body quickened, but he resisted the urge to devour her right there on the spot. For a few seconds, their faces were close together and he could smell the warm, woman scent of her, could feel her breath on his cheek, could hear the shallow gulps of air she was taking in.

"You okay?" he asked gruffly.

"No." She sniffed and another tear trickled down her cheek.

Sam lifted his hand and brushed it away with his

thumb. "Yes, you are," he said quietly. "Now let me take you home, babe."

She sat quietly while he started the car and headed out onto the Capital Beltway. He knew her address, though he'd never been there, and he needed little direction until the last few streets in her development.

"Turn left here. It's the third one on the right."

The third one on the right turned out to be a spacious town house with a bay window. It was built into a hill that fell away in the back so that she actually had three levels, he noted as he followed the curving street around to the parking area.

He helped Del out of the car and followed her closely as she went up the sidewalk. She still tottered a little on the heels and he wasn't sure if it was alcohol or simply lack of practice, but he put an arm around her waist, anyway, enjoying the feel of her slender body tucked against his side while she fished for her key in her handbag. *Soon,* he told himself, *soon you'll know everything there is to know about the body that's been hidden beneath those damn tents for all these years.*

When she came up with a small ring of keys and selected one, he took it from her hand. She looked up at him then and her eyes were dark, unreadable pools in the moonlight.

"Look, ah, Sam, I had a fair amount to drink and, ah, I mean—I know you were just kidding and I do appreciate you saving me from myself—"

"Why do you think I was kidding?"

She bit her lip. "You don't want me," she said in a small voice. "You're just trying to be nice."

He shook his head, stifling a strong urge to laugh at both her and himself. "I'm not nice." He debated with himself for a moment. What the hell. "And I do want you. I've wanted you for a long time."

Her eyes were huge as she absorbed the words. Suspiciously, she said, "You have? You're not just saying that to make me feel better?"

"I'm not just saying that."

"But why—"

"You're stalling." He put the key in the lock. "What was it you said? You weren't going to wake up tomorrow morning and still be a virgin." He opened the door, then turned to face her, taking her face between his hands and simply holding her there, examining her wide, wary eyes and trembling mouth. "You started it," he said, and his voice was rough with need, "you can finish it."

Three

He kissed her then. Holding her face cradled in his big hands, he set his lips on hers the way he'd imagined doing in countless idle daydreams. Daydreams he'd barely permitted himself to admit to having before tonight.

Her lips were soft and warm and she made a small noise as their mouths touched. Her hands came up and wrapped around his thick wrists and to his pleased surprise, she didn't fight him or passively accept. No, she kissed him back. Awkwardly at first, but she was definitely responding.

She's a virgin, he reminded himself. *Take it*

slow. And so he did, leisurely making love to her mouth alone, molding her lips with his until she was twisting and turning to meet him. He was dying to touch her, to slide his palms down her body and cup her soft bottom, to pull her up against his aching flesh until she could have no doubt about his interest in her. But he forced himself to keep his hands lightly on her face, concentrating on arousing her first. Slowly, he tasted her with his tongue, light flicking touches along the closed seam of her lips, and glory, hallelujah, she opened to him, inviting him in and even meeting him with shy tastes of her own. Her mouth was warm and sweet; she tasted of those green things she'd been drinking, and he pushed farther into the slick, moist depths, showing her what his body longed to do.

When he finally lifted his head, she sagged against him and her forehead dropped to rest against his broad chest. "You should be labeled 'explosive,'" she mumbled.

He grinned, dropping a kiss on the crown of her bent head as he let his hands fall to her bare shoulders beneath that glorious mane of hair. "May I come in?"

She lifted her head again at that, and her lips

looked swollen, glistening with his kisses. "I thought I didn't have a choice."

"You don't," he said, brushing his thumbs along the sides of her neck. She was like a drug—now that he'd finally begun to touch her, he wasn't sure he'd ever be able to stop. "I just wanted to make you feel better."

She snorted, though he noticed she didn't move away from his caressing hands. "What if I'd said no?"

"Then I'd have had to charm you with my irresistibility."

"That is not a word."

He was absurdly pleased to have his smart-mouthed, reliable Del back instead of the fragile, weeping woman he'd had in his car. "Wanna bet?"

She considered. "No."

He chuckled. He had never really thought about the easy working relationship they'd had. They'd been in sync from the very beginning, on the same page, often thinking the same thing at the same moment.

From the very first, Del hadn't been afraid to voice her opinion, to stand toe to toe and argue with him when she felt she was right. As she'd gained experience and knowledge, he'd had to concede to her more often. Hell, at least half the time her business sense was better than his.

They made a good team, he and she, he thought as he slid his hands from her shoulders down her back to her waist. He had the knowledge to offer their clients the specialized kinds of help they needed. Del had company management capabilities. They'd taught each other a lot, and their very different styles meshed well.

He knew at least half the employees were scared stiff of him. He wasn't terrific with people. *Okay, get real, Sam.* The truth was, he sucked at interpersonal stuff. He had no patience, no sense of finesse. He left that to Del. She was sympathetic, empathetic, all that "-etic" stuff, but she had a core of iron as well as a keen nose for bull and he'd bet on her in a verbal exchange of fire any day of the week.

Yes, they were a good match, playing little games like the one they just had.

And it had relaxed her. Her body wasn't tense and stiff against his anymore, but soft and pliant. He was the one with the stiff body now, he thought with grim amusement. And it was going to be a while until he wasn't anymore.

"Sam?" Del's head had settled on his shoulder,

her temple at mouth level. Without her shoes, he was pretty sure he could have rested his head atop hers.

"Yeah?"

"Can I ask you some questions?"

"Maybe," he said, "we should go inside and get comfortable."

"Okay."

For answer, he bent and slid an arm beneath her knees, the other around her back, and lifted her into his arms.

"Whoa!" She clutched at his neck. "What's with you carrying me tonight? Although I have to say this method beats the last one."

He stepped into her house and kicked the door shut behind him. There was a small nightlight of stained glass in shades of rose giving off just enough glow for him to get his bearings, and he headed for a couch along one wall. When he reached it, he pivoted and sank down with her in his lap. Not a bad arrangement, he thought to himself, tugging her closer as he yanked off his glasses and tossed them on her coffee table.

Then he remembered her words. "Okay. You wanted to ask me something?"

"Several somethings, actually." She took a deep breath that pressed her body against his and added fuel to the fire raging through his system. Her arms were still linked around his neck and he could feel her idly playing with the hair at his nape. It was an intimate, erotic action and his body responded immediately. And then her words sank in.

"Give me a break." He sat up straighter. "You were going to pick up a stranger and now you're *interviewing* me? I don't think so." Dropping his head, he sought her lips again.

Del was laughing but she quickly wound her arms around his neck, pressing her upper body against his as she opened her mouth and kissed him back. He plunged his tongue deep, seeking out the unique flavor that was Del. It seemed impossible that he really could be sitting here with her in his arms.

Not just in his arms, he thought. The rounded curve of her hip and bottom were pressed against the bulge behind his zipper, exciting him even more as the soft flesh yielded, cushioned his insistent arousal.

His free hand rested at her waist, and he spread his fingers wide, covering her flat belly. Slowly he smoothed his palm upward but before he reached the soft pillowed flesh he sought, he slid his hand back down and repeated the action, stopping just short of the swell of her breast each time.

Finally, she tore her mouth from his. "Touch me," she breathed. She took his wrist and urged it higher, and he breathed out a sigh of relief as the firm, soft mound of feminine bounty filled his hand. He shaped her breast with his fingers, then began to brush his thumb back and forth across the tiny bud of her nipple until it peaked and rose, the taut outline clearly visible through the thin fabric of the dress.

"It's time to get you out of this dress." He gathered her into his arms, then rose. She was surprisingly light, as he'd noticed before. He supposed he didn't think of Del as a small and delicate woman, but that's exactly what she was beneath all that businesslike competence. "Where's your bedroom?"

"Back down the hall on the left." She touched a finger to his bottom lip, tracing a light path around his mouth. "I didn't know a bed was required."

He strode back down the hallway and entered her bedroom. "For your first time, it's a damn good idea."

That sobered her and she took her hand away from his mouth.

"Hey," he said, "it's going to be all right."

She smiled but her lips quivered a little. "I know. I'm just…nervous."

Afraid, is what she meant. He imagined women

the world over felt very much the same way the first time they gave themselves to a man. And telling her it was going to be okay wasn't helping one little bit. He'd have to show her.

The room was dim and he didn't bother with the bedside lamp. There was enough light spilling in from the hallway as well as the moon that shone through her open curtains for him to be content, and he suspected Del would be more comfortable if it was dark, anyway.

He let her slide down to her feet beside the bed. Reaching for the hem of the little dress, he slowly tugged it up her body and over her head, tossing it carelessly into a corner.

Her hair was a loose, wild cloud spilling over her shoulders and he gently combed tresses aside, pushing them behind her shoulders until her torso was revealed. All she wore now was a lacy black strapless bra and a tiny pair of matching panties.

As he took in her slim, shapely figure, the generous slope of creamy breast and rounded hip, his palms nearly itched to touch her. "Del," he said softly. "I can't believe I let you hide from me all these years. What a dope I was."

She smiled again, a little less tentatively this

time. "I didn't exactly go out of my way to let you know I was interested."

"Were you? Interested?"

She nodded. "Very."

Very. She was right, she had hidden it well. If he'd had any idea a little alcohol would uncover the truth, he'd have taken her out for a drink a long time ago.

He slid his hands from her shoulders in toward her throat, circling her neck gently. Letting his thumbs brush downward, he skimmed the shadowed cleavage between her breasts and let his hand drop to the front clasp of her bra. It had been a long time, but he hadn't forgotten everything he knew, and he easily snapped open the simple fastening. The fabric sprang free but clung to her, caught on the peaks of her breasts, and he smiled as he slowly brushed over the satiny flesh and let the bra fall to the floor.

"Pretty," he murmured, bending his head. He set his mouth against her neck just below her left ear, kissing and tasting the tender flesh he found. "Very pretty." As his hands cupped the warm mounds, he lightly brushed his thumbs over their taut peaks, feeling them rise beneath his touch as he slid his mouth down the slender column of her throat to the delicate joining of neck and shoulder. He pulled her to him again then, turning her sideways and arching her backward over his arm as he bent his head to the breasts that jutted up at him. Lazily, he used his tongue to trace a wet circle around one brown tip, then lightly blew on the sensitive flesh, smiling when she shuddered. He flicked his tongue over her again, not missing the way she shifted restlessly in his arms, and then he couldn't wait any longer. Nuzzling his face against her, he took one nipple into his mouth, sucking gently at it, rolling his tongue smoothly around and around as he increased the suction. Her hands came up to clasp around his head and he felt her body relax. Become his. All his.

Gently, he eased her upright and knelt before her.

"What are you doing?" Her hands were rigid on his shoulders.

For answer, he tugged at the tiny panties, sliding them slowly down her smooth, bare legs. "We forgot these." It was an effort to resist leaning forward and burying his nose in the sweet, dark-curled cleft at the top of her thighs, but he reminded himself that Del wasn't used to such intimacy. So he stood, urging her toward the bed as he stripped off his shirt and kicked out of his shoes.

"Why don't we lie down?" If she were more experienced, vertical wouldn't be a problem. But he wanted her to be comfortable, to have wonderful memories of her first time. Her first time with him.

She began to slide onto the bed, but suddenly she stopped. "Aren't you going to undress?"

He nodded. "You can help," he told her, taking her hands and setting them at his belt buckle. He closed his eyes in delight as he felt her small hands fumbling with the belt, the tips of her fingers pressing against him as she found the zipper tab and slowly lowered it. She spread his pants wide and he said, "Ahhh," as his hardening shaft was freed from the tight strictures.

He looked down at himself. His stretchy briefs were…stretched, leaving little to the imagination. Putting his thumbs beneath the top elastic edge, he slowly pulled them out and down. As he freed himself completely and stepped out of the briefs, he wondered what she was thinking. Had she ever seen an aroused man before?

Just as he was about to reassure her that yes, it really would fit, Del said in a small voice, "May I…touch you?"

He smiled, trying not to look too much like the Big Bad Wolf in Grandmother's bed. "Sure."

But when she had permission, she hesitated. He reached for her hand and lifted it, slowly drawing her palm to him, wrapping her small fingers around him and holding her hand there with light pressure.

She looked up at him, eyes wide in the dim light. "It's soft!"

"No," he said definitely. "It is not."

"I know *that*," she said with a startled laugh. "I meant it feels velvety. Soft over hard." She explored a little, running her fingertips up and down and around, and he shuddered, feeling a dangerous frisson of pleasure slide down his spine. Hastily, he pulled her hand away with a rough laugh.

"I like that," he said, "but if you don't want this to be over right now, you'd better stop."

"I'm sorry," she said, perfectly serious.

"Me, too," he said with feeling.

He stepped around her and pulled the covers back to the foot of the bed. She slid onto the mattress while he donned protection, moving over as he followed her until she was on her back in the circle of his arm.

He gathered her close with one arm, the other resting at her waist. He was pressed against her soft hip, and if he'd ever known anything more erotic than this moment of sexual anticipation, he couldn't remember it. He kissed her gently, running his hands from her waist to her breast and down again. Letting himself sink into the flavor and scent of her, deepening the kiss until she attempted to turn more fully into his arms.

He slid his hand across her belly, stroking her soft skin, allowing his hand to trail lower with each movement until his fingers were stroking the soft, tight curls between her legs.

"What are you doing?" she whispered.

He knew she didn't mean it literally. "Taking it nice and slow," he told her. He eased one finger into her warm cleft. "Open your legs for me."

Her eyes were wide, searching his face, so he leaned down and kissed her again as he slipped his hand farther between her legs and found what he'd been hoping for. She was moist and slick, responding to his handling as if she'd been made for him. Probing deeper, he found her snug channel and inserted one finger.

She was tight. Very tight, and he felt sweat breaking out all over at the thought of what it was going to feel like when he was inside her. He'd better not think about that right now. "You okay?" he asked her.

She nodded. "It doesn't hurt."

He smiled tightly as he withdrew and returned, this time using two fingers.

She was breathing heavily, beginning to move restlessly against him. He smiled to himself as he bent his head and took her breast again. As he did, he slipped his fingers up through the dense nest of curls, searching out the tender bud hidden there. She gasped sharply as he pressed, then circled lightly, and her hips lifted off the bed. "Sam!"

"Del," he murmured against her skin. "Relax. Enjoy."

To his delight, she was amazingly responsive, her body reacting with every slight touch, every kiss, every breath she took. Her hands grew damp and frantic as she clutched at him, her nails digging into him as she tried in vain to pull him atop her.

He was having an increasingly difficult time keeping a lid on his own reactions. The feel of her satiny hip repeatedly pressing against him was a potent stimulant, and soon he found himself moving against her in response, pleasure shivering through his system with every subtle shift.

Finally, when he sensed she was as ready as she could be without completely sliding over the edge, he shifted his weight. Del accepted him eagerly, spreading her legs so that he could nestle himself in the warm cove of her thighs. Just the feel of her soft body beneath him threatened his control, and he quickly moved into position.

"This might not be comfortable," he warned her.

"I don't care." She urged him on, palming his buttocks and trying to pull him to her. "Please, Sam?"

He forced himself to move slowly, to enter her only one small fraction at a time before withdrawing and forging ahead a little more. Over and over again, he repeated the motion, his arms corded with the effort of holding back, every muscle in his body focused on the slick, tight glove of her body. She didn't seem to be in pain or even discomfort, her eyes shining and her warm body flowing around him. Suddenly, she arched her back, digging her heels into the bed and shoving herself up, offering him everything. The motion embedded him deeply within her, and he groaned as he felt his body slipping from his precarious control. His hips surged once, then again and again. He gritted his teeth. "Del," he ground out, "I-can't-wait."

"I can't, either," she panted. "Make love to me, Sam."

It was impossible to resist her plea. Letting his body take over, he ceased to think. Pure sensation reigned as he found his rhythm and urged her into following his lead, fiery pleasure spreading through him with each stroke. His body drew tighter and tighter as forerunners of ecstasy tap-danced down his spine. Del was moving wildly beneath him, with him, her slim body a beautiful sight.

She was making small sounds each time he moved against her, a whimpering, keening, needy sound that rose higher and higher until her body began to convulse beneath him, her tight sheath gripping him, milking him again and again as she shook and shattered. He couldn't wait, couldn't hold on, and with a rush of satisfaction he followed her, his body completing the mating ritual in the most primitive of ways, arching his spine and sending his seed forth in an explosive finish that nearly took off the top of his head.

In the aftermath, he slowly let his shaking arms relax and collapsed onto Del, burying his face in the pillow just beside her. Her arms came up around him immediately and the small motion created a warm glow deep inside him. She stroked his back lightly and as he moved to one side and drew her into his arms, he knew he was going to do his best to see that he spent a lot of nights from now on in Del's bed with her small body tucked securely against him.

Four

"Why," he said, kissing the fragile shell of her ear that was mere inches from his mouth, "haven't we ever done this before?"

He felt her shoulder slide against his chest as she shrugged. "I always wanted you to notice me."

"I did notice you. I've spent countless hours over the past seven years wondering exactly what was under those huge shirts of yours." He cupped a breast in one big palm, gently brushing his thumb back and forth across the nipple. "Now I know," he said with deep satisfaction.

"You noticed me? Why didn't you ever do anything about it, then?" She ran her fingers through the hair across his breastbone.

He shrugged. "I'm shy?"

When she hooted with laughter, he tickled her until she screamed for mercy. Then she found the single tiny ticklish spot along the left side of his ribs and he was the one begging her to stop.

"I can think of some *s* words that describe you, but shy isn't one of them," she gasped, wiping tears of merriment from her face.

"Such as?" He smoothed her hair and settled her along his side again. He sandwiched one smooth thigh between his as she turned into his arms and nestled her head on his shoulder.

"Surly," she said.

"Me?" He was too preoccupied with his body's response to her to be offended. He was already half aroused again from their tussling and teasing, and her knee was lightly brushing some very sensitive territory. Having her sweet warmth so close and so very available was a form of the most pleasurable torture, because he knew she would be too tender, too sore, to accept him again that night.

"Everyone in the office trembles when you pass," she said.

"What happened to *s* words?"

"Scary," she said promptly, and laughed when he growled. "Sexy, of course."

"Of course."

"Smart, seductive, surprising depths—"

"That's two, but I like it."

He felt her smile against his skin. Then she gave a mighty yawn. "I'm sleepy."

"Go to sleep, then."

"Will you stay?"

"Yeah," he said. "I'll stay." *Just try getting rid of me, baby.* For some reason, he thought of her earlier question again. *Why didn't you ever do anything about it, then?* Why hadn't he ever thought about asking Del out? And then he knew. "You want to know why I never asked you out, Del?"

"Um-hmm." She sounded slightly more alert.

"Because I was afraid of what would happen when it ended. You'd have left and I couldn't have stood that. I need you, Del."

She stretched up and pressed a kiss against his chin. "I need you, too."

But she didn't. She had a life that could move on quite smoothly without him in it. But if she quit and he never saw her again… "I can't imagine running the business without you." It was inadequate, but he couldn't really express what he wanted to say.

Was it his imagination or did she shrink slightly away? He didn't move, but he pondered his last words. Did she think he hadn't paid her fairly for all the work she'd done through the years? He'd tried, but perhaps they should discuss it. Or maybe it was more than that—he'd wondered, on occasion, if he should make her a partner. He had no idea if she'd ever thought about it, had no idea if she had any capital to invest, but she deserved it. PSI wouldn't exist today if it weren't for Del, he was sure.

Then she said, "Lucky for you, you don't have to. 'Night."

He knew enough about women to know a dismissal when he heard one, so he shut up. Instead, he kissed her. To his immense relief, she lifted her face to his and responded, and he gathered her closer.

"Umm," she said. "What's that I feel?"

"Me appreciating you."

She laughed, and to his delighted surprise, slipped one small hand down between their bodies, exploring him with her fingers. "I didn't think men could, ah—"

"Some men can." He moved his hips, thrusting himself a little more firmly against her hand, groaning in pleasure when she gripped him firmly. "And would love to." He rolled to his back, spreading his legs slightly and giving her complete access to his body. "Wanna explore?"

She lifted her head and smiled at him, her eyes slitted with pleasure. "I'd love to."

The next morning, he awoke to an empty bed. The clock said it was after nine, and warm sunlight streamed into Del's tidy blue-and-white bedroom. He tossed back the covers and rose, stretching, then snagged his pants from the floor and headed for the bathroom.

Afterward, he followed the smell of coffee and bacon down to her kitchen.

She was sitting at the table, nursing a cup of coffee while she read the morning paper. Her hair was down, curling around her shoulders like a living curtain, and she wore only pajama bottoms and a brief camisole top that revealed the rounded shape of her breasts in a manner none of her daily work clothes ever had.

When their eyes met, heat flared and sizzled. But all she said was, "Good morning. Did you sleep well?"

Her tone was neutral. For a second he was puzzled—and then it hit him. She probably was embarrassed about last night—about the frank things she'd said and done—and she was expecting him to make quick excuses and leave this morning, having completed his duties last night. He sure as hell hoped that wasn't what she *wanted,* because he had no intention of going back to the unsatisfying way things had been before.

He was glad last night had happened. He was tired of being alone. It had been more than eight years since he'd been with a woman who meant anything more than simple relief, and he didn't realize how much he'd missed intimacy. Hadn't *allowed* himself to realize it, he supposed.

Crossing the kitchen, he scooped her out of her chair and sat down with her in his lap, settling her against his chest. He picked up her coffee cup and took a sip, then set it down and took a length of her unbound hair in his hand, gently stroking through it. "Good morning," he said. "I slept fine until I woke up alone."

"Sorry," she said, "I thought maybe you liked to sleep in on the weekends and I didn't want to disturb you."

"Not particularly. I'd rather spend time with you." Immediately he felt her body subtly relax, and triumph surged through him. He'd been right. "What do you want to do today?" he asked.

She shrugged, her camisole slipping lightly up and down against his bare chest. "I don't know."

"Well, what do you usually do on the weekends?"

Puffs of air blasted his chest as she chuckled. "Laundry."

He grimaced. "Me, too." Slowly, he slipped his hands beneath the hem of the little top she wore and ran his palms lightly up and down her back. She made a sound almost like a purr and relaxed even further in his embrace, and he gently cupped one of her pretty breasts, slowly rubbing his thumb back and forth over the sensitive tip that rose to meet him. He cleared his throat, but his voice was husky and deep when he spoke. "I've got some ideas on how we can spend the day."

Immediately, the tension returned to her body. "I don't think I can, at least until tonight," she said, regret in her tone. She pushed against his hold and rose from his lap, picking up her coffee cup and carrying it to the sink. "I'm sure you have things to do today and I actually do have a number of errands to run—"

"Whoa." He held up a hand, unable to believe his ears. Was she really giving him the brush-off because she thought all he wanted from her was sex? He rose and caught her hand, tugging her against him. "Del, I'd still like to be with you, even if we can't make love."

Doubt shone loud and clear in her skeptical gaze. "You would?"

"Yeah."

"Why?"

How in the world could a woman this appealing not have any idea of her own charm? He intended to find out more about her life until he figured it out. "As great as it was," he said gently, "I don't just want to jump your gorgeous bones. I want to spend time with *you*. Talking. Hanging out together."

She looked completely befuddled. "But if we can't—"

Sam put a hand over her mouth. Clearly, he wasn't getting through with words. He'd just have to show her. "After breakfast," he told her, "we'll go over to my place and grab my laundry. We can do it together and then maybe catch a movie or something later. Okay?"

She nodded solemnly behind his hand. "Okay."

He took a deep breath. "Would it be okay if I kept some clothes and things here?"

She looked at him as if he'd grown two heads. "What for?"

"So I can spend my free time with you," he said patiently, although her suspicious reaction put him on guard. He'd thought she would welcome the question.

She actually thought about it for a minute and he found himself actually breaking into a light sweat. Was she seriously thinking of refusing? "All right," she said at last. "I'll clear out a drawer for you if you like."

"I like." He tried to be as casual as she, although his brain was working overtime, picking apart the mystery that was Del. He'd expected his intent would signal his interest in establishing a more permanent relationship, that she would understand now that he meant her to be more than a handy bed partner. Instead, she'd nearly shot him down. He mentally added her reaction to the list of other questions he had in his head. Why would she be so skittish about letting him share her space?

And then he realized what he'd just been thinking. A permanent relationship. Holy hell, where had that come from? Yesterday he'd been happily single, today he was pondering the best way to get Del to let him move in. It was a pretty major shift of viewpoint, but he knew what had happened. For seven years he'd been watching Del without any real expectation of getting closer. But his subconscious knew what a prize she was, and the first moment that she gave him an opportunity, he'd recognized it.

And now that he'd gotten close, he had no intention of letting her push him away again.

Monday morning came too fast, in his opinion. The weekend had been unbelievable. Del was the most responsive woman he'd ever dreamed of, as she got past her initial inhibitions. He'd have been happy to spend another week making love to her. And he would, once her newly initiated body healed enough for more frequent lovemaking. Maybe, he thought wryly, if he kept her in bed that long he'd learn a little more about her. She'd said very little more about herself since the summary of her less-than-ideal childhood on Friday night.

"What's Del short for?" he asked as they were dressing for work.

"Nothing," she said.

"Just Del?" He was openly skeptical, although he knew from her personnel report that was the only name she'd used on any documents.

"Just Del," she said firmly. "Do you prefer Sam to Samuel?"

"Yeah." No point in explaining that Samuel wasn't the name he'd been given at birth. He'd been Sam for a lot of years and he liked it just fine. It still amazed him that no reporter had uncovered his legal name after the incident.

The Incident. That's how he'd come to think of it in the years since, that stupid little label the media often used to describe horrific events.

"Are you ready?" Her question jarred him from his unwelcome introspection as she picked up her briefcase and headed for the door.

"Right behind you."

They'd picked up her car from O'Flaherty's on Saturday, but he saw no sense in them driving separately to work now. He had every intention of coming home with her again tonight. Still, once they reached the office, Del insisted on entering individually.

"Why?" The way she kept trying to keep him an arm's length away was beginning to rankle.

She shrugged. "I'd rather the entire company didn't know we have a personal relationship now."

He hooted at her prim tone. "You mean you don't want them to know we're sleeping together."

She glared at him. "Well, yes. Hasn't it occurred to you, in this age of sexual-harassment suits, that it might not be such a great thing to broadcast?"

He sighed. "Del. We both know there's no harassment involved—unless the fingernail marks you left on my behind last night count—and we're the only ones who matter."

She blushed to the roots of her hair. Finally, she smiled and a wash of relief rolled through him. "Okay. But would you just humor me? I already feel like I'm wearing a sign that says, 'Sam and I…'"

"Are doing the mattress dance?" he suggested, laughing.

"Ick!" She punched his shoulder, then reached for her door handle. "Just like a man. If you're going to be crude, I'm outta here."

"Hey." He caught her hand as she began to slide out of the car.

"Hmm?" She turned to face him.

He leaned across the seat and claimed her mouth in a brief, stirring kiss. Her lips softened and warmed beneath his before he drew away. "Thanks for this weekend."

She smiled softly, touching his cheek with a gentle finger. "I'm the one who should be thanking you."

He gave her a head start, then casually entered behind her. He paused in the outer office where Peggy reigned. She and Del already were bent over some forms on Peg's desk. "'Morning, Peg. 'Morning, Del."

"Hey, boss." Peggy glanced up at him and her eyes widened. She immediately fastened her gaze on Del. "Yee-haw!" she hooted.

"What?" Del jumped and lifted her head.

"It's about time you two got together," Peggy said.

"What makes you think we did?" Del asked.

Peggy grinned. "You're glowing and he smiled at me."

He raised his eyebrows and tried to look fierce. "And that's a sign of…?"

"Sam," said Peggy. "You *never* smile before you've had your coffee. Besides, Del's blushing."

Oh, hell. Now they were going to be the water-cooler topic of the week. He quickly escaped to his inner sanctum, leaving Del to fend off Peggy. Women were better at that kind of thing, anyway. As he closed the door, though, he heard Peggy say, "The air around you two has been sizzlin' for years. If I'd have wet my finger and stuck it between you I'd have gotten electrocuted."

Had he been that obvious? Interesting that Peggy had recognized it before he had.

At nine, Karen Munson came in to fill out more paperwork and meet the people with whom she'd be working. Since the undercover-division leader was on vacation until Friday, Del had arranged to have Walker show her the ropes and bring her up to speed on current contracts. Walker was the head of the abductions division, but he often worked closely with undercover so it wouldn't be much of a stretch.

That was fine with Sam, since he needed Del to help him work up an estimate for a new job they'd just gotten. Karen was in Del's office so when he heard Del page Walker, he got up and went to the door that led from his office to Del's.

He walked across the room with his hand extended. "Good to have you on board," he told Karen.

"Thank you." She didn't quite smile, but the serious expression that seemed to be her norm lightened a little. "I'm looking forward to getting started."

A knock on the door preceded Walker's entry.

"Come on in," Sam called. To Karen, he said, "The head of our abductions team is going to explain our procedures to you and bring you up to speed on our current contracts. Undercover employees often work closely with abductions and surveillance."

As Walker entered the room, Sam turned to him, indicating the new hire. "Walker, I'd like you to meet—"

"Karen!" Walker's shocked exclamation echoed through the room. "What the hell are you doing here?" He made the question an insult.

"I'm working here now," she said coolly, although she looked nearly as shaken as Walker was, "as you apparently do."

"No way." Walker's eyes narrowed. "This work isn't going to suit you."

"You have no idea what suits me anymore," she said sharply.

"Did she tell you she's my wife?" Walker demanded, wheeling to face Sam. His big hands were actually fisted at his sides.

"Ex-wife." Karen's tone was frosty. "And no, amazingly enough, your name never even entered the conversation during my interview. I had no idea you worked here." *Or I'd never have taken the job.* The unspoken words hung in the air like glass slivers in a broken window's frame.

"I can't work with her." Walker wheeled and stalked to the window.

Sam looked at Del, silently questioning her with his eyes. *What the hell do we do now?*

Del's eyes were the size of saucers, but as always, she rose to the occasion. "Sam, why don't you and Walker go into your office?" she said. She indicated the door to the hallway as she turned to Karen. "I'll take Karen down to her desk and get her started."

As she led Karen from the room, she glanced back at him, and he read her response. *Calm him down!*

Great. She got the lamb and he got the lion. Pushing a hand through his hair, he said, "Walker. My office." He turned without waiting for a response and entered his own office again, taking a seat behind his desk. Intuition told him authority was going to be important right now, though he'd always had an easy, friendly relationship with the bigger man in the past.

Walker followed him in, every muscle in his solid frame looking tense and taut. "I mean it, Sam," he said in a deep, furious tone. "I can't work with that b—"

"Hey," Sam said. "Walker. Chill. Take a deep breath." He took his own advice, watching Walker pace around the perimeter of the room. "I didn't know." Honesty compelled him to add, "But I might have hired her anyway. She's exactly what we're looking for."

Walker spun around and glared at him. "She's *not* what we're looking for. We need a dedicated individual who can be as flexible as we need her to be. Karen doesn't know the meaning of the word." His tone was bitter. "It's her way or no way."

"She says she'll work as long and as hard as we need her to." Sam watched his abductions expert closely, wondering what had gone wrong between the couple to make Walker still feel this way after so many years. Karen Munson must have been the woman responsible for the binge Walker had gone on that time he'd come in so hungover, but Walker had indicated then that the marriage had been over some years before he'd come to PSI.

"She's got a family," Walker said harshly. The words sounded raw and accusatory. "She's always going to put her husband and kid above the job."

Sam cleared his throat. Karen Munson hadn't stipulated that the information she'd shared with him was private. Quietly, he said, "Her child is…deceased."

Walker's angry gaze flew to his, incredulity replacing the rage. *"What?"* It was an explosion.

Sam just watched him.

"God." Walker dropped heavily into a chair and buried his head in his hands as his anger visibly drained away. "Is she still married?" he asked in a muffled tone.

Sam could answer that. After the initial interview, he'd checked out Karen's application. "She listed herself as a widow."

Walker raised his head and there was more anguish in his gaze than Sam had seen in anyone's eyes since he'd woken in a hospital bed and his commander on the teams had had the unenviable task of telling Sam he'd probably never walk again. "They're both dead?" he whispered.

"You knew she was married and had a child?"

The other man nodded. "That's why she left me. I wasn't willing to settle down." Remembered agony twisted his features. "She replaced me faster than you can say 'I do.'" He heaved a deep sigh. "God, I've hated her for years. But I never wished anything like this on her. What happened?"

Sam shrugged. "She didn't get into it. Just made us aware that she was free to work pretty much anytime we needed her."

"I don't think I can work with her." Walker sounded defeated.

"Why don't you—"

But the other man shook his head. "She cut out my heart, Sam. I just don't think I can do it." Slowly he rose to his feet, walking toward the door like a man much older than forty. "My resignation will be on your desk by the end of the day."

"I won't accept it."

Walker turned, his hand on the doorknob. "You'll have to."

But Sam shook his head. "You're the best at what you do, buddy. I'll tell Karen we can't employ her."

Walker stared at him a moment. "You can't do that."

"Wanna bet? I'm not about to lose you."

There was a taut moment of silence, humming with tension.

"Damn." Walker's shoulders slumped. "You know I wouldn't do that to her. Especially now, after…"

"I was hoping so." Sam got up from behind his desk and walked across the room to the man who'd been one of his first hires and most faithful employees. "We'll look at the structure and see if we can't work something out so you don't have to work closely together, all right?"

He held out his hand. After a moment, Walker took it and they shook. "I'd appreciate it," the big man said quietly, and left the room.

Five

An hour later, he heard Del return to her office. Moments after that, she came through the connecting door. "Hey," she said.

"Hey."

"I got Karen settled, showed her around. She's reading over the current workload for the rest of the day." She perched on the corner of his desk and blew out a deep breath. "What a bombshell."

He took off his glasses and massaged the bridge of his nose. "I sure wasn't expecting that."

She grimaced. "I had no idea they'd been married."

"I looked at her file again. It's not mentioned in there but there isn't any reason it should have been."

She picked up his glasses and fiddled with them idly. "What are we going to do?"

He shrugged. "Nothing. We hired her. Walker's going to have to deal with it if he stays. I can't just fire her because he doesn't want to work with her." He paused. "I told him we'd try to figure out something so he didn't have to work with her much."

A single elegant eyebrow rose. "You think we can manage that?"

"To some extent."

"I guess you're right." Del started cleaning his glasses with the tail of her shirt. Then she held them up to the light. A moment later, she lowered them and looked at him with a strange expression. "Sam?"

"Yeah?" He was still thinking about Walker's defeated expression. He'd felt like that for a while after Ilsa had dumped him. He never wanted to feel it again, either.

"Why do you wear glasses if you don't need them? These aren't prescription lenses, are they?"

Hell. He'd completely forgotten about that. "No," he said slowly, "they aren't."

"So why do you wear them?" she asked again.

He searched for an explanation she would accept. *Because I don't want to be recognized* was definitely not the right one. "I've found they make people take me more seriously." That was lame.

But Del's face lit up with amusement. "You mean women, don't you? Poor baby. Were you getting hit on a lot?"

He narrowed his eyes. "You think that's funny?"

"I think it's true." She was laughing. "Sam Deering. Hunk of the year."

She had no idea how accurate that was and because she didn't, he was able to laugh. He shot out a hand and grabbed her elbow, yanking her off her perch on the edge of the desk and into his arms. "So you wanna hit on me?"

She slipped her arms around his neck, running her fingers through the curling hair that lapped over the collar of his denim shirt in the back. "I might."

He lowered his mouth to hers. "Notice me struggling."

"Hey, boss, I've got—Whoops!" Peggy barged into the office and just as quickly retreated, shutting the door behind her. From the other side of the closed door, they could hear hoots of laughter.

"Damn," he said, regretfully releasing Del. "There goes my office credibility."

"What about mine?" Del straightened her shirt, blushing furiously.

"You don't have to worry. I'm irresistible, remember?"

She groaned. "Not that again." But she was laughing as she went to open the door for Peggy.

Other than that Monday-morning explosion with Walker and his ex-wife, it was the best week of his life. He and Del arose together, ate breakfast together, went to work together in the morning. At work, after the time Peggy had caught them on Monday, they were the model of propriety except for the occasional blood-pressure-raising exchange of glances.

Until they were alone together after everyone else had left the building.

Then he couldn't seem to keep his hands off her. It didn't prevent their work from getting done if he pulled her into his lap while they argued the cost estimates on a project. And it didn't slow them down too drastically if, while she was showing him the layout for the new brochure, he slipped his hand up beneath her baggy shirt and cupped one rounded breast, teasing the nipple into stiff attention until her eyes clouded and she pulled away.

"Stop," she said. "I can't think straight when you do that."

Good. He didn't want her to think straight. He wanted her to think Sam. Only Sam.

After work they prepared meals together. Del was no better and no worse than he was in the kitchen. Between them they could put together a decent stuffed chicken, potatoes and a salad.

It amazed him, when he stopped to think about it, how easily they'd fit into each other's lives. It was as if they'd been together for years. Which, he supposed, wasn't far from the truth. While they hadn't lived together, they'd worked so closely together that they knew each other's quirks and moods without speaking.

He knew her favorite kind of pizza—pepperoni—and that when she was annoyed her eyes became as green as emeralds. She knew that ice cream gave him indigestion, and that he couldn't knot his tie to save his life. Her habit of drumming her fingers on the table while she was thinking aggravated him endlessly, and when he chewed on the end of practically every pen he picked up, she fussed at him about spreading his germs to everyone in the company.

But in many ways, she was still an enigma. As

far as he could tell, her life was as solitary as his. She didn't appear to have any close girlfriends, and the calendar on the wall in her kitchen was conspicuously empty, except for a few notations about birthdays for co-workers. It appeared that her life revolved around PSI as much as his did.

That was weird. Most women were nesters in one way or another, drawing at least one or two people close even if they weren't highly social. He'd never heard Del speak of a single person who wasn't connected with the company other than her mother. And though she was close to several of the other PSI employees, particularly Peggy, he'd noticed the relationships seemed largely to end at the office door. *Except for birthday parties,* he thought, smiling to himself.

Friday evening, they took a prospective client to dinner, a West Coast actress who had been receiving death threats. Sam always invited Del along to meet prospective clients, and she usually attended. She was so much better than Sam at putting people at ease that he found her presence a welcome buffer.

As they were getting ready to go out, Del said, "Tell me again why Savannah Raines wants to hire us?"

Sam glanced across the bedroom. "Stalker," he said briefly. Then he stopped in the act of donning his charcoal suit coat. "You're wearing that?"

"That" was a shapeless black pantsuit. Now that he thought about it, he realized Del had worn the exact same outfit to every dinner meeting they'd had over the past seven years.

She glanced down at the boxy black jacket and equally loose black slacks. "Yes. Why?"

Sam walked across the room, thinking about the best way to word his objections. "You've worn it a lot before."

"So?" She was looking at him in bewilderment. "It's comfortable."

"It helps you hide, is what you mean," he said.

"Hide?" Her voice was chilly, but he didn't care. Someone, somewhere, had given Del reason to believe she wasn't attractive, and Del had been playing down her every asset ever since, he'd bet. "You hide behind glasses with useless lenses."

"You're a beautiful woman," he said, ignoring her words as he crossed to her. "That dress your mother sent you looked terrific on you the other night. This—" he indicated her unflattering suit "—is like everything else you own—designed to make you invisible."

"Maybe," she said stiffly, "that's what I'm aiming for. Maybe I like being invisible."

"Do you?"

She hesitated, and he realized she hadn't expected him to challenge her aggressive words. "Most of the time, yes," she finally said. "I have good reasons for not wanting to attract attention." Then she smiled, and he felt himself responding to the sensuality in her knowing gaze. "But I'm glad I wasn't invisible last Friday night."

"Me, too," he said, meaning it. He was willing to let the subject drop for the time being, but he knew she thought she'd successfully sidetracked him. If she thought he was going to forget about it, she didn't know him very well. She'd really piqued his interest with that simple statement: *I have good reasons for not wanting to attract attention.* What reasons could be good enough to make a woman work that hard to hide her natural beauty?

Savannah Raines's husband came with her, and over dinner they discussed her best options for keeping herself and her family safe as well as for locating the individual making the threats.

The actress was surprisingly pleasant and

down-to-earth and her husband, an architect, was nothing like some of the idiotic Hollywood types they occasionally dealt with. Sam would have enjoyed the meal except that Del was being almost monosyllabic. She wasn't rude or unfriendly, in fact she was better than he at explaining what PSI could do for Savannah. But when they weren't talking business, she sat back and seemed more than content to let him hold up the conversation, which was definitely not his strong suit. Usually, it was hers, and he wondered if she wasn't feeling well or something.

He glanced at her, sitting quietly in the corner of the booth beside him just as Savannah said to Del, "You know, dear, you look so familiar to me. Have we met somewhere?"

Del raised one eyebrow, a unique trait that always intrigued him. "I doubt it, Ms. Raines. Have you been to Virginia before?"

The question implied that Del was a Virginia girl, and Sam knew for a fact that wasn't true. She'd graduated with honors from Williams College, an exceptionally selective liberal-arts school in Massachusetts, shortly before he'd hired her. It suddenly dawned on him that he had no idea where she'd lived before that, and he cast her a sharp look. How was it they'd worked together so long and he knew so little about her formative years? He deliberately stayed quiet about his own past because he had something to hide. But it seemed that so did she: *I have good reasons for not wanting to attract attention.* The sentence kept replaying in his head.

What reason could Del possibly have for her reticence? What was she hiding? Somehow, he doubted it was anything as earthshaking as his desire not to have half the country recognize him when he walked out his front door.

At the end of the evening, they said goodbye to their guests and Sam helped Del into the front seat of his Jeep. He hadn't forgotten his thoughts from earlier in the evening.

As they drove back toward her place, he said, "You lied by omission in there tonight."

"What?" Del sounded understandably bewildered.

"You let Savannah believe you grew up in Virginia. Did you?"

"No." Her bewilderment acquired a distinct edge of irritation. "I just didn't see any point in going into my background."

"Guess where I grew up." He knew she'd get pricklier if he pressed her, and though he was determined to get some information out of her tonight, he was prepared to take his time and go about it leisurely.

She paused, apparently searching her memory banks. Finally, with an air of surprise, she said, "I don't know. California?"

The guess was incorrect, but it shook him. He'd never told anyone at the company that he'd been based in San Diego during his years with the teams. In fact, he didn't think anyone even knew he'd been a SEAL. They knew he was ex-military but he knew most of them assumed he'd come from the army and he'd never done anything to correct their impressions.

"No," he said in answer to her guess. "I lived in California before I started the company. But I grew up in Nebraska."

"Nebraska?"

He glanced across the car and was amused to see that single eyebrow raised again. "Yep. On a ranch a few miles from the South Dakota border."

"You're kidding. I never would have pegged you for a cowboy."

He grinned. "I hide it well."

"You can ride a horse?" She sounded highly skeptical.

"Of course I can ride a horse. On a ranch, everybody rides. I learned to drive when I was thirteen, though, because my dad got thrown and broke a leg that summer."

"I didn't learn to drive until I was in college," she said.

"Why?" He was startled. That was far more unusual than learning to drive early.

She shrugged. "Never really needed to before that. Are your parents still in Nebraska?"

He nodded, aware that once again she'd neatly avoided talking about herself. "And my younger brother and sister. David and his wife have three sons and they live in the house where I grew up. My sister, Rachel, lives about twenty minutes away with her family. Mom and Dad moved into a smaller house on the property a few years ago."

"So you're the only one who moved away."

"Yeah." He took a deep breath. "I joined the navy."

This time she turned fully in her seat to stare at him. "You're full of surprises tonight. I thought you were army."

"Nope."

"Why the navy?"

"I wanted to be a SEAL."

She was silent for a moment. Finally, she said, "That explains it."

"Explains what?"

"The way you seem to know everything there is to know about the weird military stuff."

He was amused again. "Weird military stuff. Such as?"

"Such as every kind of explosive on the market, weapons I've never even heard of, the best ways to get people in and out of places they shouldn't be in the first place." She took a breath. "You always consider the worst-case scenario and plan for it. That's one of the reasons we're so successful. When we take on a job, it gets done even when something unexpected forces us to alter the original plan."

He didn't quite know how to respond to that. He'd never really thought about it before. "Building this company has been exciting," he said, "but we never would have become what we are today without you. I'd better remember to thank Robert someday for recommending you."

"How did you meet Robert?" she asked.

Yikes. He wasn't quite ready to go there yet, although he supposed that someday he would have to tell Del about his past.

"A year or so before I started PSI, I had an injury that ended my navy service," he said. It was true enough; he just didn't mention how he'd been hurt. "I was trying to decide what I was going to do with my life. So there I was, lying on a gurney in the hospital waiting for some X rays and this guy starts to talk to me. He was there for knee surgery and we both had to kill some time until they came for us. Turned out he once was married to an actress—he had all kinds of advice for me about how to avoid losing my privacy."

"Robert." Her voice was quiet. She'd become very still while he'd been speaking and he wondered what she was thinking.

"Yes," he said. "So how did you know him? When he recommended you, I got the impression he'd known you for a long time."

"He was a family friend."

"A friend of your mother's?"

"Um-hmm."

"He's a great guy." And Sam couldn't imagine the distinguished, elegant Robert hooking up with the woman Del had described. But who knew?

"Were you injured during a mission, or whatever you call it?"

The question caught him off guard, though he

supposed he should have expected it. She'd seen the bullet wounds the first night they'd made love. The one that had ripped through his bicep didn't look too bad.

But the other one told a different story. The slug had entered just above his left hipbone and torn its way through his body to exit through his back. It had nicked his spine and though he'd lost bits and pieces of several organs, that hadn't been the damage that worried his doctors the most. He'd experienced temporary paralysis. Of course, no one had known it was temporary until it began to fade, and he'd spent weeks adjusting to the thought of life as a paraplegic.

And as a man who'd been dumped when he was no longer the able-bodied SEAL his fiancée had wanted.

He still could barely stand to think about those days. But she needed an answer.

"Sort of," he said briefly, hoping she wouldn't pursue the topic.

"Your injuries look as if they were serious."

"They were." He didn't have to dissemble about that.

There was a moment of silence. He didn't look at Del, but he could feel her gaze measuring him. Finally she said, "I'm glad you didn't die."

They had arrived, and he pulled into the parking lot and cut the engine before responding. Then he reached for her in the dark interior of the vehicle, hauling her into his arms. Just before he took her mouth, he said, "I'm glad I didn't die, too. I'd never have met you."

She kissed him back with all the fire and passion he'd come to expect, but when he lifted his head, she didn't say anything more.

"Shall we go in?" he asked.

She nodded. "Let's."

As they started up the steps together, it occurred to him that they had never had any kind of conversation that hinted at future plans. She'd reluctantly agreed to let him bring over some of his things, and throughout the week he'd gradually brought more and more, until he had enough changes of clothes that he didn't have to go home for a week if he didn't want to. She had to have noticed, but she hadn't protested, and he'd taken that as a good sign.

But sudden uncertainty pulled him to a halt in the hallway just outside her door. "Del?"

She glanced up at him, smiling as she extracted

her key from the purse she'd carried this evening in a departure from her usual backpack. "Hmm?"

"Are you okay with this? With us?"

The door swung open, but she continued to look at him. "Yes. Are you?"

She'd answered him, so he didn't know why he felt unsatisfied. Maybe he hadn't asked the right question. "Yeah," he said. "I am."

But something within him wanted more. More what, he wasn't sure. But he definitely wanted more from Del and he wasn't at all sure she was prepared to give it.

That night, for the first time in more than six months, he had the dream.

He was walking down a street not far from the utilitarian apartment in San Diego where he lived when he wasn't on an op. He was carrying a sack of groceries he'd picked up at the corner store.

It was a sunny Saturday afternoon in November and the temperature was shirtsleeves pleasant. There were tourists crowding the seafood market and checking out the little boutiques that had overtaken the rougher elements of the neighborhood a few years ago. It was a perfect day.

And then a madman opened fire.

He instantly recognized the rapid, distinctive sound of shots and reacted. But as he went rolling for the dubious cover of a nearby parked car, he felt a punch in his left shoulder, followed moments later by a searing pain.

He'd been shot!

And whoever had done it was still shooting.

Dammit. In his years with the navy, he'd never suffered more than cuts and bruises and once, a concussion from a blast that had gone off a little too close for comfort. And here he was, at home on leave with a bullet wound in his shoulder. God must enjoy a good joke.

Cautiously, he peeked around the fender of the car. A lone man was strolling down the street at an almost leisurely pace, about twenty-five yards away. Three people lay sprawled on the pavement behind him, unmoving. At least one, a man, was clearly dead, Sam was sure, from the awkward angle at which the body had fallen. Another woman knelt on the pavement not far from where the guy was walking, a child cradled in her lap.

The shooter raised his pistol and shot her through the head.

Sam recoiled, his brain rejecting what he'd just

seen. He heard another shot, a piercing scream and then another shot. The screaming stopped instantly.

God, this guy was executing people! Instantly, his mind went into what he privately thought of as protection mode, automatically seeking and assessing his chances of eliminating the enemy while saving his own hide and those of all the other people around him.

He glanced behind him, down the street in the other direction. Several people lay where they'd fallen when they'd been hit. Most of them were moving. And Sam would bet there were more people who'd taken cover just like him. This could be a massacre of devastating proportions.

In a doorway opposite him, a woman in a shopkeeper's apron crouched, her eyes wide and terrified. A kid in the baggy pants and backward ball cap of a teenager lay a few feet from her, blood staining his pant leg and the pavement beneath him. He was trying to drag himself to the shelter of the shop's doorway.

Sam could hear the gunman's footsteps approaching.

"Hey, buddy," the guy called to the bleeding kid. "What's amatter? You afraid?" He laughed, a chilling cackle that Sam would hear in his head for

*the rest of his life. "Lotsa people gonna die today,"
he said in a singsong voice.*

*Sam gathered himself, every muscle in his body
quivering, raring for action. The guy wasn't close
enough for a grab; he was going to have to sprint
to get to him. And if he wasn't careful and accurate—and fast—the woman and the injured boy
would die next.*

*The gunman took a few more steps. This was as
good as it was going to get.*

Sam launched himself from behind the car, directly at the man with the gun.

*The guy turned at the sound of Sam's footsteps
but by the time he'd swung his gun around, Sam
was on him. Both men went tumbling to the pavement, elbows and heads striking the unforgiving
surface as they fell. Another shot rang out and
Sam felt a tremendous kick in the region of his left
kidney. As he wrestled with the insane killer, a
small part of him registered that he'd been shot
again. But no pain. Not yet. He didn't have time
to worry about it as he struggled to immobilize the
man before he could kill anyone else.*

*The guy still had a death grip on the gun and
he was shooting wildly. There were so many people around he was almost guaranteed to kill some-*

one else.... In a split-second decision, Sam did what he'd been trained to do. With one powerful arch of his body, he broke the gunman's neck.

The silence was shocking after the noise of the weapon.

Sam lay where he was, the killer's limp figure half atop him. As his concentration receded, he began to hear sounds. Sirens, people sobbing, several people moaning and screaming. The kid nearby was softly crying for his mother.

The woman who'd been crouching in the doorway ran to the boy's side. "Lie still," she said. "You're going to be okay."

"I'm a nurse," shouted an unfamiliar voice as footsteps ran toward him. "We need to identify all the wounded and prioritize them by who's most critical."

The shopkeeper said, "I can put pressure on this boy's leg. He didn't hit a major blood vessel. But that guy over there—the one who stopped him—he might need help. He got shot when they were fighting."

The footsteps came closer. He shoved at the gunman's dead weight, rolling the body ignominiously to one side in a careless heap. The movement sent a nauseating wave of red-hot pain ripping through his abdomen, rippling out to every cell in him.

Gritting his teeth against the agony, he raised his head and looked down at himself. The second bullet had hit him in the lower left torso. Blood darkened his shirt and his jeans and was beginning to pool on the sidewalk around him.

He tried to gather himself, but his legs weren't cooperating. The woman who'd said she was a nurse knelt at his side. "Hang in there," she said. "Help's on the way."

And it was. Sam could hear the sirens drawing to a screaming halt, doors slamming and gurneys clattering as medics rushed toward the injured.

"This one first," his comforter yelled.

Sam caught her eye. "That bad, huh?" It came out a hoarse whisper.

She shrugged, but she met his eyes and he saw the truth there. "Not so good," she said, "but you can't die on us, you're a hero."

Six

Two weeks later, they had settled into a comfortable routine. Since the night they'd made love for the first time, they had been together nearly every minute. They worked together and then came home, usually to her place, together. They ate together and slept together, although neither one of them was getting nearly as much sleep as they needed. Sam had gradually moved darn near every important piece of clothing he owned—as well as a few books and all his toiletries—into her apartment.

They were sitting on the couch watching television on a Sunday evening when he finally decided to get it over with. He'd been wanting to talk to her all weekend about their living arrangements and had been putting it off like a big sissy.

"Del?"

He had his arm around her and she lazily turned her head against his shoulder until she could see his face. "What?"

"Do you like it here?"

He got The Eyebrow. "Here, as in Northern Virginia, or here as in on this couch this very minute?"

Trust Del to pick apart the semantics.

"Here as in this town house," he said.

"Well, yeah, or I wouldn't be living here." She sat up and looked at him questioningly. There seemed to be a hint of suspicion in her voice, or maybe that was just his own paranoia kicking in. "Why?"

He shrugged. "We seem to be spending all our time away from work together, and it seems kind of a waste to have two places to live." He stopped and held his breath.

She searched his eyes. "You mean you want me to move in with you?" She sounded sincerely stunned.

"Or I could move in with you," he said hastily.

She was silent for so long he was already steeling himself for a refusal when she said, "It took me a while to find a place I like. How attached are you to your apartment?"

He felt a surge of hope. She'd been to his apartment and she knew it was nothing but a basic box with a kitchen and bathroom. "Not at all," he said. "If you'd like to keep this place, I could give up my apartment and move in here with you."

She was silent again, and he caught himself nervously jiggling his leg, a habit he'd outgrown in about the eighth grade. Was she going to say no?

He cleared his throat. "Is it such an awful suggestion that you don't know what to say?"

She didn't laugh, as he'd hoped. "It's a big step," she said seriously. "May I have some time to think about it?"

"Sure." He swallowed the urge to insist that she let him move his recliner in tonight. He made a production out of checking his watch, waited five seconds. "Was that long enough?"

"Very funny." She wrinkled her nose at him, hesitated, then spoke again. "Sam, it's not that I don't want you—"

"I'm aware of *that*," he said dryly.

She couldn't hide her smile, but she kept speaking. "—but you're talking about something that's sort of permanent."

And marriage would be even more permanent.

Marriage? The idea had lain just beneath the surface of his thoughts for a while now, he realized. If he and Del were going to be together long-term, he wanted her to marry him. Wanted to know she'd be his forever. He was a little surprised at the rush of satisfaction the notion gave him. Del. His. Forever.

Yeah, he liked it. But apparently, she wasn't feeling quite the same way, judging from her reaction to his suggestion of merely moving into a place together. He hated to think of how she'd have reacted if he'd asked her to marry him. "What if we did it on a trial basis?" he said. Mentally, he said goodbye to the notion of moving his furniture anytime soon.

"That might work," she said. "Like a month and then see if we still think it's working?"

He shrugged, feigning indifference. "A month would be a good start."

"And you wouldn't give up your place until then, at least," she added.

He didn't like the sound of that, but figured he'd worry about his lease in a month. By then, maybe he could convince her that living together—forever—was a good idea.

* * *

Monday morning had been underway for exactly two hours when the thing he'd been dreading for years occurred.

The phone rang in the outer office. He barely noticed it. The phone rang all the time, but Peggy took the calls, routing them to whoever they were meant for.

A moment later, though, her voice came over his intercom. "Sam, line one is for you. She wouldn't give her name, just said she was a potential client."

"Thanks, Peg." He pushed away from his keyboard and punched the button on the phone system, taking a moment to stretch. "Sam Deering, may I help you?"

"Don't you mean Sam *Pender?*" It was a woman's brassy tone. "I'm calling for *PEOPLE* magazine. Are you the Sam Pender who stopped that gunman in San Diego?"

It shook him. How in the hell had they found him? He'd been so damn careful, had sealed the records of his name change and even changed his social-security information. "Wrong last name," he said, reaching for brisk cheerfulness. "Sorry."

"We want to do a piece on you," the woman said

in a rush. "A sort of where-are-they-now kind of thing. We'd need to—"

"Sorry," he said again, firmly. "I'm not Sam Pender." *Anymore.* "If you require the firm's services, please call again."

He punched the button to end the call. Then he clasped his hands before him on his desk, noting only distantly that they were actually shaking, for God's sake. Publicity. He'd evaded it for seven years. How had they found him? Or had the journalist been fishing, adding a few facts and hoping they equaled the right answer? Maybe that was all it was.

He drew a breath and spun around again to face his monitor. The company had just gotten a kidnapping case that was going to require coordination from several of PSI's departments, since it involved European travel and recovery of an American national in another country. Not to mention getting the child safely away from the noncustodial parent.

He shook his head briskly to clear it. He had other things to worry about. That phone call probably had just been a fishing expedition. No way could they be sure it was him.

After work, he had to go by his apartment to pick up clothes and a few other things he thought he'd need next week. Del went straight to her town house because, she said, she wanted to wash her hair and let it dry by itself. If she used a hair dryer it would get too frizzy.

He'd never noticed Del's hair looking frizzy in seven years. It must be a woman thing, he thought as he unlocked his door. Either that, or in seven years she'd never used a hair dryer a single time.

His apartment had a faint air of disuse. It should. He had hardly been here except to pick up his mail and occasionally grab some clothes since he'd been with Del the first time. And it was going to stay that way if he had anything to say about it.

The answering machine was blinking and he crossed the room to press the button and play the messages. The first one was from his mother in Nebraska. He'd call her tomorrow and give her Del's number. He imagined his mother would jump up and down at the thought that he was living with a woman. She'd be dreaming of more grandchildren with no encouragement at all. While he was at it, he'd better caution her about the reporter who'd called. His family protected his identity but it was best not to be blindsided.

The second was from his sister, reminding him of his niece's fourth birthday. Thank God she also had some suggestions for gift ideas because he didn't know squat about little girls.

His dentist's office had left the third message. It was time to schedule his six-month checkup.

The fourth was from Robert Lyon. He stood in shock as the cool, elegant, masculine voice floated into the room. He hadn't seen Robert in over a year. What were the odds of the man calling mere weeks after Sam and Del, the two people he'd introduced, had become lovers? Uneasily, he wondered if the man had ESP as he listened to the message.

"Hello, Sam. It's Robert Lyon. I'm in town for a few days and thought you might have time for dinner." He named the hotel where he was staying and left his number. Sam stood staring at the phone, then picked up the handset and punched the callback button. He knew from the little Del had spoken of Robert that she was fond of him. It would be a pleasant surprise for her if he took her out to dinner with Robert.

Del agreed to go out on Wednesday evening for dinner as easily as he'd anticipated. But he didn't tell her they'd be meeting Robert.

That night, she wore the little black dress that

had changed their relationship. He'd finished dressing ahead of her and gone out to the living room to check his e-mail on the laptop he'd brought over. He was just closing the program when Del walked into the room.

"Whoa," he said. "I like it even better the second time around."

Del smiled, tossing her long, unbound hair back from her shoulders. "I thought you might."

"Come here." He beckoned but she shook her head.

She knew what he wanted; he could see the heated awareness in her eyes. "No. We'll be late."

"So?" He stood, beginning to walk slowly across the room.

She backed away, putting the table between them. "Sam, we have reservations for seven!" The sentence ended in a shriek as he feinted left, then moved right when she dodged. He caught her by one elbow and whirled her to him, clasping her against him and running his hands over the silky fabric of the little dress and her curves beneath it. "I wanted to do this that night in the bar."

"You did?" There was amusement in her voice, but beneath it he detected a hint of vulnerability. Del had hidden herself away for so long she honestly didn't know how appealing she was.

"I did." Dropping his head, he sought her mouth and her resistance died as he plunged his tongue deep, finding her breast with one hand and covering the plump mound with one hand. He rotated his palm, the rising peak beneath his hand fueling his growing arousal. Her arms wound around his neck and her fingers speared into his hair, holding him to her. "Mmm," she murmured. "I guess we can have a quick appetizer."

He wanted her again. Badly. Tugging the hem of the dress up one smooth thigh inch by inch, he could feel himself growing harder and readier by the second. As he slipped his fingers beneath the little dress and around her thigh, he ground himself against her soft mound. Pulling her one leg high around his waist, he pressed himself even more intimately against her. He thought he might just die of pure pleasure. He trailed his fingers along the rounded globes of her bottom and the sweet crease he found until he touched her there in the heated V he'd exposed.

And holy heaven, she wasn't wearing any underwear!

"What…?"

"I wanted to surprise you." She tore her mouth from his and nipped his earlobe, then sucked hard on the tiny sting. The small sensation shot straight through his throbbing body, making his pants uncomfortably tight.

"Consider me surprised." He could barely get the words out. He released her for a moment and shoved his hands between them, opening his pants and pushing them and his briefs out of the way.

She was making tiny mewling sounds, trying to climb his body, and he obligingly lifted her, breath surging in and out of his lungs like a winded marathoner as her legs clasped his hips and her moist, heated female flesh caressed him.

"Inside you," he managed. "I need to be inside you."

She suckled his ear again. At the same time, her small hand burrowed down between them and she wrapped her fingers around him, sliding up and down gently as her thumb whisked over the ultrasensitive tip.

He almost lost it right there as she continued to caress him. Gritting his teeth against the urge to simply let himself relax and go with it, he gripped her soft buttocks in his big hands and lifted her higher, rubbing her over him.

She made a small sound of delight, her hand faltering in its task as he angled her against him so that she would feel as crazy as she was making him.

She moaned and clutched at his shoulders as he turned and braced her against the wall. He was almost ready to enter her when he realized he hadn't used protection, and he swore.

"Wait! We can't—"

Del made a shocked sound as he set her down and fumbled in the pile of clothes around his ankles until he came up with the small package he sought. He covered himself with frantic haste and then, with one slick, swift motion, he lifted her and positioned himself again, then thrust inside her. She was hot and wet and smooth and tight; he was out of control, pounding toward the pinnacle of his pleasure. She made a small noise with each motion of his hips, her body impaled by him, and he realized she was as close as he was. "Come to me, baby," he said hoarsely. "Let go and come to me."

"Sam," she said, her voice trembling. Her fingers dug into his skin as he felt sweet internal contractions begin to ripple through her. Her body arched; her heels dug into him. He threw his head back, shuddering as he felt his own body gathering, and then he couldn't think at all, could only feel as her body gripped him like a hot, tight glove, squeezing an earthshaking response from him that left his knees trembling and his entire body drained. Slowly, he dropped to his knees on the floor, still holding her.

"Wow," she said. "I'm not sure I'll be hungry for the main course."

He laughed, savoring the sweet intimacy of their position. "It's possible the main course will be delayed for a while after that." He lifted her off him, then staggered to his feet. "I'm not sure I can walk."

"I'm the one who should be saying that," she pointed out, reaching for the box of tissues on the counter. "Let me," she said when he reached for one.

Her fingers were soft and gentle as she cleaned him. By all rights he shouldn't be able to get hard again for a week after that. But amazingly, he felt a renewed stirring of desire beneath her hands.

"We really do have to go," she said, smiling.

"I know." He began to restore his clothing to order. "But I can't seem to tell *him* that."

She laughed aloud. "I'll be ready in a minute," she said as she walked toward the bathroom. "I'll hurry."

He glanced at his watch. "We're not late. You even have time to put on some underwear." He couldn't wipe the silly grin off his face as she rolled her eyes at him, then disappeared through the door. Satisfaction invaded his every pore. He'd needed that, to bond her to him, to make her his again. At least, he was sure of one thing: she still wanted him as badly as he wanted her.

So badly that you almost forgot something important, pal.

The voice in his head snapped him back to reality with a jarring thud. Holy hell. Birth control. The thought hadn't entered his head until he'd been poised and ready to take her. Unbelievable. If he'd ever known such a total loss of... He'd always thought he'd have kids someday, but after Ilsa had informed him she couldn't live with a man in a wheelchair for the rest of her life, he'd put that dream away. The fact that he wasn't wheelchair-bound was inconsequential; he simply hadn't wanted to get involved with anyone again.

Now, though, the thought of seeing Del with a baby—a baby they'd made together—was unexpectedly appealing. Apparently he hadn't buried those dreams as deeply as he'd assumed.

The moment they entered the restaurant, a tall, silver-haired man rose from a table where he'd been waiting and waved at them.

"Robert!" Del's voice held delight and amazement. "What are you doing here?"

Robert smiled as he embraced her, then shook Sam's hand. "I'm in town for a few days and when I called Sam, we thought it might be fun to surprise you."

"You were right." She smiled at Sam. Then she appeared to realize that Robert didn't know about them, and her whole face pinkened.

"Sam tells me you two are dating or something," Robert said as he held her chair and smoothly seated her.

"Or something," Sam said as the men sat.

Robert grinned. "So how's business?" he asked.

The meal was pleasant. They spent most of it discussing PSI in generalities, since confidentiality was a hallmark of the business. Robert knew a few of their clients because he had recommended them, but he was equally interested in some of the other work the firm had begun to do.

"I had good preliminary talks with a German firm that trains dogs for protection work," Sam told him. "We've had so many requests to add guard dogs to the security measures we offer that Del and I thought the time had come."

"We flew to Germany and visited three training

centers," Del added. "One clearly offered a superior product and they're interested in working with us. Essentially, we'd act as a middleman. When dogs are requested, we'll bring them straight from Germany to the client's home. We're adding a trainer to our staff who will evaluate all requests. If they're approved, he'll travel to Germany to transport the dogs. He also will stay with the client for a few days to ensure the proper setup is in place and there's someone responsible for the dogs."

Robert whistled. "Sounds like a big step."

Sam shrugged. "It is and it isn't. We offer every other type of home security on the market, but some people still feel more secure with dogs around."

"I can understand that," the older man said. "Evvie wouldn't be without our two."

Evvie was Robert's wife. They'd been married shortly after Sam had met the man and he'd also met Evvie on one or two occasions. A pretty, youthful-looking woman of about Robert's age, Evvie was a horsewoman and a dog person, as well. The couple had two large Dalmatians.

"How is Evvie?" Del asked. "She was getting a colt ready for the Preakness last time I talked to her."

"She's still horse-mad," Robert said with a

smile. "She recently invested in a new colt who's a several-times-great-grandson of Man O' War and she has high hopes for the Triple Crown."

Del's eyebrow rose. "Those *are* high hopes."

"Wish her luck from us," Sam said as the waiter appeared to remove their salad plates.

After the main course, Del rose and excused herself to freshen up. The moment she was out of earshot, Sam turned to Robert. "So I understand you know Del's mother."

Robert smiled, but there wasn't real humor in it. "I ought to. I was married to the woman."

"You're kidding." Sam was stunned. He tried to imagine Robert and the sort of woman Del's mother clearly was, and failed. "Before Evvie."

"Well over a decade ago. It didn't last two years," Robert said. "And the only reason it took that long for me to decide to leave was because I was brought up to think one never quit working at a marriage." He sighed. "But she wouldn't meet me halfway. Hell, she wouldn't even take the first step." He shook his head, and to his surprise, Sam detected a fond note in his voice. "She was a spoiled brat, but she could charm the socks off any man she met. Still can, for that matter."

"You're on good terms now?"

Robert nodded. "Once she got over the fact that for once *she* hadn't been the one to call it off, we were able to be civil. She's even had dinner with Evvie and me a time or two."

Dinner with Robert and Evvie? This was getting stranger and stranger. "What attracted you to her?" Sam asked, still trying to fathom Robert's interest.

Robert looked at him. "You're kidding, right?"

Sam shook his head.

Robert smiled. "Del's personality is very different from her mother's. Imagine Del dressed to kill, fluttering her eyelashes and deliberately aiming all that sex appeal at you."

"Ah." Sam smiled wryly. "It probably wouldn't have taken us seven years to get together."

Robert laughed. "Yeah. I could barely remember my own name." He took a sip of wine. "So tell me about you and Del."

Sam shrugged, picking up his own wineglass. "We've worked together for a long time. One day we realized we had…good chemistry." The understatement made him smile.

A moment later he realized Robert was regarding him with less than enthusiastic regard. "Del is a wonderful young woman," Robert said softly, "and I would do my utter best to tear your heart out if you hurt her."

Sam would have laughed except that Robert's blue eyes carried not a hint of humor. "I'm not planning on hurting her," he said evenly.

"At the risk of sounding paternal, might I ask what your intentions are?"

Holy hell. The man was serious. "I, ah, consider my relationship with Del to be a permanent one," he said, feeling his way through the minefield that suddenly had developed, "and I hope to convince her to marry me eventually."

The steely expression on Robert's face eased significantly and his eyes warmed again. "I see. Del isn't keen on marriage?"

Sam shook his head. "She doesn't even want to talk about next week, much less anything permanent. I've convinced her to let me move in on a trial basis, but that's it."

"Del hasn't seen many examples of successful marriages," Robert said regretfully. "But keep after her. I imagine you'll get an 'I do' one of these days."

Del returned then and both men stood. She eyed them curiously as she slid into the booth. "You two look guilty," she said. "Keeping secrets?"

Sam laughed. "When was the last time I managed to keep a secret from you?"

She smiled demurely. "True."

But he *was* keeping a secret from her, and his amusement faded as he thought of the phone call he'd received. Someone wanted to find Sam Pender, and if he wasn't careful, the quiet life he'd created for himself was going to be blown right out of the water.

After coffee, they rose to leave. Del preceded the men from the restaurant and Sam put an arm around her waist as they crossed the parking lot. At the car, Robert kissed her before Sam put her into the passenger seat and closed the door.

As he rounded the hood, Robert kept pace with him. "Thank you for bringing Del along. It was wonderful to catch up with both of you."

"No problem." Sam stopped and held out his hand. "I can tell Del adores you. Thanks for joining us."

Robert smiled as he clasped Sam's hand. "If you ever talk her into marrying you, let me know."

Sam nodded. "Don't hold your breath. She's still pretty skittish." He glanced fondly at the small woman sitting in his vehicle. "But I'll wear her down eventually."

Robert followed the direction of his glance and raised a hand in farewell when she waved at him. "Does she know you love her?"

Sam paused, going still. "I didn't say that."

"You didn't have to." Robert clapped him on the back. "I recognize the signs."

Sam opened his mouth to respond. But what, really, was there to say? He watched as Robert walked across the lot to his dark rental sedan and drove away with a final wave.

He loved Del. And Robert had seen it before he, Sam, had even been able to admit it to himself. The mere thought made him literally begin to sweat.

He *did* love her. Her quirky eyebrow and the baggy clothes she often wore, that stupid baseball cap and the way she impatiently flipped her braid back over her shoulder. Her ready sense of humor and her quiet stubbornness when she thought she was right. Her firm no-nonsense approach to handling their employees and the warmth he didn't have that she brought to the company.

His chest felt too small to contain his swelling heart as he stood there with his car keys gripped in his hand and his whole world sitting there five feet from him.

God, when he'd thought he'd been in love with

Ilsa, it had been a manageable, controllable emotion, subject to his will. When she'd left him, he'd been a little hurt, but a lot humiliated and even more angry that she would desert him when he most needed someone.

Loving Del wasn't manageable at all, he realized. If she ever left him, he would be devastated. His pride wouldn't even come into play, and perhaps that was the most telling thing. Abruptly, he spun and yanked open his car door, sliding into his seat and turning to Del.

She was looking at him with a humorous question in her eyes, but he couldn't explain. Leaning across the console, he cradled her head in both hands as he set his mouth on hers, kissing her with all the tenderness of the feelings rolling through him.

When he finally lifted his head, her eyes were soft and dreamy. She touched her lips with one finger. "What brought that on?"

He shrugged as he inserted the key into the ignition and turned on the engine. "Nothing in particular. I just thought you needed kissing."

It was her turn to lean over the console as she kissed him on the cheek. "You thought right."

He smiled as he put the car in gear and started home. He'd lied when he'd said nothing in particular. He might love Del, but he wasn't stupid enough to tell her so. As cautious as she was, she'd head for the hills before he could get out the third word.

No, it was going to take time to woo her, to make her see that she couldn't live without him, either. To make her relax those ever-present guards around her emotions and love him back.

Time. It wasn't as if he was going anywhere.

Seven

In the middle of the night, he woke up sweating. His heart was pounding, adrenaline rushing through his system as the remnants of the dream receded.

Damn. This was the second time in less than a month.

Del was sitting up in bed beside him, one hand lightly clasping his arm. "Hey," she said. "You were having a bad dream."

After the first time, he'd had the dream over and over again, whenever he closed his eyes. Only in the dream, sometimes the gunman turned and pointed his weapon at Sam before he could get to the guy. It had been months before he'd gotten a decent night's sleep. As the years had passed, though, it had ambushed him less and less frequently, so much so that now he was surprised when it recurred.

"Want to tell me about it?"

He hesitated. He still wasn't ready to tell her all about his past. Being called a hero made him cringe. He'd only been doing what he'd been trained to do that day; he'd known he had a moral obligation to try to stop that killer.

But if he was going to continue to be with her she deserved to have some explanation.

He pulled her down into his arms, enjoying the way she instantly softened and draped her body over his. "It's a recurring dream. I've had it for almost eight years now."

"It has to do with your injuries, doesn't it?"

"Yes." He stroked her back, absorbing the silky texture of her smooth skin. Somehow it wasn't as hard as he'd expected to talk about this with her, lying here in the dark, quiet room. "But I wasn't wounded in combat."

"Then how did you get shot?" Her voice was intense and puzzled. "Those *are* gunshot wounds."

And she would know. One of their bodyguards had been winged a couple of years ago, and just last year a member of the abduction team took a bullet in the thigh while reuniting a little boy with his custodial parent after he was taken out of the country by the other parent.

He took a deep breath. "I got shot by a nut job on the street. It was kind of ironic—I'd never been wounded in combat, but a day after I get home on leave, I get nailed right on the street." That was all true. It just wasn't the whole truth.

"This one—" she lightly touched the puckered scar above his left hip "—must have done some damage."

"It nicked my spine," he said tersely. "I spent a couple months at a rehab center."

"Rehab center?"

"Learning to walk again." He could feel the muscle clenching and unclenching in his jaw. "For a while they thought I was going to be paralyzed. I had no feeling in my legs for about three weeks."

She gasped and her hands moved in an unconscious gentling circle on him. "No wonder you have nightmares. That must have been terrifying."

"It was. Luckily it only lasted a short time." He

dismissed the fear and abject terror, the budding despair of those three weeks with one sentence.

"I'm so glad you weren't permanently paralyzed." She stretched up to kiss his chin, then lingered, pressing light, soft kisses against his throat and working her way down his chest until she found one small, flat nipple.

He forgot his somber thoughts as pleasure instantly ricocheted through his body. Del didn't seem to want to talk, didn't seem to need additional explanation. And that was fine with him.

Way more than fine. She was soft and warm and eminently arousing as she squirmed into better position atop him, and he found himself swiftly, completely aroused, hard and full and aching for the sweet oblivion she promised. He reached down and pressed against her inner thigh until she parted her legs on either side of his body.

He sucked in a raw breath of need as he grabbed protection from the bedside table. "Wait a sec," he growled as he deftly covered himself. Then he moved into place, inching himself into her at an excruciatingly slow pace. When she moaned and wriggled, trying to push herself down onto him, he held her hips in his big hands and kept it slow and leisurely.

"Sam," she pleaded, "please...please..."

"Please what?" With one quick move, he rolled them so that she lay beneath him. The motion had nearly dislodged him, and her hips surged restlessly as he braced himself above her and resisted her urgings.

"Please..." She was panting, her fingers digging into his hard buttocks as she tried in vain to pull him closer.

"Please...this?" He lowered his weight onto her abruptly, driving his hips forward, embedding himself deeply within her as she arched up to meet him, her arms tightening as if to hold him there forever.

"Yes." The word was a bare whisper of delight.

He looked down at her, silhouetted in the moonlight that shone through her window. Her dark hair was a wild spill across the pillow. Her eyes were closed and her lips were full and soft from his kisses, lightly parted now with passion.

God, she was beautiful. And she was his.

He and Del were meant for each other, meant to spend the rest of their lives together. They complemented each other in so many ways. He couldn't imagine his life without her, couldn't predict a future that didn't have her in it.

He was determined to have her in his life.

Now all he had to do was convince her. She was wary and as skittish about commitment as he'd been just days ago, but he was going to change that, he vowed. He was going to marry her.

The following week, Del popped her head into his office toward the end of the day and said, "We're celebrating Beth from bookkeeping's birthday this evening. Do you want to go?"

He hesitated. *No* was on the tip of his tongue but he wanted to spend the evening with Del, and he supposed this was her indirect way of telling him she planned to go. "I guess since I went to one, it might cause ill will if I didn't go to them all now," he said with a grimace. "Right?"

"Probably," she said in a cheerful voice. "It would be a nice thing to do, too."

He stared at her. "I am not nice."

She laughed. "All the more reason for you to go and be civil."

Which is how he found himself sandwiched between Del and the new woman, Karen, at a round table in a small Italian restaurant, singing "Happy Birthday" to Beth from the bookkeeping department. They had just finished the song when the door to the restaurant opened and Walker entered.

"Sorry I'm late," he said. "Happy birthday, Beth."

Sam felt both Del and Karen stiffen. It was hard to miss, smashed between them as he was in the bench seat. Women, he supposed, had an internal radar for relationship trouble. And that was what had just walked through the door.

Walker had the top-heavy, intellect-light redhead with him again. His tie was crooked—very— and the redhead's lipstick was smeared across one cheek. Her hair looked as if someone had set off a small explosion beneath it. There was little question what the pair had been doing. God, he hoped he and Del were never that obvious.

Both of them looked as if they'd had more than a few drinks. Even if Karen had divorced Walker a long time ago, it probably still was no fun seeing your ex make an ass of himself with a woman young enough to be his daughter.

"Thank you," said the birthday girl. "Pull up a seat."

Walker grabbed a chair from a nearby empty table one-handed, swiveling it around so that he could sit. Then he grabbed the redhead and tugged her down onto his lap, winding a brawny arm about the girl's waist as she giggled. "Jennifer, everybody," he said, waving a hand. "You met some of them before. Everybody, this is Jennifer."

"Hi." Jennifer waved like a beauty queen on a parade float. She turned to Walker. "Which one is Karen?"

"That would be me." Karen raised her hand, her voice cool and casual.

Jennifer examined Karen for a long silent moment, then turned to Walker. "You said she was old. She's *pretty*," she said in a sulky voice.

Walker looked as though he'd swallowed his tongue. "Sorry," he mumbled, and Sam wondered if he was talking to Jennifer or Karen.

Around the table, curiosity was as strong a presence as the new guests. No one else in the company, other than Del and he, knew Walker and Karen Munson had been married once, as far as Sam knew.

At his side, Karen stirred and spoke into the uncomfortable silence. "Could you excuse me, please? I need to get going."

She stood and Sam stood automatically, pushing Del before him so they could let Karen slide out of the seat.

She paused at the edge of the table and smiled

at Beth. "Happy birthday," she said. "Thank you for inviting me."

"We do it all the time," Peg said. "You'll soon be good and sick of us inviting you to celebrate birthdays. We might as well just glue this on our thighs." She indicated the piece of chocolate cake on her plate.

There was a general ripple of agreement and a few chuckles, and Karen smiled again. "See you tomorrow."

She was already turning to walk away when Jennifer-the-redhead said, "Why's she leaving? I thought you said she didn't have a family anymore." Although she was speaking to Walker, the words carried across the table.

Karen stopped abruptly. "Pardon me?" She turned back to the table, her face carefully expressionless.

"Well," said Jennifer, "Walker said you didn't have a husband or a kid anymore, so—"

"Jennifer, shut up," Walker growled.

Karen looked as though someone had punched her in the stomach. Tears sparkled in her eyes, but after one scathing glance at Walker, all she did was smile again at Beth, though her lips quivered. "I hope the rest of your evening is wonderful," she said. One tear trickled down her cheek but she didn't wipe it away before she turned and walked steadily out of the restaurant.

"Well," said Peggy brightly, "I think it's time we all headed out, don't you?"

Subdued murmurs of agreement greeted her words, and the table was suddenly a flurry of activity as people gathered personal items and rushed off. A few of them cast dark looks in Walker's direction as they left.

"Dammit, Walker," said Sam, "that was completely out of line."

Jennifer spoke. "Sorry," she said in that ridiculous baby-doll voice. "I didn't mean to hurt her feelings."

"Of course not," said Del in a voice that left no doubt of her opinion.

"If she can't take the heat," Walker said aggressively, "she should get out of the fire."

Whoa. Now he'd done it. Sam had been around Del long enough to know when the match touched the fuse. It didn't happen often but when it did, there was no stopping her.

Del leaned forward, her expression set in stone. "That's *kitchen,* you moron. 'Get out of the *kitchen.*'" She stood, almost shaking with fury. "You had no business sharing Karen's personal difficulties with that twit." She didn't even look at the redhead as she slid her arms into her jacket and picked up her briefcase. "Your life," she added in an icy tone, "is your own business. But when you inflict someone on us who's so offensive that she can ruin an entire evening in one sentence, it becomes *our* business."

She stood, then jabbed Jennifer in the shoulder with a stiff forefinger. "If I ever see you at a PSI party again, I will pull out every fake red hair on your empty head."

"And you." She transferred her attention to Walker. "Don't bother coming to any more of the office parties unless you're sober and single."

Walker was glaring at Del, a muscle in his jaw ticking uncontrollably. "Sam?" he said, not looking away from her angry face.

Sam sighed. "She's right. You showed up and everyone left. That ought to tell you something." He put an arm around Del, feeling the anger vibrating through her as he hustled her out of the restaurant before she completely lost her temper. He didn't really want to have to bail her out on assault charges.

He held her car door until she settled herself with rigid, angry motions, then climbed into the driver's side and started the engine without speaking. A smart man knew when to keep quiet. As he drove out of the lot beside the restaurant, he could feel Del still simmering.

Finally, about halfway home, he said, "Every fake red hair on her empty head?"

There was a moment of tense silence and for a minute, he thought she might be about to take *his* head off. Then Del snickered. "I thought it was fairly poetic."

He laughed aloud. "That wasn't quite the first word that sprang to mind."

"So what was?"

"Sincere," he said, "It sounded like you meant it. I think if I were Jennifer, I might not be anxious to cross your path again."

Del sobered quickly. "I can't believe that bimbo said that. I *really* can't believe Walker was dumb enough to tell her that he was married to Karen once."

"And believe me, I'm sorry I mentioned it to him."

"You should be," Del said seriously. "That's personal information and we don't have any right to talk to anyone about it. You think she'll quit?"

"I hope not. Frankly, I'd sooner fire Walker than lose her. She's been working her butt off this week, and she's about ten times as diplomatic as Mr. Foot-in-Mouth has ever been."

Sam grinned. Walker did have a reputation for telling it the way he saw it. They didn't often let him deal directly with clients. "I hope we don't lose either one of them."

Del was quiet for a moment. "Why do you suppose she ever married him?"

"I imagine he had his good points at the time."

"I guess." She sighed.

"People can be deceptive," he said, thinking of Ilsa. "A little chemistry can blind you to someone's less-charming traits."

From the corner of her eye, he caught the abrupt motion of her head as she turned toward him. "You sound as if you have firsthand experience." It wasn't a question and yet he knew it was.

"I was engaged once."

He heard her suck in a sharp breath. "But not married?"

"No." He was glad he was driving. It was easier than facing her when he went through this story. "She changed her mind pretty fast when she thought she might be stuck with a paraplegic for life."

"I'm sorry," she said quietly.

"It was no big deal," he said. "If she wasn't

going to stick, better I found out before the vows." But when he glanced over at her, her brown eyes held a well of sympathy, and he suspected she didn't believe his profession of unconcern. "I can't even remember what she looked like anymore," he said, and was surprised to find it was true. Since he'd gotten involved with Del, the past had faded into insignificance.

"Still, it must have hurt when she cut and ran." There was anger in her tone.

"Look," he said, feeling cornered, "I'm sorry I didn't tell you before—"

"I'm not mad at you!" Her eyes went wide with surprise. "I'd like to rip her heart out, though."

Amazingly, he was able to laugh again. Ilsa really *wasn't* important anymore, and the knowledge was like emptying his pockets of a load of rocks. "Your bloodthirsty side is showing tonight." He reached over and laced his fingers through hers, drawing her hand onto his thigh. "Lucky for you, I like bloodthirsty women."

Her hand turned over in his, then slipped down between his legs and a jolt of electric sexuality ran up his spine. He wanted to whimper aloud when her fingers began to explore, and he felt himself begin to pulse and fill. "Lucky for you," she said, her fingers exploring the growing bulge behind his zipper, "this bloodthirsty woman likes you. In fact—" she glanced down at the evidence of his desire for her, plainly outlined in the khaki pants he'd worn to work "—she can't wait to get home."

He gave a hoarse laugh which turned into a moan as his zipper opened with a soft hiss and she slipped her hand inside. "Much more of that and we won't make it home."

The next morning at work, he couldn't ignore the buzz of gossip in the hallways. Everyone was talking about what had happened the night before. If he heard, "I had no idea they used to be married!" once, he heard it a dozen times.

Karen had puffy dark bags beneath her eyes, but she worked with the same efficiency he'd begun to notice she brought to all her tasks, presenting him with a study of the manpower it would take to covertly watch a home in Rio where a client's child was believed to have been taken by her noncustodial ex-spouse.

Around three o'clock, he was standing beside Del's desk going over flight reservations for a visit to the German canine people to finalize the deal, when Peggy appeared in Del's doorway with a vase of flowers. "Check it out," she said. "Karen got flowers!"

"From who?" Del went around her desk and tried to look at the card but the tiny envelope was sealed.

"Don't know. But I already called her to come get them, so we won't let her leave until she spills the beans," Peggy said cheerfully.

Sam snorted, and both women looked at him.

"What was that for?" Del asked.

He shook his head, grinning. "No reason. I just don't get what the big deal is."

Peggy shot him a pitying look. "Receiving flowers is *always* a big deal."

Karen stuck her head in the door at that exact moment and both women turned to her, but Sam remained rooted to the spot where he stood. Guilt, strong and forceful, rushed through him.

He'd never given Del flowers. Hell, he'd never even taken her out to dinner unless it was work related. He'd intended to, but somehow they always seemed to get sidetracked by a mattress when they weren't working.

In fact, that was pretty much *all* they did, he thought with a pang of regret. They worked, ate and fell into bed together. They damn near burned up the sheets every night, and neither one of them had gotten enough sleep since her birthday, but he wasn't complaining.

And neither had she. He wondered if she really didn't mind the fact that he'd never once taken her on a real date. If she did, she hid it so well he'd never caught a hint.

"What's it say? Who's it from?" He tuned back in to the conversation as Peggy began to pester Karen.

With an odd, frozen look on her face, Karen silently passed the card over to Peggy.

"That rat bastard!" Peggy wasn't shy about voicing her opinion.

Del, crowding over her shoulder, said, "At least he realized he was way out of line."

Karen didn't say anything. She just stood there, holding the vase of pretty pink-and-lavender flowers with a blank, bewildered expression on her face. Sam reached out and snagged the card from Peggy, reading the simple message.

I'm sorry. Walker

"Hey," said Peggy, "You okay, honey?"

Karen sighed. "As okay as I'll ever be with that jerk on the same planet," she said. She shoved the arrangement back at Peggy. "You can keep these. Brighten up your office. Pitch 'em. I don't care."

She turned and started toward the door, then turned back and plucked the card from the arrangement. "But I think I'll keep this. Just to remind me he isn't a complete and total waste product."

Sam was pretty impressed that she managed a smile in response to Peggy's and Del's laughter before she left the office.

Eight

He lay on his back in bed that evening with Del curled against his side. Her fingers idly combed through the hair on his chest and he decided that with very little effort he could be persuaded to make love to her again. But first, there was something he wanted to do.

"What do you think," he began, "about dinner and a movie on Saturday night?"

Her fingers stopped moving. After a moment, she said, "I think lots of people probably will be doing that."

He slid his hand down over her hip and pinched her backside. "Smart-ass."

"Hey!" She lurched against him before settling back down with a grin. "Oh, did you mean what did I think about the two of us having dinner and then going to a movie?" she asked with false innocence.

"Or I could invite some other girl."

"Not if you want to have any shot at sleeping in this bed again." They both chuckled, but her casual words warmed him.

That was the first time Del had ever alluded to a future of any sort. She was generally extremely careful about *not* defining their relationship, to the point that for the past couple of weeks he felt as if they'd been dancing around some enormous piece of furniture, pretending it wasn't there.

"So," he said, "would you like to go out?"

Del turned over and levered herself above him, propping her arms on his chest. "I would love to," she said, as her hair fell around them in an intimate curtain, "but may I ask what prompted this?"

He shrugged. "I just thought it would be fun."

She digested that for a moment. "Yeah," she said softly, "it would be fun. We don't take much time for just enjoying ourselves, do we?"

"Outside of this bed?"

She smacked his chest with the flat of her hand.

He captured her hand and pulled her down closer. "You're right. I think it's time we started to think a little more about getting to know each other outside the bedroom."

"Or the office," she added.

He smiled, running a hand over the smooth hair that spilled down around them. "Yeah."

She laid her head on his chest. "Dinner and a movie would be nice." She paused. "Your heart is beating really fast."

"My heart always speeds up when you're around," he said without thinking.

Del went still.

He realized what he'd said. Oh, hell.

Then he felt her body relax against his again. "My heart beats faster when you're around, too," she said softly.

He was so relieved that for a minute he couldn't speak. And by the time his vocal cords were functional again, he'd let it go too long, so he didn't say anything.

But long after her breathing slowed and evened out as she slipped into sleep, Sam lay awake wondering. What had she meant? Had she only been thinking in physical terms or had she understood that he'd been speaking of emotion?

They slept in the next morning until nearly ten. Unlike most of the Saturdays they'd spent together, he awoke before she did. He put on some coffee and grabbed a quick shower, then stepped into a pair of jeans before heading back to the kitchen. Pouring a cup of coffee for himself and one for her, he carried them to the bedroom.

After setting the cups on the bedside table, he bumped her hip with his until she grumbled and slid over far enough for him to take a seat on the edge of the mattress. Del wasn't a morning person, he'd discovered with some amusement. Until she'd had a cup of coffee, there was no point in even trying to hold a conversation or expect her to frame a coherent answer.

"Good morning." He braced his hands on the mattress on either side of her body and leaned down to nuzzle her throat, seeking out the warm, sweet woman fragrance he'd discovered was strongest there. When her arms came up around his neck and she arched her body up to his, he smiled against her skin. "I have coffee."

Immediately, one arm left his neck, hand outstretched. "I am your slave forever."

Forever. He liked the sound of that. A lot. And he wished she meant it, but he suspected it had simply been a trite phrase. Well, that was okay. He had plenty of time to make her see how good they would be as husband and wife.

He was flipping eggs when the shower cut off and he grinned in satisfaction. Perfect timing.

Then the doorbell rang.

Puzzled, he automatically headed for the entryway. Who in the world could be at Del's door? She appeared to have no close friends and didn't do anything other than work that he'd been able to see.

He checked the peephole, but could only catch a glimpse of an artfully tousled blond head of hair and a bit of a woman's profile. Relatively satisfied that whoever it was presented no imminent threat of physical harm, he flipped open the dead bolt and turned the knob.

"Darling!" The woman came at him with her arms outstretched, then halted abruptly. "Well," she said, smiling coquettishly. "You're not the darling I had in mind, but you'll do." She let her gaze drift over his bare torso. "You'll do quite nicely." Then her smile sharpened as she dropped the vamp act and she held out a hand. "You must be Sam. It's wonderful to finally meet you."

He couldn't have spoken if his life depended on it. He'd recognized her the moment she'd turned to face him.

Aurelia Parker. *The* Aurelia Parker!

The woman standing before him was one of Hollywood's darlings, an actress who'd been making men drool since he was old enough to spell the word *woman*. Possessor of an Oscar and a couple other awards he couldn't name, a nominee several times, a guaranteed box-office star worth millions, Aurelia Parker had to be nearly old enough to be his mother but she looked hotter than a lot of women his own age in a slim black pantsuit beneath which a simple white shell showed a surprisingly decorous hint of cleavage.

Silently, he held out his hand.

The actress took it and he was surprised by her firm, no-nonsense grip.

"I am," he finally said. "Sam." Wow, that was brilliant. He cleared his throat and stepped back. "Please come in." *And tell me what the heck you're doing here and how you know my name.*

She gave him a dazzling smile. "Now I see why Del has kept you to herself for so long. I was so thrilled when I heard about you two. I had begun to despair of her, I tell you." One finely arched eyebrow shot up. "I know I shouldn't ask, but Del will never tell me. Is there any chance you two are thinking of starting a family soon?"

Huh?

"Sam, don't answer my—" Del stopped dead in the entrance to the living room, her face a study in shock and dismay. All she wore was a large navy bath towel wrapped around her, with a smaller white one wrapped turban-style around her wet hair. The bloom he'd put in her cheeks earlier vanished instantly as she took in the scene. "Mother. Hello."

Mother? Aurelia Parker was Del's mother?

Now he knew what the expression *thunderstruck* meant because that's exactly how he felt. As if he'd been struck by a bolt from the blue. Only that would be lightning-struck, wouldn't it?

He supposed that single arching eyebrow should have been a clue, he thought, immediately recalling the expression. And just what the hell had Del told her mother—*good God, could Aurelia Parker really be her mother?*—about the two of them? He'd been under the impression that Del and her parent rarely talked, but apparently Del had confided in her sometime during the past few weeks when he wasn't around. Which wasn't often.

"Hello, dear!" Aurelia Parker crossed the room and threw her arms around her daughter. "Happy belated birthday! I hadn't seen you in so long I thought it would be lovely to surprise you."

"But I told you this weekend didn't suit," Del said in a tone that would have frozen a polar bear.

Aurelia Parker straightened her shoulders, her feathers clearly a little ruffled at Del's reaction. "If I waited until it suited you, I'd be in a nursing home." The voice was crisper than anything he'd ever heard her utter on the screen, and for a moment, mother and daughter simply stood and measured each other.

Studying the two women, their resemblance was startling, although their differing styles played down the similarities. Someone who wasn't looking for it might not even realize they were related.

But to him, it was clear. Del's chin was a little more determined, and she mostly ignored her assets while her mother enhanced her eyes, her lips, her skin and damn near everything else that he could see to the maximum. Their figures were similar although her mother seemed a bit top-heavy considering how petite the rest of her was. Then again, that probably was the result of a clever bra or surgery.

"Fine. Come on in and make yourself at home." Del's voice was resigned. She seemed to have recovered a little, but even through the anger that was rapidly replacing his shock, Sam could see that she was deeply upset. "I've asked you never to drop in without calling, remember?"

"But, darling, it wouldn't have been a surprise if I'd called! And this way, I got to meet your adorable Sam. He's been out of town every other time I've come by."

Out of town? What other times? He looked at Del, who was even paler than she'd been when she'd first seen her unexpected guest.

"Uh, Mom—"

"Honestly, Del." Aurelia glanced at him and smiled, then turned back to her daughter. "I thought I was never going to get to meet your husband."

Husband? It was a good thing Aurelia wasn't looking at him, because his mouth fell open.

"Mom, make yourself at home," Del said hurriedly. "Sam and I need to get dressed." She snagged his hand with the one that wasn't holding her towel in place and towed him toward the hallway that led to the bedrooms.

He let her, not because she actually had any hope of moving him, but because getting Del alone seemed like the quickest way to find out exactly why in the hell Aurelia Parker thought he was married to her daughter.

Del dropped his hand the second they stepped into her bedroom. Crossing her arms defensively and hugging herself, she said, "I guess you'd like an explanation."

"You mean I'd like to know why your mother—whom you neglected to mention is a world-famous actress—believes you're my wife." His voice cracked like a whip and he saw her flinch. But hell—all he could think of was what a disaster this was. He'd spent seven years in blissful anonymity, and the first time he took a full-time lover she turned out to be the daughter of a star who rarely went a day without making some publication somewhere. What were the chances that he was going to stay anonymous now?

Hell, he'd even been thinking about marriage. Wouldn't that have been just peachy?

"I needed a husband," Del blurted. Her color was coming back in a big way as her cheeks flamed with what he could only assume was embarrassment at being caught in her lies. "Not a real one. Just a fictional one to get her off my back and make her stop trying to set me up with every man she came across."

"So you used me." He couldn't control the rage and hurt seething beneath his set expression.

"Well, yes." She looked completely ashamed. "It was easier if I talked about you than if I completely made a guy up. This way, I didn't have so many details to worry about, since I already knew you."

"How long?"

She didn't pretend to misunderstand. "Almost six years now. She thinks we have an anniversary coming up in two weeks."

"Hell!" He raked a hand through his hair. Aurelia Parker was Del's *mother*. He'd be lucky if there hadn't been tabloid photographers outside Del's door this morning taking pictures of him in his unbuttoned jeans.

Del flinched again at the succinct curse. "I didn't think you'd ever really meet," she said, her voice shaking. "I mean, it wasn't as if…"

"We were lovers," he finished grimly. "Didn't it even occur to you *recently* to tell me who your mother was?"

Tears were standing in her eyes now. "Yes. No. Oh, I don't know. I've spent my entire life trying to get away from being Aurelia Parker's daughter. I was afraid if I told you, you'd…look at me differently or something. Or not want to be with me at all."

He was too angry to be careful with his words. "You're damn right about that. The last thing I want is to be hooked up with someone whose name is going to get in the papers."

Del put a hand to her throat, a blatantly defensive gesture, but her voice was steadier when she spoke again. "You have something specific against fame or is this just a general policy?"

Ah, what the hell. He'd been going to tell her soon anyway. "Eight years ago I stopped a gunman on the street in San Diego before he killed more people. I spent the next year trying to get away from the publicity it generated."

"The San Diego shootings," she whispered. She looked absolutely stunned. "He killed seven people before he was stopped by a Navy SEAL on shore leave. That's *you?* Sam Pender?"

"Was," he corrected. "I even had to change my name."

"Why? You should be proud of the lives you saved that day."

"I am," he said. "But I didn't need all the hoopla

that came with it. I was just doing what I was trained to do. What I *knew* I needed to do to stop that guy." He shook his head, looking into the past. "At first, there were reporters all over the hospital where I'd been taken. They would have followed me to the rehab center if I hadn't changed my name—"

"They said you would never walk again," she said, almost to herself. "They were wrong."

"Yeah, and the last thing I want is to have to start running from the press again."

"Oh, Sam, I'm so sorry." Del looked stricken, but he was too angry to care. She slumped down onto the edge of the bed, her lower lip trembling. "I'll go out and explain to her that I've been lying to her. You can leave if you like. I wouldn't blame you if you did."

He turned away from her and paced the room. "Why in the *hell* didn't you tell me?" He was repeating himself in his agitation.

This time, a hint of the Del he knew emerged. Her spine straightened. "Why didn't you tell me your secret?"

"I was planning to!" he roared, and she flinched. "If you'd been straight with me from the beginning—"

"I didn't think it was any of your business in the beginning," she flared. "We might be sleeping together but that doesn't mean I have to share my life story with you."

The words hit him with the force of a blow. He stopped moving, his back to her as he absorbed the implications of her terse response. Clearly, she hadn't been seeing their growing closeness in the same light he had. In her mind, all they were doing was sleeping together. She couldn't have made her position more clear.

"You're right." His voice sounded stiff and rigid even to him; he had to force the words out through a throat so tight he could barely speak. "It isn't any of my business."

There was a silence behind him as he stalked over to the dresser and yanked out an old university sweatshirt, his standard Saturday attire. As he tugged it over his head, she said, "Sam..." in a trembling voice.

But he was done with the whole mess. "I'm leaving," he said. "You can tell your mother whatever you want."

He slammed the bedroom door behind him and snatched his keys off the kitchen counter as he headed for the door.

Del's mother half rose from the couch where she'd taken a seat. "Sam...."

He didn't bother answering.

He didn't know where else to go, so he went to the office. It was pretty damn pathetic, he thought, when a man didn't have a single friend he could call on at a time like this. But it was true. He'd immersed himself in his business so deeply that even his family had been excluded gradually. It had been too painful to stay in touch with his buddies still in the teams so he'd let their overtures and persistent calls go unanswered until they'd finally given up.

Del was the only other person who knew him anymore. Under normal circumstances he might have considered calling Robert, but this situation was far from normal, and besides, Robert couldn't be expected to be objective. The man might not be related to Del by any legal or biological means, but it was clear that he was the closest thing she had to a father figure.

And Robert had been married to Aurelia Parker. *That* was going to take a while to compute.

As he let himself in and reset the security system, he berated himself for being four kinds of an idiot. He almost snorted aloud as he thought of how wrong he'd been in his mental vision of Del's mother.

Your mother didn't want kids?
She was afraid they'd ruin her image.

What an ass he'd been! He'd assumed she meant that her mother was worried about regaining her figure and still looking young. He'd half feared her mother had been a hooker, dependent on her looks for her income. When, in fact, Del had literally meant that a child might ruin the sexpot image Aurelia Parker projected as her stock-in-trade.

God! He threw himself into his executive chair and spun around to face the window. What the hell was he going to do now?

What did it matter? He doubted Del would keep his identity from her mother, and even if she did, what were the chances he could hang around Aurelia Parker's daughter without everyone in the world seeing him? Someone would eventually recognize him, and then he'd be right back to that crazy place he'd been in eight years ago, with women everywhere angling to meet him. He knew how the reality-TV bachelors felt—the only differences were that he hadn't chosen to make himself America's bachelor, and he hadn't gotten a million dollars for it.

Just one hell of a lot of aggravation and a total loss of privacy.

The beeping of the security system interrupted his thoughts, and he swiveled his chair back around, moving the mouse so that his computer monitor screen saver vanished and the programs were visible. Clicking on the state-of-the-art program, he saw that Walker's ID had been confirmed by the scanner that surveyed his employees' irises.

Moments later, he heard the subdued *whoosh* of the elevator doors opening and Walker's footsteps marched across the carpet toward his office. Hell. The last thing he wanted to do was put on a pleasant face today.

"Hey, boss." The big man loomed in the doorway. He leaned a shoulder against the frame and crossed his arms. "Thought I'd be the only one in here today."

"Nope. Beat you to it." He didn't feel like answering questions so he asked one instead. "What are you doing in here on a Saturday?"

Walker shrugged. "I wanted to check over the plans for the child-recovery op next week one last time, be sure we've got contingency plans to cover every sort of foul-up." He shifted from one foot to the other and his gaze slid away from Sam's.

And suddenly Sam thought he knew what was eating at the guy. Karen Munson was going undercover on that op.

"She's going to do fine," he said quietly. "Her references are terrific. I wouldn't send her if I wasn't confident of her abilities."

"I know." Walker didn't pretend to misunderstand. "I just want to be sure nothing goes wrong."

Sam nodded.

"I mean, I've been thinking…" Walker's eyes met Sam's. "I'm not sure putting Karen on cases involving kids is such a good idea. If something ever goes wrong, she's going to take it hard."

The man might have a point. "But I can't pick and choose her assignments," he said to his buddy.

"I guess not." Walker sighed. "She knew coming in that a lot of recovery work deals with kids."

"She did."

"And it's not my job to worry about how she's handling that."

"It's not," Sam agreed.

"It's just that…she's hurting," Walker said. He looked thoroughly ashamed. "I've already hurt her more. And I don't want to add to it."

"I don't, either, but I can't just yank her off every case involving a kid, with no explanation. Everyone else would see what was going on and they might resent her getting special treatment." He met Walker's gaze with a cool one of his own.

"Most of them don't know about her past. Or they didn't before the other night."

Walker's face turned a dull brick-red. He put up a hand and massaged the back of his neck roughly. "I was an idiot," he said. "You probably should have fired me."

"I thought about it," Sam said honestly.

"The thing is," Walker said, "she said she loved me. But when we couldn't agree on our lifestyle, she bailed. Couldn't get away from me fast enough. I couldn't let that go."

"And now?"

Walker sighed heavily. "And now I have to face the fact that I've destroyed any chance at a relationship with the only woman I've ever loved." He let his arms drop to his sides as he slowly straightened. "Guess I'll check over a few things before I take off." He aimed a halfhearted wave in Sam's direction as he moved off down the hallway toward his own office.

Nine

Now I have to face the fact that I've destroyed any chance at a relationship with the only woman I've ever loved.

As Walker's footsteps receded down the hallway, Sam sat frozen in his chair.

God, was that what he, Sam, had done? He'd lashed out at Del, worried about himself rather than thinking about her feelings. She hadn't told him about her mother at first because she hadn't wanted to lose him. She'd probably been afraid—and with good reason, given her past—that he'd be happier with his connection to the famous star than he was with her daughter. How could she have known how the news would affect him? A sense of shame crawled through him. She hadn't been the only one keeping secrets. Why should he have expected her to trust him more than he had allowed himself to trust her?

But…he *did* trust her. With the sparkling clarity of hindsight, he saw that over the past seven years, he had trusted Del with far, far more of his company's intimate workings and secrets than any mere employee normally would warrant. He'd always known, in his heart, that she would never betray him. Long ago, something in him had recognized that she loved him, even though she'd always been careful and correct in his presence.

She loved him! Realizing that should have made him the happiest man in the world. But he'd screwed up royally when he'd walked out on her. She'd needed him, he saw now. Needed a buffer between her mother and her. She'd created an artificial one over the last few years with their fictitious marriage, but now, when she needed protection the most, he wasn't there.

Abruptly, he surged to his feet, rolling his chair back so hard it banged against the wall. He had to get home and apologize. He didn't want to be

Walker, screwing up his life so thoroughly that he could never straighten it out with the one woman he really loved.

As he headed down to his truck, he thought of Del and his confidence returned. She loved him. She had to, or she couldn't be so tender, so responsive. She couldn't finish his sentences and read his moods unless she was totally tuned in to The Sam Channel all the time, just as he was able to discern her thoughts before she opened her mouth half the time.

She loved him! And it went both ways. He hadn't been ready to recognize or define his feelings for Del before, although he didn't really know why. He'd already acknowledged the fact that Del was very different from Ilsa. If she had a self-centered bone in her body he had yet to see it.

Something contracted in his heart as her face came into his mind again, a certain knowledge he'd never felt before with anyone. He loved her, and he'd better get back there and tell her so.

But…when he did see her again, what was he going to say to her?

Marry me. The answer was right there in front of him, and it was so simple he was amazed he hadn't seen it before.

They'd tell her mother the truth, and invite her to the wedding. He almost smiled when he thought of telling Del he wanted to make her marriage real. She was wary and cautious about relationships, but he'd already bulldozed over most of her fears. He'd just tell her she didn't have a choice.

Once, he'd thought Ilsa had cured him of any desire to put a ring on a woman's finger. By now, though, the betrayal and hurt he'd once felt had altered, become nothing more than thankfulness that he'd escaped such a shallow relationship. It wasn't marriage he'd been avoiding, he'd realized. It was putting your heart in someone else's hands.

Now he was ready to hand Del his heart in a wrapped box.

He stepped into Del's apartment fifteen minutes later, filled with anticipation. If her mother was still there, he'd apologize. He'd grovel, if that was what it took to get Del to forgive him.

But as the door swung open, there were no voices. No lights. No smell of the scented candle Del loved and faithfully burned whenever she was at home. The apartment felt empty, and he knew before he even called her name that Del wasn't there.

Maybe she'd taken her mother to her hotel.

Maybe they'd gone shopping. He reached for acceptable alternatives to the terrible fear that was spreading through him.

Behind him, another key scraped in the lock and the fear began to ebb. He whirled—but it wasn't Del who stepped through the door. It was Robert, looking unusually grim.

"Hey," Sam said. "What are you doing here?"

"Get your things and give me your key to this place." Robert's face was granite hard, his tone far less than friendly.

Sam was stunned. "Where's Del?"

"She asked me to come over in case you returned," Robert said. He handed Sam a plain white envelope.

With a sense of foreboding, Sam tore it open and extracted two sheets of paper. Del's familiar handwriting covered the top page.

Sam—
Enclosed is my resignation, effective immediately. I'm sure you'll find someone to replace me quickly. Sorry to leave this way, but I can't imagine working together anymore. I'm sure you agree.

Again, I apologize for not being straight with you.

> Thank you for making my first love affair so very special. I will treasure the memories always.
> Del

Every little sliver of radiance that had begun to shine in his heart dimmed and went out. She'd thought he wasn't coming back. Because in her world, when people ended a relationship, it was over forever. They moved on.

And now she'd moved on, too.

God, please don't let it be too late. Their relationship was barely beginning. It couldn't end like this.

He reread the note, disregarding Robert's chilly stare. *Love affair.* He clung to that small phrase as if it were golden. She hadn't called it a "sexual encounter" or even simply an affair. She'd called it a love affair.

"No," he said. He ripped both sheets of paper in half and let them flutter to the floor, focusing on Robert again. "She's not leaving the business and she's not leaving me. Where is she?"

Robert shook his head. "Don't ask me that."

"I *am* asking, dammit!" he roared. "I want her back."

"Why?" Robert was watching him closely.

"Because..." He floundered, reluctant to expose his newly discovered feelings. This was between him and Del. "Because I do."

Robert shook his head. "Not good enough. You can find another reliable employee."

"I don't care about the work," he said harshly. "I want *Del*."

"Again," Robert said, "why?"

The hell with his stupid concerns. If he had to shout his feelings from the rooftop in order to get her back, that's what he'd do. Sam cast Robert a furious glance. "I love her. That's what you want to hear, right? Well, there you go. I love Del."

Robert's frozen expression relaxed and he almost smiled. "It's not me you need to convince."

"Then tell me where she is and I'll tell her, too." He didn't care if he begged. "Please, Robert. I have to find her. I hurt her feelings and I wasn't fair to her. I need to apologize." He swallowed, and for the first time he truly realized that there might not be a future for him with Del. "Even if she doesn't want to come back, I still need to apologize."

Robert hesitated. Finally he said, "She went to Aurelia's hotel. They're planning on flying out in the morning."

"Flying out where?"

"Back to California."

Shock rippled through him; he had trouble taking a deep breath. "She doesn't belong on the West Coast. And she hated living with her mother. Why would she go back?" Panic was making it hard to get the words out.

The older man shrugged. "What is there to keep her here?"

Sam winced.

"Apparently she and her mother had an honest talk. Aurelia's a forceful personality: I don't think she realized just how she intimidated Del as a young child. This was the first time she ever really understood just how much Del hated having men thrown in her path all the time. Aurelia wanted Del to be happier than she's been. It might sound misguided to you and me, but she honestly thought she could help Del meet the right man."

"And instead it pushed her away. Clear to the other side of the country." He felt even worse. It had taken Del years to come out of her shell and take a chance on him. He looked at Robert. "What hotel?"

Thirty-five minutes later he was at the exclusive hotel in the heart of the capitol where Aurelia had commandeered the most luxurious suite they had to offer.

Robert had given him directions to the hotel as well as the suite number, and he strode to the elevators and rode up to her floor without incident. His heart was pounding as if he'd run the miles from Fairfax.

He'd considered calling to let her know he was coming, but he was afraid she'd leave again. When he knocked on the door, he stayed well out of range of the small peephole through which she might look.

"Who is it? Aurelia isn't here at the moment."

He supposed he was glad she was cautious, and smart enough not to simply open the door to anyone, but now the moment of truth had arrived. What if she refused to talk to him?

He cleared his throat. "It's Sam," he said. "I'd, ah, I'd like to talk to you, Del. Please," he added belatedly.

Silence. Not a single sound issued from her side of the door.

"Del?"

"Go away." Her voice was tight. "I don't have anything to say to you."

"Then you don't have to talk." He attempted to keep his voice low and reasonable.

No answer.

"I'll talk. All you have to do is listen."

Again, silence.

"Let me in," he said forcefully, "or I'll stand out here and yell until you do."

The words were barely out of his mouth when the locks clicked and the door swung inward. "Be quiet!" she hissed. "There are probably journalists camped in every room around here waiting to report something about my mother."

"If you'd let me in when I asked nicely, I wouldn't have had to shout," he pointed out as he moved forward.

Del skittered backward and he caught the door with the flat of his hand before it could hit him. Gently closing it behind him, he followed her down a wide hallway toward a sitting room.

She was wearing jeans and a T-shirt but they weren't the baggy kind she wore at work. These were clothes she'd bought in the weeks since their first night together, clothes that showcased her slim figure, the jeans hugging the curve of her bottom. Her hair was down, gently swaying as she moved, and he closed his eyes briefly, undone by the mere thought of never having the right to run his hands through those marvelous, silky tresses again.

He forced himself to concentrate on his surroundings when he realized his hands were actually shaking. On the right were bedrooms, on the left, a dining room and a powder room. Holy cow, this was an entire apartment. All it appeared to lack was a kitchen and he wouldn't be surprised if there was one of those, as well.

For one swift, surprising moment, the differences between his own barely middle-class ranch upbringing and her far more luxurious one loomed large between them and he almost faltered. It shocked him a little. He'd never thought himself particularly class-conscious, but Aurelia Parker's wealth was pretty damn intimidating.

Then he remembered that Del had left all this behind. She lived in a modest apartment—by these standards, anyway—worked at an average job and did her own errands and chores. She lived like him. No one ever would have guessed at her silver-spoon beginnings. She didn't want, didn't need wealth to make her happy. He hoped to God he was right in thinking he knew what would.

Del had taken a seat in an armchair near an enormous black-marble fireplace. He took another and pulled it forward so that he was sitting mere inches from her. She didn't actually move away, but her averted eyes and the way she seemed to curl herself into the smallest shrinking ball imaginable spoke loudly enough.

He didn't know how to begin, so he said the simplest thing. "I'm sorry."

Her forehead wrinkled and for the first time since she'd met him at the door, she met his gaze squarely. "*You're* sorry? But I lied—"

"I lied, too. By omission if not literally." He took a deep breath. "I didn't think about how you felt. I didn't understand."

Del linked her fingers together. She looked away again and he saw her chin quiver before she pressed her lips into a tight line.

"Will you tell me about it?" he asked quietly. "Your childhood?"

Again, she didn't speak, and he realized she was trying not to cry.

Pain cleaved a hot wound through his heart. He'd caused this.

"From the things you said about your mother," he prompted, "I thought she might be a hooker."

He got a reaction: The Eyebrow quirked in response. "A hooker?" She almost smiled, but it faded fast. "No. She was just a lot more preoccupied with her career and her image and her love life than she was with her child. You know she's been married four times, right?"

He shook his head. He wasn't much for keeping track of celebrities' lives. He had enough trouble with his own. "Wow."

"And there were a lot of wannabe Mr. Parkers in between them. My father, Pietro Caminito, was her first husband. After he was killed, she married and divorced three more times." She went on without waiting for his response. "She wasn't a bad mother, not abusive or anything like that."

He remembered what she'd said about the parties. "What about the man who almost attacked you?"

She shrugged. "Mom was having a cast party after one of her films wrapped. Everyone was supposed to be outside, but this guy was wandering around inside the house. I had come out of my room to see if I could watch the party from the upstairs gallery windows." She took a deep breath. "I was looking out the window when he grabbed me from behind."

Sam couldn't prevent the deep, primitive sound that rose from his throat as he thought of a young Del, defenseless against an adult male.

"Robert stopped him," she said quickly. "He was my stepfather at the time. I think it's the first and only time I've ever seen him really, really furious. He knocked him down and called the cops. My mother had the guy arrested and she swore he'd never work in the film industry again. And she never had another house party without hiring bodyguards to keep people in the party areas."

Sam snorted. "But she didn't stop having parties."

Del smiled faintly. "No. Are you kidding?"

There was a short silence between them.

"You changed your last name," he said abruptly. "Why Smith?"

"It was my grandmother Parker's maiden name, except she had an *e* on the end," she said. "I didn't want anyone to treat me differently because of who my mother was so I had it changed legally." She shook her head. "Mom thought I couldn't possibly be happy without a husband. You can't imagine how many potential spouses she tried to tempt me with." She made a doubtful face. "Like I was supposed to want to get married after watching her all my life."

He supposed, between watching her mother bounce from husband to husband and growing up in the false environment of Hollywood, that Del had good reason not to believe in marriage.

"It's not that I don't love her," Del said. "She's

not a witch. She just didn't get it for a long time. That's…that's why I made up a husband." Her brown eyes were wide and earnest. "Sam, I never would have involved you on purpose. I had no idea she was coming to town. If I had known about the San Diego shooting…"

"We both had our secrets," he said, "and good reasons for keeping them."

She nodded, but her gaze had slid away again and her face was a lovely, remote oval. Her shoulders moved slightly in a helpless gesture. "At any rate, I'm sorry, as well." She seemed to think the subject was closed.

"So you'll come back?"

Her eyes flew to his, and he thought there was a flicker of hope amid the pain and sadness there. Or maybe that was just wishful thinking, because she shook her head. "No."

Well, okay, Sam, stop dancing. She's gone for sure if you don't say something. At least this way you'll know you tried. He took a deep breath. "You don't have to come back to work if you don't want to, but I want you to stay."

She started to shake her head but he leaned over and put his hand over hers, and she froze.

"Marry me," he said. "I need you. I've needed

you for years and I was too dumb to figure it out. Since the night of your birthday, my life has been perfect. Well, almost. If you marry me for real, it really will be perfect."

Del's eyes were huge, riveted to his now.

"Say something," he blurted. "If you can't stand the thought of marriage, we can just live together."

He read the refusal in her eyes before she spoke. "I can't, Sam." She rushed ahead when he tried to break in. "I appreciate the offer, but I couldn't do that to you. Do you know how your life would change if people found out…?"

"I've been thinking about that," he said urgently. "If I'm married I won't be exciting anymore. Besides, being a hero is nothing to be ashamed of."

Del shook her head, smiling pityingly. "Maybe not, but together, the hero of San Diego and Aurelia Parker's daughter would generate some headlines. Don't kid yourself about that."

"It won't last long. We'll let your mother take us out to dinner and get it over with. We'll be old news the second the next Hollywood starlet gets engaged."

But she didn't smile, didn't say anything. Her expression was both sad and skeptical.

Desperation rose. She was so close, and yet she

might as well have been on the moon. "Del, I *want* the world to know we're married. We can live in a glass bubble as long as we're together." And then he realized what he'd forgotten. "I love you."

She actually pulled away from him. "You don't have to say that." The tears were back, trembling on the brink of her lower lashes.

"I'm not just saying it." He leaned forward, took her hands again, noticing with distant disinterest that his own were still shaking. "I love you, Del. If you can look me in the eye and tell me you don't love me back, I'll walk out of here now." He took a deep breath, tried to smile although it felt crooked and pathetic. "It might kill me but I promise I'll leave you alone."

One single tear spilled over and trickled down her cheek. "Oh, Sam, are you sure?" she whispered.

That surprised a laugh out of him. "Sure it would kill me? Yeah," he said. "I'm sure. I've seen the way Walker and Karen still eye each other when they think the other isn't looking. I don't want to mope around like that for the rest of my life, wishing I hadn't ruined my chance at a life with you. I want my ring on your finger. I want a house, a dog, even some kids if you think you could deal with that."

"Children…"

"But I'm flex on that," he said hastily. "I want *you*. I love you," he added again, "and that's all that matters to me."

She took a deep breath and suddenly launched herself forward into his lap. "I love you, too," she said, wrapping her arms around his neck in a stranglehold. "Oh, Sam, I love you, too."

Relief rushed through him, so strong he would have dropped to his knees if he'd been standing. He pulled her close, burying his nose in her hair, running his hands up and down her slender back. "I thought I'd lost you," he confessed, knowing his voice was shaky and not caring.

"I thought you didn't want to be with me anymore after you found out who my mother was and how it might affect your life." She ran her fingers through his hair and pulled back to smile at him. "I'm so glad I was wrong."

"Is that a *yes?*" He still wasn't sure enough of her to assume anything.

"Yes." Perched on his lap, she gazed into his eyes. "To marriage, to kids, to all of it."

"Thank God." He almost sagged with relief.

"I could never imagine being married except to you. I dreamed of it for so long and told myself it would never happen, I guess I was afraid to let myself hope."

"Now you don't have to hope anymore."

She smiled, nodded, dashed away a tear. "I promise we'll do our best to stay out of the spotlight."

He shrugged. "We'll deal with it. And it won't last. We're not exciting enough."

She tilted her face up to his. "You're plenty exciting enough for me," she told him, her voice going low and husky as she pressed herself against him.

Sam lifted her into his arms and started back down the hallway. "Is one of these bedrooms free? You haven't seen exciting yet, babe."

Del laughed, pointing to a doorway. "That one." She put her hand against his face, the look in her eyes so loving and tender that he actually felt his heart stutter. "I love you, Sam. Why don't you show me how exciting we can be together?"

Epilogue

The flight to Las Vegas with Del's mother hadn't gone as badly as he'd feared. Aurelia Parker Caminito Haller Lyon Bahnsen could carry a conversation with minimal help from another person just fine.

She had told them all about the movie she'd just made, and the recent parties she'd attended. She'd talked about who was rumored to be doing illegal substances and who was currently in rehab. She'd talked about Del's father, the Italian race-car driver who'd died in a frightful, fiery accident on a track in Europe in front of thousands of horrified onlookers, and about husbands two and four. Husband Number Three, Robert, sat across the cabin from them with a laptop open in front of him, oblivious to his former wife's chatter. He'd called his wife, Evvie, before they'd left and she was catching a flight, planning to meet them at their hotel before the service.

A Vegas wedding had been Del's mother's idea, largely because the lack of preplanning wouldn't alert the media. That held some appeal. But it had appealed to Sam because he didn't want to wait one day longer than necessary to marry Del.

He couldn't imagine his life without her now. Not waking with her in his arms in the morning, not watching TV at night with her nestled in his lap, not bumping into each other in her small kitchen as they made a meal. Not ever feeling her smooth, silky skin again, never parting her legs and finding her warm and ready for him, never sinking into her so deeply he felt as if they were one.

Thanks to the vows they'd just exchanged, he never would.

Holding Del's newly ringed hand in the small, amazingly tasteful chapel Aurelia had found, he glanced down at his bride yet again, feeling the familiar shock of love, attraction and tenderness welling up within him.

She was radiant in a simple white-satin gown that caressed her curvy body and swept to the floor to trail behind her. A circlet of pearls and shining beads crowned her loose, flowing hair and a sheer white veil floated down from it to kiss the hem of the gown. Her mother had worn the ensemble when she married Del's father—the only white gown she'd ever worn, she pointed out—and when they'd announced their plans and the idea of the Vegas wedding had taken shape, Aurelia had had the dress overnighted to the hotel. It was there when they arrived, along with a seamstress who did some minor alterations so that it fit Del like a second skin. He still couldn't quite wrap his mind around the advantages that truly amazing amounts of money could provide. Thank God, Del didn't seem to care about it.

"Right over here," the minister said, interrupting Sam's preoccupation. "If you'll just sign the marriage license, we'll be through here."

Oh, boy. He took Del's elbow and steered her toward the table. "You first."

His new bride signed her name in the firm, rounded script with which he was so familiar. Then she straightened and handed him the pen.

He bent over the legal contract. He blinked as he looked at Del's signature and started to chuckle.

She glared at him, balled her fist and hit him solidly in the shoulder. "It's not funny."

"Oh, but it is." Laughing even harder, he bent and signed his own name, then laid the pen down. "Don't those look nice?" he asked her.

The Eyebrow rose at the inane question. "Lovely," she said dryly.

"Look closer," he suggested.

She shot him a puzzled glance, then focused again on the marriage license. "What's the big deal?" She glanced over the form, then her gaze drifted down and she read their names. *"Are you kidding me?"* She was already starting to laugh.

He shook his head. "My parents named all their children from the Old Testament. It's my given name."

Del was shrieking with laughter and the minister was regarding them as if they might need to be hauled away in straitjackets. Robert, Evvie and Aurelia hurried over to examine the license, and a moment later they all were laughing like a pack of hyenas.

"What are the odds…?" Del was still chuckling.

He shook his head. "No way could this happen again in a million years."

And as he took his new bride's hand and they started into the rest of their life together, he cast one final glance at the marriage license in his hand.

Delilah Aurelia Smith, it read. And on the line for her new spouse to sign: *Samson Edward Deering.*

* * * * *

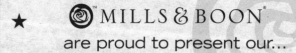

are proud to present our...

Book of the Month

The Wicked Baron
by Sarah Mallory
from Mills & Boon® Historical

The *ton* can talk of nothing but Luke Ainslowe's return from Paris – and his reputation as an expert seducer of women. Innocent Carlotta Durini refuses to become the Baron's next conquest, but what if the Wicked Baron refuses to take no for an answer?

Available 2nd October 2009

Something to say about our Book of the Month? Tell us what you think!
millsandboon.co.uk/community

On sale 6th November 2009

3 NOVELS ONLY £5.49

Sleeping with the Sheikh

Featuring

The Sheikh's Bidding
by Kristi Gold

Delaney's Desert Sheikh
by Brenda Jackson

Desert Warrior
by Nalini Singh

Available at WHSmith, Tesco, ASDA, Eason and all good bookshops
www.millsandboon.co.uk

MILLS & BOON
Spotlight

Spend the holidays with a sexy, successful, commanding man!

Snowbound with the Billionaire by Carole Mortimer

Twins for Christmas by Alison Roberts

The Millionaire's Mistletoe Mistress by Natalie Anderson

Available 16th October 2009

www.millsandboon.co.uk

THREE SUPER-SEXY HEROES...

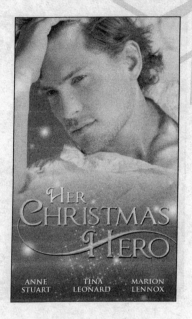

Taken by the cop...

Romanced by the ranger...

Enchanted by the bachelor...

...three unforgettable Christmas romances!

Available 6th November 2009

www.millsandboon.co.uk

Five great Christmas romances from bestselling authors!

A Spanish Christmas by Penny Jordan
A Seasonal Secret by Diana Hamilton
Outback Christmas by Margaret Way
Miracle on Christmas Eve by Sandra Marton
The Italian's Blackmailed Bride by Jane Porter

Available 6th November 2009

www.millsandboon.co.uk

millsandboon.co.uk Community
Join Us!

The Community is the perfect place to meet and chat to kindred spirits who love books and reading as much as you do, but it's also the place to:

- **Get the inside scoop from authors about their latest books**
- **Learn how to write a romance book with advice from our editors**
- **Help us to continue publishing the best in women's fiction**
- **Share your thoughts on the books we publish**
- **Befriend other users**

Forums: Interact with each other as well as authors, editors and a whole host of other users worldwide.

Blogs: Every registered community member has their own blog to tell the world what they're up to and what's on their mind.

Book Challenge: We're aiming to read 5,000 books and have joined forces with The Reading Agency in our inaugural Book Challenge.

Profile Page: Showcase yourself and keep a record of your recent community activity.

Social Networking: We've added buttons at the end of every post to share via digg, Facebook, Google, Yahoo, technorati and de.licio.us.

www.millsandboon.co.uk

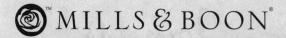

www.millsandboon.co.uk

- All the latest titles
- Free online reads
- Irresistible special offers

And there's more...

- Missed a book? Buy from our huge discounted backlist
- Sign up to our FREE monthly eNewsletter
- eBooks available now
- More about your favourite authors
- Great competitions

Make sure you visit today!

www.millsandboon.co.uk